PRAISE FOR
PAMELA DUNCAN'S *MOON WOMEN*

"A touching story about what it means to be family."
—*Booklist*

"So hilarious, so heart-rending, and so honest that I
sometimes had to shake my head in satisfaction while reading
it. . . . *Moon Women* is the kind of book that becomes beloved."
—Silas House, author of *Clay's Quilt*

"In the tradition of Fannie Flagg and Rebecca Wells comes
a Southern-fried debut. . . . Duncan shows promise as a
from-the-heart, quirky storyteller."
—*Publishers Weekly*

"Add newcomer Duncan to your reading list of Southern
women writers. . . . Duncan expertly demonstrates that
ordinary lives are worth illuminating."
—*Library Journal*

"Pam Duncan has a perfectly tuned ear for the rhythms and
ironies of speech and a vast wisdom when it comes to the
twists and turns of the human heart. These talents shine in
Moon Women, a novel brimming with energy,
compassion and humor."
—Jill McCorkle,
author of *Carolina Moon* and *July 7th*

Also by Pamela Duncan

MOON WOMEN

PLANT LIFE

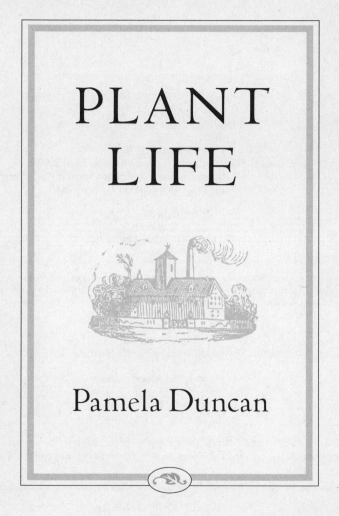

Pamela Duncan

DIAL PRESS
TRADE PAPERBACKS

PLANT LIFE
A Dial Press Trade Paperback Book

PUBLISHING HISTORY
Delacorte Press hardcover edition published April 2003
Delta trade paperback edition published May 2004
Dial Press Trade Paperback edition / February 2007

Published by
The Dial Press
A Division of Random House, Inc.
New York, New York

Cover image by Melody Cassen

Book design by Lynn Newmark

The Dial Press and Dial Press Trade Paperbacks are registered trademarks of Random House, Inc., and the colophon is a trademark of Random House, Inc.

Library of Congress Catalog Card Number: 2003040961

ISBN: 978-0-385-33526-3

Printed in the United States of America
Published simultaneously in Canada

www.dialpress.com

BVG 10 9 8 7 6 5 4 3 2 1

For
Pat Eaton,
Marie Moore Neese,
Jamie Pryor,
and mill workers everywhere,
the best people in the world

And for
Kelly Jerome Duncan
and
Aaron Wade Henderson

"It is not just work. It is as if the blood these people shed at their machines, and the fibers they ingested over time—'eatin' cotton,' they call it with a smile—have made the mill a part of them and them a part of it, all mixed together, metal, cotton, flesh and bone."

Rick Bragg

First Day Photo
by Jane Hicks

Summer closes, hot gardens contained
in sparkling rows, mowers soon parked,
windows soon shuttered against endless outside
chores. First day pictures, a bottle-thick squint
into August dew shine. Fifth grade awaits a cornsilk
ponytail poised to bounce just so. The stiff
JC Penney three-for-ten dollar shirtwaist indicts
an early puberty, white Keds sparkle, fresh
Blue Horse binder with a zipper pocket,
three hand-sharpened pencils, and virgin white paper peek
from beneath a battered Agatha Christie, her summer best friend.

Red brick heaven waits, chalk dust her perfume,
multiplication a mantra, a world she wants to rule
when the new century turns her timeline. The
town mill wants her, escape route blocked by early
marriages, a steady wage against mama's old age, dervish
machines winding out threads of Fate. Many grill
orders, dirty dishes, and milk cows stand
along the fits and starts journey to the kingdom of the
mind. No hair nets, no uniforms, no punch
clocks, no gold watches for brown lungs, just dreams of
clean boards, new books, and fresh faces when summer closes.

"We have a few old mouth-to-mouth tales; we exhume from old trunks and boxes and drawers letters without salutation or signature, in which men and women who once lived and breathed are now merely initials or nicknames . . . we see dimly people, the people in whose living blood and seed we ourselves lay dormant and waiting . . ."

William Faulkner, *Absalom, Absalom!*

PLANT
LIFE

ALBERTA

There's a reason folks cries at weddings. I tried to tell Laurel the day she got married, tried to stop her. All them years I thought she was listening when I said, "Don't never get married, honey. Stay single and love them all if you got to, but don't never get married." She'd laugh and say, "But, Maw Bert, you got married. Why didn't you take your own advice?" Well, that just goes to show how much you know when you're that young. You don't know nothing, and what makes it worse is you're at the mercy of your own fickle heart. It wants what it wants and the more you try and deny it, the harder it wants. Same with the body. I would've been so much better off if I'd been born without no skin, no mouth, no hands, no arms or legs, wouldn't never have gone crazy over no man, wouldn't never have give up my own dreams just to have him love me, have him touch me.

I like to went out of my mind that whole summer before Laurel went off to college, her dating that boy Craig and so crazy in love I just knowed she was going to do something foolish, just like her mama done, run off and get married and start right in to having young'uns. Of course, Pansy was suited for that, didn't know no better. But Laurel, she's like me, she's got a good head on her, could've made something of herself. And I thought she would too, when that boy took up with another gal. I never was so glad in my life as the day I watched her going down the road to college. I thought to myself, Finally, finally at last. And it was like I was in that car with her, pushing my foot down on that gas, going faster and faster the further away I got.

But then what did she do but take up with the first boy to ask, married him just about five minutes after she got that diploma, and what was the point of all that work then? It broke my heart; I don't care how much she said she loved him. I could tell the first time I seen them together who was running that show, and it wasn't Laurel. That's when I seen her future plain, all down the years, not much different than mine or Pansy's, except Laurel ain't had no young'uns, which is a blessing 'cause young'uns is a heavier weight to bear than any man.

The day of Laurel's wedding I had made up my mind to try one more time talking some sense into her. Till the preacher said them words, I knowed I still had a chance. When we got in the Sunday-school room together that day, getting ready, I sent Pansy out to get me some more panty hose, told her I had a run, which I didn't. After she left, I set there a minute, just watching Laurel. It was real quiet, not a sound but the ticking of the clock, and Laurel humming a little tune to herself. She'd been so jittery all morning, busted out crying one time, but she seemed real calm then, setting there in her petticoat, trying to cover up that red nose with foundation. That's when I said it, that about folks crying at weddings. It just come out my mouth without me even knowing I was going to say it. She turned around and looked at me kindly surprised and said, "Huh?"

I wasn't quite sure what to say after that, but I figured if I opened my mouth something would come out. Nothing did at first and Laurel said, "Maw, are you all right?" and got up and come over to me. When she set next to me on the piano bench, I took hold of her hand and held on. I said, "Honey, I want you to think about what you're a-doing. Think real hard, because once you do it, ain't no going back." Well, then she put her arm around my shoulders and talked like I was the one fixing to jump off a cliff. She said, "Maw, it's all right. I have thought about it. I love Scott. I really do. Just like you loved Grandpa Dill."

Her grandpa died before she was born, so all she knowed was what she heard from her mama. Myself, I didn't see no reason to talk about the dead. You can't know somebody just from hearing about them, but Laurel, she'd built her grandpa up in her mind to where she thought she knowed him, just like she thought she knowed me. Right there I decided I had done wrong by not telling her about Dill, about me and Dill. I knowed then I had to tell it all, tell her everything before it was too late, but quick as I opened my mouth, in come Pansy with them panty hose in her hand.

And then it was too late, too late to tell about my own wedding day and how I was just as foolish as Laurel, all worked up, thinking there wasn't nothing could ever separate me from Dill or the life I wanted for myself. Me and him stood up so proud in Mama and Daddy's front room, said our vows right out loud, and when he slid his mama's wedding band on my finger, I thought my heart would stop. We didn't have a pot to piss in, but it didn't matter because we was married.

If I'd known then all the ways that one little promise would bind me and come near to choking the life out of me, I never would've done it. Never, never, never. And I always wondered, why didn't somebody try and stop me? Why didn't Mama or one of my aunts, one of them crying women, why didn't they tell me the real reason they was crying? Of course, the way I had done lost my mind over that man, might be I wouldn't have listened, might be I would've just laughed, same way Laurel did when she said, "But, Maw, I love him." Ain't no point wasting breath when a woman gets like that. She's got to figure it out herself, just like I done. The hard way.

I

LAUREL LOVED GROCERY STORES, LOVED COMING IN out of the heat and strolling into that delicious air-conditioned comfort, putting the workday behind her. She loved the extra blast of cool air and the smell of carnations and roses when she opened the cold case across from produce, loved the beautiful colors of peppers and eggplant and apples and lemons. She loved going up and down all the rows, taking her time, looking at everything, losing herself for just a little while in that clean, orderly world. She loved the variety, loved the way something she'd overlooked a million times would suddenly one day jump out at her, full of possibility. Like the time she picked up a bag labeled *masa harina* just to see what the heck it was and ended up having a ball making tamales for supper that night.

Scott had hated those tamales. God, was everything always going to remind her of him? She'd never been kicked in the stomach before, but that's what it felt like every time she remembered after not thinking about it for a while: a physical blow. And when she turned a corner and saw him there at the other end of the aisle, she thought, Oh, great, now I'm seeing things. My subconscious wants to see him so bad that I've hallucinated. After all, how could she possibly do the shopping without him? It was something they'd always done together, every Thursday after work. They'd meet at the grocery store, spend an hour shopping, then pick up burgers and eat supper in front of the TV. But, no, he didn't go away when she blinked hard, didn't turn into some other man who only looked like Scott.

Last time—had it really been months?—she'd found him in that same spot, reading spaghetti-sauce labels. Laurel had always liked to take her time, compare prices and ingredients, plan menus in her head, but Scott would get bored and go on ahead of her. She'd caught up with him, gone up and poked him in the middle of his back, and he'd turned, grinning that *oops you caught me* grin, and put his arm around her. He'd asked why she insisted on making homemade sauce when this stuff was just as good and wouldn't take nearly as much effort, and she pretended to be hurt that he didn't like her sauce, and he said, *You know what I mean,* and they laughed, and she said how much she loved cooking for him, and they put the jar back on the shelf and turned the corner. That's how it should be, had been, so many times.

And now this, this holding herself back. It would not sink in, the fact that she no longer had any right to do what she wanted so badly to do, which was go to him, put her arm around him, rub his back, smell him, gather a fold of his shirt in her hand and hold on. She wanted him to put his arm around her, walk with her, pushing the buggy side by side, bumping hips and laughing like they used to. He looked so adorable, so helpless, picking up first one jar and then another. Seeing him unexpectedly had always affected her this way, made her stomach jump, or was it her heart? All her vital organs sat up and paid attention. Wanting to touch him was a physical ache in her joints, a longing in every muscle. She looked down at her hands, at the white circle around her ring finger, the wedding band and engagement ring now hanging on a chain under her blouse.

Then, just like that, it was a specific Thursday, this Thursday, the third Thursday of not being his wife, of him not being her husband, and she wanted to turn away but it was too late. He'd seen her, had smiled his old, carefree smile before catching himself, before realizing. It was still new to him too. Laurel smiled back, not wanting to feel that fluttering of hope in her chest but moving toward him anyway. She wondered where Deedee was, then shook the thought off. For just one minute she would allow herself to pretend there was no Deedee.

At least she looked nice since she'd just come from work, her favorite yellow linen suit still relatively unwrinkled, and she'd put on fresh lipstick in the car. Her hand went automatically to her hair, wondering if the French braid had come loose, wondering if he'd notice the new gray hairs mixed in with the brown. He was wearing an outfit she didn't recognize, khaki pants and a dark blue golf shirt that brought out the color of his eyes. At least Deedee was dressing him well. He'd never liked Laurel's taste in clothes, and she'd kept her mouth shut about his. He reminded her of Clark Kent, with his tortoiseshell glasses and that glossy black hair—Elvis hair, her daddy had called it when he first met Scott, although Laurel failed to see the resemblance and Scott did not appreciate the comparison. "Elvis *dyed* his hair," Scott had said, as if male hair coloring might be a crime.

"Hey," he said, the smile not so wide this time. He glanced over his shoulder, then turned back to her. "How are you?" He said it so seriously, as if she'd just got out of the hospital.

"Fine," she said, shaking her head. Not her first lie of the day in response to that question. She hadn't told people at work, hadn't wanted to get into it with them. When she said fine, they believed her and left it at that, just like Scott was doing.

"What you got there?" She nodded at the Newman's Own he held in one hand, Ragú in the other, then noticed the wedding band on the Ragú hand. She looked up, confused. She'd taken hers off the day they signed the papers and thought he had too. He opened his mouth to say something, then looked past her and smiled and waved. Laurel turned, already knowing, already dreading. It was her—Deedee. *Deedee* sounded like some kind of bird, something stupid that tweeted all day and drove you crazy. Deedee took her time, sashaying her tight white T-shirt and white jeans-wearing, blond-headed—that would be *bleach* blond, by the way—self down the aisle, turning her cart to face Laurel's. What is this, Laurel thought, a game of chicken?

"Honey, I got the cereal you like," Deedee said, turning her face up to Scott's like a little girl waiting for Daddy's approval. Laurel had to look away, couldn't stand seeing them side by side. She took a quick inventory of her cart to see what she still needed, then looked at theirs. Oh, God. She glanced at Scott to see if he'd noticed, but he was too busy checking the cereal box Tweety Deedee had handed him. Laurel checked the buggies again. They had the same groceries, right down to Scott's favorite salad mix, his favorite blue-cheese dressing, his favorite pasta, his favorite cookies, his favorite everything. She hadn't even realized she was doing it. Pure habit, that's what it was, one she'd had for so long she didn't even think about it anymore. Please God, she thought, don't let him see, don't let him notice anything.

The cereal must've passed inspection, because Scott tossed it in the buggy. Deedee, satisfied, turned, gave Laurel a fake smile, held out her hand. "Have we met? I'm Deedee."

Laurel's spine stiffened. She ignored the hand and showed her teeth. Bitch! she thought. You know exactly who I am and I know you, right down to your conniving little bones. "I'm Laurel," she said, surprised not to see lightning flashing between them after that shared look of pure animosity. Deedee's cheeks turned red and she turned to Scott, who had his back to them.

Laurel glanced down, saw the hands again, saw the rings. Diamond solitaire, two carats at least. And the clincher, a wedding band that of course she could now see matched the one on Scott's hand. Time froze while this information processed through her brain, then headed for her guts. Married. They were married. Score, Deedee, she thought. I sure didn't see that coming. Willpower alone stopped her from slapping that hand, breaking those long French nails, which for the record were *too* white, bordering on tacky, especially against that dark tan. Ten years, maybe even five, Deedee could be dead of melanoma, and then where would Scott be?

Scott had turned back to his spaghetti sauce and refused to make eye contact. Laurel decided a quick exit was called for, but she made the mistake of looking into their buggy again, and even thinking *their buggy* made her mad. This time she noticed avocados, cilantro, tomatoes, limes. Guacamole? She did a double take, then looked at Scott, knowing he wanted to run and hide. He hated confrontation and so did she. Well, maybe he hated it a little more than she did. But it was one of the things they'd liked about each other, both quiet, peace-loving homebodies. No muss, no fuss, no fighting, just the occasional disagreement about who forgot to take out the trash or where to go for dinner. How could he do this to her? How could he not tell her, not give her fair warning? And now they'd ruined her nice quiet shopping trip, not to mention her life, and she could feel Mount Saint Laurel building up, ready to blow. She wouldn't blow, though. She would remain calm, behave in an adult manner, handle this with class, pure class.

Laurel showed her teeth again. "I'd just like to know one thing," she said as sweetly as possible considering she wanted to slash that smirk off Deedee's face with a claw hammer. "Can you tell me please, what the hell is this?" She pointed to the groceries.

"What?" Scott said. "What is what?"

"This!" Laurel grabbed the plastic bag of avocados and shook it in his face. She made sure to lower her voice a little. "This, you son of a bitch. What is this?"

"It's avocados," Deedee said, trying to be helpful.

Laurel turned away from Deedee's pitying look, a look that said, *How sad. The little hick from North Carolina has never seen an avocado before.*

"Really?" Laurel said, staring at Scott, willing him to look at her. He became fascinated with the cans of sauce on the bottom shelf and squatted down for a closer look.

Deedee nodded enthusiastically. "Yes, Scott's never had guacamole before, so I'm going to make some tonight."

Scott's head appeared above the buggy as he rose to his feet and Laurel turned on him. "Liar!" she said. "What have you been telling her? God, you make me sick. Why don't you tell her the truth? Tell your sweet little coed that, oh, yes indeed, you most certainly have had guacamole before, made by my own two little hands, and tell her what else. Tell her how you spit it out after I spent an hour making it. Tell her how you said you hoped I wouldn't waste good money on crap like that again." She flung the avocados back in the cart. "Tell her you don't like guacamole, you never have liked guacamole, and you never will like guacamole!"

An old guy who looked like the only thing holding him up was his buggy pushed slowly past them, staring, and Laurel stared back, saying,

"Well, he doesn't!" The whole store must've heard but she didn't give a damn, she'd never shop there again. In the shocked silence, she had the urge to laugh, followed by the urge to cry, followed by total calm. I'm losing my mind, she thought, and it's not so bad.

Scott and Deedee stared at her, looking for all the world like her old Barbie and Ken dolls, and just as speechless. She realized now she should've listened to her brother all those years ago. Cecil was all the time wanting her to let Barbie go out with his Big Jim doll and she'd always said, *No, you idiot, Barbie and Ken are a couple.* She'd never questioned it, never given it a thought, didn't even know at that age what being a couple meant, just went along with the advertising: Barbie and Ken go together, end of story. How could she have been so blind? Maybe Big Jim didn't have the wardrobe or the fancy sports car, but he had that great RV and he knew how to survive in the wilderness. Big Jim could take care of a woman, and he'd never even think of leaving her stranded in the middle of the desert all by herself. God! Ken was a selfish bastard.

"You know what?" she said, shaking her head and spinning the cart around. "Never mind. Let her find out the hard way like I did." Keeping her head down, she pushed the buggy to the pet-food aisle and left it there. She hadn't even made it to the refrigerated and frozen foods yet, so nothing would spoil. Some poor clerk would find it later and put everything back just the way she'd found it, just like she'd never been there.

SHE HADN'T realized she was waiting for them until they walked out, Deedee holding Scott's arm, only two grocery bags in his other hand. Not a week's worth, then. She and Scott had always shopped for the whole week. Maybe Deedee didn't plan ahead the way Laurel did. Maybe Deedee didn't like to cook either. The way Scott was looking at her, though, he didn't care what Deedee couldn't do.

She put the car in drive, her foot on the brake. They hadn't seen her. She could press the accelerator and they'd be dead in seconds, squashed as flat as Deedee's narrow little ass. She could drive into the desert and ditch the car and walk into the mountains until she found a cave, and there she would make her home, become a feral woman and live off the land and never see another human soul. Or she could swerve slightly and kill only Deedee, leaving Scott alive to visit her in prison until she got out early for good behavior, and then he'd never ever make the mistake again of leaving her for another woman. He'd love and cherish her as he'd promised to do at their wedding.

But it was too late. They were safe in Scott's Jeep Cherokee, the very Jeep Cherokee her paycheck had helped make payments on. Before Scott started the engine, he leaned over to kiss Deedee, and Laurel closed her eyes. She knew that feeling, the warmth of his face so close, his hand on her neck, then his soft lips on hers, the smell of his cologne so blended with the smell of him that it made a completely unique scent that could never be found in a bottle. She loved to breathe him, loved sitting back from the kiss wrapped in that heat, feeling so safe and so wanted.

When she opened her eyes they were gone.

Driving toward home, she watched an arm hanging out of the driver's side window ahead of her, watched the cigarette on the end of that arm, the hand disappearing inside every few seconds. That's what she wanted, what her mouth and fingers itched for. That's what would make it all better. It must be like riding a bicycle: Once you learn, you never forget, no matter how long that bicycle's been in the shed.

At the next convenience store, she stopped, went in, and asked for a pack of Kools. The clerk, a sixtyish redhead who looked like she could've been a showgirl in her younger days, turned to scan the cigarette rack above her head. She spoke to Laurel over her shoulder. "You must be from the South."

Confused, Laurel looked up from digging change out of her purse. Did they sell Kools only in the South? She could've sworn she'd seen some at the grocery store before.

"Your accent, I mean," the clerk said.

Oh, Laurel thought, and said, "Yes, ma'am," throwing the *ma'am* in for flavor. She thought she'd lost her accent years ago, not deliberately, but by being gone so long, following Scott's jobs. Scott, who had taken a class to get rid of his Charleston accent—a liability, he called it. Her family said he sounded like a Yankee and she would too before it was all over. She felt suddenly glad that she hadn't lost that, at least.

Laurel tore the wrapping off the pack the clerk handed her, pulled out one cigarette, and slid the pack back to the clerk. "Keep the rest," she said.

"Well, thanks." The clerk took a lighter from the pocket of her smock and held it out. After she lit Laurel's cigarette, she fired one up herself and they took a long drag in silence. Laurel coughed and decided to wait a few seconds before trying again.

"Been a long time since I had one of these," the clerk said. "I usually smoke the generics. Cheaper." In spite of hair a shade of red that did not occur naturally, she was still a very attractive woman, with impressive makeup talent. Pink and purple shadow swirled together on her lids halfway up to her eyebrows, false eyelashes out to there, black mascara making them look like spider legs. It was a work of art, really. And her nails: They were gorgeous, long, and dark pink, no chips, no rough edges. The hand holding the cigarette looked so elegant, she could've done an ad for Kools. It reminded Laurel of her mama's hands, only her mama kept her nails shorter because of work.

"So, where you from?"

"North Carolina." Laurel took a second drag without coughing.

The clerk nodded as if that narrowed it down enough for her. "Mayberry, right? Like the TV show?"

Amazing, Laurel thought, noticing that the clerk's little plastic name tag said Shirley, how people believed Mayberry really existed. But she didn't want to be the one to burst Shirley's bubble, tell her the ugly truth, that the South wasn't all one big theme park full of Andy Griffiths and Waltons. Her head spun from the nicotine buzz, so she put a hand flat on the counter. There, grounded. The third drag went in smooth, the dizziness passed, and she was back on the bicycle. "Oh, man," she said, closing her eyes and breathing out smoke. "This feels just like coming home." The muscles in her back, her legs, her shoulders began to relax.

The clerk laughed. "That's the difference between you and me. I never wanted to leave home in the first place."

Laurel opened her eyes. "Me either," she said, the gnawing craving she'd felt all evening finally quieted by the nicotine. She realized it wasn't a cigarette she really wanted, but it would have to do, at least for now. Not that she'd be starting back—no, she was glad she'd quit, glad for her lungs anyway, and without Scott she'd probably be up to two packs a day by now, on the road to emphysema like her grandfather. Scott had never liked her smoking, even when they were dating in college and he took an occasional drag himself. He used to wrinkle his nose and wave the air even though she was always careful to blow it away from him. It really pissed her off but she never said anything, because she knew he was right, knew she should quit. Then one night they'd been lying in bed after too much wine and not bad sex, having one of their long talks about anything that popped into their heads, when Scott got the brilliant idea they should each tell one thing about the other that really bothered them. She'd played it safe, picked the least insulting thing she could think of, said she didn't like that he never had to study as hard as she did to get good grades, which was true. There were lots of things she could've said, though, complaints about him throwing his laundry in with hers every Saturday while he went to play tennis, him always eating onions when he knew she never did, him never offering gas money when she drove them to the beach for the day.

"Sorry," he said when she told him, and when he kissed her cheek she felt him grinning in the dark. "Can't help if I'm brilliant."

"Okay, your turn," she said, pulling the sheet up to her neck.

He'd obviously been thinking about his answer, probably long before the conversation even started, because it popped right out. "The smoking," he said, turning on his side to face her, his hand on her stomach. "I hate to be the one to tell you this, but it makes you smell bad."

Laurel wanted to pull the sheet all the way over her head, wanted to kick him out of her bed and send him home, wanted to die of embarrassment. She smelled bad?

"Don't be mad," he said. "It's just that I don't want you to kill yourself with those things."

Yeah, she thought, but somebody who smells as bad as me probably deserves to die, right?

He grabbed her hip and pulled her toward him so that her chest was against his, the sheet between them. "Come on," he said. "You know what I mean."

She was so glad for the dark, glad he couldn't see the hurt in her face.

"I love you," he said in that whiny I-know-I've-been-bad voice that got on her last nerve. It was the same voice he used when he canceled a date so he could go to a bar with his buddies.

Finally she'd managed to say, "I know," then rolled over and pretended to sleep. Five minutes later he started snoring and she snuck out of bed and took her cigarettes to the kitchen, sat there crying and smoking for an hour. When she got up to go back to bed, she put the rest of the pack down the garbage disposal and hadn't picked one up since. Well, no, there had been that one time—her wedding day—but that didn't count. If she hadn't smoked then, there would've been no wedding at all. Which meant she could've saved herself a whole lot of heartache if she'd never given up the damn Kools, because Scott was the kind of guy who would've kept nagging her about it until she either quit or broke up with him. He was the kind of guy who liked things a certain way and if they weren't, well, then he moved on to something else. What she couldn't seem to figure out now was what she'd done wrong to make him move on to Deedee. Hadn't she been the perfect wife, supporting him through school, going where the jobs took him, accompanying him to thousands of boring faculty gatherings where Scott and all the stuffed-shirt MBAs from the business school stood around talking about money and politics and golf?

"Sweetie, take this," Shirley said, holding out a cigarette. "You look like you could use another one." She lit them both again, then leaned her elbows on the counter, chin on her hand. "Don't tell me," she said. "There's a man in it somewhere."

A sound came out of Laurel's throat that could've been a laugh but sounded more like a cough. It'd been so long since she really laughed, she couldn't even remember what it was supposed to sound like. "Bingo," she said.

"And another woman?"

"Are you psychic?"

"Nah, just know the look. Personal experience."

Laurel made a sympathetic face, though she didn't really have the energy to feel sorry for anybody but herself right then.

"That's all right," Shirley said. "He's right where he belongs now, six feet under."

She didn't laugh when she said it, so Laurel didn't either.

"That bastard's the reason I'm working here instead of sitting home on my nice fat retired ass, excuse the language."

"What happened?"

"Oh, honey, what's the oldest story in Vegas, or in the world for that matter? Screwed around on me, blew everything we had gambling, drank himself to death after I divorced him."

Surreal was the word that came to mind as Laurel listened to Shirley and glanced around at the coffee machine, the coolers full of beer and sodas and bologna lining the walls, the racks full of shiny potato-chip bags, candy bars, and barely concealed porn magazines. Poor Shirley, poor woman. And yet, for some reason, she herself was beginning to feel a little bit better.

"Yeah, he left me in a fix, all right," Shirley said, her hand shaking a little as she tapped off the ash on her cigarette. "Let me tell you something, sweetie. Men are the craziest, most exciting, most fun creatures God ever thought up. They're good for a lot, make your life easier in some ways, harder in others. But even if you get lucky and find Mr. Perfect instead of Mr. Will-Do, the one thing you don't ever want to do is give up your girlfriends. That's what really gets you through in the end, plus they live longer than men. What's wrong, sweetie? You've turned green on me."

A wave of nausea rolled from Laurel's stomach up into her throat. Uh-oh. Time to give up smoking again. She stubbed the cigarette out and pushed away from the counter. "Oh, Lord," she said, her hand on her stomach.

"Hold on," Shirley said. She hurried over to the cold case, grabbed a Coke, hooked a nail under the tab, and had it open by the time she got back to Laurel. Shirley was a good woman, Laurel thought as she took a sip. She could just tell, the way she helped a perfect stranger like that. She'd fit right in in the South if she ever did decide to go.

Two guys in mechanics' coveralls came in, looked Laurel up and down before asking Shirley to fix them some hot dogs. Laurel asked how much she owed for the Coke, and Shirley waved a hand in the air. "On the house, sweetie," she said. "Us girls got to stick together."

Laurel smiled on the way to the car, thinking about the Jimmie Rodgers double thumbs-up Shirley had given her on the way out the door. She hadn't thought about that in years. Her daddy loved Jimmie Rodgers, and thinking about him made her sad again, sent a wave of homesickness through her so strong she wanted to jump in the car and drive until she was back in North Carolina, back in Russell, which was about as close to Mayberry as you could get in the real world.

Lord, her daddy, the world's biggest country music fan, who loved Faron Young and Randy Travis and Don Williams, the Gentle Giant, and poor Jimmie Rodgers, the singing brakeman who died tragically young of tuberculosis. She hadn't thought about that in years, hadn't gotten the double thumbs-up from her daddy since . . . when? At college graduation probably, when she'd found him in the crowd, thumbs big as spoons framing the big smile on his face. No, her wedding, that was the last time, when she met him in the vestibule, ready to finally head down the aisle on his arm. He'd taken her right to Scott, but she couldn't blame him or her mama: She'd made her bed, as Maw Bert used to say, and now she had to lay in it.

COMING HOME to a dark house made her feel even more alone than she already was, and Laurel could've kicked herself for forgetting to leave the lights on. It made her feel better to see a warm yellow light in the window, to fight off the moths under the porch light as she unlocked the door. In the pale light from the nearby streetlamp, she found the keyhole and got the door open, then went through the condo turning on every light in the place. In the bedroom she stripped, threw her clothes in a pile on the floor, put on her favorite big T-shirt, and went to the kitchen to find something for supper. All the happy memories of being in the kitchen, waiting for Scott to get home, listening to the radio, chopping vegetables or making a casserole—had she been happy because she knew her husband would soon be there, or because she was just naturally happy and loved being in the kitchen, loved to cook? The thought of cooking a meal now made her feel like crying, so she opened a bag of barbecue potato chips, grabbed a can of diet soda, and went to sit on the couch, clicking through channels on the TV and stopping on *Santa Claus Is Coming to Town*, which made her think of Cecil and her mama and daddy and Christmas and home. It was ridiculous, the way they started running the Christmas shows so soon after Thanksgiving. She clicked around some more, finding a rerun of *Matlock*, but that made her homesick too because it was her daddy's favorite show. She went back to the Christmas show and sat there watching and getting potato-chip crumbs all over the front of her shirt. Did it matter if she was a slob when there was nobody around to see?

The crunch of the chips sounded so loud inside her head that she started laughing, then felt crazy for sitting there laughing by herself. It seemed unnatural, like drinking alone. Scott used to hear her and would come grinning out of his study and say, "What's so funny in here?" and then sit with her and watch the show and they'd laugh together. Laurel put the chips on the coffee table and wrapped her arms around a big pillow. Sometimes she laughed into the pillow so the neighbors wouldn't think she was crazy. They had to know Scott was gone—you could hear everything through those damn paper-thin walls.

God, it was quiet, so quiet it roared in her ears, like standing next to a waterfall. She looked around the room, noticing for the hundredth time all the things that were missing, all the empty spaces, the bare walls where wedding and honeymoon and vacation photos used to hang, as well as the framed sampler her mama had embroidered with their names and wedding date. She'd taken those down herself, thrown them in a box and stuck it in the storage closet behind the old vacuum cleaner. He hadn't wanted any of them. Then there were the holes he'd made—the empty spot by the end of the couch where his recliner sat, the gaps on the shelves where his books and golf trophies had been, the smooth pecan top of the coffee table cleared of his business journals and newspapers. She even missed the hideous green piggy bank he'd had since he was five and insisted on keeping by the door so he could drop his change into it when he got home from work.

How many times had she wanted to break that damn piggy bank, accidentally drop it during one of their moves? *Oh, Scott, honey, I am SO sorry.* He would've gotten over it, and she would've gotten him one of those great big clear glass jars like the one her daddy put his change in. And she would've talked Scott into keeping it out of sight in the corner of the bedroom like her mama had done with her daddy, and him just as happy about it as a pig in mud. That was how a marriage worked. She knew that. But she'd messed up. She should've done what felt right to her instead of listening to him, but now it was too late and the pig lived with Deedee.

And now she had to worry about running into them at the grocery store, any public place. He was the one who ran off and she'd be the one stuck sneaking around, trying to avoid them. God, she wished she could do some running off for a change. She should've found herself a sweet little cabana boy and run off to Mexico, that's what she should've done the minute he walked out, see how he liked that. She should've called him up from Puerto Vallarta and said, *Hey, Scott, honey, I'm down here on the beach getting a tan with a half-naked muscle boy rubbing oil on me every fifteen minutes and bringing me piña coladas when I'm thirsty, and we're eating guacamole by the gallon. Now, you be sure and tell Deedee I said hey.* Scott hated the beach, hated piña coladas, but would he even care about the cabana boy?

The problem was, she didn't want a muscle boy. She'd been perfectly happy with the man she had. And anyway, a muscle boy would probably just get on her nerves and she'd have to start smacking his hands and telling him to go play in the sand so she could read her book. Then again, she thought, sitting up straight, who said she had to have a muscle boy to run off? Not to Puerto Vallarta, of course, but somewhere, anywhere but here, where she'd be worrying about running into Scott and his concubine every blessed day.

The pillow slid off her lap onto the floor and she left it there. Wait a minute, wait just a cotton-picking minute. She didn't need a buddy, or permission, or anything. She could leave. She could leave anytime she wanted to. She was a grown woman, and if she didn't want to live in Las Vegas, she by God didn't have to. She'd only come out here on account of him anyway.

Laurel picked up the pillow and sat back, glanced at the TV, and turned up the volume. The Winter Warlock was singing about putting one foot in front of the other. Christmas. It was so simple. She'd put in her two-week notice at work, let Scott handle selling the condo, load all her stuff in a U-Haul, and head home for Christmas, just like always, only this time without Scott. Of course, she'd have to tell the family everything then—they didn't even know about the divorce—but she'd cross that bridge when she got to it, or go around it, or blow it up, hell, she couldn't think about that right now. And once she got home, it would come to her what to do next. She couldn't think that far ahead, just one step at a time.

Hugging the pillow tightly to her chest, she felt the heaviness that had weighted her down for months begin to lift, just the tiniest bit, just enough to let her know she must be doing the right thing. I'm leaving, I'm leaving, she thought. It ran through her mind like a song, and she closed her eyes and let it play.

WINTER

This, too, shall pass.

2

It wasn't that the plant really looked like a prison, not like the one where her daddy worked anyway, but it reminded her of prison—the chain-link fence, the guard in the gatehouse, the bricked-up windows—and the isolation of the place combined with the gray winter day only added to the effect. It was a place for keeping those who belonged in and those who didn't out. In which case, why were they letting her in? She smiled from the backseat as the guard waved them through, thinking she ought to remember him. He looked old, old enough to have been there all those years she came to plant Christmas parties as a kid with her parents. A name popped into her mind—Odie. Or was it Opie? Then her mama said something to her daddy about Opie getting ready to retire in another year. Opie. Like on *The Andy Griffith Show*. She'd always wondered if that name was short for something else. So Opie was retiring soon. She turned and looked out the back window at the tiny white guard shack, the Plexiglas window he sat behind. Laurel felt sorry, thinking of him spending his life in what amounted to nothing more than a glorified phone booth. Talk about prison.

She bounced and turned as the car went over a speed bump. Studying the back of her daddy's square head with its thick black hair—no gray hairs yet, thank goodness—and the top of her mama's brown head just visible above the headrest on the front passenger seat, she imagined them as jailers with herself as the prisoner being transferred to minimum security. What would it feel like to know you were going in but maybe never getting out?

Oh, God, she thought. I'll probably be the only adult who doesn't actually work here. Nobody else's kids still come to this thing. Grandkids, maybe, but not the grown kids. Cecil certainly wouldn't be caught dead here. But the alternative hadn't appealed either, staying home in that empty house. She'd tried distracting herself with a book but couldn't for the life of her concentrate on anything for more than a few minutes. It was hard work, this not thinking business she'd assigned herself, not thinking about anything but right now.

"Here we are!" her mama said, her voice excited as she opened the door to cold air and a silence that struck Laurel as strange, almost eerie, until she realized what it was. With the plant shut down for the coming holiday week, the machines had been turned off. The droning hum, which became a whining, deafening roar once you got inside, had been temporarily suspended, thank God. That was the one thing above all that would've driven her crazy, aside from the dirt, the dust, the being on your feet all day. She didn't know how her mama stood it.

Laurel got out of the car and sucked in a deep breath, the icy air burning her nose and making her think of snow. Snow would be nice, something to blanket the world, cover up the ugly parts, a nice white cushion that would force them to get off the roads, stay home, and curl up on the couch and drink hot chocolate and watch old movies on TV in between trips to the window to see out.

The cold made her shiver and wish she'd worn something under the Christmas sweatshirt borrowed from her mama. At least she'd had the good sense to pick the less flamboyant snowman. The entire front of her mama's bright red sweatshirt was covered with a waving, smiling, sack-laden Santa, while the back featured a fireplace with just his black boots showing as he whisked up the chimney. Laurel thought of the time she told Cecil that Daddy was going to light a fire in the fireplace on Christmas Eve. Instead of crying as she'd hoped, Cecil got in the fireplace, perched on a log, and refused to move even when Mama and

Daddy both promised not to light the fire. "She knows where the matches are," Cecil said, pointing at Laurel. Finally they made her go to bed and Cecil came out, but only after they promised he could sleep in a sleeping bag next to the fireplace. Of course, when he came by her room later with his pillow, Laurel had to holler, "I bet Santa Claus takes one look at you and goes right back up that chimney, fart face."

"What you giggling at, Little Bit?" Her daddy put his arm around her shoulders and she leaned into his warmth.

"Cecil," she said, nodding toward Pansy's back, and Dan looked and laughed too.

"Be careful, now," Pansy said, handing each of them a bag of Christmas presents from the trunk. "There's breakables in there."

Laurel and her daddy smiled and rolled their eyes behind Pansy's back and followed her into the plant. Christmas was Pansy's big thing and she wanted the whole world to celebrate with her, starting right here with the Revel Mill Christmas party. It had signaled the official beginning of the holiday season ever since Laurel could remember, and she figured even after her mama retired, she'd still come to this party. The plant was like a family that way. Once you belonged, you belonged forever, and so did anybody connected to you.

Even before her mama opened the door to the warehouse, Laurel could hear the noise of people, lots and lots of people, talking and laughing. They stepped through the door and into the middle of chaos. Hundreds of men, women, and children in jeans and Christmas sweaters or sweatshirts like her mama's milled around, and the roar from their talk was nearly as deafening as the machinery they ran when the plant was open. Wooden pallets holding plastic-wrapped packages of yarn for dyeing had been stacked around the walls, leaving the floor open for tables covered in white cloths, one long one loaded with food and the rest surrounded by folding chairs. As they passed the food table, two middle-aged men in white T-shirts and aprons lifted tinfoil off big aluminum trays, and a wonderful smell of fried chicken and ham and bread and potatoes wafted out. Laurel took a long sniff, grateful no one could hear her stomach growling. She'd had a bowl of cereal at about seven o'clock that morning and it was long gone. She eyed the long line snaking around the food table, reaching back almost to the huge Christmas tree at the other end of the warehouse. Even if they got in line now, it would be half an hour before they ate.

When they got to the table where her mama's friends sat, Pansy and Dan were immediately pulled into conversation. Laurel hung back, shy all of a sudden, until a tiny woman with white poofy hair came over and stood in front of her, squinting up through glasses too big for her face.

Laurel smiled down at her and said hey, remembering Lottie May mainly because she remembered her oldest daughter, Nellie Belle, who used to follow the kids around at Christmas parties and Labor Day picnics, getting right up in their faces and talking too loud, wanting to play their games and freaking them out because she was big and didn't belong with them. Laurel hadn't understood about Down syndrome then, and Nellie Belle scared her to death.

"It's good to see you, Lottie May. Where's Nellie Belle?" She glanced around, thankful not to see her.

"She had to work today," Lottie May said, "but I got Nisco with me." She pointed toward the Christmas tree, and Laurel saw Santa Claus on the same old plywood throne beside the tree with a line of children waiting. When she was six years old, Laurel had cried and cried about having to sit on Santa's lap because she knew it was the plant manager under that beard. Cecil had told her. And she knew from hearing Mama and Daddy talk about him that he was a bad man. She wondered if it was still John Dollar under there, whiskey on his breath, bouncing the kids on his knee so hard they bit their tongues.

"Nisco?" Laurel said.

"My grandbaby, honey. Nellie's boy. See, yonder he comes."

Nellie Belle had a son? Laurel didn't know Down syndrome people could have kids. And what a son. A little brown boy rushed up then and grabbed Lottie May around the hips, all excited about Santa Claus promising him a pony. He was around six years old, with kinky reddish-brown hair, green eyes, and freckles all over his face. How did blond, blue-eyed Nellie Belle produce this child?

Lottie May turned Nisco around and started pushing him toward the other side of the table where she'd been sitting. "I'm going to beat that John Dollar," she said over her shoulder. "Promising young'uns like that."

Pansy and Dan had already taken seats, so Laurel pulled out the chair next to her mama and sat down, the big sack of gifts on her lap like a shield. It was always weird to see these women in person, like meeting somebody from a book or a movie, somebody she'd heard a lot about but didn't really know. Maxann, who sat on the other side of her mama, was still beautiful even in her early fifties, though she looked a little haggard. Laurel had a vivid memory of Maxann, sometime in the 1960s, wearing a white minidress, white boots, and a white fur hat, her long, white-blond hair like silk down her back, sitting on Santa's lap after all the kids got through. She'd found Laurel crying behind the Christmas tree, afraid to tell Santa what she wanted, and promised to tell him for her. Laurel never knew if she did or not, sensing even as young as she was that Maxann wanted to sit on Santa's lap for reasons of her own that had nothing to do with Christmas.

She had no specific memories of Percilla, the fat one with a mean streak who supposedly fooled around with any man who asked, or Idalene, the tall old lady with a dark red modified beehive hairdo and a face like a white raisin, long and wrinkled.

Her daddy had moved to the other end of the table and sat talking to Rex, his best friend and the only other husband in their group, which struck Laurel as odd. All the husbands this group had had, and only two left. Maxann was divorced, divorced, widowed, and divorced, Lottie May widowed and divorced, and Idalene never married. It amazed Laurel that of them all, Percilla—the one nobody really liked but they all tolerated, the one who looked a little bit like the female Tasmanian Devil on Looney Toons—was the only one besides her mama with a man. Then she felt evil for thinking that, for judging Percilla like that. What was it made women do that to one another, especially considering they were hard enough on themselves already?

"Where's that good-looking husband of yours?" Percilla asked, leaning across the table so Laurel could hear her. "Did you leave him at home?"

Laurel, unable to think how to answer, felt her mama get still beside her, waiting to see what she'd say, and she fought the urge to get up and run. Both her parents knew there was more to the story than what Laurel had told them, which was that Scott was spending Christmas in Charleston with his parents. They let her leave it at that, but their curiosity had become an almost physical presence between them. And since she hadn't even told her mama and daddy what happened, she sure as hell wasn't going to discuss it with Percilla, mother of her high-school nemesis, that boyfriend-stealing bitch Carmen Dover.

"He's in Charleston," Laurel said. "His daddy's in bad health."

Pansy leaned forward, looking at Laurel. "What's wrong with his daddy? You didn't tell me that."

Oh, shit, Laurel thought. What now? She put a hand to the back of her head, patting her braid. "I didn't?" she said.

"No," Pansy said, drawing out the *o* sound longer than necessary. "You didn't."

"Is he dying?" Percilla said.

Laurel broke away from her mama's stare, turned back to Percilla. "No, oh, no, he'll be fine." She actually liked Scott's father, didn't want to kill the poor guy off just because his son was a jerk. He'd always been kind to her, maybe to make up for Scott's mother being so lukewarm.

"I hate it when people die on holidays," Percilla said. "It just ruins it. Rex's daddy died Christmas Eve, and then his mama up and died the very next Easter."

How inconsiderate, Laurel thought, glancing down the table at Rex. He looked like Boo Radley, skinny and pale and unhealthy with his white hair sticking straight up, looked a hundred years older than her daddy. It hurt to look at him, so she let her eyes slide over to Nisco, who sat eating with the kind of concentration only a small child could give a piece of pumpkin pie. Lottie May watched him too, then caught Laurel's eye. "How long you staying, hon?"

That is the $64,000 question, isn't it? Laurel thought, her mind racing to come up with a safe, acceptable answer. Lottie May waited, and Laurel could feel her mama listening with one ear even as she carried on a conversation with Maxann, but Laurel couldn't open her mouth, because if she did, she knew she wouldn't calmly say, *Oh, I'll be joining my husband for New Year's, thank you.* Instead, the words, *Help me, I'm homeless*, would leap out and the entire room would fall silent and they would all know her shame and stare and maybe even a few would snicker over how pathetic she'd become and she'd have to run, sobbing, out into the cold.

But then she opened her mouth and the words came out so smooth, so easy, as if she really did plan to spend New Year's with Scott's family, just as they had every year of their marriage. They didn't need to know that this year it would be Deedee sleeping with him in that beautiful green and gray guest room overlooking the water, eating crab cakes Scott's father had made, sitting in front of the fireplace in that living room lined with books. Then again, Deedee would also be the one stuck listening to Scott's mother as she held forth on everything from politics to gardening. The woman never drew a breath, never gave anyone else a chance to jump in and add something to the conversation. She also didn't know how to have fun, never just relaxed and gossiped about stupid stuff like TV shows and tabloid headlines and what the neighbors were doing. Laurel used to watch her, hoping for just a crack of a smile, some sign that she had a sense of humor, but it never came. She began to believe that if Adele Granger ever did let a smile slip onto her face it might trigger a massive explosion of the woman's head. There, now she was feeling better. Let Deedee deal with Charleston this year. She had it coming.

"Well, you ought to come out with me one night instead of staying home with the old folks," Maxann said, grinning at Pansy and tossing her long hair back over one shoulder. "We'll go out to the Ponderosa and party."

Oh, yeah, Laurel thought. That'll be the day. It sounded snobby, she knew, but Maxann was a redneck—a skinny, gorgeous, natural-blond redneck, but a redneck nonetheless. And if she hadn't already planned to leave early, Laurel couldn't think of anywhere she'd rather be on New Year's than sitting home with the old folks, watching Dick Clark, eating popcorn, and drinking ginger ale just like they did when she was a kid.

Fortunately, Pansy jumped in and said since Laurel wouldn't be home long, they were being selfish and keeping her home. All Laurel had to do was shrug and smile apologetically.

"Oh, Lord," Idalene said. She'd been sitting twisted around in her seat, watching the crowd around the Christmas tree, and she turned back to face them. "Here comes John Dollar. Now, I want to know, why does he have to strut around acting like God Almighty?"

Laurel watched Santa making his way down the room, stopping at the head of each table to say a few words, every once in a while reaching up to scratch under his Santa beard. When he reached their table, Nisco ran over and hugged him and wouldn't let go, so Santa stood there patting the boy's back. "Ho, ho, ho," he said. "Is everybody having a good time?" He had to really work to get his naturally high tenor voice down to Santa's range and kept coughing as if the effort tickled his throat. Finally he sent Nisco off to the elves for a Christmas present and turned to Laurel. "And who is this lovely young lady?" Another cough. "You can't be Pansy's girl?"

When Laurel nodded, he slapped his thigh, stepped closer and put his arm around her shoulders. "Well, I'll be dogged. I haven't seen you since you went off to college, honey." Laurel smiled up at him, feeling as if her face would crack if he didn't move away soon.

"Listen," he said. "Why don't you come on down here and work for me? I'll treat you right." And he winked, actually winked at her. Yeah, Laurel thought, I just bet you would. As if she'd even consider staying in Russell, much less working at the plant. That's what she'd left home to get away from, wasn't it?

"We better go get in line," Pansy said, rescuing her again. "I been listening to Laurel's stomach growl ever since we got here."

"Right," John said. "Y'all go on and get you something to eat. Santa's got to mingle."

"Thank you," Laurel said when he was out of earshot. Her stomach growled again and she put her hands on it as if to muffle the sound. She leaned toward her mama and whispered, "I didn't think anybody could hear that in all this noise."

Pansy looked at her like she'd just said the stupidest thing, and answered back in a nonwhisper. "Well, I'm not just anybody," she said. "I'm your mama."

WITH A belly full of fried chicken, ham, sweet potatoes, green beans, broccoli casserole, corn, collards, biscuits, and blackberry cobbler, Laurel leaned back in her chair and wished she had the nerve to un-button her britches like her daddy always did when he ate too much. The world was so much easier on men than women in some ways. When a man unbuttoned his pants at the table, people thought it was cute. If a woman did it, she was trashy.

At first she tried to follow the conversation with her mama and the other women, but they were talking about work and people Laurel didn't know, so she let herself zone out. That food had been so won-derful and it had been so long since she'd eaten a good southern meal where the fried chicken was just the right balance between crispy and greasy, the collards chewy and not slimy, and the green beans cooked with fatback till they were soft enough to swallow without chewing. She was tired of living in places where they ran green beans under hot tap water and considered them done. Green beans were a delicacy when cooked right. They needed good seasoning, needed time to start cold and heat up slow and spend hours marinating over low heat with fatback and salt and maybe a few new potatoes. Not that she wanted to eat like that every meal, of course not, but a person couldn't watch her cholesterol every goddamn minute. Well, one person could, but she didn't have to cook for him anymore, thank God.

Okay, she thought. Time to move, do something. Can't sit here and marinate or ruminate or anything like that. Down the table she saw her daddy and Rex with their heads together, then they stood up, stretched, yawned. Rex veered and wandered off toward the door while Dan came and stood behind Pansy, his hands on her shoulders as he waited for a break in the conversation. Pansy kept smiling at something Idalene was saying as she slowly tilted her head back against Dan's stomach and looked up at him. Laurel stopped breathing, wanting to freeze that mo-ment, preserve it. There, in that small gesture, that was their marriage. That slow tilt toward his solidness and strength spoke of vulnerability and trust and love and comfort and ease, and oh, God, she wanted that, wanted it so bad it was like a bitter taste in her mouth.

"Honey," Dan said. "I'm sweating like a mule. Me and Rex is going outside for a while."

Laurel jumped to her feet. "Can I go?" She felt like a little girl, begging to go with Daddy. But she had to go, do something. That feeling kept coming over her, that heaviness that made her want to sink down on the floor and never move again.

"Sure, Little Bit." Dan put a hand to the small of her back to guide her out. "Come on, we'll show you the river."

"What river?" she said as they crossed the warehouse floor and headed outside. After the heat and noise inside, the cold quiet outside was a relief, like a cold shower after getting all sweaty mowing the grass.

"Honey, this place used to run on water power." They followed Rex down a long walkway on the side of the building and around back to a small concrete loading dock.

When she saw the water, Laurel said, "I thought that was a creek." She'd crossed over it a million times on her way to and from school, never realizing it was a river.

"It's the Catawba River," Rex said. They joined him at the railing and leaned on the yellow metal bars. Beyond a narrow tree line and down a steep red-clay bank lay the river, shallow, reddish brown with mud, and frothy as it ran over big rocks scattered throughout the riverbed.

"It's high," Rex said. "All that rain we been getting."

"We sure needed it too," Dan said.

Huge trees grew along both banks, their bare black branches like wrought iron against the gray sky. It was probably beautiful in the summer, the green of trees mirrored in the water, grass and shrubs hiding the liquor bottles, beer cans, Styrofoam containers, and cigarette packs that littered the banks. Laurel shivered and put her hands in her pockets. This was bringing her down. "I never even knew this was back here," she said.

"You ought to come in the spring and summer," Rex said. "We used to take our smoke breaks out here, and before they put in these railings we'd sit on the edge of the dock and watch for whistlepigs."

"Whistlepigs?"

"Yeah. Big fat ones."

"Groundhogs," Dan said.

Laurel nodded. "Oh." She thought groundhogs only lived up north somewhere, like the one that predicted if there'd be six more weeks of winter. "Why do they call them whistlepigs?"

" 'Cause they make this squealing noise sounds like they whistling," Rex said. He leaned over the railing and waved his arm toward the opposite riverbank. "See them holes? That's where they live. Dig way in up under them trees and make a little nest. They probably in there asleep right now." Rex sounded like he wished he could crawl in there with them. "Lord," he said, laughing. "One time I come out here and seen something run in the top of that drainpipe over yonder. Well, I went over and looked down to see what it was, and this whistlepig popped its head up in my face and started squealing and I about shit my britches." He ducked his head. "Excuse the language."

It tickled Laurel to hear a man apologize for cussing in front of her. If he only knew some of the things she'd heard her own husband say and had said herself. She leaned out and pointed downstream at what looked like a low rock wall across the river. "What's that?"

"The dam," Rex said. "There's a sluice that used to route water from the river to power the mill. Course, they don't need it no more. Everything's electric. That was the beginning of the end, you know, electricity. Pretty soon they won't need people at all. Just one feller to run the computer."

They leaned on the railing for a while, looking at the water, enjoying the sound of the river and the wind in the trees, or so Laurel thought. Rex kept sneaking looks at her from the corner of his eye and every once in a while nodded and muttered, "Yep," as if in conversation with someone they couldn't see. He was the same age as her daddy, only fifty-seven, yet he acted like an old man. And Dan, who could always be counted on to hold up his end of a conversation and then some, had let a silence fall. Laurel began to sense that maybe she wasn't wanted, maybe her daddy and Rex had come outside to talk and they couldn't in front of her. She tried not to smile. It was just like a man to try to outwait a situation instead of just being direct. Wasn't that what Scott had done with their marriage, waited for her to find out about Deedee?

But she wouldn't make her daddy wait. She pushed away from the railing. "Daddy, can I borrow the car?" she said, feeling sixteen again and just as uncertain, just as anxious to get away.

"Sure, Little Bit." Dan pulled the keys out of his pants pocket and handed them over. "Where you going?"

She had no idea, just somewhere away from here. "Just loafing," she said, knowing he'd understand since it was something he'd done every Saturday morning of her life. He'd take the trash off and meet his buddies for breakfast at Hardee's and drive around visiting the auto-parts store, the hardware store, the Pantry, staying gone just long enough for Pansy to get the big weekly housecleaning done. "Don't worry, I'll come back for you," she said.

"I can run y'all home," Rex said.

"Oh, that's all right." Laurel knew her mama would not want to be stuck in the car with Percilla. "I'll be back in about an hour."

On her way out the gate, Laurel slowed down to wave at Opie, maybe stop and chat for a minute, see if he remembered her, but he wasn't there. Oh, good, she thought, he got to go to the party. She hated to think of him trapped there, having to ask somebody to cover for him just so he could go to the bathroom. She'd had a receptionist job like that once. It was humiliating as hell and she didn't stay long, just until she found something better. No grown person should have to ask permission to go to the bathroom.

Laurel looked both ways at the road. Left would take her through the countryside and out to the high school. She turned right. There was more to see in town, and it'd been a long time since she'd been. She probably should've gone back and sat with her mama, but she could only take those women in small doses. They were nice, but it freaked her out that they knew so much about her, especially since she'd only seen them a couple times a year. That's what women who worked together did, though: group therapy. Her whole life had probably been dissected over lunch in the canteen—grades, illnesses, boyfriends, braces, college, marriage.

Of course, the reverse was true too. She'd heard all their stories over the years as her mama and daddy sat and talked about work after supper. Did they even think about the fact that everything they told each other at work got taken home and told again with no regard for privacy or discretion? Would they care? Maybe because of that, Laurel had made a point of keeping her personal life out of the workplace, and it had been easy, especially since they never stayed in one place long enough for her to slip and start confiding in anyone. She talked to Scott, to her parents, her brother and his wife, and Sally, her best friend from college who lived in London now. Of course, she realized that everything she told her mama got told at the plant. It was a vicious cycle. No, not vicious. Just unrelenting. As soon as she told her mama about the divorce and all, they'd find out the next day. She had to accept that. Coming home to Russell, privacy was the first thing to go.

Not far beyond the plant she started passing rows of little white mill houses. There were so many of them, all basically the same structure but differing in cosmetic ways. Some had porches with white wooden railings, some had black wrought-iron railings, some had shutters on the windows, some had carports or screened porches or extra rooms added on the side, some had fences all around the yard, some had sidewalks to the front door, some had gardens out back. She passed three churches within two blocks of each other, each a little bigger, a little fancier than the one before. The Baptist and Methodist churches, small white clapboard structures with brick fellowship halls behind them, sat close to the road, probably so passersby could read the signs out front with messages like *Do not be an idle worshiper*, and *Where will you spend eternity, smoking or nonsmoking?* The Presbyterian church sat back in the middle of professionally landscaped grounds like a huge, imposing brick ark, above the need for signs or add-on fellowship halls. Her favorite, though, was the Pentecostal Holiness church, housed in what looked like an old dry cleaner's, which had a sign out front reading, *My Jesus can whip your devil*. Just about any night of the week you could ride by there and look in the big plate-glass windows and see religion going on right out in plain sight, not hidden behind stained glass like in the other churches.

Mill Road dead-ended at the intersection with Main Street and Laurel turned right again, passing dry cleaners, printers, banks, florists, accountants, grocery stores, a big new Eckerd's pharmacy. And, good Lord, there in the same spot where there used to be an empty lot, the very place Uncle Wendell used to sell his pumpkins and gourds and apple cider at a makeshift stand every fall, right there was a Chinese restaurant. A Chinese restaurant in Russell. She almost pulled over to see if there were actual Chinese people inside, unable to imagine them finding Russell, much less making a life here.

When she reached the traffic circle at the old courthouse, Laurel stopped and checked for oncoming cars, then drove halfway around the circle and out the other side, into the original downtown. This was the Main Street she remembered—the same buildings, but instead of Belk's and JC Penney and Butler's Shoes, the brick buildings now housed offices for lawyers and developers, accountants and insurance agents. An antiques store had replaced Butler's, and the old dime store was now a gift shop with sun-catchers and porcelain dolls and ceramic teapots in the window.

Thank God the Russell Cinema was still here, her old friend, the place she'd spent nearly every Saturday afternoon of her childhood, sitting in the balcony fantasizing about being a jockey or a spy or a movie star or a nurse. And the City Café still sat in its same old spot next to the theater. She'd always loved the city skyline painted in gold on the windows of the café. The tallest building in Russell was only three or four stories, nowhere near the size of those skyscrapers, but maybe back in the forties when the place first opened they'd had hopes of the town growing as big as Charlotte someday.

She pulled into one of the diagonal spaces in front of the café, got out, stretched, and couldn't help smiling. The café reminded her of back-to-school shopping days and Christmas shopping days with her mama. She had loved the excitement of being in town with all the people, going in all the stores, and eating in a restaurant, which seemed a very grown-up thing to do then.

The bell over the door jingled as she entered the café, and the man behind the counter in the back looked up from his newspaper. "Afternoon," he said. He looked about sixty but wasn't anybody Laurel remembered. He wore a green golf shirt under a gray apron stained with what looked like coffee, and his pudgy cheeks and bald head glowed pink under the fluorescent lighting. As cold as it was outside, he still looked hot, like he'd been working over a barbecue pit all day.

"Hey," Laurel said, setting her purse on top of the counter. She glanced at the menu on the wall behind him. "Hot chocolate, please." She didn't need snow to go ahead with the hot chocolate, did she?

"Yes, ma'am, large or small?"

Large, huge, jumbo, give me the biggest you've got, she thought, and the more chocolate the better, a big hit of comfort. "Small," she said, deciding to favor her hips over her feelings. The man went down the counter to make the hot chocolate, and Laurel turned around to take a better look at the place. It hadn't changed much, still one table by each of the front windows, red vinyl booths lining the walls on both sides of the long room all the way back to the counter, then five stools at the chrome-edged counter. There were three decorative themes that shouldn't have blended but actually did: old Coca-Cola signs and trays with pictures of old-fashioned girls; big black-and-white photos of Elvis, Marilyn Monroe, Buddy Holly, and James Dean; and smaller, autographed photos of race-car drivers. Laurel remembered the Coke and the rebels, but the NASCAR was new.

After paying for the chocolate, she picked a booth near the back and sat facing the door. Scott had always laughed at her because she couldn't sit with her back to the door, called her Doc Holliday whenever they went out to eat. Maybe it was because of how Cecil used to always sneak up behind her and gooch her when they were kids. She'd be reading or listening to records and, next thing she knew, he'd poke her in the sides and run, laughing. It drove her crazy, never knowing when he might get her. Whatever the root, she just always wanted to see what was coming. She hadn't seen Deedee coming, though, had she?

The chocolate was too hot and she set it aside to cool, then pulled a paperback from her purse. She'd learned long ago to never leave home without something to read, something to keep her company in line at the bank, in the doctor's waiting room, in traffic, at lunch. Just by reading in the car while waiting for Scott to finish his night class three times a week, she'd managed to get through all but the last twenty pages of *Anna Karenina*. Sometimes she wondered if she'd been silly not to finish, but the end of the book had coincided with the end of her marriage and the two were so entangled in her mind now, she knew she'd never go back. Besides, Tolstoy was a big downer. Life was sad enough. She wanted drama, but she also wanted a happy ending and had recently gone back to historical romances. She'd read them compulsively in her teens, then gave them up during college, mainly because she didn't want anyone to see her reading them. But since the breakup with Scott, they were the only books that distracted her.

She was right at a good sex scene when she had the weirdest feeling somebody was staring at her. There was only one other person in the café, an old man playing solitaire in a booth near the front. She went back to her book but couldn't shake the feeling of being watched. A minute later she heard footsteps and felt somebody heavy drop into the booth behind her. Laurel turned to look over her shoulder, and a face was so close to hers that all she could see were eyes, big blue ones. Startled, she jerked back.

"Hey," the woman said as she got up and came to sit across from Laurel. She looked middle-aged, although it was hard to tell with Down syndrome people, their faces were so round and smooth. But there were wrinkles around her eyes, and her blond hair was streaked with gray. Wait a minute, Laurel thought, remembering her conversation with Lottie May, remembering the face in front of her from her childhood.

"Nellie Belle?" she said.

The woman nodded. "You was afraid of me when you was little."

I still am, Laurel thought, ashamed of herself. She hadn't known Nellie Belle could tell she was afraid. Sometimes she worried that some people really could read her mind and so tried to be careful what she let herself consciously think, though of course trying to hold back a thought only made it come back even stronger. Now she felt awful and tried to think good thoughts about Nellie Belle, but like white chalk on a blackboard, all she saw in her mind were the words, *Please go away and leave me alone.*

"Where you been?" Nellie Belle asked.

She wasn't sure how to answer that, plus Nellie Belle's unblinking stare was making her nervous. "Well. I don't know. I guess I've been a lot of places since the last time I saw you."

"I seen you last year at the mall with your mama."

"You did?"

"Yes, but y'all was way on the other end, and me and Mama and Nisco was going to eat at the K&W. Are you moving back home?"

The fake smile fell off Laurel's face, and she ran her tongue over her dry teeth. Hell, it was probably safe to tell Nellie Belle the truth. She could say, *I have no earthly idea what I'm doing. Isn't that awful?* But, no, Nellie Belle could tell Lottie May, and Lottie May could tell Pansy, and so on and so on. "No, I'm not moving back. Just here for a visit. You know, for Christmas."

"Oh," Nellie Belle said, staring.

Jesus H. Christ on a cracker, Laurel thought. Was she going to have to sit and talk to Nellie Belle Gamble until it was time to go? Please, God, she thought, I can't take that. All I want to do is get Mama and Daddy, go home and eat supper, watch some stupid Christmas crap on TV, take a Trazodone, and go to bed. Please, God, that's all I ask.

"Well," Nellie Belle said at last, standing. "I got to start the chicken."

Thank you, God, thank you, Laurel thought as Nellie Belle disappeared. I do appreciate it. She wrapped her hands around the cup to warm them, then took a sip of the hot chocolate and burned her tongue. That's what she got for thinking bad thoughts about the mentally retarded. Or was it mentally handicapped? Mentally challenged? If that was the term, Laurel felt like she might qualify herself.

The bell over the door rang and she looked up to see what appeared to be a Greek god strolling into the café. But, no, as he stepped into the light she could see it was only a man, but what a man. And while Laurel was not the least bit interested in men at this point in her life, she couldn't help appreciating him on a purely physical level, his black curls, blue eyes, cleft chin—oh, how she loved a cleft chin and had always longed to put her tongue in one but couldn't because Scott's chin had no cleft or dimple or even a dip. This guy's cleft, while more a crease than a dimple, still counted. He had an athlete's build—a baseball player, maybe—with wide shoulders, big hands, narrow hips. In his navy suit, he looked more like a banker, though, a liberal banker with that purple paisley tie. The high shine on his shoes glinted under the fluorescent lights as he walked toward her in what seemed like slow motion. She tried to make herself look away, look down, not stare, but she couldn't. My God, she thought. He can't be from around here. I would've remembered him. As he came abreast of her booth he slowed, looked, nodded, smiled, hesitated, then walked on.

Laurel blew out a breath. She didn't usually pay that much attention to other men, but maybe it was time she did. Maybe this was a first step toward enjoying being single again.

"Hap!" the man at the counter called out. "What can I do you for, buddy?"

Hap? His name was Hap? Laurel turned around just to make sure nobody else had come in without her knowing. No, just the counter man and the god. What in the world kind of name was Hap? He most certainly did not look like a Hap. A Steve, maybe, or a John. She glanced down at the romance novel she'd been reading, the cover featuring a half-naked couple on their way to all-the-way naked. The hero's name was Byron. That's what he looked like, a Byron, somebody strong and self-assured and yet tender and poetic. Which meant, of course, he was probably a jerk. Nobody could live up to that image.

The man's voice, deep and smooth as he answered the counterman, gave her a little thrill. What in the world was wrong with her? Here she sat lusting—was it lust?—over a man she'd only just seen. It reminded her of the huge crush she had on John Travolta when she was sixteen. She didn't know him from Adam, but she loved him, she knew she loved him. At that age, she hadn't known the difference between love and infatuation. Knowing the difference didn't make it any less appealing, though, the instant physical response to male beauty.

Not that looks were all he had going for him. He looked prosperous, and if he wasn't a banker, she'd bet on a lawyer, either one a good profession, good provider. And there it was, her mama's voice, the database of advice and commentary she hadn't even realized was being stored inside her until it started sending up little messages, like now, reminding her that a man should not be a freelancer or freeloader, that no woman should allow herself to end up with a man who couldn't provide for her. Her mama had never liked Scott and hated the fact that Laurel worked to put him through grad school. And apparently her mama had been right. For an MBA, he was terrible with money. They never saved a dime, spent everything on new cars, vacations, a condo they couldn't really afford, and, of course, he'd spent money on Deedee, no telling how much. The rings alone . . .

She slapped her hand down on the book, hard, and it slid across the table and knocked her cup over. Hot chocolate poured out, soaking her book, her purse, and running off the edge of the table onto the shoes of the man named Hap, who'd chosen that moment to pass her booth with his cup of coffee. Oh, shit, she thought. Those shoes looked expensive. Could she afford to replace them?

"You could've just said hello," he said, looking amused instead of pissed.

"I am so sorry," she said, watching as he pulled out a handkerchief, lifted his feet, and wiped the hot chocolate off. It'd only gotten on the toes, not bad at all. He balled the damp hankerchief up in his hand and smiled down at her. God, those teeth were white.

"You got my attention, though."

Laurel's head drew back on her neck. He did not just say that. He did not stand there and accuse her of deliberately trying to get his attention. Suddenly he didn't seem nearly so handsome. As a matter of fact, he had thin lips, a downright cruel mouth—almost sneering, really.

Her disgust must've been obvious, because he laughed. "No, no, sorry, that was just my lame attempt at a joke."

She wasn't sure she believed him, but his face had turned pink, so maybe he wasn't a total jerk.

"Look," he said. "Let me get you another hot chocolate."

"No, that's okay."

"I insist." And he had her cup and headed for the counter before she could protest again. When he got back, he stood there holding their cups, eyebrows raised as he glanced at the seat across from her, and said, "May I?"

She hesitated a split second, then said, "Sure." It wouldn't kill her to bump knees with this guy for a while. She glanced at the clock. Still half an hour to kill before she needed to pick up her parents. He'd be a pleasant diversion, that was all. Lord knows, she could use something pleasant in her life right now.

Laurel felt him studying her as he sipped his coffee, and it made her nervous. It'd been so long since she sat across from a man like this. What did her hair look like? Her makeup? And she would have to be wearing this hideous snowman sweatshirt. God, she hated this part, the constant worry of whether or not she looked good enough. Five minutes ago she'd been perfectly content to sit here and be invisible and read her book.

"I thought I'd seen just about everybody in Russell by now," he said.

She had to look at him then, into those light blue eyes that seemed to be laughing at her but not in an unkind way. "I'm home for Christmas," she said. His eyes went to her ring finger, and for the first time she was glad she'd taken the rings off, even though they still hung from a gold chain around her neck. Her hand went to her chest, but she knew he couldn't see them under the sweatshirt. It'd been almost like an amputation, taking those rings off, and she still couldn't make herself part with them completely.

He stuck out his hand, and without thinking she took it. "I'm Hap," he said, "Hap Luckadoo, and Dave back there can vouch for me." Without taking his eyes off her, he raised his voice and said, "Can't you, Dave?" His hand felt warm and dry as it slid away from hers, and she put her hands in her lap.

From behind the counter, Dave hollered, "Watch out for him, ma'am. He's a lawyer, lower than whale feces at the bottom of the ocean, if you'll pardon my French."

"I thought so," she said.

He blinked and said, "Excuse me?"

"I mean, I thought you might be a lawyer."

He pretended to wipe his brow. "Whew. Thought you might be one of those people who believe all lawyers are the spawn of Satan. You're not, are you?"

"No," she said, and laughed. "It's just that anybody wearing a suit in this town must be either a lawyer or a banker or an insurance salesman. What kind of law?"

"Whatever comes my way, really. Hard to specialize in a place this small. Actually, I just moved here about a year ago from Charlotte."

While he talked he turned his cup in circles, his long fingers tan against the white ceramic. Where'd he get a tan in December? she wondered. Lord, surely he didn't go to a tanning bed. That was one of her pet peeves, that and men who wore necklaces or bracelets, especially gold chains. Or Speedos. God, she hated to see a man on the beach in a Speedo. She did a quick check of his wrists. Nothing but a simple silver watch with a black leather band.

"Why did you come here?" she asked.

"Lots of reasons. Starting with divorce."

"Oh," she said, surprised by his answer. She'd noticed his ring-free hand earlier and pegged him as a hard-core bachelor rather than a divorcé. "Me too."

He held up his cup. "Let's drink to that," he said.

She took a sip of hot chocolate to hide her face. He was flirting with her and she had no idea what to do next. Remain calm, she told herself. Flirting is easy. Flirting is fun. "So," she said, "I've never heard the name Hap before. Is it short for something?" There, she thought, that was harmless enough.

"Francis Marion Luckadoo."

Laurel squinted at him. "How do you get Hap out of that?"

"You don't," he said. "But I had to do something. Remember that song 'A Boy Named Sue'?"

"Sure." She nodded. "My daddy loves Johnny Cash."

"Well, imagine what happens to a boy named Francis Marion in school."

"Right," Laurel said, nodding again. There had been a boy named Beverly in her class who was picked on all the time by the other boys, until he got himself a tough nickname, Spike or Digger, something like that. But Hap? That didn't sound tough at all. "I still don't understand where Hap came from."

"My mother. When I was little, she called me her hap, hap, happy baby, so my older brother thought my name was Hap, and everybody else started calling me that too."

"It's funny, isn't it," she said. "How little kids can end up having the power to name things like that, without even trying. So, Hap is short for happy, is it?" And that's flirting, she thought, like getting back on a bicycle.

He put a finger to his lips, said, "Ssshhhh, don't tell," and she thought maybe his mouth didn't look cruel after all. Then he gave a cocky little smile that let her know he knew exactly how attractive he was, knew the effect he had on women, and enjoyed every minute of it, but it was also a smile that said, *I'm interested in you*, which went a long way toward balancing out the cockiness. The recently cast off and divorced, sensible part of her wanted to squash him like a bug, but the girly, feminine part said, *More, more.*

"Listen," he said, looking at his watch before reaching into his breast pocket. "I've got an appointment in a few minutes, but here's my card."

"Thank you," she said as she took it, held it in her palm, ran her fingers over the raised black letters of his name. "Actually, I could use some advice. I've been thinking of changing my name back."

"I'm your man, then," he said. "Give me a call sometime."

Oh, no, Laurel thought. That's not how it's played here in Russell. Maybe in Charlotte, in the big city, but not here. She found a pen in her purse, wrote her number on the back of the card, and returned it to him along with her biggest smile. "I've got to run too," she said, thinking of her parents. She grabbed her purse and scooted out of the booth, and he scooted out and stood next to her. He was taller than her, though not quite six feet, and looking up she could tell she'd surprised him. Good, she thought, hearing another of her mama's tapes. Maintain your mystery, because the minute a man thinks he knows all about you, he gets bored and then it's just a matter of time before he's looking somewhere else. She wouldn't make that mistake again.

"It was nice meeting you," he said.

"You too." She brushed past him and headed for the door. That's it, girl, she thought, leave him wondering. Only when she was pulling through the gates at the plant did she remember the wet romance she'd left on the table, horrified for a moment to think he might've seen it, knowing she'd have to go back and pick it up, because it was a good one and she wanted to find out what happened next.

PANSY COULDN'T figure out what had her so irritated. She wanted to be happy and have fun, but she wasn't. And as awful as it was to admit, she knew it was because Laurel was there. She ought to be happy to have her daughter with her, happy that she wanted to join them. It wasn't that Laurel had said or done anything, but somehow Pansy knew, could just see in her face how plain and ordinary and pitiful this party had looked to her. After being out in the world, this place was bound to come up short in her eyes. Laurel was probably used to Christmas parties at fancy hotels or restaurants with wine and candles and soft music and elegant people in their best clothes, and pâté, and all them other kinds of food they didn't have in Russell, parties like people on TV had.

She tried to think how it must look to somebody who hadn't been coming there every day for the last thirty-nine years. Good Lord, could it really be that long? She'd been thinking about being married to Dan for thirty-nine years because of their anniversary coming up, and she started at the plant the same year they got married. She'd never admit it to Dan, but somehow the marriage seemed to have lasted longer than the working. Not that she didn't love Dan, hadn't loved being with him all these years, but taking care of a man and young'uns had took a whole lot more out of her than this job ever had. When the kids was little, she used to be glad to come to work just to get a break.

Her first day at the plant wasn't really a clear memory, more a feeling of being scared and coming home tired, and there had been so many days here since then that they all blurred together. What she did remember clearly was the Saturday before she started work, when she got home from a graduation beach trip with her aunt Eloise. It was her first time seeing the ocean and she couldn't wait to get home and tell her mama about it, couldn't wait to show her the pictures, pictures she wanted to paint as soon as she got a chance. But her mama had met her at the door, no smiles or open arms, just said she'd got her a job at the plant starting Monday so she better get her clothes ready.

Pansy had known all along that after graduation she'd have to go in the mill, because they needed the money. With her daddy gone and all the boys married and gone, it was just her and Mama left. She was expected to help out and she wanted to, was glad to. But she'd never thought it would mean giving up things she loved, like painting, and making pretty clothes for herself, and going to the movies sometimes. Her mama said there wasn't money for things like that, said they needed every penny to pay the bills and eat. If it hadn't been for Dan, she wouldn't never have got out of the house. He saved her, and she'd always be grateful for that.

This party, with its fluorescent lights, cement floors, fold-up tables and chairs, country cooking, and stacks and stacks of yarn pallets holding up the walls, was bound to be a disappointment. When Laurel was a little girl, of course, none of that mattered. All the kids cared about then was Santa Claus and presents and sweets. But now, now it mattered, now she was bound to notice, and that bothered Pansy, though she couldn't think why. Even if Laurel was disappointed, she'd be leaving in a few days. And besides, this party wasn't for Laurel, so what did it matter if she thought it was country and plain?

"Wake up, Pansy," Maxann said, plopping down in the next seat. "It's time to open presents." She pulled a pack of Salems and a lighter from her purse, glanced around the room to see if anybody was watching, then lit up, her cheeks sinking in as she inhaled. She held the cigarette down beside her chair so no one would see.

"I thought you were going outside to do that." Pansy hated cigarette smoke and Maxann knew it.

"Well, I'm sorry, but it's too damn cold out there. Don't worry, I'll blow it away from you."

"And watch your hair. It's swinging right over the tip of that cigarette." That was another smell Pansy hated, burning hair. Maxann was too old to be wearing her hair long and straight like that, the way she did back in the sixties and seventies when she was young enough for it. She was still so pretty, but her skin was getting that leathery look from too much sun and smoke. A couple more years and the wrinkles would come calling and take over that face, and it would be a shame if she ended up looking rode hard and put up wet.

"Thank you, Mama," Maxann said, pulling the hair across her other shoulder and grinning at Pansy as she bent low to take another drag.

Lottie May came back from the bathroom and sat on the other side of Pansy, fluffing the hem of her blouse out over her hips like a hen settling her feathers. "Where's everybody at?"

"Idalene's over there talking to Mary and Bonnie and Anita. I don't know where Percilla got to."

"I bet I know," Maxann said, moving her eyebrows up and down. She was the only one of them who'd actually seen Percilla in action with one of her many boyfriends at the plant, claimed she saw her kneeling in front of Willie Ledford back in a dark corner of the opening room one time. Because of the bad blood between the two of them, Pansy didn't know whether to believe it or not.

Lottie May scanned the room. "Did Laurel not come back in yet?"

Pansy shook her head. "No, I reckon she wanted to stay with her daddy." She always had been a daddy's girl. But then, Pansy had been one herself, so she understood Laurel's attachment to Dan, that safe feeling only a daddy could give you. Or a good husband.

"Well, that's a shame about Scott's daddy," Lottie May said. "I sure hope he'll be all right. I can't believe she flew out here all by herself. I'd have been scared to death."

"She drove," Pansy said. It still made her mad to think about it. Pansy wouldn't even drive to the mall by herself after dark. The world had got too dangerous. Laurel should not have done it, and she didn't bother telling anybody until after she got home. She'd said, "What would've been the good of you knowing ahead of time, Mama? Did you want another scoop of worry to add on top of all the other worrying you do?"

"They Lord," Lottie May said. "Scott should've never let her do that."

"My God," Maxann said. She dropped her cigarette on the floor and mashed it under her foot. "Y'all talk like two old women. Laurel's grown. She can take care of herself."

"We are old women," Lottie May said.

"You said it, not me," Maxann said. "What I want to know is, what's really going on with her and that husband of hers? I can tell that ain't the whole story, that sick-daddy excuse."

Pansy sighed. That was the other thing bothering her, wondering what in the world Laurel wasn't telling, and it made her tired just thinking about it. "I don't know what's going on with Laurel," she said, then felt an elbow in her side and turned on Maxann, about to get mad until she saw where Maxann was nodding. Percilla was headed their way and they knew without saying a word it was time to change the subject. If she heard them talking about Laurel, she'd have to start in to talking about her daughters, especially Melanie's upcoming wedding, and they'd all heard that tune till they could sing it themselves: how Melanie was marrying a doctor, and Melanie was having a huge church wedding and then a big reception with a band at the country club, and Melanie was going to live in Hunter's Ridge where all the doctors and lawyers and dentists and contractors lived, and Melanie wasn't going to have to work after the wedding unless she wanted to keep her job just until her and the doctor started having babies.

"I'm here," Percilla said, as if that was what they'd all been waiting for.

The woman really ought not wear horizontal stripes, Pansy thought. Especially not red and white. She looked like a piece of that puffed-up peppermint candy shaped like a little pillow.

Percilla glanced at the empty chairs beside Lottie May and Pansy, then pulled up the chair next to Maxann. Pansy didn't think she'd ever seen the two of them sit so close before. Years ago people used to say that if you put Maxann and Percilla together, they'd make the perfect woman. Maxann had a beautiful face and she was funny and smart, while Percilla had a body that practically made men cry. *Had* being the operative word. No telling where that body was under all that fat. The sad thing was, she thought she still had it, dressed like she did, acted like she did. And funny thing was, that confidence did get her a lot of attention. If more women understood what Percilla had seemed to know from birth, that men can be fooled into thinking confidence is beauty, they'd quit all their dieting and aerobics and plastic surgery and anorexia and just be happy the way they was, and their men would be happy too and never know the difference.

Pansy pushed a cookie around her plate, an oatmeal cookie hard enough to break a window. Must be one of Maxann's. Bless her heart, the girl could not cook worth a durn. It was a wonder her boys hadn't starved to death. That was one thing she'd been able to do for Laurel, teach her to cook and clean. Pansy had started working around the house from the time she could walk, had to, for there was always too much to be done. And because sometimes her mama just wasn't able; sometimes she just sat in her chair and rocked, and it was up to Pansy to get supper and do the wash. She'd never ever left Laurel to do her work for her, but she taught her just the same. Little girls grow up, and they got to know how to take care of a house.

Percilla leaned forward to see Pansy better. "Where's our husbands at, you reckon?"

"Probably out in the car drinking beer and listening to that shit-kicking music." Pansy wiped crumbs off her hands, thinking she probably shouldn't have said *shit* at a Christmas party. "Will somebody go get Idalene? We got presents to open." This was always her favorite part, but she couldn't seem to work up her usual enthusiasm. Pansy made herself act perkier than she felt, jumping up and sliding the piles of presents down to where they could all reach.

"Here comes Idalene," Percilla said. "Look at her limping. Lord, you'd think her leg was broke."

This must be a day for seeing things with new eyes, because it seemed like all of a sudden Pansy saw Idalene as old when she never had before. She hadn't turned old overnight, had she? No, it was happening to them all but so gradually they forgot to notice. That come from working together so long, knowing each other so good, paying more attention to the inside person than the outside. Pansy wanted to look away but she couldn't. She didn't want to lose her old way of seeing Idalene, the way she'd seen her through the years—that tall, bony woman with hair the color of oak leaves in the fall, that dark dark red, a woman strong as a tree herself, always with her chin up, them blue-gray eyes flashing, eyes that could stare holes in the plant manager one minute and turn laughing and kind with Pansy the next. Idalene had been the one to train her, the one she turned to again and again when she didn't know how to do something. Pansy had already lost too much this year, losing her mama and going through the change. She didn't want to see Idalene walking so slow. The woman had never walked slow in her life. Pansy used to have to run to keep up with her on the floor. She didn't want to think about Idalene having to leave the plant next April when she turned seventy-five either, but there was no getting around it. That tired feeling come over her again and something in her spine gave way a little bit, brought her chin closer to her chest.

"Hey, girls," Idalene said when she reached them. She put her hands flat on the table, leaning so hard it wobbled a little. "Well, I believe I've eaten too much today. I'm going to have to go home and lay down." She rubbed her belly, then turned a sharp look on Pansy, a look with a question in it, asking without speaking, "What's the matter with you?"

Good old Idalene, she could always tell when something wasn't right. Maybe that come from being quiet, paying attention instead of always running her mouth like the rest of them done. "We better get to these presents, then," Pansy said. They'd started exchanging gifts a long time ago, the five of them, just little things at first, sometimes gag gifts like a laughing box or a Magic 8 Ball, but then gradually switched over to real gifts. Pansy got more excited opening presents with these girls than she did with her own family. As much as Dan and the kids loved her, she knew they seen her only as what they wanted her to be, wife and mama and grandma. At the plant, she was Pansy, she was her own self, and that's how her friends seen her too.

"Yeah," Maxann said. "We better enjoy it while we can 'cause there might not be no next year."

"Oh, Lord," Lottie May said. "What've you heard?"

Pansy could've wrung Maxann's neck, bringing that up at the Christmas party. Lottie May already worried too much about pink slips, ever since her daughters got laid off from the weave room last year. They all needed to forget the rumors about layoffs and the plant shutting down. That's all they was, anyhow, rumors, every year the same, and nothing ever come of them. She gave Maxann a look that shut her up.

"Nothing," Maxann said. "Never mind. Now, how about handing me a present?"

"I got ambitious this year, girls," Lottie May said, handing out packages, big boxes wrapped in green or red foil paper with gold bows. She'd bought a case of that paper at a fire sale years ago, and Pansy figured she'd never run out.

Pansy tore the wrapping off quick as she could, racing with Maxann to see who could get theirs open first. Percilla always picked the tape off hers with her long fingernails, peeled it back and then unwrapped the present real slow and folded the paper to save it. Pansy figured she just did it for the attention. If she had all that paper stored up in her house, it'd be a fire hazard.

"Oh, my God, Lottie May! You made this?" Maxann held a sweater—black with red stripes around the bottom—up to her chest and looked down at it, then up at Lottie May. "It's beautiful, honey."

Pansy's was her favorite color, a soft pinky-peach. "I love it," she said, smoothing her hands over the soft yarn.

Percilla had finally got hers open. "Would you look at that?" she said, holding the reddish-brown sweater away from her so they could see. "It looks store-bought, don't it?"

"Just like your hair," Maxann said.

Pansy bent her head and concentrated on refolding the sweater to keep from laughing about Percilla's wardrobe of wigs. Today she had on what looked like a Tammy Wynette sixties' special, a blond beehive with bangs swept to one side.

"Hardy har har," Percilla said, stuffing her sweater back in the box and reaching for another present.

"These are a hundred percent better than anything store-bought," Maxann said. "I'm putting mine on right now." She stood and lifted the hem of the sweater she had on.

"Good Lord, Maxann," Pansy said, looking around to see who might be watching. The crowd had thinned some, but a lot of people sat talking over their empty plates still. Maxann didn't care, though, and Pansy wondered if she was missing the modesty gene. Thankfully, she wore a T-shirt underneath, a tight one with no bra underneath that. One of the guys at a nearby table whistled, and Maxann flipped him the bird before pulling Lottie May's sweater over her head.

Pansy noticed that Idalene hadn't even taken hers out of the box, just sat with her hands folded on top of it. She reached across the table and patted the box. "What color is yours, honey?"

Idalene lifted hers by the shoulders, leaving the bottom half still folded. It was a beautiful blue-gray that matched her eyes. "I declare," she said. "I don't know where I'd ever wear it." She laid it back in the box and put the lid on.

Lottie May looked like a door had slammed in her face. Pansy couldn't remember ever seeing Idalene wear the things Lottie May made for her. It wasn't like she made ugly stuff either, the kind of things you said you loved when you opened them and then stuck in a closet or under the bed and forgot about. She always made something pretty, something they could really use. Her hands always had to be working every minute of the day, and Pansy bet even in her sleep they was never still.

"Well, goddamn, Idalene," Maxann said. "You could at least say thank you."

Idalene looked surprised. "I thought I did."

"That's all right, don't worry about it," Lottie May said. "Now, Percilla, you go."

Percilla always give them perfume, and she had a knack for picking the awfullest-smelling stuff in the drugstore, stuff that could walk around by itself, it was so strong. Pansy had a whole shoe box full of it under the bathroom sink at home. And that's right where this year's selection—Jontue, a big old bottle of it—would end up too. Pansy couldn't believe they still made that stuff, but she remembered how Percilla had always loved the commercial on TV, the one with the man on the horse looking for the woman and singing in French.

Idalene, being more thoughtful than Percilla, give everybody something they could really use, gift certificates to the Western Sizzlin' in Smith River.

Pansy always give something homemade and something bought. This year it was nice bedroom shoes, the good kind from Belk's, and some of her homemade blackberry jelly. She felt bad because it was left over from summer before last, but after her mama died last spring she hadn't ever got around to making a garden, much less doing any canning. It had been all she could do to get to the store this year. Seemed like whenever she got home from work it took the last little bit of strength she had left just to get supper on the table.

Maxann's gifts was the ones Pansy liked best, because they was always a lot more thoughtful than what you would expect from somebody like Maxann, who lived for the moment and not much else.

"Is this your way of saying I need to cut the fat?" Percilla said when she finally got the paper off a big George Foreman grill.

Maxann gave a little laugh and shook her head. "No, Percilla, that's my way of saying Merry Christmas. That thing'll cook a steak in ten minutes without you having to stand there and turn it, and it'll taste just like you cooked out on the grill. Rex still likes steak, don't he?"

"Yeah, not that we can afford it anymore since he lost his job."

"Well, it'll cook chicken and fish too." Maxann smiled the biggest old smile at Percilla, almost like she really meant it.

"Well, thank YOU," Percilla said, and smiled right back at Maxann just like she really meant it. Pansy wondered sometimes if they even remembered why they didn't like each other. She couldn't remember herself, if she'd ever known.

Idalene got a foot massager and Lottie May a coffeemaker, the kind that could be programmed to have the coffee already made when she got up in the morning.

"Now, Lottie May," Maxann said. "I know you're still using that damn hundred-year-old drip pot on that woodstove of yours, but you just try this one time and I swear you'll never go back."

Pansy opened hers last, a set of four ceramic kitchen canisters, four different sizes, white with yellow lids and pretty yellow flowers painted on them.

"If you don't like them, well, too damn bad, because I got them at the Craftiques Show after Thanksgiving and there's nowhere to take them back to."

"No, honey, I love them." A lot of times Pansy thought Maxann's taste was all in her mouth, especially when it came to her wardrobe, but the canisters really were pretty and the perfect shade for her kitchen.

"Now, they ain't brand-new, but they're clean. I washed them out with Clorox." Maxann lit up another cigarette, not even bothering to try and hide it at this point. "The man said he got them off a family in Greensboro. This old couple had died and their daughter sold all their stuff at an estate sale. She said them canisters had been in the house from the time she was a little girl, and she was fifty-some years old, which he said makes them antiques. Which I reckon makes me one too." Maxann laughed, and then the laugh turned into a coughing fit. It always worried Pansy to hear Maxann cough like that, and she wondered, didn't the woman ever worry about lung cancer or emphysema? Dan's daddy had smoked for forty years and died of emphysema, and it'd been awful to watch a man not be able to breathe like that. But it was a waste of breath to say anything. Maxann would just ignore her.

"You know," Maxann said when she could talk again. "I'd done made up my mind to buy the things, but this guy, he just loved the sound of his own voice. He says, 'You're making a smart purchase with these canisters, ma'am. They come from a good family, and they'll bring you good karma.' I just looked at him. I said, 'What the hell do I need with karma? This is America, buddy.' "

"I don't even know what karma is," Pansy said.

"Oh, karma," Percilla said. "Karma's . . . well, it's like your horoscope, honey. It's your future."

"Jesus H. Christ, Percilla, it ain't no such a thing." Maxann shook her head and gave Percilla a mean look that would've hurt Pansy's feelings, but Percilla had always had a thicker skin than the rest of them. "Karma is this Indian—India the country, I mean—word for getting what's coming to you. Don't you remember nothing about the sixties?"

"Well, excuse me," Percilla said, drawing herself up straight. Maybe her skin wasn't as thick as Pansy had thought. "I reckon I missed the sixties. I was too busy working my ass off and having babies. I didn't have time for no karma or none of that other hippie go-go shit like some people."

And there goes Christmas fellowship, goodwill, and peace on earth, Pansy thought. "Now, girls," she said. "It's Christmas." And with those two words she all of a sudden felt too tired to put up with any more from anybody. Usually they had to be run out of the Christmas party so the cleanup crew could get to work. Even though they seen each other every day, they still loved to sit and talk after the party, tell about their Christmas plans. But the party was over and it had been a long day, a long week, hell, a long year. It was time to go home. They all looked surprised when she stood up and started gathering her things, but then Idalene spoke up and said, "I reckon it is about that time, girls."

Lottie May stood up too and looked toward the corner where Nisco lay asleep on a pile of coats. "Yeah, I better get Nisco home. He'll be wanting his supper soon."

As she was putting her coat on, the door opened and Dan came walking in and Pansy felt so relieved she didn't have to go looking for him. She wanted to go home, wanted to lay down and rest for a while. Christmas was right around the corner and she had so much to do, but all she could think about right now was laying on the couch and closing her eyes for just a minute or two.

Rex followed Dan and the door shut behind him. Where was Laurel? That worry returned, that nagging feeling that she should know what was bothering her own daughter, should be doing something about it. There were so damn many shoulds in her life—she should be taking better care of Dan and Laurel and Cecil and the grandbabies and her friends and her house and her neighbor. No wonder she felt tired all the time. When was somebody going to take care of her?

IN HER daddy's workshop in the shed out back of the house, surrounded by his tools hanging neatly on pegboard, the clutter of different sizes of lumber in the corner, the smell of sawdust and machine oil, the sound of his drill or his sander drowning out any need for talk, Laurel felt the safest she had in a long time. As a little girl she loved to come out with her dolls and watch him work, just be with him, as he put together a bookshelf or a table. He always had something to show for his work, something you could see and touch and use every day. It must be so nice to be able to make useful things that could also be beautiful. She'd never had any hobbies other than reading and riding horses, and what good did that do anybody except her? Sewing, painting, musical instruments—she'd tried it all and given up after only a few weeks, bored with trying. Her daddy even tried to teach her woodworking, until she nearly caused him to cut off his finger with the Skil saw. And now here she was without even a job, a parasite, a drain on society.

"What are you making?" she said, when he cut the sander off. He pushed his safety glasses up on his head and started brushing sawdust off the wood.

"Your mama's anniversary present. Potting bench." Dan set the board down and, acting nonchalant, said, "I reckon she got me that new drill I been wanting."

Lord, the man was worse than a child when it came to presents. Every year until they were old enough to keep their mouths shut, he'd tricked her and Cecil into telling what he was getting from them, from Mama, from Santa Claus. "Forget it, old man," she said, shaking her head.

"That's all right. I still got time." He winked and pulled the glasses down over his eyes.

That was one of the many things she loved about her daddy, how good-natured he was, never moody or hard to figure out like her mama, who had seemed even more so this visit. She picked up a hammer, held it upside down, and let it swing back and forth like a pendulum. "Is Mama all right?" she said, watching the hammer. "I mean, she looks like she's lost weight, and she seems sort of, I don't know, moody."

Without looking up, Dan said, "She's just tired. You know Christmas wears her out."

"She never used to get that tired."

"Well, honey, I reckon we're getting old." He grinned like the thought didn't bother him at all and turned on the sander, drowning out anything else she might've wanted to say.

Laurel had never given much thought to her parents aging before, and she didn't want to now, but there it was, staring her in the face. They were still young, only fifty-seven, but the fact of them getting old seemed more real now. Would they someday not be able to care for themselves and have to go into a nursing home like Maw Bert? Scott's parents had already bought a condo in a fancy retirement community in Charleston. They were a few years older but still in good shape. Yet they'd sold their house and gladly gone to live with the other old folks. Laurel couldn't see her parents doing that. They loved this place too much, they'd worked too hard for it, not to mention the fact that they were too independent to ever live in a nursing home, if they could even find one that would take them.

It scared the shit out of her, thinking of them getting older, herself getting older. The responsibility of looking after them would probably fall on her since she was single, the spinster daughter who'd be expected to stay home and look after the old folks, and when they died she'd get the house and spend the rest of her lonely days holed up here until she was found by the mailman or a neighbor, dead in the middle of the kitchen floor in her nightgown, laying in a puddle of spilled milk.

Aside from the fact that she loved her parents and would miss them terribly, she guessed what it boiled down to was the comfort of having another layer between her and death. When her parents died, she'd be next in line. She wondered if they ever thought about things like that, how there was no layer left for them, they were it, the top of the pile, the next in line to be scraped off by the big D. Good God, I'm being morbid, Laurel thought, watching her daddy work and feeling guilty for thinking him into old age and death like that, glad he still had that full head of hair and didn't look one bit like an old man.

He turned off the sander and ran his hands around the edges of the wood again. "Smooth as a baby's butt," he said.

"What part is that?"

"A shelf for the top." He brushed the board off, put wood glue on the ends and back edge, then tapped it into the grooves in the bench. "She can keep her gloves and Miracle-Gro and all up there." He dragged the bench from behind the table where his sander and saws sat. "What do you think?"

"She'll love it. How'd you get that heart cut out in the top panel?"

Dan waved his hands in front of his face. "Magic," he said. "Come on, Little Bit, let's go before she comes looking for us."

"Why don't you give it to her now?"

"Tomorrow's our anniversary and that's when she gets her present. Don't you go telling her what it is, neither."

"I'm not a tattletale." He gave her a look. "Not anymore," she added. He wasn't the only one she and Cecil had told about their presents.

"We'll see," he said.

Laurel went out ahead of him and he stopped to lock the door, something he never did.

"You're serious about this thing, aren't you?"

"Your mama can be nosy." He put the keys under the mat and took a deep breath. "Smell that clean air. Come on, let's go up front and look at the Christmas lights again."

He was so proud, he'd dragged her out every night to admire them. On a normal night, they could stand in the middle of the road and never worry about getting run over, but the traffic always picked up at Christmastime because her daddy went crazy decorating the yard and people drove by for the free show, so they had to stand by the mailbox to keep from getting hit. People would roll down their windows and tell them hey, or good job, or man, I'd hate to have your power bill. Her mama thought it was tacky and had managed to keep only white lights on the tree in the house and the candles in each window, but her daddy liked color. A little trash and flash at Christmastime was good for the soul, he said. Every bush along the front of the house had been draped in lights, as well as the lower branches of the two maple trees in the middle of the yard. He outlined the windows and doors with lights and hung those icicle lights from the gutters. The collection of life-size lighted yard art included Santa and Mrs. Claus, Santa in a sleigh, Santa in a car, Santa in a helicopter, Santa in a canoe with a black bear, a group of ten carolers, two snowmen, and a Nativity complete with baby Jesus in a manger, Mary, Joseph, wise men, camels, sheep, donkeys, and an angel on top of the little wooden stable. It was a production. The funny thing was, he'd never done this when they were kids. He stayed out of Christmas pretty much altogether, except for opening his wallet. Christmas had always been Mama's holiday, while summer vacation was Daddy's.

She noticed that this year he'd added lights on the roof of the house. They spelled out MERRY CHRISTMAS in great big letters, and there was a big X next to the chimney so Santa couldn't miss it. Cecil's kids loved it, and Laurel envied them that wonderful Christmas buzz that used to hit at Thanksgiving and last until she fell asleep Christmas night clutching that year's doll or book or both. Why did that have to disappear when you grew up? Although, if her daddy was anything to go by, it came back in middle age and then some, second childhood with a bank account to back it up. He put his arm around her and squeezed. "Well, what you think of my masterpiece?"

"You're keeping Duke Power in business, that's for sure."

He groaned and put a hand to his heart. "The great ones are always unappreciated until after they're gone."

She put her arm around his waist and laid her head against his chest. His heart beat big and slow and steady, and she wanted to keep her ear there and listen to it forever. "I appreciate you, Daddy," she said.

He squeezed her closer. "Wish you wasn't leaving tomorrow."

"Me too," she said, pulling away from him, overcome with evil-daughter guilt. He'd been dropping hints for days about her staying for New Year's. Maybe since Scott wasn't around to oppose, he thought she'd cave in. And God, it wasn't as if she wanted to get in that car tomorrow morning with no idea where to go after that. But with no alternative, all she could think to do was follow the original script. Too late for revisions, even if it meant watching Dick Clark in a Motel 6 by herself. Stick to the plan, stick to the plan, stick to the plan. Maybe if she said it enough times, an actual plan would appear in her head like a map, something with directions, something to show her the way.

3

DÉJÀ VU, LAUREL THOUGHT. WAS SHE GOING TO END up one of those pitiful people who lived in their car because they had nowhere else to go? If she could only think of a destination, she might be able to actually leave the driveway. There was no reason to keep sitting here, suitcases and gifts in the back. Her daddy had loaded the car for her and started it up so it would be nice and warm when she got in. He was so sweet to her. Didn't look at her with all those unspoken questions like her mama did. Christmas Eve she'd overheard him saying they should just leave her alone, let her tell them in her own time. It almost made her cry, how sweet he was.

Trouble was, she'd tried and tried to figure out where to go and what to do next, tried to make some kind of plan, but her mind just slammed shut, said don't go there, it's not looking too good right now.

If her watch was correct, she'd been sitting here for ten minutes. She reached over and turned the heat down. It was so cold that her mama and daddy hadn't come out with her to say good-bye. They'd shut the door and gone about their business. Or were they watching out the window now, wondering what was taking her so long, afraid to come out and see about their crazy daughter? They probably couldn't wait to get the house back to themselves, and Laurel didn't blame them. She wouldn't want to be around her either. All she did was sleep and watch TV and mope around in her pajamas like she was sick. No wonder her mama kept making grilled cheese.

It wasn't as if she didn't have a plan. She had a plan. The plan was to back out of the driveway and go until it got dark, then stop at a motel and get up the next morning and go again. Eventually it would come to her what to do after that.

Now it had been fifteen minutes. Weren't they wondering what she was doing just sitting out here? She kept intending to put her foot on the brake, put the car in reverse, and step on the accelerator. Something was interrupting the signal between her brain and her feet, though.

Her daddy's pickup sat in front of her, the back loaded with Christmas trash to take to the landfill later, but right now he was probably in front of the TV, watching some weird show about buffalo or volcanoes or rubber bands on the Discovery Channel, while her mama messed around in the kitchen, already trying to decide what to make later for lunch, even though they'd just finished breakfast an hour ago.

The heat in the car really was unbearable now. She couldn't stand it anymore, opened the door and got out, leaving the engine running. The cold felt good against her cheeks and she pulled her gloves off to feel it on her hands. She wandered down the driveway, letting her hand slide along the chipped paint on her daddy's truck, his good old truck he'd had forever and would never part with even though it looked like it had been through a war or a tornado. She stood under the basketball net where she and Cecil had played a million games of horse, wishing for a ball so she could try out her old granny shot that never missed. Then she saw the shed and realized that was what she wanted, to see her daddy's workshop one last time. Just a quick look and then she'd go. She got the key and let herself in.

It was cold without the space heater on, but she wouldn't be there long enough to need it. She got up on the stool behind her daddy's worktable, reached out and ran a hand down the side of her mama's new potting bench. He was right, smooth as a baby's butt, and she was going to love it. They were so lucky. Did they even realize? They had this great marriage that would last them all their lives. They never had to worry about being lonely, never had to sleep with a light on because they were afraid to wake up in the dark alone, never had to sit watching TV at night wishing they had somebody to laugh with, never had to give up cooking because cooking for one was just too much trouble, never had to wonder who'd drive them to the emergency room in the middle of the night if they ever got sick, never had to sleep holding a pillow in their arms instead of a real person, never had to walk into a restaurant or a movie or a department store and feel conspicuous because everybody in the world had somebody, everybody but you. Oh, God, oh, God, she thought, please help me, please.

She didn't know how long she'd been sitting there like a zombie, watching her breath make little clouds, when her mama found her.

"Laurel?" she said, peeking around the door as if she was afraid she might be disturbing her. It almost made Laurel laugh, the way her mama's head jerked when she saw her. Who did she think it was? All signs point to Laurel—car door open, motor running, no daughter in sight.

"Laurel." Pansy came all the way in the room then but stood with her body angled toward the door, as if she might need to run for help any second.

Laurel didn't say anything, didn't know what to say, just waited.

"Honey, what are you doing? It's cold in here."

"I'm not cold." Laurel pulled a warm hand out of her coat pocket and touched her nose. It felt like a little ice cube. The problem wasn't that she was cold. The problem was that her whole body kept shaking. What would her mama do if she just fell off this stool like a dead bird off its perch? Why didn't she say something, for God's sake? Did she have to spell it out? Why couldn't they ask her so she wouldn't have to sit there like an idiot?

"So. I guess you've been wondering what's really going on with me and Scott," Laurel said finally, surprised because she hadn't known she was going to say that. What a segue.

Pansy moved closer and stood on the opposite side of the worktable, her eyes busy searching Laurel's face for clues. Sorry, Mama, Laurel thought. The outside is smooth and flawless. It's the inside that's all screwed up. Pansy was the one who looked tense as she started brushing sawdust onto the floor. "What about you and Scott?"

Too late Laurel remembered the potting bench beside her, which her daddy had meant to be a surprise tonight after supper. Maybe her mama wouldn't notice, but no, she'd seen it, seemed to be appraising it, as if she already knew about it anyway. She probably did. Didn't she always know everything? She knew when Laurel lied about denting the car, knew it wasn't some hit-and-run in the Sky City parking lot, though Laurel had never told her what really happened, that she backed up without looking and hit a tree. She knew when Craig dumped her for Carmen, though Laurel had told everybody she dumped him. Her mama always knew. So why, then, didn't she know now? Had she forgotten how to pay attention?

Actually, she felt ridiculous for not just calling and telling them when it happened. Not telling them had made it into such a stupid big deal. She could've gotten this all over with on the phone and wouldn't be sitting here now, freezing her ass off, scared to death to ask her own mama for help. It wasn't that she didn't think her mama would give it. She knew they'd do anything for her if they could. It was just so damn humiliating, running home to Mommy and Daddy with her tail between her legs, especially since they'd never liked Scott in the first place.

Laurel realized she was breathing through her mouth as if she'd been running, and the cold air burned her lungs. She put her lips together and sucked air in through her nose, and a sharp pain flashed inside her head. Her mama must be getting really worried now, because she stepped around the table and put her arm across Laurel's back. "Honey, you're shaking like a leaf. We can talk just as good in the house. Come on, let's go."

With her mama trying to ease her off the stool, Laurel felt something inside her shift, about to break open, the way a frozen river will crack when warm water starts running under the ice. She almost laughed again, thinking of herself as a river, frozen solid, only not, because now she was crying in her mama's arms, remembering a time she'd been riding her bike and hit a bump and flew over the handlebars and skidded down the road on her belly, her head bouncing on the pavement. Those were the days before helmets and pads. All she had on was a T-shirt and a pair of culottes. She got up and ran, just ran, finding her house and her mama by pure instinct, and her mama had made everything better. Laurel didn't hold out such hope this time, not for the long haul, but for now her mama was doing a pretty good job, holding her, letting her cry, making those mama noises children need to hear sometimes, even grown children.

"All right," she said. "I'm here. I've got you."

When she calmed down and could think straight again, Laurel would tell her everything, tell her daddy too. She'd let them decide what she ought to do and she'd do it, just for a little while, just until she figured it out for herself.

THE MORNING sun blinded Laurel as she followed Pansy out of the shed, then ran smack into her back. "Mama. What did you stop for?" She stepped to the side and put a hand up to shade her eyes, using her other hand to wipe under her nose. God, she hated crying. She saw then what her mama had seen, a police car in the driveway behind her car, a tall policeman standing next to it talking to her daddy. "Is that one of Daddy's buddies?" she said, thinking there was something familiar about the guy.

Dan saw them, raised a hand, then went back to talking to the cop. "Lord, I don't know," Pansy said, and turned toward the house. "Probably. Let's go in. It's freezing out here."

Laurel was about to follow when her daddy hollered for her to come over. Oh, shit, she thought, am I going to have to go over there with raccoon eyes and a nose like a blister and be charming to Daddy's friend? He was waving her over now and she couldn't pretend she hadn't seen. What the hell? She didn't know the guy from Adam, didn't care how she looked for some dumb cop.

As she got closer, she couldn't help staring, not sure why she had such a strong feeling that she knew him from somewhere. He looked about her age, not bad-looking, but with his hair cut so short and his collar buttoned, his face looked a little puffy. Probably looked better out of uniform, maybe in a V-neck. "Hey," she said, rubbing her arms to let them know she was cold and wanted to wrap this up and go inside.

"Honey," Dan said. "This is Joe Clark. He's with the sheriff's department."

Joe cleared his throat, tilted his head in her direction. "I believe we went to school together."

So that's where she knew him from. "I thought you looked familiar. You went to Jackson?" It was coming back to her now, the image of a scrawny boy in her class, flattop haircut in a time when most boys wore their hair long. Old Joe Clark, who was teased mercilessly because of his old-man shirts buttoned up to the neck and high-water pants and white socks and brown brogans. She hadn't known him, not really. They traveled in different circles, she with the Beta Club crowd and he on the vocational track, the early work-release crowd, the people that she, in her college-bound arrogance, had thought of as losers. Wasn't it nice he'd turned out to be a cop, and wasn't it weird that he ended up in her driveway?

"Honey," Dan said, taking a good look at his feet before looking back up at her. "Joe here got a call from the manager of Wal-Mart this morning. Said they's been a U-Haul parked out there about a week now. The U-Haul people give him your name and this address."

Laurel's mouth fell open in a silent, *Oh*, and she closed her eyes, thinking, shit shit shit. Embarrassed did not begin to cover how she felt at that moment. Exposed, pathetic, humiliated—that might do it. Who was the loser now, huh, Laurel? The gainfully employed and respected public servant, or the homeless, destitute, out-of-work slug whose few remaining worldly possessions now sat as abandoned as their owner in a U-Haul at the local Wal-Mart?

"I am so sorry," she said, her voice coming out in a croak. She looked up at Dan, her eyes pleading with him to go along, to not ask for an explanation until after Joe left. "I was going to get it today, I swear."

"Well, it's not a problem," Joe said. "Just wanted to make sure it wasn't stolen."

Dan, feet spread wide apart, crossed his arms over his chest, all business now. Such a man pose, Laurel thought, surprised he didn't spit off into the grass too. He said, "We'll go out there this morning and take care of it. Appreciate you stopping by, Joe."

"Yes, thanks." Laurel hesitated, then added, "Joe."

"You're welcome." He smiled then, and the transformation was amazing, changing him instantly from sober lawman to mischievous little boy, little boy with a real dimple in his chin. What was this, Laurel thought, remembering Hap, a smorgasbord of clefts after wandering in the desert without them so long?

"I better get back on the road," Joe said. "Y'all have a happy New Year."

As he backed out of the driveway, Laurel smiled and waved, wondering if his personality was as black and white as his face. She suspected not. Something told her there were layers.

The way her daddy was looking at her, she knew she had some explaining to do, but the first thing she had to do was hug him, hang on to the solidness of him for a minute. Then she'd tell him about Scott and the divorce, tell him she'd be staying awhile if he didn't mind, and he wouldn't. That was one of the few things she knew for sure. Her mama and daddy would always want her.

PANSY WONDERED how she always got stuck both putting up the tree and taking it down by herself. It was Dan's tree too, but he always found some excuse, some errand he had to run, like now, taking Laurel to pick up her U-Haul. He was a master at getting out of work, although what he was doing now counted as work, she reckoned. And at least she had the house to herself for a little while. With Laurel home, and Cecil and Lisa and the kids over so much this week, several times Pansy had felt like screaming at them all to get out. And it wasn't over yet. There was still their anniversary and New Year's, and then no telling how long Laurel would stay after that. It had broke her heart to see Laurel so tore up, but there was also a tiny little voice in a back corner of her mind that said, How could she let that happen to herself?

She got the plastic tubs out of the bottom of the hall closet and dragged them into the living room next to the tree. Her mama always said it was bad luck to leave the tree up after New Year's and told a story about a woman who left the tree up till her son come home from the army and he got killed on the way, and it was all the tree's fault. Still, it didn't hurt to be careful. Every year Pansy took their tree down New Year's Eve day, but this year she didn't feel like waiting. Today or tomorrow, it was all the same. Christmas was done and over with, time to get the house back to normal. She wanted all the decorations packed up, the couch moved against the wall, and the tree out of here in time for Dan to take it to the dump before it closed. But instead of starting on the tree, she plugged the lights in and sat on the couch to look at it one more time. She and Dan used to sit there every evening after supper, just looking at the lights and listening to Bing Crosby and Johnny Mathis Christmas albums, but this year they'd missed that. Laurel wanted the TV on, watching them crazy Christmas shows she'd seen a million times when she was little. Was that what Christmas meant to her, TV? If so, Pansy felt ashamed of herself for letting it happen. But only people in TV families had time to do all that Christmas stuff they showed in magazines—baking cookies, going caroling, making homemade wrapping paper. Working people didn't have time for that. They had done fun things with the kids, though. They drove all over town looking at lights, sat around the kitchen table playing Rummikub and eating fruitcake cookies, wrapped presents together with the Christmas music playing. They'd done a lot of family stuff, and still Laurel's favorite part seemed to be the TV shows.

When she was little, her favorite part of Christmas was going to get the tree. Her and the boys would go with Daddy and cut it down, and on the way back she got to sit on the tree while they carried it. The boys would bounce her up and down, but Daddy wouldn't let them throw her off. Her mama would have the lights and ornaments all set out and start decorating as soon as Daddy got the tree set up. She'd let them help, handing them the glass balls one at a time, gold and silver and red and green, the hook already attached so all they had to do was find the perfect spot and hang it. The boys usually got bored quick and went outside to help Daddy, so it was Pansy and her mama putting on the ornaments and the garland, always silver because gold was tacky, and the final step, a good spray of canned snow over the whole thing. Pansy had to stand back while her mama sprayed, didn't want her breathing the stuff. Pansy always wondered if her mama didn't care about her own lungs, or if it was only children who could be hurt by it.

Her mama walking around and around the tree, spraying that snow, was one of the few memories Pansy had of her without that pinched-up look on her face, the two lines across the middle of her forehead making her look like she was having trouble seeing. As she watched that snow drift and settle on the tree, she seemed to step into another world, a place she went all by herself and Pansy couldn't go, so she just watched and waited for her to come back. She'd always had the feeling that part of her mama wanted to leave them, just get on a bus and never look back, and because of that part, she was never completely there with them. There was always that part of her mama wanting to be gone, and not just at Christmas. Seemed like fall was the worst time, and her mama would get so nervous with summer coming to a close, watching them all go off to school or work at the mill, leaving her by herself. Pansy had to run straight home every day and see about her mama, for the boys wouldn't do it, couldn't stand all that crying. They'd stay out doing chores and Pansy would be in the house, making sure the supper didn't burn, praying, *Please be on time, Daddy, please,* while her mama sat in that rocking chair, big tears sliding down her face, waiting on him to come from the mill. Even with her mama right in the room, and the boys right outside, Pansy would feel like the last person left on earth, a lonesomeness like water closing over her head in a dark pond, and by the time her daddy walked in that door, it was hard to tell who was happier to see him, her or her mama. To this day, Pansy still got to feeling sad when the light changed in August, the way it does when summer starts giving way to fall, the days shorter and the sun tilted just enough to make the world look different.

That all changed when her and Dan started dating, though. She'd known him her whole life, all through school, and thought he was nice and nice-looking but never noticed him that way, not till he noticed her first, and then she couldn't remember a time she hadn't been crazy about him. He took her to football games, basketball games, the movies, out to eat, riding in the country. That was the best, them rides when she'd roll down the window of his truck and let the wind blow her hair back and just be free for a little while.

Her mama hated Dan, and the only reason Pansy could figure was because being with Dan meant she wasn't home, stuck in that house. She hated to think it but couldn't help wondering if her mama didn't want her to be happy. Dan, he had saved her in so many ways. He loved her, and he got her away. She probably would've never had the guts to leave without him. When they eloped, a big rock lifted off her soul and she felt free for the first time in her life. She wished Laurel could find somebody to make her feel like that. She hated to think of her going through the rest of her life alone. And she certainly didn't want her to end up here, taking care of them in their old age.

Pansy stood up, opened the plastic tubs and took out the stacks of ornament boxes, then started taking balls and Hallmarks off the tree and packing them away. She didn't have many Hallmarks, because she could get a box of twelve balls for the price of one Hallmark. But she'd splurged on a few over the years. There was Laurel's Barbie—the original blue-eye-shadowed Barbie, not that trashy Malibu version—Cecil's fire truck, Dan's Model T Ford driven by Santa, and hers, a little artist mouse. She held the ornament up by the hook and twirled it, the mouse so cute in a little green smock and red beret, holding a paintbrush and palette.

Then the colors blurred together and she was standing there crying for no good reason. No good reason, she thought, which scared her so bad she sat back down. What on earth was the matter with her, crying over a Christmas ornament? She laid it beside her on the couch and put her face in her hands. Oh, Lord, please, she thought. Please don't let me be losing my mind. She wiped her eyes and stood back up. Dan and Laurel would be home soon. They'd come in all cheerful and happy the way they always done, wanting lunch, and Pansy would have to act like this never happened, like she hadn't wanted to curl up in a ball and cry herself to sleep.

She reached for a Kleenex from the box on the coffee table and blew her nose, then looked up at the tree. In the brightness of the midday light coming through the sheers over the big windows, it looked so different than it did at night. It'd been up since Thanksgiving, and the limbs drooped and needles were falling off. It looked like she felt, old and used up. She went to the bathroom and washed her face in cold water, then came back and started taking off the rest of the ornaments, deciding that after that she'd go start lunch and let Dan and Laurel deal with taking the lights off. She'd always hated that part.

4

WORKING IN THE SHED SEEMED LIKE FUN AFTER DOING
nothing for a week but laying around on her butt, eating too much and
talking even more to various relatives making their Christmas visits, all
wanting to know the same thing—where was Scott?—as if she'd appeared this year with an arm or a leg missing. The solitude of the shed
was wonderful in spite of the cold and dust and dirt and mildew. The
shed's storage room had no electrical outlet, so she'd dragged her
daddy's space heater as close to the door as the cord would allow and
turned it on full blast. It didn't help much, so she kept moving, dragging boxes and bags of junk across the concrete floor and stacking them
on one side to make room for her stuff on the other.

Some of it was Maw Bert's stuff, boxes that had been packed up
when she had to move to the nursing home after the stroke. Laurel had
no clue what was inside. She and Scott had just moved to Vegas then and
she'd just started a new job and couldn't leave to come home and help
her mama. She lifted the flaps of one box and saw pots and pans, Blue
Willow dishes in another. Looked like they'd cleaned out the entire
house, kept everything. Why didn't they have a yard sale and get rid of
some of this junk? Though of course she was glad in a way that she'd get
a chance to go through it all and see if there was anything she wanted.

The grime that had accumulated in such a relatively short time was unreal, and Laurel felt it on her hands, her hair, her face, even in her mouth. In the dim light from the little window, Laurel checked her watch, wanting to make sure she finished in time to clean up for her parents' anniversary supper. Her daddy was cooking steaks on the gas grill, and she and Cecil had ordered a big cake, which he was supposed to be picking up. She'd need to call and make sure he didn't forget.

In addition to Maw Bert's stuff, her mama had packed away stacks of boxes and bags too, each one neatly labeled with a list of the contents. *Blankets. Shoes. Toys.* Things her mama didn't need anymore but couldn't bear to part with. One box said *spring/summer linens, curtains, place mats.* Since when had her mama taken to changing the decor with the seasons? Maybe she'd been watching Martha Stewart, probably got the labeling idea from her too. It did make sorting through things a lot easier, though, and Laurel decided that sometime in the next couple weeks she'd get out here and inventory Maw Bert's stuff and label it too. What else did she have to do, except look for a job, something she dreaded? But her cash was running low and no way she'd take money from her parents. It was bad enough she had to live with them for a while.

When she'd cleared one wall in the storage room, she went out to the U-Haul to get her stuff. There, inside the smallest trailer they made, was her life in almost literally a nutshell. She hadn't even been able to fill it up, so it didn't take long to move everything out. Dan and Pansy had gone to the grocery store, thank God. Laurel didn't think she could've stood for them to see what her life had been reduced to. Only last year she'd counted her blessings because she had so much—a husband, a home, a job. And now, none of the above.

When the U-Haul was empty she went back to the storage room to take a last look before closing it up. There it sat against the wall, her life. When would it see the light of day again? She couldn't imagine where she was going to end up and therefore had no place to imagine her things. They wouldn't be staying in Russell, that was for sure, although there were worse places they could end up, but she couldn't think of any at the moment. She was a cliché, a grown woman forced by circumstances beyond her control to move home with her parents. The humiliation of that alone might be enough to kill her.

She wiped dust off Maw Bert's rocker, the only furniture she'd kept, the only piece she really cared about, then pulled it over next to Maw Bert's boxes and sat rocking and studying her own. They didn't need labels. She knew exactly what each one contained. The big one held pillows and blankets, the medium-size ones held linens, kitchen stuff, clothes, shoes, and doodads. The smaller ones held books, boxes and boxes of her treasures. She missed them, missed seeing them, missed skimming the spines, looking for old friends or something new to discover. She collected books the way some women collected dolls or thimbles or bells, or angels, like her mama. There must be a hundred angels in that living room now, all shapes and sizes and made out of everything from porcelain to wood to plastic to pecan shells. The weird thing was, they weren't tacky. The way her mama displayed them, they seemed a natural part of the room, small groupings of them on tabletops, on a small bookshelf by the front door, and in a lighted curio cabinet in the corner.

She leaned back and closed her eyes, just rocking, trying not to think about anything, thinking maybe she'd take a little nap. It was too cold, though, and she kept rocking faster and faster, her muscles tightening, trying to stay warm. Her hand dropped down to the top of the nearest box and she stopped rocking and pulled open the flap. Leaning over to peer inside, she recognized Maw Bert's pocketbooks, the big old-fashioned kind that hung from the crook of a lady's arm, nearly big enough to carry a baby. There were three of them, one red, one black, and one tan. She'd carried those same leather bags for as long as Laurel could remember, didn't believe in buying a new one when the old ones still had plenty of wear, regardless of whether or not they were in style. Laurel used to play with them, loving the feel of the metal clasps opening and closing in her fingers, carrying the bag in the crook of her arm even though it banged against her shins. She opened the one on top, hoping to find some forgotten treasure left by Maw Bert, but found only a few still-sweet-smelling Juicy Fruit gum wrappers, a receipt from the A&P and one from Woolworth's—both closed now—and an old Avon lipstick, one of the tiny white plastic samples. Laurel held it up to the light to read the color: *Passionflower.*

When she opened the tiny tube there was still some lipstick in it, a rich dark red that she remembered seeing on her grandmother's mouth every time she fixed up to go to town. Laurel had always watched the transformation in awe, loving the way her plain old practical old Maw Bert rolled her hair, put on bra, girdle, hose, dress, heels, makeup, costume jewelry, and transformed herself into a whole new person, someone Laurel hardly recognized. This woman had a shape like an hourglass, not the round, lumpy figure of her Maw Bert, and this woman looked glamorous and sophisticated, like the ladies who worked at the bank. It also had made Laurel a little afraid, seeing Maw Bert so changed, and she was always relieved to have her back barefoot in a cotton housedress with pockets on the front that held safety pins and buttons and butterscotch for Laurel to reach in and take whenever she felt like it.

She sniffed the lipstick, wondering if it was still good, then dabbed some on and rubbed her lips together. Passionflower. She said it out loud. *Maw Bert in Passionflower*. No, Maw Bert would not wear that. Maw Bert put Vaseline on her lips to keep them from getting chapped. But Alberta Marie wore Passionflower, and it suited her. Laurel had always wished they had pictures of Maw Bert as a child or young woman, but the youngest she'd ever seen was a studio portrait when she was in her forties. God, Laurel thought, here I am, sneaking up on forty myself. It scared the shit out of her. It wouldn't be so bad if she had something to show for her life, something like her mama and grandma had, a family, a home, something.

A wave of longing came over her then, and she realized that almost as much as she missed Maw Bert, she missed herself, herself as a child when everything was simple and everybody loved everybody and there was no such thing as grief or time. The feeling of loss washed over her as it had done every so often in the last year, just when she thought it might not come again, and she let herself cry, quietly but hard just like yesterday with her mama. She cried it all out, a luxury she hadn't allowed herself in Las Vegas because, alone as she was, she was afraid once it started it might never stop. Here it felt safe, though, and she was almost proud of herself for having two good cries in as many days. It must be healthy.

She regretted it for only a moment when she realized her mama would take one look and know she'd been sitting out here crying, but so what? Crying was a great release, and her mama would probably benefit from a little more of it herself. Laurel had seen her cry only at funerals. Didn't she ever allow herself a good, hard cry to clean out her system? Pansy had always seemed above that somehow, and Laurel didn't know if it meant she felt less than other people or if it just meant she didn't believe in sharing her feelings and dealt with them in private. If that was the case, she must not deal very much, because when did the woman ever have a minute to herself? Between husband, kids, grandkids, neighbors, job, church, she was pretty much booked solid. Her life would drive Laurel crazy, never a minute to sit quietly and read or think or just be.

She pulled out the other two pocketbooks and found more Juicy Fruit wrappers—no wonder the woman lost most of her teeth, all the sugar she consumed. There were more receipts, some hairpins, and that was it, no treasures. She was about to put the pocketbooks back when she saw a small wooden box, one of those cedar boxes high-school girls used to get from some furniture company for graduation. Laurel had gotten one herself, had no idea whatever happened to it. She wiped dust off the box with her sleeve, then put her nose down to the top of it, catching just the faintest, faintest smell of cedar. The beautiful red-gold color was gone from the wood because it had dried out and faded, but the smell had hung on just enough to remind her of something, she didn't know what, maybe days when she still believed anything was possible.

She tried to lift the lid but it was locked. She shook it. Sounded like it was full of something. She used both hands to pull at the lid, but it wouldn't open. On some level she knew it was wrong to look since it wasn't her property, but she looked around the shed for something to pry it open anyway. Pandora, that's what Maw Bert used to call her, because her curiosity could never be satisfied.

She went into her daddy's workshop and found a small file in his tool chest. Maw Bert was dead and couldn't possibly care anymore, and what her mama didn't know wouldn't hurt her. She took the file back to the storage room in case somebody walked in and caught her pilfering. It didn't take long to insert the file in the crack between the lid and the rest of the box and saw away the lock. It was a shame to ruin it, but the box was in bad shape anyway, warped and faded. A little thrill of excitement made her take her time lifting the lid. What did she expect to find? Money? Jewels? No, this was Maw Bert. It was probably more gum wrappers and receipts.

The musty smell that hit her nose as she opened the box convinced her it hadn't been opened in a long time. And, just as she thought, a bunch of old papers. She lifted the top paper, a grocery list written in Maw Bert's hand on the back of a Duke Power envelope. Onions, taters, bacon, lard. Under that was a stack of old bills from Tompkins Seed and Feed from the thirties and forties, and under that, old pay stubs for Grandpa Dill and Maw Bert from Revel Mill. She'd forgotten Maw Bert worked there when she was young. Under that were photographs, and Laurel pulled these out to look at more closely when she got where the light was better.

There was a rabbit's foot, dried flowers—probably from Grandpa's grave—a bunch of her mama's report cards, an old library card, some black thread taped to an index card, and newspaper clippings yellowed and crisp with age. Laurel unfolded the one on top, a photo labeled: FIVE CHILDREN ORPHANED, MOTHER KILLED, no caption, no article. Laurel looked at the back and saw an ad for a sale at Woolworth's. Aha, that's what Maw Bert had saved. The woman dearly loved Woolworth's and took Laurel there all the time when she was little. They'd shop, eat at the lunch counter, watch people go by. Laurel always felt so grown up, taking the taxi to town with Maw Bert and carrying bags for her.

Under the clippings was Pansy's certificate of baptism from Gum Springs Baptist Church, a blue ribbon with no indication of what it was for, and, stuck to the very bottom, a letter from Mount Holly College in Statesville addressed to Pansy Dillingham, postmarked June 1957. Laurel pulled at the edges and ran her fingers underneath so she could pull the letter out without tearing it. The top of the yellowed envelope had been slit with a letter opener, something she didn't think anybody in her family even owned. They just tore into the mail with their fingers and threw the envelopes away. Her mama had taken special care with this particular piece of mail, though. She turned the envelope up-side down and the letter slid out into her hand. There was no way she could stop herself from reading it now.

Dear Miss Dillingham, it read, and it was so weird to see her mama being addressed as anything but Mrs. Champion. *We are pleased to inform you that you have been accepted to Mount Holly College, and we are further pleased to inform you that you have been awarded the Mary C. Tuttle Scholarship for Most Promising Student of Art. This scholarship will cover tuition, fees, and all living expenses for your four-year program here at Mount Holly.* The letter went on to detail everything Pansy needed to do before arriving at Mount Holly, almost identical to Laurel's letter from Chapel Hill.

She laid the letter in her lap, stunned. Her mama applied and got accepted to college? And won a scholarship? For art? She'd told Laurel and Cecil how she used to love to paint when she was in school, but Laurel had never heard anything about this. She looked again at the name and address on the envelope and on the letter. Yes, Pansy Dillingham. How could she not know this? How could her mama not have told them? And what was worse, her mama had never gone to college; Laurel knew that much because the whole family always bragged about her and Cecil being the first generation to go. Why? What happened?

Pansy went to work in the mill the summer after graduation, and not long after that she got married and started having babies. Maybe she just forgot about the letter. But wouldn't she have remembered when Laurel was getting ready to go to college? Especially when her mama knew how scared she was to leave home and go off by herself and leave everyone and everything she loved behind. Didn't Pansy realize it would've helped Laurel to know that she had faced the same fears? It did make sense, though, Pansy's insistence that Laurel and Cecil both go. Laurel couldn't remember specific instances where her mama told her she was going to college; she'd just known it all her life, aware on some level that this knowledge came, somehow, directly from her mama. Maybe she wanted her kids to fulfill a dream she hadn't been brave enough to follow herself.

More likely, though, was that Pansy deliberately didn't tell them, probably because she was ashamed and embarrassed that she made them do something she was too scared to do herself. Part of Laurel wanted to run to the house, wave the letter and say, *Your secret's out, Pansy.* But didn't she have to respect her mama's privacy, especially since she valued her own so much? Her mama hadn't pushed her to talk about Scott, had let her tell it in her own time, and Laurel would return the favor. Of course, that didn't mean she couldn't do a little digging in the meantime, ask a few questions and see what came out.

She put the other papers back and picked up the photos, but the light from the window was nearly gone. She got up and went to stand directly under it, squinting in the dim glow. One picture showed a teenage Pansy sitting with Maw Bert on that old galvanized-metal glider in the backyard under the chestnut trees, next to the garden. The corn behind them rose tall and thick, and a white cat lay on its side in the grass beside the glider. They were looking at the cat and laughing, Maw Bert's mouth wide open showing her crooked teeth, her mama's mouth closed, lips curving up, cheeks rounding under her eyes. She looked like she had a secret, but then again, didn't most teenagers?

Another photo showed an unsmiling Grandpa Dill and Maw Bert in a studio photograph from the forties. Grandpa Dill, a short, slender man, wore a wool suit, white shirt, and striped tie. The brim of a big black hat shaded his piercing eyes, high cheekbones, and thick salt-and-pepper beard, making him look like an outlaw. The way he stood next to Maw Bert, it looked as if he might be holding a gun to her back, while she appeared to be his plump, unhappy captive. She wore a plain black coat over a white blouse, her dark hair styled close to her head and emphasizing the roundness of her face. No makeup, no jewelry, and apparently no corset, because her bosom hung halfway between her neck and her hips. Why would she get all dolled up to go to town when Laurel was little but not bother for this picture? Laurel figured if she had a husband, a farm, and eight children, she'd look like that too, as if she didn't care if Grandpa Dill did shoot her.

There were several school pictures of the boys—her uncles—and one of her mama, not a studio picture but one taken in the front yard before the road was paved. It ran behind her, a chalky dirt ribbon running perpendicular to the length of her body, winding away into the distance. Behind her lay the same pasture that Laurel could step out-side and see today, hilly and backed by tall pines and cedars. Pansy looked about fifteen, her eyes and mouth smiling from between dark curtains of hair on either side of her face, wearing shorts, tank top, and no shoes, holding in front of her a picture, what looked like a painting of two people on the porch of a house. Laurel held it closer to her face, trying to see who it was, but the painting was too small. But there it was, evidence of the artist, right there, in a picture she'd never seen be-fore in her life.

The Pandora urge rose in her stronger than ever, but it was getting late, her parents would be home soon, and she still had to shower and dress. Their present, an enlarged and silver-framed photo of them on their wedding day, leaning back on the hood of her daddy's old Ford af-ter they'd run off to South Carolina to get married, wasn't anything fancy, but they looked happy and that was what counted. All she had to do was compare her own wedding photo to her parents' to see that clear as a bell. In all her photos she looked like she'd been crying, which she had, and those two little lines in the middle of her forehead made her look much older than twenty-two.

And that was her signal to get up and move, stop thinking about her wedding day or anything even remotely connected with it. She stood and quickly packed everything back into the little cedar box, then tucked it under her arm, turned off the heater, and hurried to the house. She didn't want her mama to catch her pilfering, didn't want the look and the lecture about how nosy she was. She'd put the box in her bedroom and later she could look at everything again, try to figure out if Maw Bert had saved it all on purpose or had simply used the box as a catchall, like her old pocketbooks. It would give her something to think about as she went to sleep, something besides herself.

THE HOUSE was chaos, but Pansy didn't mind. She'd grown to love the peace after the kids left, but the quiet still didn't feel right. Not that she wished the kids back. Lord, no. It had taken her a good year to get used to having the house to herself, but now she enjoyed it and couldn't imagine it any other way. It was almost like the early days of their marriage, just her and Dan, no noise, no messes. But it made for a nice change having the house full sometimes, having Laurel home too.

She looked around the table at them talking, Dan listening as Cecil and Lisa told about going camping at Lake Lure last summer. Cecil's three had gone into the living room to watch a video, and Pansy hoped they wasn't messing with her angels. They loved to get them down and play dolls even though they'd been warned not to. Taylor, Tucker, and Miller—Lord, them names just grated on her nerves sometimes. They seemed too uppity, too much name for little young'uns, but she figured Lisa's fourth one due in a couple of months would end up afflicted the same way, named Smith or Jones or some other last-name-sounding name. Still, if their names was all she had to complain about, she counted herself a lucky woman. Everybody was healthy and doing good, except maybe Laurel. Getting over a bad husband probably didn't take as long as getting over a good one, but it still took some getting over. She'd find her somebody new, though, somebody better. Pansy was sure of it.

The kids had ordered a beautiful cake, white with yellow icing roses. Pansy loved yellow roses because that was the first flower Dan had ever given her, plucked from a bush in his mama's yard on his way to their first date. She'd had to put Mercurochrome on his thumb where a thorn stuck him. That was when it struck her, holding his hand between both of hers. She knew just that quick he was the one, same way she knew when the wind whipped up on a cloudy day she better get the clothes off the line. Something had whipped up in her blood and told her, *Don't let go this one's hand, Pansy.* How quick it had happened, that going from carefree girl to woman in love, from all the possibilities of the world to only one desire.

"Mama, you look like you're off in your own little world," Laurel said.

Pansy smiled and leaned back in her chair, felt Dan's arm resting along the top behind her head. "I'm just thinking I can't believe I'm old enough to be married thirty-nine years."

"Tell us about your wedding," Lisa said, leaning forward, elbows on the table, chin in her hands, looking too young to be the married mother of three. Sometimes Pansy felt old as water, especially around

Lisa, who was always so perky and happy. She didn't see how Cecil stood it all the time, but then again, maybe she wasn't like that at home. Nobody knew what went on between a man and a woman behind closed doors, which was the way it ought to be. Private.

"Not much to tell, is there, Dan?" Pansy said, looking up at him. "We run off to Spartanburg and got married and come home the same night."

"No honeymoon?" Lisa said, a horrified expression on her face.

"Well," Pansy said. "We was going to spend the night at a hotel, but it started snowing and we figured we better get on back home. We had to work Monday and I was so afraid we wouldn't make it, the snow was coming down so thick. But it sure was pretty driving through it at night, the way them big fat flakes dropped down in front of the headlights. I couldn't see nothing but white all around. There wasn't no other cars on the road, and it felt like we was the only two people in the world. Didn't it, Dan?"

"Mmhm," Dan said.

"How come y'all to run off like that?" Cecil said. "You would've killed me and Laurel if we hadn't got married here."

Pansy looked in Dan's eyes and they didn't need any words, they was both thinking the same thing. Their reason for running off had seemed right at the time, and Pansy didn't have no regrets. They'd started talking about getting married after they graduated but decided to wait until the next year, save up their money, and have a June wedding. All that summer and fall, Pansy worked at the plant six days a week, coming home dog tired after being on her feet all day long. She didn't have the time or energy to do much except work and eat and sleep, and once or twice a week she and Dan would go out on a date.

One night she come home feeling so tired and lonesome for her daddy, she went straight to her room without speaking to her mama and reached under the bed for the old cardboard coat box where she kept her paintings from school. There was plenty of snapshots of him in the album, but they didn't show her the daddy she wanted to see, the way he looked when he was looking at her or something else he loved. When her hand couldn't find the box, she lifted the bedspread to look. No box. She sat up on her knees and thought for a minute. Last time she'd got the box out was in May when she put the latest painting, a picture of her art teacher, Mrs. Young, in there. She hadn't touched it since. Maybe her mama had wanted to look through it and forgot to put it back.

Pansy found her in the living room, in her rocker reading another romance. She must go through five or six of those things a week, Pansy thought. She'd never read one herself and didn't see the attraction. Maybe romance in a book was better than nothing.

"Mama?"

Bert looked up, her eyes taking a minute to focus on Pansy.

"Mama, have you seen my picture box? The one under the bed?"

Bert folded the corner of a page to mark her place and closed the book. She stared down at the cover, a picture of the head of a blond woman in a nurse's cap, a tall dark doctor standing in the background. Finally she said, without looking up, "It ain't here no more."

A bad feeling started under Pansy's ribs then, like what came before the dry heaves. "Mama?" she said, like she was talking to a child who had got caught doing something bad.

"Don't take that tone with me." Bert spoke calmly, then started rocking, slow and steady as she stared off in the corner like she was looking at the Christmas lights. "We got to get that tree took down tomorrow. It's bad luck to leave it up till New Year's."

Why in hell was she talking about the Christmas tree? Pansy took a deep breath, trying to remain calm. She was probably making a mountain out of a molehill. Her mama had just put the picture box in the closet, that was all. She never had liked having nothing under the beds, because it made it harder to sweep. "Mama, just tell me where it is, please?"

Bert stopped rocking and darted a quick look up at Pansy, then looked away again. "Now, Pansy, you don't need to be fooling with none of that and you working and fixing to get married. It was just taking up room in the house, collecting dust. So I throwed it out."

"Oh, my Lord, Mama." Pansy's voice came out so calm when what she really wanted to do was scream. She had a hard time stopping herself from yanking her mama out of the chair and shaking her. "Them was my things. You didn't have no right to do that. You didn't have no right!" Her voice got louder and louder until she was hollering, and then Bert stood and her hand landed against Pansy's jaw.

"You hush that mouth. I'm still your mother and this is my house and you'll not speak that-a-way to me."

Pansy touched her face, the side her mama had slapped hot and tingling, and closed her eyes, breathed in deep. She had to keep calm, at least for now, had to find out what her mama had done with her pictures so she could get them back.

Bert sat back down, her hands smoothing the wood arms of the rocker. "Now, I'm sorry, but it had to be done. And don't go thinking you'll find it because I done burnt it."

Her mama's lips kept moving, but the blood banged so loud in Pansy's ears, it drummed out the words. She couldn't have heard that right. Her mama did not burn her pictures, the one thing in life besides Dan she got any pleasure from. She wouldn't do that to her own child, would she?

Bert's face looked up at her, softer then, as if she hadn't just ripped out her daughter's heart and stomped on it. "Honey, I done it for you. Holding on to things like that ain't good for you."

Pansy couldn't remember ever hating a single soul in her whole life, but at that moment she hated her mama with every ounce of life in her body. Hated her and wished her dead. She turned and walked back to her room and quietly shut the door. She didn't cry then, didn't move, just lay on the bed in the dark listening to the house settle, listened to her mama get up, go to the bathroom, lock the doors, get in bed, turn out the light. The bedsprings creaked as Bert tossed and turned a long while. Finally everything was still and Pansy clicked on the lamp, sat up, got her suitcase from the closet, and started to pack. Lugging that big old suitcase, she walked two miles through the pitch dark to the nearest gas station and called Dan from a pay phone. At first his mama wouldn't get him out of the bed, but when she heard Pansy crying, she got him up and he come and got her. He was so mad then he wanted to drag her mama from her bed, but Pansy calmed him down and it didn't take long for them to decide what to do. When they got back from South Carolina, married, they moved in with his parents, and her mama acted like nothing had happened. They never talked about it again. But Pansy didn't think she'd ever quite forgiven her.

"Hello?" Cecil snapped his fingers. "Did you hear me?"

Pansy turned to him. "What?"

"We was in love," Dan said. "We didn't want to wait."

"That's right," Pansy said, still foggy-headed. Seemed like she couldn't concentrate on nothing very long these days. She took a deep breath and sat up straighter in her chair. "Besides, we didn't want to spend all our money on a wedding."

"Did they play music at your wedding?" Lisa said.

"Yeah, what was your song?" Laurel said.

"Our song?" Pansy blinked, then looked at Dan. "They did put on a record at the wedding, didn't they? What was it?"

Dan shook his head.

"No," Laurel said. "I mean your song, something that was special to you. Something you danced to, something romantic."

Good Lord, Pansy thought. After all the girl had just gone through with Scott, she still wanted romance? "I don't think we had one."

"You've got to have a song," Lisa said. "Mine and Cecil's is 'Always and Forever' by Luther Vandross." She turned to Laurel, and Pansy thought, Oh, Lisa, honey, don't, but it was too late. "What was your and Scott's song?" She realized her mistake right away, her hands flew up over her mouth, and she said, "Oh, Lord, Laurel, I'm so sorry. I forgot."

"That's okay," Laurel said, lifting her tea glass to her mouth and hiding behind it. But Pansy saw her eyelids flutter, knew Lisa's question had twisted the knife and wrenched her insides once again. Laurel took a long swallow, then put the glass down. "We didn't really have a song. Well, I did, but he hated it."

Cecil laughed. "How can it be your song if he hated it?"

"It was playing on the radio the first time he called to ask me out, and I kept hearing it at dances and in the car when we were together. I thought it was a sign, you know? Stupid, I know."

"No it's not," Lisa said. "What was it?"

"The song?" Laurel hesistated. " 'When I Need You,' that sappy Leo Sayer song from the seventies."

A small silence fell over them then, until Dan piped up and said, "I used to have me a song."

"Oh, Lord," Pansy said.

"I did. Don't you remember me singing it to you? *'I want to live fast, love hard, die young, and leave a beautiful memory.'*"

"Don't sing," Pansy said. "You'll set the neighbors' dogs to howling."

"Now, you talk about some good music," Dan said, ignoring her. "Faron Young could sing."

"Do y'all still have Daddy's Rodeo?" Laurel said.

"You mean Randy's Rodeo?" Cecil said.

"Oh, yes, every Friday night," Pansy said. "He finally got over that Randy Travis fit, thank goodness. If I got to listen to that shit-kicking music, I at least want some variety."

"Daddy, you still owe me about five hundred dollars for all the times you promised me a quarter if I'd change the record for you." Laurel held her hand out.

"Put me on the installment plan," Dan said, and dropped a quarter in her palm.

"Mama," Cecil said. "You mean to tell me in all these years you still ain't learned to love country music?"

"I didn't like it then," Pansy said, "and I don't like it now. But, it's your daddy's house too, so it's only fair he gets to play it sometimes. That's why I got him that CD player. And the headphones."

"Speaking of which," Dan said. "It is Friday." He left the table and went into the living room.

"Y'all go on with your daddy," Pansy said. "I'll clean up."

"No, we'll help you, Mama," Laurel said.

In the kitchen they got the giggles because they could hear Dan playing Faron Young and singing along with the record: *"I want to leave a lot of happy women a-thinking pretty thoughts of me."*

"If he just wouldn't sing along, it might not be so bad," Pansy said. "The man can't carry a tune in a bucket."

There was silence for a minute, then a slow song led by fiddles and steel guitar came on.

"Pansy!" Dan hollered. "Come in here and dance, honey."

She looked at Lisa, then Laurel, shook her head, but couldn't keep the smile off her face. "I believe your daddy's had too many beers tonight," she said, wiping her hands on a dish towel before heading to the living room.

Dan swayed with the music, singing with Faron, *"Crazy arms that long to hold somebody new."* He held out his arms and like always Pansy went to him, couldn't resist him when he got like this. She looked over his shoulder at Cecil and the boys sitting on the couch, their attention glued to something on TV. The sound was turned off but they watched anyway. They looked like zombies, like the Culhanes on *Hee Haw*.

Pansy laid her cheek against Dan's chest and closed her eyes. When he had his arms around her like this and she couldn't see his face, couldn't see the lines or the way his hairline was just starting to slide backward off his head, it didn't feel any different than the first time they danced together all them years ago. She felt a little bit sad just thinking about it. The passage of time just didn't seem fair, taking so much away. But it gave too, gave her children and grandchildren. She should be counting her blessings instead of wishing she was upstairs in the bed with her head under the covers, the door locked so nobody could come in on her. She held on to Dan as hard as she could, scared all of a sudden he was the only thing in the world keeping her from falling.

"COME ON, Little Bit," Dan said, grabbing Laurel's hand before she could follow Pansy and Lisa back to the kitchen. "Dance with your daddy."

The song was "Sweet Dreams," and Laurel looked up into his happy, slightly drunk face and thought of all the times they'd danced when she was young. God, she missed dancing. Scott refused to, said he couldn't, but Laurel knew he was just afraid of looking foolish. How sad was that? Would she ever dance with anyone besides her daddy again?

The pity party that had taken up residence in her stomach like a parasite rose up once again, but her daddy wrapped his arms around her and swayed with her and after a few minutes she forgot about Scott and being sad. She was her daddy's little girl, and she could pretend for a few minutes that she'd never left this safe place to go out into the world and have her heart stomped on. For now it was enough to know that her daddy and her brother would gladly kick the shit out of Scott or anybody who tried to hurt her. They loved her even if nobody else did.

At the end of the song when her daddy dipped her, he staggered a little bit and Laurel squealed and grabbed his shoulders to keep from falling. They must've blocked the TV, because Cecil yelled for them to move. So much for chivalry, she thought, and that reminded her of the tall, lanky guy in Kingman, Arizona, who'd held the door open for her as she came out of a Subway sandwich shop. She'd stopped there for lunch the day she left Las Vegas to drive home to Russell. When she first saw the guy in a hard hat and dusty jeans and T-shirt, she'd hesitated to walk past him, afraid he might say something crude, just like most construction workers she'd ever come across. He looked different, though, almost elegant in spite of the dusty clothes, and she thought he must be part Indian, with that dark hair and cut cheekbones, not hard on the eyes at all. Still, she was prepared to skewer him with a look if he did say anything as she walked on through the door. He didn't smile, just gave an elegant bow and said simply, "Chivalry is not dead." It surprised her so much she didn't know what to say back, so she just hurried to her car. Once it sank in, a part of her wanted to run back into the Subway, find the guy, and thank him, maybe even sit with him while he ate his sandwich. Surely a man who would say that to a stranger must really mean it, must know what it meant. So few men did anymore. It wasn't that she couldn't open a door for herself. But having a man do something like open a door or take your arm while walking was a sign of respect, the same signs she'd been raised to show her elders.

Laurel had even dreamed about him when she finally stopped at a hotel for the night. She'd fallen asleep to the sound of the ice machine down the hall dropping its load, to the lights of passing trucks flashing across the closed curtains, to the glare of the TV in the darkness of an anonymous hotel room where no one knew her or even cared. In the dream she was falling through a dark sky, no moon or stars, feeling the terrible panic she'd felt ever since Scott left. She landed unhurt in the driver's seat of her car, which in the dream had become a con-vertible. She looked up and there was Mr. Chivalry, smiling at her through the window. He knocked but she couldn't make herself roll it down even though she knew he was safe, even though the top was down and he could simply reach over and grab her. But he didn't reach over. Instead, he took a small silver tube of lipstick in her shade of brownish-red and wrote something backward on the glass so she could read it. It said, *This, too, shall pass. Keep on trucking.*

And she had, all the way home. Where was he now, the man with the messages, Mr. Chivalry? She needed him to tell her what to do next.

She watched her daddy bending over the stereo, humming to him-self as he looked through his new CDs, and loved him so much in that moment for always being there, for never changing, for being someone she could always count on. And now she was going to cry and felt like a complete idiot. He still had his back to her, and Cecil and the boys were wrapped up in the TV. They wouldn't miss her. She let herself out the front door and wandered around the yard for a while, but it was too cold to lay on the grass looking at stars like she used to when she was little. She went around the house to the back-porch steps and sat down. The square of light from the kitchen window lay on the ground at her feet, and she could hear her mama's and Lisa's voices and every now and then the clink of dishes. It made her feel safe, and she was able to keep herself from crying.

There was a rustling of the bushes at the corner of the house, then Cecil said, "Boo!" and came to sit next to her. He must've followed her just like he used to do when they were little. Everywhere she went, he wanted to go too, at least until junior high when they became too cool to be seen with each other outside the house. They'd been so close in age—Irish twins as Maw Bert used to say, only sixteen months apart—and she hadn't realized until that moment how much she'd missed him.

He bumped shoulders with her, then put his hands under his arms. "Ain't you cold?"

"No," Laurel said. She'd pulled her arms out of the sleeves of her sweater and wrapped them around her waist, so really the only cold part was her face, and she liked the sensation on her cheeks. It made her feel awake and clear-headed for a change.

"Mama and Daddy's fixing to cut the cake. Mama had to go to the bathroom first."

"Okay." No details please, Laurel thought.

"Ain't you going to come in and watch?"

"In a minute." Laurel didn't look at him, just kept staring up at the stars, hoping he'd go back in. She hated to hear him talk the way he did. Just because he'd stayed in Russell didn't mean he had to use bad grammar. If she stayed here long enough, would she go back to talking that way?

"You got to be in the pictures too or Mama'll have a fit."

"Damn, Cecil, I said I'd be there in a minute, okay? Can't I have one minute to myself?" Even at thirty-four years old he still acted like the baby brother, driving her crazy. She had trouble believing the boy could run his own business.

"Whoa!" he said. "Excuse the hell out of me."

Hell, Laurel thought. Now I'm going to have to apologize. They sat without talking for a couple of minutes.

"I'm sorry," Laurel said finally. "I didn't mean to take your head off. I'm such a bitch these days and I can't seem to help it. I yelled at Daddy this morning for waking me up to tell me breakfast was ready."

"Did he give you a whipping?"

"No, the evil-daughter guilt was punishment enough."

"You still in that club?" Cecil stuck his long legs out straight, resting his heels on the bottom step. "Daddy told me about you and Scott."

"I figured he would."

"Do you want to talk about it?"

"Nah. I'm sick of talking about it."

"Okay." He leaned back to look at the sky. "There's Orion," he said, pointing. "That's the only one I can ever remember, that and the Big Dipper."

"Me too," Laurel said, leaning back next to him. "Oh, and Taurus the Bull. And the Pleiades. Right there." She pointed.

"Show-off."

"I can't help it if I got the brains in the family."

"Brains ain't everything."

"Don't I know it and didn't I learn the hard way?" Laurel said.

Cecil laughed. "Goda'mighty, you sound just like Maw Bert. That was her A side, wasn't it?"

"Shut up," Laurel said, though he was right. Maw Bert always had two key responses to any issue. *Don't I know it and didn't I learn the hard way?* and *I don't know what I ever done to deserve this.* Her daddy used to call them side A and side B of her one and only record. Laurel figured saying things like that was the only way her daddy survived the stress of having to be in the same room with a woman who hated his guts and ignored him even when he spoke directly to her.

Had Maw Bert always been like that? Surely there'd been a time in her life when she wasn't so damn bitter, but if there was, Laurel didn't remember it. She'd always had mixed feelings because for some reason Maw Bert had singled her out of all the grandchildren for special attention. She didn't yell at Laurel and shoo her out the way she did the others when they went to her house. It had always made Laurel feel special and guilty at the same time, though Cecil and their cousins never seemed to want to spend time with Maw Bert anyway. "She's such a old heifer," Cecil would say, and then Laurel would have to smack him for insulting Maw Bert even though he wasn't actually wrong.

She scooted closer and leaned against Cecil because she was starting to feel a little cold. "I found some stuff in the shed today. This box with old papers and stuff in it. There was a letter addressed to Mama."

"And you read it," he said, shaking his head at her. "Bad girl."

The light from the kitchen went out and it took a minute for Laurel's eyes to adjust to the dark. Her mama and Lisa must be done with the dishes and were probably sitting at the table now, talking about babies, waiting for Cecil and Daddy to come looking for cake. Laurel felt relieved that at least one of them had come through with grandchildren, which took some of the pressure off her. Cecil's three and soon to be four would have to make up for her deficit. Didn't look like she'd be reproducing anytime soon.

"Well." Cecil nudged her with his elbow. "What did it say?"

"Did you know Mama won a scholarship to college? To study art?"

"She did not. I never heard that."

"Me either. What I don't understand is why she never told us." It had never really occurred to her that their mama might keep secrets.

"She probably just forgot about it."

"Cecil. A person does not forget about winning a scholarship."

"Well, maybe it just doesn't matter anymore. Except to nosy heifers like you." He put a hand on her shoulder and used it to push himself to his feet. "I'm going in and get me some cake. You coming?"

"I'll be there in a minute."

She watched the back of his white sweater disappear around the corner of the house. Did the boy have absolutely no curiosity about his own mother? He said maybe it didn't matter anymore, but how could it not? She didn't know about the rest of the junk in Maw Bert's box, but Laurel knew that letter was important, though she couldn't have said why at that moment.

She'd been watching her mama all night, trying to see inside to the girl who used to be an artist. Whenever she told them how she used to like to paint, it was usually at a time when she was trying to get Laurel and Cecil to be quiet and color. Laurel never thought her mama really meant it, that she loved painting. What kinds of pictures had she made? Did she still have any of them? And the biggest question of all, the one Laurel didn't have the nerve to ask, at least not yet, was why didn't she go to college?

The kitchen light blinked on then, and a minute later the back-porch light started flicking on and off, on and off. God, Cecil. He could be such a pain in the ass, but she couldn't help smiling to herself in the dark. Somebody knew where she was. Somebody cared. She hadn't realized how much she missed that feeling until right now.

"All right, Cecil, you idiot," she hollered as she pushed her arms into her sleeves and stood up. "I'm coming."

Alberta

Everything I kept, I kept for a reason. Put it in that little box for Pansy to find someday. So she'd understand what all I sacrificed for her, what all I done to make sure she didn't suffer like me. It don't pay to want nothing in this life. It don't pay at all, because wanting leads to not getting, which leads to disappointment and heartache, nothing but trouble. I wanted Pansy to understand that from the get-go, but I don't believe she ever did. I had hopes that during my lifetime we'd come to some sort of understanding of each other, but it never did happen. She went along with me, but she didn't always like it, that's for sure. What she didn't seem to understand was that I'd been there before her. I knowed what it was like to want something so bad you can taste it and then you don't get it and it breaks your heart so bad you want to die. I spent my whole life trying to get over disappointment and never did. It just don't go away.

When I married Dill and started having children, it was like the final closing of the door on the life I had wanted for myself. I have never been able to quit looking back, wondering what if. What if we wasn't poor? What if I had been able to go to school like I wanted? I was smart enough. Everybody said so. From the time I was a tiny child, that's all I wanted, was to go to school. That first day I loved it and never stopped. My whole world up till then was our house and the farm, and that schoolhouse was like a magic carpet.

The teacher, Miss Shinn, she liked me right off. I believe she just took one look at me and could tell how smart I was, how much I wanted to learn. The other children called me teacher's pet, thinking it would make me mad, but I liked it. She left at the end of my third year, though, went off and got married. She kept me after school one day and talked to me about it, because I'd been so mad at her I wouldn't speak in class, and I always was the first to raise my hand.

I set in to crying, so she got me up on her lap and I said, "Why, Miss Shinn? Why do you want to go and get married? I don't understand. If I was a teacher I would never quit."

She said, "Alberta, honey, someday you'll be a grown girl and you'll understand. You'll get married and raise a family of your own."

"No," I said. "I never will. I'm going to be a teacher like you and live in my own rented room and not have to share a bed with nobody, not my sisters or nobody. You watch and see if I don't." And then I couldn't help myself, I started crying harder, and she petted me till I calmed down.

Before she left, she give me a rabbit's foot for good luck. She said I didn't really need it, it was just to remind me that if I wished and worked hard enough, all my dreams would come true. It worked for a while too. I got to stay in school all the way up to the tenth grade, which was all they had then, and started making plans to go to the teachers' college in Greensboro. Every teacher I had told me that's what I ought to do. But when the time come, Daddy told me no, we couldn't afford it. I begged and pleaded and told him I'd get a job and work and he wouldn't have to pay for nothing, but he still wouldn't let me. He said I'd had enough school and it was time to go to work in the mill because the family needed me.

I could see he was right about that part. We had a time keeping all of us fed. So I done what he said. I went in the mill, thinking I'd work real hard and save and save and someday get to go to school and be a teacher. Of course, that was foolishness. Times was hard, and I had a lot more than most, a bed and something to eat and a roof over my head and kin that treated me good.

Somehow, though, I never could leave off wanting more. It was like I had a disease and there wasn't no cure. Many a time I wished I could cut out that part of my heart that refused to be satisfied. I would have too, cut it right out. A big hole would've been a whole lot easier to live with than that craving I had, that empty feeling that never went away and made me feel like I might lose my mind. And at night when I'd lay there crying, I'd wish to my soul I hadn't never listened to that Miss Shinn or none of them other teachers. And that's something I never could get Pansy to understand, how sometimes it's just better to stay ignorant and not know what all else is out there in the world, what all you might like but won't never get to have for yourself.

5

HAD SHE BEEN SLEEPING? OR DID HER MIND WANDER? Pansy had been sitting there listening to Percilla, Maxann, and Idalene for what seemed like hours, listening but not hearing a word they said. Half her sandwich was gone, so she must've eaten. The others didn't seem to notice she wasn't all there, so she must look normal. Pansy glanced around the canteen, surprised to see every table full of talking, eating, laughing people. How had she blocked all that out? She put her hands under the table, fingers to her wrist, and checked her pulse. It didn't race, just the same slow, steady throb, so she probably wasn't having a heart attack or stroke. If it was spring she could blame her foggy-headedness on allergies, but it was too early for hay fever. She didn't know what it was making her feel so tired and tense all at the same time. When Percilla's arm bumped hers as she leaned forward to look toward the door, Pansy's whole body jerked.

"Why, Lottie May Holt, what happened to your head?" Percilla yelled as Lottie May crossed the canteen. Maxann and Idalene looked up from their sandwiches.

Lottie May put a hand to her head self-consciously as she scooted into the booth next to Pansy. "What do you think, girls?" Her hair had been cut in short locks that clung to her head like a cap and looked even whiter than before.

"I think it looks wonderful," Pansy said. "You look like a different person."

"She's little enough to get away with that kind of haircut," Percilla said. "If I got one of them my head would look like a pearl onion setting on top of a cantaloupe."

"It sure would," Maxann said, and Percilla shot her a mean look.

Lottie May opened her lunch sack and took out a sandwich, then folded the paper bag and fanned her face with it. "Lord, they got that thermostat turned up again? It's hot as a firecracker in here."

"Tell me about it," Pansy said. Sweat trickled down the middle of her back, and she would've loved to tear off her sweater and run outside in her bra just to cool off.

"Maybe you're having hot flashes like Pansy," Percilla said.

Pansy ignored Percilla and focused on Lottie May. "What made you decide to get it cut?"

Lottie May quit fanning and rested her hands on either side of her sandwich. "Well, I'll tell you. Saturday morning me and Nebraska and Nellie Belle was over at Wal-Mart and I went to get me some hairspray and Nebraska looks at me and says, 'Mama, the beehive hairdo is OUT. Don't you know that?' I just looked at her. I know she's my daughter, but I swear, she looks terrible with that long stringy hair hanging down her back. It was fine in the seventies, but she's too old for that now."

Pansy had to force herself not to look at Maxann when Lottie May said that.

"Well, then Nellie Belle speaks up. You know she can't stand nobody giving me a hard time. She says, 'I like Mama's hair. It looks like a big thing of cotton candy.' Then Nebraska laughs and says, '*Gray* cotton candy?' and Nellie Belle says, 'No, white. White cotton candy. And Mama's body is the stick.' Well, Lord, that set me and Nebraska laughing so hard we like to fell on the floor. But I tell you, it put a picture in my mind, and wouldn't nothing do but for me to go in the walk-in place and get it cut that very day. Nellie Belle cried and cried when she seen it, but I kind of like it myself. My head feels like it lost a hundred pounds."

"You'll have to start wearing you a toboggan when you go outside," Idalene said. "You'll catch your death without no hair up there to hold in your body heat."

Lottie May looked so pleased at that, if she'd had a tail it would've been wagging.

"Where you been all morning?" Percilla said.

Lottie May waited till she'd swallowed a bite of her bologna sandwich. "Had to take Nisco to the doctor. He's got a ear infection. I swear, that boy gets them things all winter long."

"Mine was the same way," Maxann said. "You reckon boys is more prone than girls for some reason?"

Lottie May laughed. "I do believe men's and women's ears is different. That's how come men are able to hear only just what they want to."

"Ain't that the truth," Percilla said. She drained her can of Pepsi, then stood up and gave a little wave. "Well, girls, I got to see a man about a dog." She dropped the can in the trash on her way out the door.

"She must be going for a record, most hand jobs in one lifetime," Maxann said after Percilla had got out of earshot.

"Maxann!" Pansy said.

"Lord have mercy, Maxann, you got a mouth on you. Why don't you put that sandwich in it and put it to good use?" Idalene said.

"I feel sorry for her," Lottie May said. "She's too old for that and them men ain't interested in her, just want something for nothing. Ain't that a terrible way to be?" She looked over at Pansy, the sandwich in front of her face like a white beard. "Honey, what's the matter with you? You look like you done lost your best friend."

"What?" Pansy blinked, staring at the white bread, wishing Lottie May would go ahead and take a bite. She didn't see how she could stand to eat that stuff. Pansy had switched to grain bread a couple of years ago for the fiber and because that white bread stuck to the back of her front teeth so bad. "Oh. Nothing. I'm just thinking." She picked up the other half of her own sandwich, then put it down again. "Anybody want this?"

"Well. If you ain't going to eat it," Idalene said, and pulled the sheet of wax paper holding the sandwich over to her. "I love tuna fish."

"You been awful quiet lately," Lottie May said.

Pansy looked off at the drink machine. Trust Lottie May. She was always the one to notice every little thing and not let it go unmentioned.

Pansy was so afraid for anybody to see how bad she felt, she couldn't look Lottie May in the eye for more than a second or two. She didn't even think she could put into words what all was going on inside her right now. Finally she said, "I'm just worried about Laurel, is all. She's still moping around the house, pilfering in everything, making messes, driving me crazy." Lord, she sounded so aggravated. It wasn't Laurel's fault she didn't feel good, hadn't felt good in a long time.

"She still looking for work?" Maxann said.

"Yes, she's applied all over town and can't find nothing."

"That's too bad," Idalene said, and popped the last bite of sandwich in her mouth. "Why don't she apply here? I know they're hiring in the winding room. She could do that awhile, couldn't she?"

Pansy sighed. "She could, but you know her. Sometimes I think she'd rather dig ditches." There was a moment of silence. If Laurel wasn't kin to Pansy, they would've started in on her then. *Who did she think she was? Too good to work in a mill? Did she think she was better than everybody else? A job was a job, and that girl was in no position to be picky.* And Pansy would've joined right in with them. But secretly she'd always been glad Laurel didn't want to work in the mill. She was proud of her for doing something different, for not getting stuck in a rut.

"Laurel just gets notions of what things are like sometimes and don't really know what she's talking about." Pansy felt disloyal, saying that about her own daughter, but it was the truth.

"Well, I don't think John Dollar was kidding when he told her to come down and see him about a job," Maxann said.

"I know," Pansy said. "She's just not thinking straight these days."

"That's what a damn husband'll do to you," Maxann said. "Of course, Pansy, you got you a good one. And Percilla does too, which is something I'll never understand. And she sure does have him trained, don't she? Don't even have to tell him to jump. He sees her coming and just starts jumping on his own and then waits for her to tell him when he can quit."

Pansy smiled and it felt strange, as if her cheek muscles had got rusty and stiff. "When me and Dan started talking about getting married, Mama said I better set him straight on who owned the milk before he bought the cow."

"Hunh," Idalene said. "If you girls had a lick of sense, you'd have done like me and stayed single."

"I won't argue with you on that score," Maxann said. "I can do without a husband. Trouble is, I can't seem to do without a man, you know? I don't see how you've stood it all these years, Idalene. Course, it ain't none of my business."

Pansy waited, knowing Maxann was hoping for details on Idalene's private life, details she'd never get. It was a losing battle. Even as close as they were, Idalene had never told Pansy anything much more personal than her favorite food, which was barbecue.

Idalene stood and gathered her trash together, then gave Maxann a look that would've struck the fear of God into anybody else. "You're right, Maxann honey, it ain't none of your business." Pansy watched her march across the canteen, tall and straight and strong as always, if a little slower. Thank God for Idalene, she thought. Thank God for somebody who stayed the same, who never had any surprises, who never needed taking care of.

LAUREL HAD always gone into the plant through the employee entrance with her mama, straight into the noise and activity and work of the place. Coming through the front, she entered a whole different world, a hushed world of plush gray carpet, gray cubicles, botanical prints, silk ficus trees. Not her taste at all but very much the generic, modern office look sold out of a catalog. And the greatest luxury of all: quiet. As she sat waiting for John Dollar, all she could hear was the murmur of voices, a phone ringing, a copier running. Familiar sounds, a comfort zone in this foreign world.

She listened and relaxed, took a good look around his office, curious to see what personal items a man like that would surround himself with. Leaning forward, she turned a double five-by-seven silver frame around and looked at the photo of him with his wife and three children. On one side, John had a receding hairline, his wife was skinny, and the kids were little. On the other side, John's hair seemed to have made a comeback and changed from brown to black, his wife had gained fifty pounds, and the kids were grown. She'd gone to school

with the oldest boy; what was his name? Johnny maybe. He'd been a
football player, FFA, one of those guys bound to end up a big fish in a
little pond. Her mama had told her he ran an insurance agency in town,
probably lived at the golf course, drove a Lincoln Town Car, spent his
vacations at Myrtle Beach or Hilton Head—a good Russell life. What
was wrong with that? And yet Laurel was aware of looking down her
nose at him, at his life, and she didn't like that about herself, didn't like
it one bit. Besides, she was in no position to judge, here to beg for the
last job in the world she ever wanted.

Everything else looked and smelled brand-new, especially the carpet, which was making her sinuses act up. She took a tissue from the
box on the desk. They must've spent a fortune renovating—new carpet, new furniture, new blinds. It looked nice enough, but aside from
the photo, there were no personal touches. Men didn't seem to need to
nest at work as much as women. Laurel had always spent part of the
first day of every new job making her space—whether it was a cubicle
or an office—homey and comfortable. Her philosophy was, if you have
to spend eight or more hours a day in a place, you might as well have
your things around you. She wondered where they'd put her if she got
a job here. She hoped for at least a cubicle. It would be awful to have to
sit out there in that open area where the receptionist sat, with constant
interruptions and no privacy. How sad, that her greatest hope for this
new job was a dismal little cubicle to call her own.

"Here I am, honey," John Dollar boomed from the door, as if he
thought she'd been waiting breathlessly for his appearance. She hadn't
heard him come in and he must've seen her jump, because he laughed
and said, "Did I scare you?"

I'm not scared of you, you old fart, she wanted to say. But deep inside,
a little voice said, *He's right, you are scared, though not for the reasons he
thinks.* She was scared all right, downright terrified to be here for a job.

John went behind the desk and his chair squeaked as he dropped
heavily into it and swung around to face her. "So," he said, and glanced
at her application. "Everything looks good." He smiled and leaned back,
looking like the fat cat he was. "When can you start?"

"Oh," Laurel said, stunned. It was all happening too fast. She stalled
for time by forcing a smile, hoping for cute but fearing she just looked

sick. "Uh, great. But shouldn't we . . . I don't know, maybe discuss the particulars? Such as, what would I be doing? And . . ." She hesitated, had always hated to ask about money. "And salary and benefits. That kind of thing. Don't we need to talk about that?"

"Well, sure," John said, leaning forward, his pink, meaty palms waving to reassure her. "I just wanted to relieve your mind a little bit, that's all. I know you been having trouble finding work and I didn't want you to think we was going to turn you away."

Laurel's whole body stiffened where she sat, and why shouldn't rigor mortis set in now? Hadn't she just sold her soul to the devil? Oh, God, she thought, I am now officially a loser. She took a deep breath, repeating over and over in her mind, *I will not cry, I will not cry.*

John bent over to read something on his desk, then looked up at her through his half-glasses. His stiff, unnaturally black hair gleamed under the fluorescent lights, reminding her of Elvis. Elvis hair. She couldn't take her eyes off it, knew she should be making eye contact, presenting a confident front, and she did manage to move her eyes lower, but they slid past his eyes to his tie, a really beautiful paisley print that perfectly matched his gray suit. She wondered if his wife picked out his clothes for him.

When it became clear she wasn't going to speak, John said, "Well, honey, what I got in mind for you is a job here in the office. With your education, you'd be perfect for this type work."

"Right," she said, her brain beginning to function normally again. "I've worked in several offices," she said. "My last job was with the English department at the University of Nevada at Las Vegas. I was the executive administrative assistant to the department chair."

He stared blankly, as if trying to translate what she'd just said into his own language. Maybe he was. She could just imagine what he thought. Woman in office equals secretary. Welcome aboard, my little secretary, and if you want to call yourself administrative assistant, wink wink, you go right ahead.

"Well, I'm real sorry," he said finally. "But Linda's our office manager and I don't think she's going anywhere anytime soon. But you stick around long enough and do a good job and who knows? You're young, and she's got to retire sometime." This time he really did wink at her.

Laurel kept the smile on by willpower alone. "And what would the job be?"

"Office assistant is what we need. Somebody to type and file, open mail, that kind of thing. Oh, and you'd also be responsible for the company newsletter. I thought that's where your college would come in handy." He beamed at her, so proud to be the one offering this great opportunity. "And you'd be helping Linda with company events like the management retreats, the Christmas party, and the picnic at Labor Day. It's going to be real big this year, our ninetieth anniversary. We're thinking about having fireworks."

"And how much does it pay?" Laurel blurted the question before she even thought how mercenary it sounded.

He laughed. "Okay, getting down to the important stuff now. That job pays eight dollars an hour to start. Pretty good money around here."

Eight dollars an hour? She could make more than that as a hotel desk clerk in Vegas. "Excuse me," she said. "But is there any room for negotiation about the pay? I mean, that's a little less than I was hoping for."

"I did see on your salary history that you was making quite a bit more at your last job." He squinted at the résumé on his desk. "You know a little town like Russell can't compete with big-city money." He shook his head, gave a little smile. "You was in Las Vegas, right? You ever play craps? I hear that's a high-roller game but you can win a lot of money."

For the first time during the interview he actually seemed to see her as a real person and not Pansy's little girl. "I didn't go to the casinos much," she said. "I couldn't afford to waste money."

"Ah, it ain't wasted if you're having a good time."

"Listen!" she said more sharply than she intended. "Don't you have anything that pays better?"

He gave her that I'm-translating-what-you-just-said look again. "Well, we got two openings in the winding room, but I don't think you'd like that."

"How much does it pay?"

"Ten dollars an hour to start, then it goes up to fifteen an hour when you start making production."

Almost double the money for a job requiring half the education. God, she was a snob, but it was hard to take after being conditioned to believe a college education equaled more money. "What does that mean, production?"

"You mean to tell me your mama's worked here all these years and you don't know what making production means?"

When she shook her head, he said, "Well, honey, what it means is there's a certain amount of work the average operative should be able to produce in a day, and if you make it, you get fifteen dollars an hour. If you don't, you get ten, and if you don't make production over time, you get let go."

"Can I try one of those jobs?"

He pulled his head back on his neck, looking as if he might be worried about her mental health. "Like I said, I don't think you'd like it."

"Why not?"

"It's hard work, it's dirty, it's noisy, you're on your feet all day. You're used to sitting at a desk, ain't you?"

"I'm in good shape. I'll get used to it."

"You don't have any experience."

"Does anybody when they first start here? I can learn." When he saw that she wasn't going to be talked out of it, he changed tactics on her.

"All right, then. Tell you what. Let's you and me take a little walk down to the winding room. You can look for yourself and then make up your mind."

"Fine," Laurel said. Did he think she was such a wimp she couldn't take a little hard work? Sure, she'd spent most of her career sitting down, but she could get used to anything. Couldn't she? She thought of that old Yiddish saying she'd seen on a calendar once: When one must, one can.

The further they went from the front of the plant, the shabbier it got. The nice rest rooms near the office seemed to mark the boundary, and past that, down the long gray hallway, there was no carpet, no pictures, no plants, just tile flooring and dirty gray walls and the noise getting louder and louder. When they reached the winding room, John held the door open and she stepped inside, or rather she was sucked in by the whirlwind of noise and activity filling the room. The sheer magnitude of it seemed almost overwhelming at first. Where was it coming from? Those machines—winders, were they called? Rows and rows of them, or was it all one big machine? And the air-handling system overhead, filling the space created by those high ceilings. The room itself seemed massive as well, the size of a football field, or maybe half of one.

She saw Idalene, an apron around her waist, standing in front of one of the machines, her hands hidden inside it. As she watched, Idalene seemed to become part of the winder. No, not part of it, but another sort of machine altogether, working in tandem with the winder. What was she doing? How did she make her hands move so quickly, so surely, while the rest of her body remained almost motionless? Even as she admired Idalene's efficiency, Laurel couldn't help wondering, Is that what's going to happen to me? Will I become a machine too, an automaton like Idalene and Lottie May and Percilla and Maxann and Mama and all the other women in here? For it was mostly women. Her mama said the men worked mainly in the dye house or the warehouse.

What do they think about all day? Laurel thought. What happens to their minds? Not that her old jobs had been brain-busters, but at least she had to think when doing a spreadsheet, composing a memo, writing a report. What kind of thought did this require? Once you learned it, your body just took over. At least, that's what it looked like to Laurel. Your body went through the motions, leaving your mind free to . . . what? Stagnate? Think about what you watched on TV last night, what you're making for supper tonight? What?

"You think too much," Scott used to tell her. "Too much thinking can make you crazy, don't you know that? Can't you ever just *be*?"

As John led her through various huge rooms, explaining what machines called bale pluckers and carders and drawframes and spinning frames and winders did, she noticed they were being watched constantly. Not that anybody ever turned and openly stared, but she could feel their eyes watching, wondering, as their hands continued to work. There was a tension in the air, and Laurel realized it was because of John. He was the man, and they didn't like it when he came on the floor. Her mama said he'd never worked in the mill like his daddy and granddaddy had, starting as a sweeper and working his way up, and how could these people respect somebody who'd never got his hands dirty?

When they got back to the office, her indecision must've shown in her face, because John smirked at her and said, "Well?"

She thought about telling him she'd take the winding-room job just for spite, but then she remembered the noise. What it came down to was a choice between money or her hearing, money or her sanity. "Can I think about it and let you know tomorrow?" she said, desperate to get out of his office, out of the plant, and be by herself for a while to think.

He told her no problem, then sent her to Personnel to fill out tax forms and health-insurance forms and just generally to sign her life over to the plant. Whichever job she chose, she'd be here, in this place. When she finally got done, Laurel went and sat in her car, just sat there staring up at the building. Oh, God, she thought. I can't do it. I can't go in there day after day. It'll kill me. The voice in her head, the one that never had anything good to say, taunted her with, *What doesn't kill you makes you stronger.*

"Oh, shut up!" Laurel told the voice, then looked around. The parking lot was full of cars but no people. Nobody had seen her talking to herself. She'd been doing that a lot lately. The sinking feeling in her stomach seemed strong enough that it might pull her all the way down through the floor of the car, through the pavement, and into the middle of the earth, where, if her daddy was right, she'd meet a Chinaman coming the other way.

It was only for a little while, right? Just until she figured out what she wanted to do with the rest of her life, no big deal, and then she'd be out of there. I am not cut out for this, she thought. I am moving on to better things just as soon as I can.

Laurel started the car and turned the radio on loud. She had a decision to make, but she couldn't think about that right now. All she could manage for the moment was driving, which felt like the best kind of freedom, maybe her last taste of it for a while.

USUALLY PANSY wasn't one to let herself drift off while she worked, but today she just couldn't seem to help it. Lord knows it was mindless work most of the time, but she never liked to think of a single moment of her day as wasted. She was not one to wish her life away like some, daydreaming or clock-watching. She liked to focus on every movement, every task at hand. Some folks said the repetition made them feel like a machine, and maybe that was true. But a machine served a purpose, was useful, and that was something Pansy cared about, being useful.

She jumped at the tap on her shoulder, looked around, seen Grady standing behind her. He leaned in to her ear and hollered, "Can I see you in the office for a minute?"

She pulled back, irritated at him for bothering her. What in the hell did he want now? Surely he wasn't going to give her another talking to about her production being low? He'd already called her in twice in the last three weeks. She was perfectly well aware that she wasn't keeping up her usual pace and didn't need him or nobody else giving her grief about it.

He just stood there, waiting, staring with them big old puppy-dog eyes, that look he usually reserved for Maxann. Pansy couldn't tell if he disapproved of Maxann or was in love with her. Maybe a little bit of both. Anyway, Maxann didn't appreciate that look and neither did Pansy. It was what they called his preacher-daddy look, like they was his flock of children or something.

"I'm trying to get caught back up, Grady," she hollered. It took a combination of hollering and lip-reading to communicate in the noise of the winding room, and they was all good at it. But Grady was also good at reading faces, and she knew he could tell she didn't want to leave the floor, knew she was embarrassed because everybody could see. It was humiliating being called down to the office like she was one of them lazy witches that hid in the bathroom to keep from working.

Grady didn't say anything, just jerked his head in the direction of the office and started walking. Pansy looked around too, though she already knew they were the center of attention. The only one not looking was Idalene. She never stopped work to look, but you could tell she was aware of everything that was going on. It was like her whole body was one big eye.

"Fine," she said to nobody in particular. Grady had stopped and turned to look at her, so she caught up and followed him. The quiet once he shut the office door made the ringing in her ears seem even louder. She pulled her earplugs out, letting them dangle by the string around her neck, and sat on the edge of a chair, ready to get up and go as soon as he let her. Grady went behind the gray metal desk, sat down, picked up a stack of papers, then set them down again. She knew they had nothing to do with her. She hadn't done anything bad enough to be written up.

He looked so nervous, sitting there with his hands on his little pot belly, his ears turning red. She wondered how many golf shirts he had, because that was all he ever wore. She wondered if he even played golf. He didn't seem the type. From what Maxann said, he mostly just worked his land when he wasn't at the plant. He did have that permanent farmer tan. Even now she could see a little line of white skin where the sleeve of his shirt rode up.

Grady cleared his throat. "You want a pop?" he said. "I can get you one from the machine."

His stalling was making her nervous too. Just get it over with, Grady, she thought. She said, "What I want is to get back to my job." The fluorescent lights overhead buzzed, and one kept flickering like it was fixing to burn out. "How do you stand that noise?" she said, looking up at the lights. "That'd drive me crazy."

He looked up too. "You get used to it," he said. "You can get used to just about anything, I reckon." He rubbed his palm across the top of the desk, raking off invisible eraser lint or dust or something that Pansy couldn't see. Her daddy used to do that same thing. After every meal the family would sit around the table talking and he'd run his hands across the table, raking off crumbs for Mama to sweep up. He must've done it purely for the feel of the wood, because it sure wasn't helpful.

"Grady," she said. "Say what you got to say, all right?" She couldn't sit still much longer, would have to jump up and run and scream or something to relieve the pressure that felt like it might split her wide open.

Grady pulled his hands in toward his chest and held them like he was thinking about praying. "Pansy," he said, a pained look on his face. "I ain't doing this to get onto you. Honey, I'm worried about you."

Honey. Grady didn't call nobody honey. Pansy felt a clutch of panic in her gut, which made her mad. She had to stop this, had to get back to work before something bad happened. "You listen to me, Grady. I do my job and I do it well. Just because I get a little behind every once in a while don't give you cause to call me in here like this."

"That's just it, though, Pansy. This ain't never happened to you before. I've had the other girls in here from time to time, but never you. You're like a machine, woman. Your production's always been regular as a clock, and you don't never mess up. That's what's got me so worried." He looked down at his hands and started wiping the desk again. "Is everything all right?"

There it was again, that puppy-dog preacher-daddy look. God-a'mighty, what did he think she was going to do, spill her guts right there? To him? Not hardly. What would he do if she did? What if she said, *Well, Grady, I'll boil it down for you. My mama died and even dead she's still driving me crazy, my young'un is suffering and I can't do nothing to help her, and I'm going through the change of life whether I like it or not—you know what that is, don't you?—and now I can't even seem to do my job no more.* Her head felt like it was spinning, or maybe the room was. She closed her eyes.

"Pansy," he said. "The only reason I brung you in here is to see if there's anything I can do. I know something's wrong. You think after all these years of working with you, seeing you every day, I can't tell when something's wrong? I may be half deaf and dumb as a rock, but I ain't blind. You been walking around like a zombie for weeks now, just going through the motions. You don't have to tell me no details, but don't sit there and deny something's bothering you." He stopped and took a deep breath. "You know I'll help you if I can."

Pansy kept her eyes closed. She'd heard that old saying about the last straw, and now she understood how it worked. Things just built up and built up and your burden got heavier and heavier and you just kept on going, like a faithful old mule, until one day some little thing, something as simple as an unexpected kindness, like your bossman asking if he can help you, trips you up and knocks the whole thing off balance and that's it, you're falling, falling, falling, and seems like it takes forever to hit the ground. She heard a sound of heavy breathing, like somebody walking up a steep hill, and opened her eyes. Was that her making that noise? Grady was watching her, and the look on his face was purely comical, like somebody juggling eggs and the first one just hit the floor and now he's afraid the rest are fixing to follow. Then it felt like her backbone just dissolved from all that water, all them tears pouring down her face. She hadn't even realized she was crying, and when it hit her, she just crumpled in on herself, covered up her face with her hands, and bawled.

"Shhhhh, now, hush, don't cry," Grady said, his chair slamming against the wall as he jumped up and come around the desk to her. He patted her back carefully, like he was afraid his hand might go right through. "Let me run get one of the other girls in here," he said. "I'll be right back."

On some level Pansy heard him, and when she felt him leave the room, she tried to make it stop, tried to pull herself together. But it kept coming back on her, like water through a busted dam, and she was alone, so alone, with nobody to help stop it.

Hours later it seemed, or maybe it was only a minute, she heard a tender voice say, "Oh, honey," and looked up to see Idalene and Maxann coming through the door. Thank the Lord, they didn't look scared like Grady. She was sick to death of coddling men, making sure they didn't worry, making sure everything was all right in their world no matter what was happening in hers. They didn't care and neither did she.

Idalene stood next to her and petted her shoulder, while Maxann knelt down and handed her Kleenex. That should've made her feel better, having somebody give her what she needed, but it didn't. It just made her feel guilty and she could not quit crying and finally she managed to calm herself enough to look up at Idalene and say, "I want to go home." What she really felt like saying was, *I want my mama*, and Idalene seemed to understand, because she put an arm around Pansy's back to help her up and said, "Come on, honey, I got you."

IF RUSSELL had a bar, she'd be in it right now, even though it was the middle of the day and even though she wasn't much of a drinker. She thought about going to the Apple Banana Candy Store, as her daddy called it, but didn't feel like a whole bottle of anything. Maybe she could get some of those little bottles they sold at the counter, though, tiny Jack Daniel's and Bacardis she could drink in the car. The prospect of the hangover made her turn the other way down Main Street instead, where she pulled in front of the café. It was still lunchtime and she decided to eat the biggest, fattest cheeseburger and fries they had, washed down with the economy-size chocolate milk shake, a carbohydrate pick-me-up with the added benefit of no hangover. Nothing like a little grease and sugar to take her mind off her future in textiles.

The café was busy with the downtown lunch crowd, lawyers and accountants and bankers and their secretaries, talking fast, gulping food, in a hurry to get back to their important jobs. These women were the reason she ended up at the mill. They knew a good job when they got one. These pretty, perfectly pressed and made-up and accessorized women in suits and pumps. She didn't remember this well-dressed clientele from when she was a kid. When she and her mama came to town for back-to-school shopping and ate lunch at the café, they saw mostly people like them, people from the mill or salespeople from the downtown stores or bank tellers.

She ordered at the counter, then settled into the booth furthest from the door, looking around without being too obvious to see if Hap might be in one of the other booths. No sign of him, which was just as well. She wouldn't want to make a pig of herself in front of him.

While waiting for the food to come, she studied the life-size black-and-white picture of Marilyn Monroe on the wall beside her. It was the famous photo of her in a white halter dress, the wind from the subway grate below blowing her skirt up around her hips. She was definitely a full-figured gal by today's standards, but not fat or even plump. Simply full-figured. Laurel was no bigger than Marilyn, but she still had that damn cellulite on the backs of her thighs. That wasn't supposed to happen, was it? What did Marilyn have that she didn't? Airbrushing? A really good masseuse? A secret anticellulite formula from monkey glands, like that stuff Loretta Young used to stay young? The fact that she remembered that little detail about Loretta Young proved she'd read entirely too much *People* magazine in her lifetime. Maybe if she'd read the smart magazines like *Time* and *Newsweek* she wouldn't be sitting here now, planning on giving up and getting fat like Maw Bert.

Oh, Lord, she thought. Why am I sitting here envying the life of a dead movie star? She hadn't been able to keep a man any better than Laurel could, not Joe or Arthur or JFK. And if Marilyn couldn't keep one, what chance did she have? But at least Marilyn had been immortalized on film. Who would remember Laurel Granger? No husband, no kids, no one to look after her in her fast-approaching old age. She was going to turn into a dried-up old spinster like Idalene Stevens, living alone with nothing to show for her life. Her body would go first, falling apart in stages—varicose veins, broken capillaries, arthritis, deafness, wrinkles. Her mind would follow soon after, and next thing she knew she'd be sixty-five with a dyed red beehive and a wardrobe of sensible shoes. She'd probably have to take up smoking again just to deal with the stress, which would lead to lung cancer and a mercifully early death. That's what working in that winding room would do to her, she knew it, and she made her decision right then and there to take the office job.

When the food arrived she sat and looked at it, the ketchup and melted cheese oozing out around the edges of the bun, and couldn't eat. Instead, she stuck a straw in the shake and drank half of it in several quick gulps. God, it felt good going down, the cold sweetness soothing her dry throat. If she could always have chocolate, maybe she could stand it. Chocolate made just about anything bearable—PMS, a bad hair day, a scary new job, getting left by your husband. In the weeks after Scott left she'd kept a drawer at work piled high with Hershey almond bars and ate at least two a day.

The bell over the door jingled and she looked up, but it was only a couple of big-haired secretary types in high heels and full makeup. Why was she so interested in seeing Hap anyway? Hadn't she just decided that chocolate would become her one true faithful love? She sipped the shake and thought about calling him. It would be easy to find his number in the book and dial it. He had obviously wanted her to. The question was, did she want to get involved with anyone right now? No, but she didn't want to sit home with her mama and daddy every Saturday night watching TV either.

She found a pay phone in the back hall of the café, between the rest rooms, and dialed the number. When the secretary took her name and put her on hold, she almost hung up, but a voice in her head yelled at her to buck up, quit thinking too much, have a little fun. It might've been Scott's voice, she wasn't sure, but whoever it was was right.

"Hello," he said, his voice warm like whiskey going down slow. Definitely not a lawyerly tone of voice.

Oh, Lord, she thought, wanting to hang up. It had been too long. Had she ever even called a man before? She heard her mama's tape, the little voice telling her the woman never ever calls the man. It is his responsibility to call you.

"Are you still there?"

Business, that's what she needed to remember. He was a lawyer and she had called about a business matter. "Hey. Yes, I'm here. It's just hard to hear. I'm in the café. I don't know if you remember what we talked about, but I was wondering—"

But she didn't have to go on, because he interrupted, still using that same low, intimate tone, as if whatever he didn't already know about her, he intended to find out and soon. "Listen, I'm right down the street from you, on the second floor of the old Butler's building. Why don't you come on over and we can talk here?"

His office was in the building where she used to buy Hush Puppies and Converse for school? Maybe it was a sign, a sign for her to walk on down there and just see what happened.

"Now?" she said. It would take her a few minutes to clean up, brush her teeth, check her hair and makeup. It was exactly this kind of thing that made her carry a huge purse with all the necessities of life in it. She never knew when she might need to floss or cut a hangnail or sew on a button.

"Whenever you're ready."

Whenever you're ready. What a lovely phrase, especially the way he said it, teasing, flirting. He would wait for her, he would help her change her name back to Champion, and he would ask her out, she just knew it, could feel it in her bones, and maybe this wouldn't be so hard after all, this getting back in the saddle, back on the dating bicycle. And next Saturday night she would have a date with him. Maybe, just maybe, having that to look forward to would get her through the first dreaded week at the plant. That and just a little bit of chocolate, she thought, eyeing the rest of her milk shake as she walked past her booth and out the door.

PANSY SAT at the kitchen table snapping green beans into a bowl, inhaling the sweet clean smell of the beans. She despised the tin-can taste of store beans. Even when she rinsed them and cooked them with fatback, they still had a whang to them. She also felt funny about buying fresh beans at the store, but she hadn't had any of her own to can last summer, even if she had felt like canning then. She worried about using these beans because they shipped that produce in from other countries and no telling what all kind of germs and pesticides were on them. Pansy always washed everything real good, but it still made her nervous. This year she'd have to get back in that garden, though this very minute the prospect wore her out, thinking of all the work that went into it. She must be getting old. She'd never felt tired all the time the way she did now. Seemed like this whole last year she'd had to make herself do the things that used to come easy. She sighed and concentrated on breaking the beans into nice even pieces.

Every snap took her further and further into her life here at home and away from life at the plant, and how she'd embarrassed herself, crying like that, and how bad her legs hurt, and how the ringing in her ears had got louder this last year. All there was in the world was her kitchen and the table Dan built for her thirty-some years ago, still holding up good, like him, like them, still strong and useful.

She looked around at the way the last of the light coming through the window made the kitchen seem almost like church, glowing and bright. In a few minutes she'd have to get up and turn on a light, although she had no doubt she could break beans and even cook the whole meal in the dark if she had to. Laurel would think she was crazy if she caught her sitting in the dark. Would she understand if Pansy tried to explain how something as simple as breaking green beans into a blue ceramic bowl that had belonged to her mama at an oak table that her husband had made for their fifth anniversary made her feel safe?

Pansy smiled to herself, thinking she must be getting senile, getting all worked up like that. But it all mattered so much, and she didn't want to take none of it for granted. Not this kitchen, not the house or the yard, not even the plant. Even there, she found something beautiful just about every day. The rhythm of the backwinders, the hands tying off threads, pulling cones, faces concentrating, laughing, talking. It was almost like a dance they did there every day, and there was beauty in it. The tears came then, again, as they had nearly every day since her mama died. How was it that beauty made her sad, and being a fifty-seven-year-old orphan made her cry? She didn't need a mama and daddy no more, but that feeling of loss kept coming back on her.

Now when she looked at the picture of herself that lived in her head, a picture big and layered enough to hold her whole life and all the people in it, it was like part of that picture had been erased, leaving little white spots not just where her parents had been but where she had been with them, and there was no way to get it back and she'd never felt such a sadness in her life as she did over them missing pieces. Living in the world without them felt wrong somehow, made her feel like the net holding her down to this life had got holes in it and she was afraid sometime she might slip through one of them holes and go floating off in space.

Pansy jumped when the light came on. She hadn't heard anybody come in.

"Lord, Mama," Laurel said. "What're you doing sitting here in the dark? You scared me half to death."

Pansy wiped under her eyes, but Laurel had seen her crying.

"Mama?" She sat down across from Pansy and leaned toward her. "What's the matter?"

Lord, Pansy thought. Am I never going to have any privacy again? Ever since Laurel got home she hadn't had a minute to herself. She stood up and carried the beans to the sink and turned on the water. "Nothing, everything's fine. Why don't you go watch TV till supper's ready?" Oh, that sounded mean, and she knew it even as the words was coming out of her mouth. Going from sad to mad so quick scared her to death, but she couldn't seem to help it. Laurel didn't deserve to have it took out on her, though.

She turned around and Laurel looked like she might cry herself. Poor thing, she wasn't used to seeing her mama cry. When Pansy was little, her mama cried so much she swore she'd never do that to a young'un of hers. Pansy stepped behind Laurel's chair and squeezed her shoulders, her come-on-buck-up-now squeeze. "You ever just have one of them days?" she said, patting the top of Laurel's head before she went back to the sink to finish washing the beans.

"You work too hard, Mama. You need to take a break."

Uh-huh, Pansy thought. Like you, been here almost two months and don't have a job yet? And that was mean too, but as long as it stayed in her head, she didn't worry. Maybe if Laurel had a job she wouldn't follow Pansy around all the time. The girl was forever wanting to go somewhere, out to eat, to the movies, to the mall. Going and spending. Hadn't they raised her better? But it could just be that generation never having to do for themselves, didn't cook or sew or make a garden or nothing. If it was to come another Depression they'd starve and go naked.

"Mama? Did you hear me?"

"What?" She turned off the water, shook the colander, and set it back in the sink.

"I got a job today."

Pansy turned, surprised. Here she'd been thinking bad thoughts and Laurel had gone out and found her a job. "Well, that's good, honey. What is it?"

"I start at the plant Monday morning. I'm the new office assistant." She tried to sound perky about it, but Pansy could tell she was depressed. She felt depressed herself. The plant was the last place she expected Laurel to get a job. She'd been applying at law firms and banks and all kinds of places like that. And this was the best she could find? What was the point, then, of all that college? The tiredness came over her strong then, and she had to turn back to the sink so Laurel wouldn't see.

"Mama?" Laurel had got up and come over to her. "You're white as a sheet. Why don't you go lay down and let me get supper ready?"

Pansy looked down at her hands resting on the green beans. She scooped up a handful and let them fall though her fingers back into the colander. "All right," she said, making up her mind that Laurel was right, she did work too hard and she did need to rest. Hadn't what happened today proved that?

"Thanks, honey," she said. "Don't forget to put the fatback in the beans."

"I know, Mama."

In the doorway between the kitchen and living room, Pansy stopped and looked back. It didn't look the same in artificial light. As she watched Laurel getting the fatback and the thawed chicken from the refrigerator, it felt like she was saying good-bye. She went into the living room and turned on the TV to drown out the sound of Laurel humming, then laid down on the couch. Something inside her had been winding tighter and tighter over the last few months, and as Pansy put a pillow under her head and closed her eyes, she felt whatever it was start to unravel, a feeling like a crochet hook slipping out of the loop, the thread being pulled, all the work coming undone loop by loop until there was nothing left but the plain old thread laying tangled in a wad.

How could something as simple and quiet as walking out of the kitchen and laying down on the couch make her feel like her life had changed? She laid there waiting, for what, she had no idea. Something was happening, something she had no control over, and the worst part was, she didn't care. She'd always held on so tight, making sure everything run the way it should, and now she just wanted to let it all go, the laundry, balancing the checkbook, vaccuming the carpet, dusting her angels, cooking the meals. Even the thought of getting up off the couch took more energy than she had to spare, so she just laid there. After a while, her eyes closed and almost immediately she fell into a deep sleep.

6

First days were the hardest. Laurel knew that, but it didn't help. It also didn't help thinking of all the first days she'd survived before this. First day of trying to ride a bike, first day of school, first day of her period, first day of college, first day of marriage, first day of every other new job she'd ever had. But the first day of this new job seemed harder than any of the rest somehow.

Then again, maybe it was just the same old fear she felt about just about everything except brushing her teeth. What if she couldn't do it? What if she failed and there was no hiding it and everybody knew just how bad she did? Here she'd gone off to college thinking she was too smart for this little town, and now what if she couldn't do it? And the other biggie, the one that had pissed her off so bad at all those secretarial jobs—what if she was really good at it? What if everybody loved her, loved her work, wanted her to stay? Just because she was good at clerical work didn't mean she wanted to do it the rest of her life. But she hated to let people down, and she liked to feel needed. Weren't those the two things that had held women down for centuries?

"Good morning!"

Laurel winced at the perkiness hitting her smack in the face so early in the day. The nameplate on the desk said *Stephanie Terrell, Receptionist*, but she looked more like a Bunny or a Susie in that pink flowered dress, perfect makeup, and blond *That Girl* flip. How had Laurel missed her the day of the interview? Maybe she'd been out at the perky store getting a refill. Linda must've had a fit when John hired this one, because she was younger, prettier, and a natural blonde.

"Good morning," Laurel said, trying to set a good example for poor Bunny by speaking in a normal tone.

"Welcome to your first day." Stephanie turned on a thousand-watt smile. Oh, yes, Laurel thought, Linda better watch out. "John and Linda aren't in yet."

God, she was young, maybe twenty, twenty-one, and so excited about her very first office job. Laurel remembered being that bright and shiny and new, vaguely.

"That's okay," Laurel said, hoisting a box against her chest. "That'll give me time to get settled in." She went through to her cubicle, set the box on her desk, and pulled out a big spider plant, a small white plastic fan, a framed picture of her family, a box of her favorite pens she'd swiped from her last job, a roll of peppermints, hand lotion, a sewing kit, and an extra pair of panty hose—all essentials, she'd discovered over the years.

It didn't take long to set up her desk, then there was nothing to do but sit and stare at the gray fabric-covered walls and wait for John and Linda. She decided to hit the bathroom before they arrived in case they wanted to meet with her right away.

She had the bathroom to herself and took her time, fixing her hair, freshening her makeup. It occurred to her that she could stay in there all day, just hide out. Stuff was on her desk, her light was on; maybe they'd think she was taking a solo tour of the plant. She'd had a boss like that one time, a guy who came in, turned on his light, hung his jacket on the back of his chair, then disappeared for hours at a time. Nobody ever figured out where he went or what he did, yet he made twice what she did. It taught her that the working world doesn't reward the conscientious. The ones who got ahead were the ones who could produce the most bullshit on a consistent basis. The ones who actually worked were too busy working to get ahead.

God, she didn't want to go back out there and face the day. But if she stayed here they'd come looking for her eventually, and that would be more embarrassing than going out there and screwing up. They'd have to send her to Broughton for testing if she refused to come out of the bathroom because she was scared to start a new job. They'd put her in a rubber room. It was times like these she wished she still smoked. It didn't help much to remind herself that this was only temporary, only until she figured out what she wanted to do, because she had no inkling what that might be.

DAN LET the phone ring thirty times before he got disgusted and hung up. Why wasn't Pansy answering? Even if she was deep asleep, thirty rings should've woke her up. Even if she was in the bathroom, thirty rings was enough time to get to the phone. Something might be wrong, but he'd hate to take off work and go home just to find her asleep in the bed. Besides, he had work to do. He picked up the phone and dialed again. This time he hung up after twenty rings. What should he do?

If only Laurel hadn't started that job, he wouldn't be having to worry like this. She could've been watching her mama. Of course, he was glad she'd found a job, though he didn't much like the idea of her working in that plant. It was all right for Pansy. She was used to hard work, and them women she worked with was like her, tough country women. He just didn't see how Laurel would ever fit in with that bunch.

For one thing, she was spoiled. He admitted it was mostly his fault. That was part of a daddy's job. And Pansy had been the one to spoil Cecil. A lot of times Dan wondered that Pansy didn't spoil Laurel too. He'd figured she might, after the way her own mama was. That old Bert, Pansy always made excuses for her, and so did people who'd known her her whole life, like Kitty. Kitty said Bert had a hard life and a lot of disappointment, but to Dan it looked like pure meanness on her part.

It struck him then. He could call Kitty. She could run next door and check on Pansy for him. He'd locked the door behind him when he left that morning, but Kitty knew about the key in the freezer on the carport. She could use that to get in if Pansy wouldn't come to the door.

Kitty answered on the second ring. "Hello, Kitty Cone speaking."

Dan always thought her voice sounded all wrong for her name and her shape. She was a tiny little woman, about five feet nothing, bones like a bird, but with this husky deep voice that sounded like she could boss a whole platoon of Marines.

"Hey, Miss Kitty," he said. "How you doing today?"

"You left kind of late for work this morning."

"Yes, ma'am, Pansy ain't feeling too good."

"What's wrong with her?"

"I wish I knew. She's tired all the time, but then has trouble sleeping at night. And she gets these terrible headaches where all she can do is lay in a dark room and wait for it to pass."

"They Lord, I didn't know. I seen her car in the driveway all week, but I figured she rode to work with Laurel. Reckon she'd like some of my vegetable soup? I could carry it over to her."

"That's exactly why I called, Miss Kitty, to see if you wouldn't mind going over and checking on her. I been calling and calling and she don't answer."

"Give me your phone number so I can call you back."

While Dan waited at his desk for Kitty's call, he leaned back in his chair and stared out at the prison yard. It was a beautiful day, not a cloud in the sky, but cold. Not a soul outside. He figured they was all huddled up in the TV lounge watching soap operas or talk shows. It still got his goat that they allowed so much TV-watching. In the old days, prisoners earned their keep out on chain gangs, which wore them out enough that they didn't have as much energy to cause trouble at night. Now they could watch TV, write a book, even get a college degree if they wanted to. It just didn't seem right that they was better off in here than out there. Prison was supposed to be punishment. Part of his objection was he hated being at a desk, missed being outside, on the road or wherever the work took them.

He jumped when the phone rang, then tilted his chair down and reached for the receiver. "Hello?"

"Dan, honey, it's Kitty. I'm over here with Pansy, and she said she just felt too tired to get out of the bed and answer the phone. But she's all right."

Too tired to answer the phone? Dan rubbed his hand on his pants leg, because it had started sweating all of a sudden. Then he switched the phone to that hand so he could wipe the other one. This was not good.

"I'll stay with her awhile and make sure she eats something."

"All right, then. Thank you, Miss Kitty."

Dan sat back down and tried to concentrate on the monthly reports, but his mind would not leave Pansy. He kept seeing her as she'd looked that morning, her face pale, dark circles under her eyes, hair mashed up against her head. It'd scared him to see her looking so unlike herself. She'd looked almost old, almost like her mama. He threw down his pen and went to the men's room, came back and sat down for two seconds, then got up and started pacing around the office. A few minutes later Ralph Sprinkle came in. Just what he needed, his supervisor catching him walking in circles around his desk like an idiot.

"What you doing?" Ralph said, leaning his hip against the doorjamb. He had his cup of after-lunch coffee and Dan could tell he was settling himself for a visit, as if that wall needed his skinny butt to hold it up for a while.

Dan stared at him, unable to think of anything to say for a minute. "Nothing," he said finally, and went back to his desk and sat down to wait Ralph out.

"Jill said you 'bout got them reports done."

Yeah, Dan thought, no thanks to Jill. He still couldn't figure out why Ralph had hired the girl. She was a cute little blonde but couldn't type worth a durn, couldn't do a damn thing but answer phones and make coffee, and even that was bad. Ralph said anything else she needed to know, she could learn on the job. But she'd been there six months and didn't appear to be learning nothing except how to talk Dan's ear off every time she come in here. That's what come of Ralph hiring his own wife's cousin. Dan missed Marie, their old secretary. He never had to ask her for a thing, because she always knew what he needed before he did, just like Pansy. He picked up his pen like he meant to work on the reports right that minute. "I'll have them ready tomorrow." Ralph didn't take the hint, though, just kept standing there.

"How's Pansy doing?"

That's what he'd come in here for, then, to find out what was wrong with Pansy. He shouldn't never have mentioned her coming home sick from work that day. Ralph was a bigger gossip than any woman. He'd go right home and tell his wife and then she'd tell everybody in town when they come in for a haircut. "She's all right." Dan wasn't about to tell what the doctor said about her hormones being out of whack and causing her to be depressed and tired all the time. Pansy would kill him if she found out he told her personal business.

"Glad to hear it," Ralph said. "Carolyn heard she's been out of work all week."

No telling where Ralph's wife got the information. He probably knew all about the doctor's visit too, then, and just wanted to make Dan squirm a little bit.

"Listen," Dan said, deciding if he wasn't going to be able to work, he might as well check on Pansy. "You care if I run home for lunch?"

Ralph lifted his cup in Dan's direction. "Not a problem. You sure everything's all right?"

"I'm just going home for lunch, that's all." Dan put on his coat and squeezed past Ralph, still standing there holding up the wall.

In spite of lunchtime traffic, he covered the ten miles home in less than ten minutes. It usually took about twenty. He went in quietly in case Pansy was sleeping and eased up the stairs to their room. She wasn't in bed. He checked the bathroom and she wasn't there either. She wasn't anywhere in the house. Her car was still in the driveway and her pocketbook was on the dresser, so she didn't go far. Kitty's. She must be over there.

Dan went down the back steps and jogged over to Miss Kitty's, his keys and change jingling in his pockets as he ran. As he came through the gap in the hedge between their houses, he noticed that Kitty already had a few daffodils blooming. The woman had the magic touch.

She met him at her back door wearing an apron that said *Kiss the Cook*. "She's on the couch eating soup and watching *All My Children*," she said. "I thought she needed a change of scenery, so I brung her over here."

Dan went past Kitty and stood in the door to the living room. Pansy looked better already, sitting up, her hair combed, slurping soup off a spoon. She even had a little color in her face. "Hey, honey," he said, feeling anxious, like he'd done something wrong when he knowed good and durn well he hadn't.

"Dan," she said, surprised and apparently not real thrilled to see him. "What are you doing here?"

"I just wanted to check on you," he said. He perched on the other end of the couch and glanced at the TV, where some man was kissing some woman and promising he'd never leave her.

Pansy saw him watching and said, "Hunh. Soap-opera promises."

"What?"

"Them soap-opera promises. I promise I'll never leave you, I promise I'll always love you, I promise you're the only one for me. People ought not promise things like that."

Now what was she on about? *Had* he done something to make her mad? Didn't it mean nothing to her that he'd took time off work to come home and see about her? "Honey, I don't know what you're talking about."

Pansy put her spoon down and wiped her mouth on a yellow paper napkin. "I'm sorry," she said, still staring at the napkin. "I don't feel good, that's all."

He sighed, relieved that it wasn't him. "Don't be sorry. Just think about all the times you looked after me when I was sick. Turnabout's fair play. That soup looks good."

"You want some?" Kitty asked from the door. "Let me get you a bowl."

"Don't go to no trouble," Dan said, making a move to get up.

Kitty waved him down. "It ain't no trouble. You set right there and talk to Pansy."

When Dan finished his soup, he carried his and Pansy's dishes to the kitchen. He offered to help Miss Kitty clean up, but she wouldn't let him, so he went back to the living room. Pansy had laid down, so there was no room for him to sit next to her. "You need anything?" he said, standing over her, blocking the TV.

She looked up at him and that tired look was still there in her eyes, like she hadn't slept in a month and might be fixing to cry any minute. "No, I'm fine," she said, and gave him a little smile.

He leaned over and kissed her cheek. "Okay, you rest. I better get on back. You know we got them reports due next week. Can you believe it's nearly March?"

She gave him another weak smile, then closed her eyes. He straightened up and stood looking down at her for a minute, not sure what he ought to do. He'd never known Pansy to be like this, to not care about her appearance, to show no interest in him or the world around her. She'd always been one to notice every little thing and remark on it.

He remembered thinking when they met how unusual she was because, unlike other girls he dated, she never looked in the mirror when they went riding. She looked out at the fields, the sky, the houses they passed. She thought the whole world was beautiful. Now she was looking at something he couldn't see, and it drove him crazy that he didn't know what it was or why she'd turned to it. What bothered him even more was wondering when she'd snap out of it and come back to him, be his old Pansy again.

"Sit down here and have some cobbler before you go back to work, Dan," Kitty said when he came into the kitchen. It felt so good to have somebody tend to him a little bit that, even though he wasn't hungry, he pulled out a chair and sat down. "I think she's asleep now," he said, eyeing the dish of cobbler Kitty set in front of him.

"Blackberry," she said. "Picked them myself last summer over behind your house. Now quit talking and eat."

He blew on a spoonful to cool it, then put it in his mouth. Lord, it was good, that dark tangy syrup of the blackberries and then the sweet cake of the crust. "Oh, Miss Kitty," he said. "This is mighty fine."

"Want a scoop of vanilla on top?"

"No, ma'am, I feel like I need something to warm me up and this is just the ticket."

Kitty sat down across from Dan. "It is cold today. I don't mean to wish my life away, but I sure do wish spring would hurry up. I can't bear to be cold."

"Me neither," Dan said. He heard a sound from the living room and turned his head toward it.

"She's just rolling over on the couch," Kitty said.

Dan set his spoon down and pushed the dish away.

"You ain't full, are you?"

"I am," Dan said, and Kitty pulled the dish over to her and started eating.

The kitchen was quiet except for the sound of the spoon clinking against the dish as Kitty scraped her bowl clean. How many times had he been in this kitchen? No telling. They'd been neighbors ever since the kids was little and never locked their doors to one another, and Dan felt as at home here as he did in his own house.

Kitty carried her dish to the sink, squirted in some dish soap, then ran hot water over it. Dan smelled lemons. Must be the dish soap. It made him think of summer and the beach. Maybe this summer him and Pansy would go to Myrtle Beach. They'd got out of the habit when the kids got grown, just took weekend trips to Gatlinburg or Lake Lure every once in a while. It'd been a long time since they went anywhere just the two of them.

As Kitty washed out the bowl, she talked to him over her shoulder. "Now, Dan, I don't want you worrying about Pansy. She's going through something all women goes through, only hers is hitting a little harder than most. What she probably needs is some hormones. A lot of women needs their hormones replaced at this time of life. They just run out and it messes up their whole system."

"That's what the doctor said, but Pansy don't want to take them. Said her mama didn't need none and neither does she." Dan had got the prescriptions filled anyway, hoping he could talk her into taking them, but there they sat on the kitchen counter, still in the little white pharmacy bag.

"Well, Bert didn't take no hormones 'cause they didn't make them back then. You better believe she would've gobbled them up like candy if she'd had any. And me and Edith too. What's the sense in suffering when you don't have to? It's the same as birth control. We done all right without it, but if we'd a had it, you better know we'd a used it. Especially Bert." Kitty hesitated, then turned from the sink. "I believe

PLANT LIFE · 125

she was one of them women not meant to have children, and there she went and had eight."

"You know Pansy," Dan said. "When it comes to her mama, you can't argue with her." Old Bert had done a real number on Pansy, but Dan wouldn't say that to Kitty. Her and Bert and Edith had all been friends when they was young.

"Well, you go on back to work now and leave Pansy to me," Kitty said. "We'll get that young'un straightened out, don't you worry."

Dan smiled at that, Kitty still thinking of Pansy as a young'un. But she'd changed Pansy's diapers, played dolls with her, watched her grow up. She was about as much a mama to her as Bert had been. "Thank you, Miss Kitty," he said as he put on his coat and headed to the door. "I owe you one."

"You come over here in a couple weeks and till up my garden and we'll call it even," she said.

ALL HER mama's friends looked up and waved her over when she appeared in the doorway of the canteen. Laurel knew that welcome wasn't really for her. They just wanted to hear how her mama was doing. But it still felt good, to be part of the gang, to not have to walk in there all alone and have people watch her out of the corner of their eyes the way they had done the past few days. Linda had told her everybody was suspicious of them because they worked in the office and they'd probably think Laurel was a spy for "the man." She'd thought Linda was an idiot, until she actually went to the canteen and saw that nobody would make eye contact.

She sat next to Lottie May, and the first words out of the woman's mouth were, "Honey, how's your mama?" Lottie May. Laurel thought it was great they cared so much, but she wasn't sure how much her mama would want her to tell them.

"She was still in bed when I left this morning." She didn't say how scary it was to see her mama laid up in the bed while she and her daddy got ready for work. Even when Pansy was sick with the flu, she'd always gotten up and gone to work. This wasn't the flu, though.

"Can we do anything for her?" Lottie May said.

"I don't think so," Laurel said, watching her peel a banana, break it into little pieces, and lay it out on her napkin. Did she have to look every bite over before she put it in her mouth? She could've eaten two bananas in the time it took Lottie May to do that one.

"How you doing, hon?" Percilla said, her voice dripping sympathy as if Laurel had broken a leg or something. "I would've come up front and said hey your first day, but that Grady's been watching me like a hawk."

"Percilla thinks Grady's got a crush on her," Lottie May said with a wink.

"Y'all hush," Percilla said, obviously pleased. "I'm a married woman."

"I notice you didn't say happily." Maxann had come up to the end of the booth. She waited for Laurel and Idalene to slide over and make room, then scooted in next to them.

"I am happily married," Percilla said. "What makes you think I ain't?"

"Not a thing. I was just wondering about Rex." Maxann peeled the plastic off her microwaved dish of macaroni and cheese and spooned up a mouthful.

"Of course Rex is happy," Percilla said. "Why wouldn't he be? I do everything for that man."

"Boy, this chicken and dumplings sure is good," Lottie May said. She looked at Laurel and winked. "Want some?"

"No, thank you," Laurel said, and took another bite of the sandwich she'd slapped together that morning. She felt about ten years old, sitting there eating peanut butter and jelly while they all had these elaborate plastic containers full of leftovers from last night's supper. She'd been in such a rush to get ready that morning, she hadn't had time to make anything else.

"Let me taste them dumplings," Percilla said, and stuck her spoon in Lottie May's dish. "Mmmmmm, they are good."

Lottie May slid her bowl a little further down the table, away from Percilla. "Nellie Belle brung them home from the café last night."

"Is that right?" Percilla said, already turning away from Lottie May. Laurel felt like a bug pinned to Styrofoam when Percilla aimed a look at her. "Honey, I still can't believe you ended up working here. Couldn't you find nothing else? You'd think a girl with a college education could find something besides working in a plant. My girl Carmen started her own business. You know that exercise place by the Food Lion? That's hers. She owns it and teaches all the classes, aerobics and Jazzercise and something with big rubber bands."

Laurel supposed she should be grateful Percilla never waited for answers to her questions. She just plowed ahead, as if she had absolutely no control over what came out of her mouth.

"Oh, Lord, girls," Lottie May blurted out, trying once again to provide a distraction. "I meant to tell you, this morning I nearly fainted. I went out on the back porch and seen three bluebirds sitting in a rusty tub."

And your point is? Laurel thought, then realized she meant that it was beautiful. It must be so wonderful to be able to take pleasure in simple things like that. Did you have to be born that way or was it something you could teach yourself? It might be worth trying.

"Anyway," Percilla said. "You ought to go out there."

"We'll see," Laurel said. Just not in this lifetime.

"I'm sure she'd give you a discount," Percilla said. "At least to start." She wiped her mouth, and the napkin came away covered with orange sauce and hot-pink lipstick. "You know, I figured sure you'd just go on back to Las Vegas. Who'd want to live here after living there? My cousin Diane went there one time about three years ago—that was back before you and Scott moved there—and she had the best time. Stayed up all night gambling in the casino, and you know they bring you free drinks, all you got to do is make sure you tip the waitress a dollar so she'll keep coming back. And Lord God, honey, the men, they was everywhere. All kinds of men. A lot of foreigners, though. But even some of them was good-looking. And of course they're all rich as Croesus. One of them took a liking to Diane and she went off with him for a while. It's a wonder she didn't get kidnapped or something, but he brung her back the next morning."

Percilla hunkered down over the table, leaned in and lowered her voice. "She said he wanted her to do it standing up in the shower. Can you imagine? You'd think a man would be more careful of his you-know-what than to take a chance on slipping and falling in the shower.

Diane told him she didn't have the muscle control to handle that and it was the bed or nothing."

The bed or nothing. Laurel had to struggle to keep a smile off her face, remembering all the times she and Scott had taken chances with his you-know-what in the shower. And on the kitchen counter, the living-room floor, the front seat of the car, in a hot tub, in the woods. Most of the time she preferred plain old bed sex herself, because it was comfortable and they could take their time, but every once in a while it felt so good to not wait, to shove aside their clothes and just go at it like rabbits, as her mama would say. God, all that seemed so long ago, when they were young and still in love. Maybe the end of the wildness should've been a warning sign to her. Maybe she should've jumped in the shower with him more often, reminded him of how they used to be. And so he got bored and got in the shower with another woman, and it was small consolation to think that what Scott had done to her, he could, and hopefully would, also someday do to Deedee.

Percilla leaned back and fixed Laurel in her sights. "So, honey, what was it made you stay here? Couldn't you face going back there and seeing him with that young thing? I don't blame you. I know it must be awful to lose your husband, especially to somebody younger."

Why couldn't Mrs. Tasmanian Devil keep her big pink mouth shut? Laurel looked down at the crusts from her sandwich and took a deep breath. She never had liked the crust. Maw Bert used to cut them off for her, but Mama never would. She told them there were poor starving children in Ethiopia who would kill for those crusts. And then when she and Cecil acted up, her mama would call them little Ethiopians and tell them to settle down. That had always confused Laurel. She'd never been able to figure out if the Ethiopians were supposed to be pitied or feared. She hadn't realized then that it was possible to do both.

"Well, Percilla," she said. "All I can tell you is what Maw Bert used to tell me whenever I'd go out to play in the woods. If you ever get lost, just sit still and wait." Let her figure that one out, Laurel thought, but she didn't have to worry about what Percilla would say. Maxann slapped her hand on the table and said, "Percilla Sue, I plumb forgot. Grady wants to see you in his office."

"What? He does?" Percilla put down her fork and stood up. "I knowed he was watching me. Y'all don't let nobody touch my cake. I'll be right back."

When she was gone, Lottie May said, "Don't pay no attention to her, honey."

"That's right," Maxann said. "She's always stirring the pot. I keep hoping one of these days she'll fall in and be in a big mess herself and then see how she likes it."

"Y'all all run your mouths too much, if you ask me," Idalene said.

It was only her first week on the job and already Laurel was exhausted from the stress and the interrogation by Percilla. Lottie May and Maxann and Idalene being nice to her was the last thing she needed. Suddenly she just wanted to bawl right there in the middle of the canteen.

"Hey, let's eat Percilla's cake," Maxann said.

"I don't want none," Idalene said. "I don't eat cake."

"She'll have a fit," Lottie May said.

"What's your point?" Maxann said, and pulled the plate holding Percilla's cake toward her. It wasn't a piece of cake anyway, more like a wedge, a hunk. She cut it into three equal sections and handed one to Lottie May and one to Laurel, then took a big bite of her piece. "Mmmm, carrot cake."

It did look good, all moist and rich with cream-cheese icing half an inch thick all over it. "Oh my God, this is good," Laurel said after the first bite. "Do you think Percilla made this?"

"Oh, yeah," Maxann said. "I got to give her credit. The woman can bake like a demon. You think this is good, wait till you taste her Italian cream cake. That'll put you in a coma."

A coma, Laurel thought. Oh, that sounded nice. Just to sleep and sleep and not have to deal with anything. She'd have to settle for a sugar coma today, though, and if the carrot cake didn't do it, she could go by the candy machine on her way out.

THE SUGAR didn't help, and actually made things worse. Plus she was hormonal. It had taken every ounce of willpower Laurel possessed to wait until she got into a bathroom stall with the door shut before she let herself start bawling. It'd been building all day, all week, and it wouldn't be denied any longer. Her nerves were so raw she jumped whenever anybody spoke to her. She'd thought as the days went on things would get better, as they always had at her other jobs. Usually the end of the first week found her exhausted but satisfied that she'd made it through and looking forward to getting the next week and the next behind her, until one day she'd wake up and realize she'd gotten used to it and wasn't anxious anymore. She couldn't understand why this time was so hard. It wasn't that the work was difficult, or that her boss was mean, although she could already tell that Linda was going to be a bitch. It was just sinking in that this was her life—home with her parents, job here—and for the last week she'd felt a constant pressure in her throat, as if she might throw up any minute. She would get used to it, she knew she would, and that scared her too. Oh, God, she thought, please show me the way.

Her nose felt the size of a fist and she turned and leaned her forehead against the cool gray metal of the stall wall. Linda was probably wondering where she'd gone, but she couldn't go back out there, not yet. She'd been a good girl and stayed glued to her desk all week. Fifteen minutes in the bathroom wasn't too much to ask. She was blowing her nose again when she heard a noise, glanced down, and saw four long fingers wiggling at her under the wall. Somebody was in the other stall, and Laurel hadn't even heard her come in. Maybe this other woman had been there all along, heard her bawling over here. God, that was embarrassing, not to mention rude. The woman should've made a noise or something.

Whoever it was didn't say a word, just wiggled those fingers, universal language for *please hand me some toilet paper*. Laurel pulled off a handful and put it in those still-wiggling fingers. They disappeared, and whoever it was blew her nose and said, "Thank you."

She couldn't be sure, but the voice sounded like Idalene's. Why would she be up here in the bathroom near the front office when there was one right across from the winding room? Maybe she came for privacy. Every place Laurel had ever worked, there was one bathroom, usually on another floor and frequently referred to as the crapper, where women went when they wanted privacy. "Idalene?"

There was no answer, just more nose-blowing. Finally a voice croaked, "Who is that?"

It was Idalene, and she sounded awful. Laurel couldn't imagine what could've upset her so, poor thing. It must've been something big. Idalene seemed like she could probably stand up to a hurricane if she had to. "It's me, Laurel. Are you all right?"

"Yes, honey, I'm all right." There was a long pause. "What's the matter with you?"

Laurel sighed. "Nothing, just a long week. What about you?"

"Same," Idalene said, and laughed, a bark that sounded like it must hurt her throat. "Lord, ain't we a pair?"

A pair of what? Laurel thought. Bookends? The before and after in the life cycle of a spinster?

"You getting along all right with Linda?"

"I don't see her that much. She spends most of her time in John's office with the door shut." As a matter of fact, the only time he left her sight was to go to meetings up at the corporate office. Linda had him thinking the office would fall apart without her, which meant all she had to do was show up and tell him what he wanted to hear and leave a list of projects on Laurel's desk. Laurel wondered what they would've done if she hadn't already known how to use the software. She felt pretty confident the only thing Linda knew about word processing or running spreadsheets was how to take credit for them with John.

"That's a blessing, then. She made poor old Betty so miserable she took early retirement. She wanted to go out at seventy-five like me, but she couldn't take eleven more years with that hussy."

Laurel assumed Betty was her predecessor. And she'd wanted to stay till she turned seventy-five? And Idalene too? Why? Whatever happened to retiring at sixty-two? God, loyalty was fine, but that was taking it too far. "How much longer do you have?"

"I turn seventy-five April first." The words came out flat, no expression, as if it was a death sentence.

"God, Idalene, that's great. Only another month or so." And she was an April Fool's baby. That was supposed to be good luck.

"Well," Idalene said loudly, as if trying to wake herself up. "What about you? I know you ain't staying here for the duration. What you going to do with yourself?"

Laurel sighed again. "I have no idea. I'm sort of taking it one day at a time, you know?"

"Well, you're too young to be crying and sighing like a old woman. Don't set around and get all rusted out. You see what I'm saying?"

Laurel laughed. "I think so. Don't worry. As a matter of fact, I've got a date tomorrow night." Hap hadn't asked her out when she went to his office last week, but he'd called soon after. One minute she felt relieved that she'd been right about his interest, and the next she was terrified of having to deal with dating again.

"Good, that's good. Can't let yourself go all to pieces over a man. They's always another'n down the road if you want one. Sometimes you don't want one, though, and that's all right too."

Laurel heard rustling next door, then the toilet flushing, then water running at the sink. When the water stopped, Idalene said, "I'm surprised Grady ain't come in here after me by now. Much as I'd love to see that, I reckon I better get on back. Listen, you keep on coming down to the canteen and eat with us if you want to. Don't feel like you got to set up here by yourself."

There was a whoosh of air as the door swung open, then shut, then Laurel was alone, feeling like crying again because Idalene had been sweet enough to invite her to join them. She hadn't even realized how alone she felt until just then. She'd been counting on her mama being there, and it had been so much harder than she thought without her.

At the sink she wet a paper towel and held it to her hot face. God, she looked awful, eyes and nose red, mascara smeared. Idalene had the right idea, them making separate getaways. If they'd gone out together, both looking this bad, it would've been like a scene from a bad sci-fi movie, *Attack of the Zombie Sisters*.

Idalene was all right, and Laurel figured maybe there were worse ways to end up than as a feisty old woman who could carry off a red beehive with no apology. It beat the hell out of letting herself turn into a wimp who sat around feeling sorry for herself all the time. This weekend she'd get in that kitchen and do some cooking. Come Monday she'd be able to hold her own in the Tupperware war at lunch, and if

Percilla started running that mouth of hers, Laurel would make sure she had something good to shove in it.

"AUNT KITTY," Pansy said. It was so quiet in Kitty's house, the quiet had a sound, a roar of nothing pouring through her ears, and it was driving her crazy. She needed something to run it out. "Aunt Kitty," she said again, this time a little louder.

Kitty stepped into the living room from the kitchen. "What, honey?" she said, shaking out a wet dishrag.

That dishrag was as cute as it could be, Pansy thought, white with red cherries all over it. Kitty had the prettiest things and always kept her house so nice. Of course, she never had no young'uns to mess the place up. Just a husband, and he'd been dead a long time. And there was Edith, but Kitty had kept her in line, wouldn't let her make too much of a mess, though everybody always said Edith could make a mess with a cough drop. "Come and talk to me," Pansy said.

"Honey, I got work to do. I can't just sit down and talk all day."

"Just for a few minutes. Tell me a story."

"Tell you a story? Honey." Kitty came and leaned over Pansy and put her cheek to Pansy's forehead. "You don't feel hot," she said, and straightened up.

Pansy smiled. "I'm not delirious. I just wanted somebody to talk to."

"Well, let me finish what I'm doing in the kitchen and then I'll set in here with you, all right?"

When Kitty settled in her rocker with her embroidery hoop, Pansy sat up on the couch to see better. "What you working on?"

"It's a dresser scarf for Edith's granddaughter. You remember Corina? She just bought herself a little house over in Smith River. It's the cutest thing, a little mill house that's been all fixed up."

"Oh, I didn't know she got married."

"She didn't. Don't you know, girls these days don't need to get married like we done. They only do it if they want to. Them nurses makes real good money, and Cori's so smart about her finances. She put down a fifteen-thousand-dollar down payment on that house. Saved up for years to do it. Plus her car is paid for. She's doing all right."

"Lord. That is something. But don't she get lonesome living all by herself?"

"Lord, no, honey. She's got so many friends and dates all kind of doctors and radiologists and fellers like that from the hospital. I reckon she just ain't ready to settle down yet. I remember what that was like. I sowed a few wild oats myself, till I met Garland, then that was it for me."

"You know, I used to tell Laurel she didn't need to worry about knowing what she wanted to be when she grew up, because her husband would take care of her. Now I think back, I don't like that I said that. I don't like it one bit. I didn't think when I said it. I just didn't think. It's what Mama told me."

"That girl has turned out just fine. You ought to be proud."

"I am. I am proud. But look at her, working in that plant. She's not using her education. She never has. Ever since she graduated, she's worked as a secretary to put that husband of hers through school and keep him in pencil money. So what good has that education done her?"

"Pansy, the girl's not dead yet. Who knows what she might end up doing? She's young. She could do anything. The point is, you done the best you could to start them young'uns out right. The rest is up to them. And considering all the awful things they could've done, like crime or drugs or unemployment, I'd say they turned out right well. I know Laurel's having a hard time right now, but they ain't a thing you can do. She's a grown woman now and she's got to make her own way."

Pansy was quiet for a minute. "I reckon I haven't done so hot at that myself," she said finally.

"What?"

"Making my own way. I reckon I never did."

"What are you talking about, honey?"

Pansy sighed. "Nothing. Just nothing. Never mind." Just that quick she'd run out of steam and could barely keep her eyes open. For weeks she'd been too tired to do anything. She was too tired to even feel ashamed of herself for not being able to work. Grady had been real understanding, and when he suggested she take a leave of absence, she hadn't even put up a fight.

Poor Dan, he was the one suffering. Pansy saw it but could only watch. It was like he was standing on the other side of a dirty window and she couldn't see him or hear him good. The best she could manage was to get out of bed in the morning and follow him to Kitty's, then follow him home again at night. There seemed to be no time in between, just one long string of getting up and laying down. Sometimes a voice in her head said, *I don't know what I done to deserve this*, and it was her mama's voice, but Pansy didn't have the energy to turn it off. It was easier to sleep. That was the only time the voice was quiet, the only time she had any peace.

ALBERTA

Seemed like from the get-go, me and Kitty and Edith hit it off somehow. Maybe because we was about the same age, maybe because we was all scared to death learning that job so different from anything we'd ever known. Kitty and Edith both come off the farm too, like I done. I was real reluctant to go in the mill, but not them two. They thought it was the most exciting thing they ever done. Everything was a big party to them.

That day we all got hired, I knowed who they was but didn't know them real well. We'd heard they might be hiring, so they was a bunch of us standing around the front gate waiting when the supervisor come out and looked us over. He pointed and said, "You and you and you." Me and Kitty and Edith was the last three picked. It was such a relief to have that job and not have to go home and tell Papa I hadn't got it again. He believed I was doing it on purpose, doing something to make them not pick me.

Being the last three, we sort of stuck together, followed that supervisor into the mill, and got to talking right off.

"Ain't you Albert and Tilly Mabry's girl?" Edith said. She was always the boldest one of us, never met a stranger. She stood a good foot taller than me and had the blackest hair I ever seen. I always figured they must've been a Indian in her family's woodpile somewhere, what with that hair and that dark skin.

"Yes," I said. "My name's Alberta."

"Alberta?" Edith said. "Well, that was original of your daddy. What do you go by?"

"You can call me Bert. Everybody does."

"This is Kitty Lavender—her real name, believe it or not."

"Edith, you're just jealous," Kitty said. She was small and fine-boned, with dark hair and eyes and the whitest skin, pretty as a doll. I felt like a mule next to her.

"Yes, I confess," Edith said. "I hate the name Edith. I'd rather have a name like Elizabeth or Victoria, a queen's name."

"Katherine's a queen's name, ain't it?"

"Yes, Katherine. But not Kitty. Sorry."

I had never heard such cutting up between two grown girls before. Men, yes, but not girls. Most girls I knowed, whenever they got together, spent their time giggling or making eyes at boys. But Kitty and Edith knowed how to have fun, and they tried to teach me. They done a fair job too, saved me from turning into a machine like the ones we worked at all day. We lived for the times the machines shut down, like Christmas, and Fourth of July, and in the summer when the weather got real dry.

That was the best times, when the water in the millrace got low and the machines quit running. We could always tell when it was fixing to happen, because there was this rock in the middle of the river that only showed when the river run low, and when we seen that thing, we knowed it wouldn't be long before there'd be this low humming noise all through the plant and the machines would slow down and then finally stop off and we'd be free for a few hours, sometimes a whole day. We called that rock the Colonel's Colonel because it was the only thing that bossed the old man, Colonel Revel.

The first time it happened, my first summer there, when we found out what was happening, Kitty and Edith got so excited they was dancing around their machines. I couldn't understand why. It made me mad because it meant losing pay, and I had nothing to do with myself. But Kitty and Edith, they fixed that. They come running over to me, giggling like crazy folks, grabbed me by the arms, and drug me out in the yard. Then they just stood there, their faces turned up to the sun like little flowers.

Some of the boys was sitting around picking guitars and banjos, and a few of the older women sat under the trees, talking. It looked like a picnic instead of work.

"Oh, Bert," Kitty said. "Feel that?"

"What?" I said, looking up, then back down because the sun was so bright it hurt my eyes. "What you talking about?"

"Freedom!" Kitty said, and started spinning around and laughing.

Edith didn't spin, but she started laughing too. "Kitty, I believe you're teched in the head, girl. Come on, Bert, let's go down to the river and cool off."

I followed Edith, and Kitty soon caught up with us.

"Kitty," I said. "I thought you liked working at the mill."

"Why, I do," Kitty said.

"Then why'd you get so excited just now?"

"Oh, Bert, it's like recess at school. You remember how that felt, don't you?"

"I never liked recess," I said, and they stared at me like I was crazy. "Well, I always liked to stay in and help my teacher, or read a book."

"You know what you need, don't you?" Edith said.

"No, what?" We had reached the river, which wasn't more than two or three feet deep at that point. Kitty and Edith got one on either side of me, grabbed my arms, and drug me kicking and screaming into the water. They throwed me down so I was on my hands and knees, then started kicking water at me till I was soaked through. I was so shocked I couldn't do nothing but stare at them, and then before I could stop myself I set in to crying.

"Oh, Lord," Kitty said.

"Oh, Bert," Edith said. "Come on, now, we didn't hurt you, did we?"

I shook my head no and got up on my feet. That old wet skirt felt like it weighed a hundred pounds.

"Well, what are you bawling for?" Edith said.

I shook my head again and started walking through the water next to the bank, in the opposite direction from the mill. I was mortified and couldn't stand for nobody to see me cry. Kitty and Edith followed me, didn't say a word. I could hear the splashes their feet made behind me. Finally I wandered up the bank and we sat in the grass under some apple trees. It was hot even in the shade, even wet as I was. When I'd calmed down some, I told them I was sorry for spoiling their good time.

"Don't you be sorry," Edith said. "We're the ones that's sorry, ain't we, Kitty?"

"Bert, we didn't mean to make you cry. We only meant to have some fun."

"I know," I said. "It ain't that." Then I told them how I'd been so disappointed about not going to college, and it just hit me when I started remembering how I loved being in the schoolroom so much I wouldn't even go outside for recess and the other young'uns called me teacher's pet. How I never wanted to be a child, I always wanted to go on and get grown and start being a teacher.

"Poor Bert," Kitty said. "Ain't there no way, then?"

"No. They need every cent I make at home."

"It just ain't fair," Edith said. "If I could I'd send you to college myself."

"Well, I wouldn't," Kitty said. "I'm selfish enough to be glad you're here with us."

Kitty always did know what to say to make me feel better. "I'm sopping wet," I said, trying to wring water out of my dress tail.

"We all are," Kitty said. "Here, let's take our clothes off and let them dry before we have to go back in."

I looked at her, horrified.

"Just our outer clothes, fool. We'll still be covered up. And way off down here, there ain't nobody to see us." Kitty pulled off her shoes and stockings, then unbuttoned her skirt and let it fall around her ankles. Her blouse hung almost to her knees then, and she looked so funny I had to laugh. Next thing I knowed, Edith had done the same, so I did too, and we hung our clothes in the lowest limbs of the trees to dry, making a little tent for ourselves in the process. Kitty started spinning again, and me and Edith followed her in that too, spinning till we got dizzy and fell down on our backs in the grass. The sky was just streaks and pieces of blue through the limbs of them apple trees, and the green apples looked so little and round and perfect and far away. With the sound of bees buzzing and the river rippling over the rocks, we soon fell fast asleep, babes in the woods, just like that old song Mama used to sing.

I woke up first and sat up and stretched. Kitty and Edith looked dead to the world, and it was so hot, I went on down to wade in the river. I had the best time, just walking up and down, looking for pretty rocks, singing that song to myself. "Now, don't you remember a long time ago, two little children their names I don't know, were stolen away, on a bright summer day, and left in the woods, I've heard people say." Oh, how that song used to make us cry when Mama would sing it to us at night, but then when she'd get done, we'd beg for her to sing it again.

I felt so free, like I didn't have a care in the world, and then I felt a tickle on my head, like a bug had got under my hair. I couldn't stand that and had to take my hair all the way down and comb through it with my fingers, but I didn't find nothing. My hair reached down to my knees back then and was dark brown and so thick it took hours to dry. I was shaking my head back and forth, watching my hair fly around my body, when I heard a cracking sound like a stick breaking. It come from the trees up above where Kitty and Edith was laying. I stopped and turned toward the sound and didn't see nothing at first, but then, right there next to the trunk of a tree, I seen him, and he was singing and smiling at the same time. I didn't see how he could do that. I couldn't make out what the song was, but he looked just like a devil there, them black eyes and hair, and white teeth, smiling that smile that looked like he could see clear through my blouse. It was almost like I forgot myself in his singing. But it must've waked Kitty and Edith up, because all of a sudden they was in the river with me and Edith was hollering, "John Dillingham, you rascal, get away from here before I take a stick to you!"

He quit singing, stepped all the way out from the tree and tipped his hat, said, "Ladies," and then turned and walked off, disappeared up the bank without looking back. And that was the first but not the last time I laid eyes on Dill.

7

FRIDAY NIGHT AND THE CAFÉ WAS ALMOST EMPTY, THE downside of not having liquor by the drink in Russell. Everybody went to Smith River on the weekends and left Russell to the old folks, and the spinsters like her. The only substance Laurel had any interest in abusing tonight was carbohydrates. She ordered a cheeseburger, fries, and a chocolate shake, glad that no one she knew was around to watch her stuff her face. She expected the old guy who took her order to bring it to the table, but when she looked up it was Charlie Cannon. He really had grown into a handsome kid, tall and lanky with a white-blond crew cut and clear blue eyes. Babyface, that's what she wanted to call him. He reminded her so much of her high-school boyfriend Craig Johnson at that age, only Craig had never been that muscular.

"What are you doing here?" she said, surprised that Maxann hadn't mentioned her son working here.

"My job," he said with a grin, and she doubted any girl under the age of twenty could resist that cocky sweetness. If most teenage boys had the first clue how really beautiful they were in all their gawky hormonal glory, they'd have to be run off the planet. Laurel noticed the class ring on his finger, big as a doorknob. "You're graduating in May?" It was all Maxann talked about at work, getting him ready to graduate, getting him ready for college. Laurel knew her nest would be awfully empty with Charlie gone, and talking about it was the only way she knew to prepare herself.

"Yeah, then I'm going to State this fall. Won a scholarship." No bashfulness in this boy. And why shouldn't he blow his own horn? There's no way he would've gone to college if he hadn't worked hard and got a scholarship. God, college, she thought, remembering when deciding where to go had been her biggest decision for a whole year.

He leaned against the side of the booth, a man of leisure, contemplating his future. "I thought about going to Carolina, but it seems like a bunch of snobs going there from my school. No offense."

Laurel laughed. Maxann must've told him about her going to UNC. "If I had it to do over again, I'd probably go to a smaller school, at least the first two years. You can really get lost at a big school like Carolina. I did, at least till I met my husband." And the rest was history. She'd latched on to Scott, followed him all through college and beyond, and never let go until he did.

"My girlfriend's going to Meredith," Charlie said. "She'll be right down the road from me."

He didn't sound real thrilled at the prospect, and Laurel suspected that relationship wouldn't survive the first semester. She'd seen it happen too many times, true high-school love wiped out by the temptations of college flings. Maybe it wasn't a bad thing to start out with somebody, though, just until you learned your way around. When Craig dumped her that summer after high school, Laurel had gone to UNC miserable and single, which may have explained how she ended up with Scott.

"Well," Charlie said, looking behind him as if his boss might be watching. "I better get back to work." He'd obviously told her everything he had to tell about himself, and that meant he had no more interest in talking to her. Oh, to be that young again, thinking the whole world revolved around you. She felt so old compared to him, old enough to be his mama, then she smiled to herself. Of course, she wasn't *really* old enough.

Wait a minute. Eighteen plus eighteen equaled thirty-six. Oh, my God, she thought. I am old enough to be his mama. If I started really young, he could even be my second child. Oh, God. There was that feeling again, that run-and-scream feeling, pure panic, the ticking of the biological clock, only it didn't tick, it bonged. *Bong, bong, bong*— echoing in her head ever since she'd turned thirty-five.

She looked down at the plate of food Charlie had set in front of her, the greasy cheeseburger and fries. She pushed the plate away, threw some money on the table, and was up and out of the booth and on the street before she knew where she was headed. She stopped and took deep breaths, decided maybe walking would help, and headed down the sidewalk. She passed the theater and crossed Pine Street, then walked quickly past the dark windows of Tilley's Dry Cleaners and NC Farm Credit. Once across Elm she found herself in front of the library and froze. It was horrible, like that scene in the movie *It's a Wonderful Life* where, without George in the world, Mary ends up a pathetic old maid. When George asks the angel Clarence where Mary is, Clarence screeches, "She's at the library!" as if it's some fate worse than death, a horrible place where spinsters go to die or simply dry up and get swept under the stacks.

Laurel backed away and hurried down the street again, walking faster and faster until she got a stitch in her side and had to stop. She saw a bench up ahead in front of the funeral home and sat down to rest. What the hell was she running from, anyway? She loved the damn library. It had been one of her favorite places as a child. Maw Bert used to bring her up there every Saturday afternoon. She'd leave her in the children's section while she went to pick out a book for herself, and Laurel had loved walking up and down the rows of books, letting her fingers slide across the spines in a slow caress because they were her books and she could take any one she chose, more than one, a dozen. It was magic—no money changed hands, just the wonderful, beautiful library card. She spent hours pulling books down, dipping into them, deciding either to put them back or add them to her stack. Maw Bert would come find her eventually with only three or four books herself, usually romances. Laurel always took home at least ten and read all her books at least once. It was an assignment she gave herself, as well as a pleasure. Cecil would beg her to come out and play with him and she'd keep repeating, "Go away, I'm busy," until he left her alone, calling her boring and stupid on his way out. He didn't really want her, anyway. He just wanted somebody, anybody would do.

And wasn't that the same thing that had happened with Scott? He hadn't wanted her. He just wanted somebody and she happened to be there. Had she really wanted him, or was she just as guilty of taking whatever presented itself, whatever happened to come along to keep her from ending up alone?

Laurel glanced over her shoulder at the funeral home behind her, a huge old lavender Victorian with dark green shutters. The place looked deserted, which meant nobody was dead tonight. Only one light burned in the front window. Maw Bert had been laid out in that house, and Laurel hoped she'd never have to go in there again. When she was a kid, the place seemed romantic and mysterious whenever she passed by. That was only from the outside, though. Inside was a different story. The hardwood floors were uneven and creaked with practically every step, and the sickeningly sweet smell of flowers and mothballs, touched with a faint hint of formaldehyde, hung in the air in spite of the ceiling fans in every room. Laurel hyperventilated the night of Maw Bert's viewing and had to go out on the porch for fresh air. The house had never seemed the same to her after that. In her mind it became the quintessential funeral home, tall and imposing and slightly creepy, shaded by huge oak trees whose fingers scratched at the windows when the wind blew. The death house.

Okay, she thought, it was getting too dark to sit on a bench in front of a funeral home all by herself without feeling like a member of the Addams Family. She headed back toward the library, stopping when she reached the front entrance again. She refused to let her silly fears keep her from going in there. A couple of teenage girls came out giggling, glanced at her, then giggled all the way to their car. God, it was annoying. I was like that once, Laurel thought. I don't think I ever giggled that much, though, but I was young and innocent and thought I had the world by the tail. Where did that confidence go, that self-assurance? She didn't want to be arrogant again, but by God she could use a shot of confidence, some hope, some direction. She couldn't even figure out if she wanted to go in the library or not.

They'd changed the doors. You didn't have to push them open any-more, they just whooshed open by themselves. Laurel missed the weight of those old doors, missed leaning against them to push her way into a world where she wanted to be. Once inside, the hushed quiet surrounded her and began to work its magic, relaxing her, making her feel at home. Funny how it could be that way even with all the people and movement. Laurel was surprised to see so many people at six o'clock on a Friday night. She was surprised to see any people at all, surprised people still went to the library, at least in a little town like Russell, where the favorite pastimes were TV and softball and drink-ing. Several teenagers appeared to be working on research papers, some smaller kids wandered with their parents in the children's section, and a couple of old men sat reading magazines in armchairs by the win-dows. It was a happening place.

First things first, she thought, heading to the counter to get a library card. The librarian was a petite blonde, a little on the plump side, who smiled so hard it looked like her dimples must hurt.

"Laurel Granger," she said when she saw Laurel's driver's license. "Didn't you used to be Laurel Champion?"

Laurel smiled and said, "Yes, I sure did." And thought, *Oh, no.*

"We had homeroom together." The librarian pointed at her name tag. "I'm Candy Carpenter. Well, Candy Webb now. I married Kenny Webb, remember him from football?"

Oh, yes, and I remember you from cheerleading, and wasn't it all just hunky-dory, the times of our lives? Laurel smiled harder. "Yes. Candy. How're you doing?"

"Doing good, doing good. We got three kids now. That keeps us pretty busy. How about you?"

"Oh, none yet. I keep putting it off. Listen, I think I'll look around a little bit and pick up my card on the way out. Is that all right?"

"Well. Sure," Candy said, flashing those dimples again. "You take your time."

God, Laurel thought as she walked away. It had been the same thing every single time she ran into somebody from high school. Seemed like everybody in the whole damn town was married with children. She hadn't met a single woman yet, except at the plant, and they were all older than her. Why did women like Candy think the first thing out of a person's mouth had to be about whether or not they had children? Laurel had started talking about Cecil's kids just so she'd have something to say. If she tried to talk about anything but husbands and kids, they always steered the conversation right back to that, or else their eyes glazed over and they just said, "Uh-huh, uh-huh," until they could get away. Maybe having kids flipped some switch that made them incapable of focusing on anything else, a single-mindedness necessary for survival of the human race.

On the way to fiction, Laurel got distracted by the children's section and wandered in. So what if she had no kids and no good reason for being there? It was a free country. Everything looked so much smaller now, the little shelves, the little tables and chairs. The books seemed bigger, though, big square thin picture books and storybooks. She remembered devouring horse stories by C. W. Anderson and Marguerite Henry and Walter Farley. She never had gotten a horse of her own, but she loved those books. On the last row of the children's section she found the big storybook of *The Black Stallion* and pulled it out. It looked like the same worn copy she'd read in first grade, with the beautiful painting of The Black on the cover. Those eyes just melted her, large and liquid and brown, so gentle, so wise.

"Are you lost, little girl?" a deep voice said somewhere above her.

Laurel's head jerked up and she found herself staring into eyes identical to those on the cover of the book. That was all she saw at first, eyes, and part of a nose behind the big shelf at the beginning of the biography section. It took her a second to recognize Joe Clark without his uniform, a big grin on his face. She'd been right, he did look better in a V-neck, though still kind of goofy with that buzz cut.

"Hey, Joe," she said and quickly slid *The Black Stallion* back into its slot.

He came around the end of the shelf where she could see all of him. Jeans, yes, he looked much better in jeans, not nearly so dorky as in the uniform.

"I was on my way to my usual corner when I saw you," he said.

"Your usual corner?"

He pointed behind him toward a section of carrels at the back of the library. "I like to sit over there and read," he said. "My grandpa runs the TV so loud I can't hear myself think."

He really did have the most beautiful eyes, Laurel thought. Not golden brown like her daddy's, but the dark brown of good garden dirt, or good chocolate.

"Did you get your U-Haul taken care of?"

Oh, right, Laurel thought, wondering how much her daddy had told him. "Yes, we sure did."

"Good, good." He nodded through an awkward little silence, then spoke up again. "So you're staying with your mama and daddy awhile?"

"For now," she said, wondering why on earth she felt so embarrassed to admit she had moved back in with her parents. According to all the magazines it was a trend. She'd become a statistic, in more ways than one. "You live with your grandpa?"

"Yeah. He's got arthritis and doesn't get around too good. Although I've been living with him since I was fifteen."

"Really? Why?" She felt bad that here she stood with a man she'd gone to school with all those years and she knew next to nothing about him. It didn't seem right.

"Well, my daddy got a job in Texas and moved the family down there, but I didn't want to go, so I stayed with Grandpa."

"Wow. That must've been hard." And she was willing to bet there was more to the story than he was telling, but it was none of her business.

He shrugged. "Yeah, but it worked out for the best."

Laurel couldn't think of anything else to say. She was tired and, nice as Joe was, she just wanted to be by herself. "Well," she said, "I think I'll find a book and read awhile."

He started backing up. "Okay, well, it's good to see you again."

She watched him walk away, thinking how weird it was that she'd run into him twice now since she got home, when she could barely remember him from high school. If her annual was anywhere she could get to it, she'd look him up, but no way was she going through all those boxes just to find out Joe Clark had belonged to Future Farmers of America. No, she didn't need to be thinking about men at all, not eighteen-year-olds and certainly not Joe Clark. She went to fiction and found a romance and sat down on the other side of the library to read. Only she couldn't keep her eyes open and eventually propped her head on her hand, face turned to the wall, and closed her eyes, just for a few minutes, just a quick nap.

There was a hand on her shoulder, a big warm hand shaking her gently, and she tried to shake it off because she didn't want to get up and go to school. "Quit!" she said, then jerked upright, remembering she wasn't home in bed, she was in the library. Joe Clark took his hand away and stepped back. "The library's closing," he said.

Laurel glanced around at the empty carrels. It looked like she and Joe were the last two left in the place, besides Candy the librarian. God, she hoped she hadn't been drooling, and put a hand to her mouth. Good, dry. She probably had creases on the side of her face, though, where she'd been laying on her arm. So much for appearing smart and aloof, reading alone in her corner.

Why was Joe still standing there, watching her? "Thanks," she said, gathering up her purse, leaving the book. It hadn't been that good, anyway. Let Candy put it back. "Thanks for waking me up. I'd feel like an idiot if I got locked in."

"I'll walk you to your car," he said.

"Oh, no, that's not necessary." God, what could happen to her in Russell? It wasn't that late.

"I'd feel better if you let me. Russell's not as quiet as it used to be, and it is Friday night."

Thank you so much, Mr. Clark, she thought, for reminding me that I just spent my Friday night in a library. Of course, so did he, so he couldn't be mocking her. Could he? She shot a look up at him, then led him toward the door, waving at Candy without stopping. She'd get her library card some other time, hopefully when a spinster librarian was manning the desk.

She walked fast, wanting to get home and get to bed. The week had seemed like it would never end, and she wanted to be rested for her date with Hap tomorrow night. The thought of it sent a little shiver of excitement through her. If she didn't have that to look forward to, she'd probably be back at the café right now, stuffing that cheeseburger down her throat.

Joe waited till she got her car unlocked and watched her get in.

"Well, thanks," she said, ready to slam the door shut.

He looked like he might be about to say something else but changed his mind. "Okay. See you," he said, and turned away.

God, she was being a jerk, and he'd been so nice. "Wait," she said, and he turned back. "Do you need a ride to your car?"

He shook his head. "No, I just live a couple streets over."

"Right, with your grandpa."

"Yep. Well, I better get on home. He pitches a fit if I'm not there to give him his medicine on time."

As she drove down Main Street she passed him and waved. She watched him wave back, looking kind of lonely on the street by himself. How did he end up a cop, and taking care of his grandpa, and an avid reader, and a seemingly nice guy? Only in a little town like Russell could a guy like that survive, the kind who always did the right thing.

8

LAUREL LEANED BACK IN HER CHAIR AND TOOK A LOOK around the restaurant, enjoying the sensation of a belly full of an expensive steak dinner that she didn't have to pay for, the buzz from several glasses of wine, and the knowledge that her date was the best-dressed and best-looking man in the place. The exposed brick glowed warmly in the light from the candles on the tables and the fire in the fireplace, the burgundy tablecloths and napkins a perfect background for gleaming silver, china, and crystal. It still surprised her, this elegance. Until now, she'd thought Golden Corral was the nicest restaurant in Smith River. She felt a little bad about the prices, but he was a lawyer, he could afford it, at least every now and then. Next time she'd tell him Golden Corral was okay with her, if there was a next time.

It was impossible for her to tell how the date was going so far, because it'd been so long, she'd forgotten how to read the signs. Was that little smile of his a sign that he wanted her, or was it covering his desperate desire for the date to be over so he could run screaming in the opposite direction? He'd been a perfect gentleman, holding doors, helping with her coat, asking her preference of food and wine. She'd told him her story and he'd told his: parents dead, brother in California, crazy ex-wife (no kids) in Charlotte. He'd gone into the

Marines straight out of high school, then college and law school, then work in a big Charlotte firm until his marriage ended and he bought the practice in Russell and moved here to try small-town living. He smiled as he ticked off the events of his life, keeping details to a minimum as if he didn't want to bore her.

She knew she should be trying harder to be witty and charming herself instead of just sitting there laughing at his courtroom stories, but she didn't have the energy. She'd spent all day cleaning the house and doing laundry, and she was tired. He didn't seem to mind carrying the show. He was having a good time entertaining her with stories about people who sounded like rejects from *The Jerry Springer Show*.

"That's not even the worst," he said. "The worst—or maybe the best, depending on how you look at it—was this guy who backed his car over his wife."

"Oh, my God. What happened?"

"He found out she was having an affair, so he gets home from work, packs a bag, and stomps out. She follows him and throws herself down behind his car, saying he can't leave her, she loves him, she just did it to get his attention. And he backs right over her, after yelling at her to move several times."

"Did she die?"

"No, luckily for both of them it had rained a lot that week and they had a gravel driveway. If it'd been concrete, she would've been a pancake. As it was, he broke her legs and several ribs. She comes to court in practically a full body cast and vouches for him, says she doesn't want to press charges, and he says he still loves her and they're getting back together. So he got probation and a thousand hours of community service."

Laurel, still laughing, shook her head. "The things people do for love."

"Or psychosis."

"Well, it was their version of love. Everybody's is different. I look at my mama and daddy—and I love them to death, don't get me wrong—but they'd drive me crazy. He's helpless as a baby about doing anything around the house, or at least wants me to think he is, and with Mama it's her way or the highway."

"They love each other, though."

"Oh, yeah." She thought about their anniversary, how, even as bad as her mama must've been feeling then, they fit so easily together dancing, totally comfortable with each other, no more surprises left. That's what made dating so hard, the not really knowing what was going on behind the other person's eyes, even when he smiled like Hap was doing now, even when he said all the right things like *you look pretty tonight* or *I really like that dress*. But in order to get to the comfort zone, she had to go through this first, maybe many times. Oh, God, it made her tired just thinking about it.

"How about some dessert?" Hap had opened the dessert menu and looked at her over the top of it.

"Oh, Lord, no, I'm stuffed," she said, patting her belly.

He refilled their glasses and turned the empty wine bottle upside down in the ice bucket. She'd regret it in the morning, but that didn't stop her from taking another sip. Tonight she'd think about tonight, and tomorrow she'd suffer.

Amazing how he was able to keep up that steady stream of funny stories, and she hoped she wasn't laughing too loudly, making a fool of herself. She looked around the restaurant to see if anyone was looking at her and noticed a couple following a waiter across the floor. The woman looked so sophisticated in a black silk pantsuit, her blond hair swept up in a French twist, silver earrings dangling against her neck. The man, also blond, was equally attractive and sophisticated, in black slacks and a black silk shirt open at the throat. Laurel felt underdressed in comparison, her white blouse and broomstick skirt seeming suddenly childish next to this sophisticated couple who looked like models, only they were probably too old. Maybe retired models. She giggled. Maybe Smith River was the place old models came to die. Hap stopped talking and followed her stare, then looked back with his eyebrows raised. "Do you know them?"

"No," Laurel said, ready to let him in on the joke when she realized she was mistaken. It had been nearly twenty years, but she did know those models. In high school they were Carmen Dover and Craig Johnson. Oh, God, she thought, they've seen me. Craig waved first, then Carmen, that fake smile zipping up her face like Miss America.

Hap saw the waves, saw them coming, and raised his eyebrows at her again. "Actually, yes," she said. "I just realized I do know them." And wanted to add, *Now please hide me.*

But she got out her Miss America smile too and waved, didn't try to stand, afraid she'd wobble because of the wine.

"Hey," Carmen said, turning it into a five- or six-syllable word as she bent to hug Laurel. She stepped back and Craig leaned down awkwardly, put an arm around her shoulders and squeezed slightly before resuming his place beside Carmen. "Good to see you again, Laurel," he said. "I heard you were back."

I just bet you did, Laurel thought. Percilla probably called Carmen and told her the minute she found out Laurel got the job at the plant. She had no doubt Carmen knew about that, no doubt she'd find a way to brag about running her own health club and make Laurel feel like shit.

"Y'all look great," Laurel said. "You haven't changed a bit."

"Well, some things have changed." Craig bent over and pointed to a little bald spot on the crown of his head. "Monk head has set in," he said, and Laurel remembered then what she'd liked about him, his sense of humor, his humility, his good nature. How in the world did he end up with a bitch like Carmen? Poor guy. She noticed then that Carmen was checking out Hap.

"I'm sorry," Laurel said. "Do y'all know Hap?"

Hap stood and shook hands with the models. "Hap Luckadoo," he said in that deep Atticus Finch voice.

"Hap's an attorney," Laurel said, loving how much more powerful *attorney* sounded than *lawyer*. Yes, Carmen, she thought, eat your little heart out. Hap has all his hair.

"Really?" Carmen reached into her bag and pulled out a business card. "Well, Craig and I own Power Town. It's a full-service health club here in town. We've got everything you could possibly need to satisfy your fitness needs." She smiled at Hap. "Come try us sometime. Oh, and, Laurel, you too," she said, laying a card beside Laurel's plate.

Before Laurel could respond, Craig had put his arm around Carmen to rein her in. Poor Craig. They started to turn away, but Carmen stopped and put a hand out, her nails like red claws on the sleeve of

Laurel's blouse. "Oh, by the way, did Mama send you an invitation to Melanie's wedding? It's really going to be something. Y'all should come." She looked at Hap when she issued the invitation.

Oh, shit, Laurel thought. "Yes, she did mention it, but I might have to work that day."

"On a Saturday?" Carmen pouted. "Oh, come on."

"Honey," Craig said. "We've bothered them long enough. Nice to meet you, Hap. Good to see you, Laurel."

"You too," Laurel said, smiling at their backs. Especially since seeing her old high-school boyfriend hadn't hurt one bit. Whatever she once felt for him was long gone. She couldn't say the same for Carmen, though. Even before she snaked Craig, Laurel hadn't liked her. Carmen was the kind of woman who didn't really see other women if there was a man in the room, the kind of woman who didn't have women friends. Of course, Laurel thought, if that's the definition of a bitch, then I must be one myself. She made a mental note to work on the friend situation as soon as possible, though she wasn't quite sure how to go about it.

"Nice couple," Hap said.

"Yeah." At least half a nice couple.

"Who's Melanie?"

"Carmen's sister. She's getting married in a few weeks. Supposed to be a big wingding at the country club afterward."

He leaned forward and whispered, "Do you really have to work?"

She glanced over at the table where Craig and Carmen had been seated, knowing they were too far away to overhear, but she leaned forward and whispered back, "No, I just don't want to go."

"Oh, come on. It'll be fun."

"You want to go with me?"

"Why not? I wouldn't mind seeing the inside of the country club." He winked to let her know he wasn't really thinking about the country club.

"Well," she said, imagining herself telling Percilla at work on Monday, making sure to mention that Hap would be her date, and then Percilla would tell Carmen. "Okay." So he wanted to see her again. He was willing to take her to a wedding, something that scared the shit out of most men, as if marriage were contagious. Here she was, on the road to comfortable, one little step anyway, and all she could think was how much she wanted to go home. Well, it had been a long day, and she wasn't used to wine. She'd feel better tomorrow, or the next day.

She'd left the front porch light on and it seemed like every moth in a three-county radius had homed in on it, swooping crazily around their heads as Hap kissed her cheek, told her he'd call on Monday, and then left once she got the key in the door. She'd been quiet in the car, so maybe he'd sensed how tired she was. When his car was out of sight, she reached in and flipped off the light, then sat on the front step and waited for her eyes to adjust to the dark.

All those stars. She couldn't see them in Vegas because of the glare, which made a sort of force field around the city and blocked out any other forms of light. It wasn't just Vegas, though. All cities were like that. Here in the country it got dark, really dark, and there was no force field, nothing between the naked eye and the stars. As a child Laurel had loved to lay in the grass and stare up at them, imagining a girl just like her living on one of those stars, wondering what her life might be like. It was easier, somehow, to wonder about that other girl's life than her own.

She slipped off her shoes, and the concrete chilled the bottoms of her feet through her stockings. She pulled her knees up to her chin and sat rocking, looking up. She'd had a nice time with Hap, enjoyed his company, definitely enjoyed sitting across from him, but something was missing. No, not missing. Something was there that didn't belong, something blocking her enjoyment. It wasn't seeing Carmen and Craig. They were harmless. And it wasn't that Hap hadn't tried to kiss her, because she'd been hoping he wouldn't. She wasn't ready for that. She wasn't ready for any of this, that was the problem. But how did she go about getting ready? Her mind knew she was divorced, but the core of her didn't accept it yet. She'd grown so used to being married, to being faithful to one man, and she couldn't just turn it off like a light switch. Part of her thought she still belonged to Scott, and she had to figure out a way to set that part straight. God help me, she thought, I don't want to feel this bad forever. She let the tears come, hoping all this crying she'd been doing lately would work like a flood and wash him bit by bit out of her system for good.

9

"JOHN WANTS ME TO TAKE YOU TO THE BASEMENT," Linda said.

Laurel looked up from a spreadsheet. The basement? They'd skipped that on the tour, but was it really important for her to see it now? She'd been here only two weeks and hadn't had time to learn the upstairs by heart yet. "What?"

Linda, wearing another pastel business suit with a skirt above her knees, shoved the desk calendar aside and sat on the corner of the desk, something she did whenever she took a break from baby-sitting John to drop off more work. Not that she really needed to move anything. Her bony tail could probably fit on a pencil eraser.

"I hate going down there," Linda whispered, looking over her shoulder to make sure John wasn't around. "It's nasty. Part of it's got dirt floors and boxes and boxes of junk and old file cabinets and all, crap they should've thrown away a long time ago. And there's no telling what all kind of vermin lives down there. We have the exterminator out once a month, but you know there's got to be rats down in there somewhere."

And you want me to go down there with you? Gee, thanks. Laurel was not dressed for a basement crawl, and she did not want to ruin a perfectly good sweater set. "Is there any way we can do this tomorrow? I'll wear jeans and a sweatshirt."

Linda looked Laurel up and down as if seeing her for the first time. "Oh. I didn't even think about you having on good clothes. Well, I would say let's wait, but I'm taking the rest of the week off and John really wants you to get started as soon as possible." She showed her teeth in a smile that dared Laurel to object again. Rumor was Linda and John were both going to be gone on some kind of retreat to Myrtle Beach and would probably not be sleeping in separate rooms.

No, he doesn't, you bitch. You're just enjoying the thought of me getting filthy while you slip off up here and spend the rest of the day filing your nails. Laurel sighed. "What exactly are we going to do in the basement?"

Linda hopped off the desk, jingling the bracelet key ring on her arm. "That's where all the files are, the ones for the anniversary. You know, for the stuff you're supposed to write for the newspaper." She headed out of the office and Laurel followed, feeling like a whipped puppy forced to follow its master.

They went out of the building, around the corner to a door about halfway back, where they went down a steep flight of narrow stairs. At the bottom of the stairs they went through another door, turned a corner, and started down a hallway where fluorescent lights seemed to stretch forever, a never-ending hallway with a concrete floor and cinderblock walls like something out of a horror movie. At the third door on the left, Linda stopped and unlocked it with one of the keys on her wrist, then twisted the key off and handed it to Laurel.

"Here you go, all yours," she said, and pushed the door open, then reached in to flick on the lights. More fluorescent bulbs flickered on, and Laurel stepped into a large room filled with old filing cabinets, cardboard banker boxes, old office furniture, lamps, and dust, lots and lots of dust. The smell hit her then, mildew and must and something sour that she hoped would not turn out to be a dead rat.

"Remember to keep it locked," Linda said. She stepped back into the hallway.

"Wait." Laurel didn't want to spend more time with Linda, but she also didn't feel like being left alone down here. "How do I know where to look?"

Linda flicked a hand toward the room. "Betty used to come down here and mess with this stuff, but I never had time myself. Just see what you can find." She sneezed, the stiff wave of hair on top of her head bobbing forward and then back. "Have fun." She waved and prissed back down the hall toward the exit.

"Have fun," Laurel mimicked as she turned back to the room. "God." It would take days, weeks, months to go through all this shit. And she didn't even know what she was looking for. John wanted historical information about the plant and its people, some kind of memorial. What the hell did that mean? Well, there was no way she was going to ruin her good clothes opening those nasty boxes today. She ran her fingers across the top of the nearest one, and sure enough it came away dirty. Great, she thought, looking around for something to wipe her hands on, then had a sneezing fit. How long would she have to stay down here before she could go back without Linda saying something to her? An hour ought to do it. Linda and John would have gone for one of their two-hour lunches by then and she could eat and read at her desk in peace.

An orange drop cord ran from an outlet by the door down the length of the room and disappeared behind a bank of file cabinets. Laurel followed it and came around the corner to find a small alcove created by a cement-block wall on one side and banks of filing cabinets on the other two. There was a desk—one of those ugly fake-wood-and-chrome jobs from the seventies—and on top of that sat a brown gooseneck lamp, a fan, neatly arranged stacks of files, a stapler, and a tape dispenser. She scooted the blond-wood swivel chair closer to the desk and sat down. In the drawers she found scissors, staples, rubber bands, glue, pencils and pens, erasers, Post-it notes, envelopes, notepads, everything a good secretary would ever need. Oh, Betty, she thought, smiling to herself as she tilted the chair back. I know you. You and I are going to get along just fine. She put her hands behind her head and studied the gray ceiling tiles, the gray-and-green file cabinets around her, the cement floor. Betty had created a nice little hideaway for herself, and Laurel was willing to bet she'd done it about the same time Linda started working in the office.

I don't blame you a bit, Laurel thought. I think I'm going to enjoy it myself for the same reason. Maybe this wouldn't be so bad after all. She could come down a couple hours a day, get away from Linda and the cubicle, do a little research. She got up and wandered down the nearest row of filing cabinets. Each drawer was labeled with a date, and it was like going back in time, the closest cabinets being most recent. Personnel files, safety reports, quarterly reports, from the present all the way to the sixties. She went to the next row and found the sixties back to the forties, and in the next row the thirties. Halfway down that row she found drawers that weren't labeled. Betty must have only made it back to, what, 1935. On the floor were boxes sorted by year and type of file, all the way back to when the plant opened. Betty must've left before she got everything into the cabinets. What a woman, so organized. Bless you, Betty, bless you, bless you. Laurel hated to think what she would've faced if Betty hadn't taken the initiative to organize this stuff. Amazing, the good that could come of avoiding an annoying coworker.

Tomorrow, Laurel thought, I'll finish up for Betty before I do my own stuff. It's the least I can do. She went back to the desk and sat down to kill another half hour before going back upstairs.

After a few minutes the quiet started pressing in on her, broken only by the buzzing of the fluorescent lights, the hum of the plant machinery overhead, and the occasional rustle that she chose to ignore. She'd need to bring a radio down here too, something to keep her company and take her mind off being alone in the basement. A maniac could come in here and cut her throat and it'd be a week before that damn Linda thought to send somebody to look for her. Oh, great, Laurel thought, and started going through the folders on the desk to distract herself, admiring once again Betty's organizational skills. How had they let a woman like that go and kept Linda instead? It had something to do with John Dollar's pecker, of that much she was sure. Even if they weren't having an affair, he was letting that thing make a lot of his decisions for him.

There was one stack of folders with nothing but newspaper clippings about the plant, one folder for each decade since there weren't that many clippings. Laurel picked up the one on top and opened it to an article from the *Russell Monitor* about layoffs at the plant last year. She remembered her mama talking about that, and it must've been then that Lottie May's daughters lost their jobs. Underneath that was an article from the business section about John Dollar celebrating his thirtieth year as plant manager. There were other articles from the *Monitor* and some from the *Charlotte Observer* covering things such as a fire in the warehouse nine years earlier, layoffs two and three years ago, renovations to the plant offices, an employee whose cousin had written a hit country song, and on and on. The folders got thinner with each decade, all except for the 1920s, which was fat with articles about union agitators and workers on strike. It looked like interesting reading, and she put that one on top so she could start with it the next day.

The next pile of folders contained photographs of various employee groups—sales, quality control, and so on, again organized by year. The newer ones were labeled on the back with the names, left to right, of each person pictured. And there, in a photo of the office staff from three years ago, there was Betty. She stood next to John Dollar and a couple of other women Laurel had never seen before, probably the receptionist and office assistant before Linda came. Behind that was another picture of Betty by herself, a pleasant-faced woman in her sixties, gray hair combed out and sprayed to perfection, big glasses that had been in style in the seventies, and no makeup except for a strong brick-colored lipstick that made her teeth look even whiter. The caption on the back said, *Congratulations on your retirement, Betty Wiggins!* These must be photos that had been taken for the newsletter. Laurel leaned the picture against the base of the lamp. Betty would be good company down here.

There were several old black-and-white photos of large groups of people standing in front of the plant, a sign in the corner reading *Revel Mill Weave Room 1940,* and *Revel Mill Winding Room 1930,* and *Revel Mill Spinning 1920.* But these had no captions, no names for the people. Laurel looked closely at the faces, some of them children, looking for anyone familiar. The thing that struck her about the old group pictures was how serious everybody looked. When had the rule changed about not smiling for pictures? Probably not until World War II. It looked like a group mug shot. Maybe they were told, Don't smile or you won't be recognizable.

She also noticed how neatly dressed everybody was. Their clothes looked plain and shabby, but the women wore their blouses tucked into their long skirts, their hair pinned up on top of their heads, and the men wore overalls or pants with suspenders and white button-down shirts. They looked like a bunch of somber, determined missionaries ready to go out and save the world, but instead they would turn around when the picture was done and go back to their jobs in the mill. Laurel tried to pick out which one might be her counterpart, the office girl who typed and filed and got sent to the basement. She couldn't see herself in any of those women. None of them looked like they had a life she would want to pretend was hers.

INSTEAD OF going straight to the office, Laurel detoured through the plant to get to the canteen. It was lunchtime and her mama's friends were bound to be there. Maybe one of them would recognize some of the people in the photographs she'd brought up from the basement.

As she walked past the muffled roar at the winding-room doors, she said thank God again she'd had the good sense to take the office job. Through the windows in the top of the door she saw Idalene walking across the floor, waving at somebody. For some reason old ladies in jeans seemed wrong, maybe because Laurel was so used to seeing them in polyester blends, or old cotton housedresses like Maw Bert used to wear. The jeans suited Idalene, though, her long skinny legs and narrow hips, not childbearing hips like Laurel's, which might be a blessing if she ever had a baby but were a pain in the ass when it came to buying pants. Idalene probably never had to take in the waist of her jeans. She looked the same width from shoulders to thighs.

The door opened and Idalene stepped out as if pushed by the sound behind her, her purse and a paper lunch sack in one hand. "Hey, girl," she said.

"Hey," Laurel said, and fell into step beside her. "I'm glad I found you. I wanted to ask you about something."

"Well, ask when we get to the canteen. We got only thirty minutes for lunch."

Laurel had to walk fast to keep up as Idalene crossed the warehouse floor and turned a corner to get to the canteen. Inside, all the booths and tables were already full, everyone talking at once. Compared to all the other massive rooms in the plant, the canteen was small and might even qualify as cozy, in spite of molded-plastic yellow chairs, orange vinyl booth seats, and scarred Formica tables against green cinder-block walls and a gray tile floor. Despite all her best intentions last week, Laurel had forgotten her lunch, figuring she'd make do with something from the bank of lighted drink and snack machines against the far wall, the familiar logos of Coke and Pepsi and Lance and Minute Maid making the room seem cheerful and bright.

Lottie May waved them over to a table where she sat with Percilla and Maxann.

"Hey, girls," Idalene said, then dragged a fifth chair over from the next table. When they found out Laurel was planning to eat out of the machines, they insisted on giving her parts of their lunches: half a sandwich, a cup of vegetable soup, a brownie, and Idalene bought her a Diet Pepsi. She felt bad taking their food, especially when she knew they worked harder than she did, on their feet all day, but they wouldn't take it back.

"You go on and eat that, honey," Lottie May said. "We got a-plenty."

"How's your mama doing?" Maxann speared a piece of pineapple on the end of a plastic fork and popped it in her mouth.

"Well," Laurel said, swallowing a bite of the best tuna-salad sandwich she'd ever had, tasting Miracle Whip and celery and something else she couldn't name. She'd have to get Percilla to give her the recipe. "Daddy took her to the doctor and he confirmed it's menopause. He said some women suffer severe depression when they go through the change."

"Oh, Lord," Percilla said. "I been going through it myself, but I ain't had no depression. Just hot flashes. Is she having those?"

"Oh, yeah. She's been running the air-conditioning full blast, and it gets so cold me and Daddy have to sleep under electric blankets."

"Pansy took it real hard when her mama died," Lottie May said. "I think she ain't got over that yet."

"That ain't something you get over," Idalene said.

Lottie May nodded. "You just get used to it. I don't know if it gets lighter, that grieving, or if carrying it makes you stronger so you don't notice it as much after a while, but either way it gets to where it don't hurt as bad."

"I think it takes at least a year," Maxann said. "At least."

It suddenly dawned on Laurel that they must've all lost their mothers by now, and she felt fiercely grateful to still have hers.

"Well, what I want to know is, what are they doing for her?" Idalene said.

"The doctor gave her two prescriptions, one for hormones and one for antidepressants, and Daddy got them filled last week but she won't take them."

"Won't take them? Well, why on earth not?" Idalene had put her sandwich down and stared across the table as if she suspected Laurel of having something to do with it. Lord, the woman could look fierce. Laurel quickly shook her head to deny any responsibility.

"I don't know," she said. "Daddy's tried, I've tried, Kitty's tried. She refuses to take them."

"She's not thinking straight, then," Idalene said. "I didn't take no hormones at my change of life, but I didn't miss no work neither. Something's got to be done."

Maxann had finished her lunch and sat with her head down, face intent, hands smoothing the folded paper bag as if trying to iron the creases out. How many times did she use it before throwing it away? Laurel wondered. "What you need to do," Maxann said, "is get it in her food somehow."

"Yeah," Percilla said, "and don't tell her."

"I don't know." Lottie May looked worried. "What if it makes it worse?"

I don't see how it can get much worse, Laurel thought, picturing her mama as she'd looked that morning when her daddy led her out the door and over to Kitty's. Laurel had watched out the window, and it took him ten minutes to get her across the yard and through the hedge, ten minutes to walk a few yards.

"Well," Idalene said. "You think about it. Now, what was it you wanted to ask me about a while ago?"

Laurel explained her assignment to them and opened the file folder so they could see the photos.

"Poor old Betty," Maxann said. "She wasn't but sixty-four, but I wouldn't have stayed another eleven years in the same office with that bitch neither."

"I myself do not plan to be here when I'm that old," Percilla said. "I'm going to quit while I'm still young enough to enjoy myself."

"I think you done missed that boat," Maxann said as she flipped through several of the photos. "What you need to do is put these in the newsletter and ask if anybody can identify these people. I bet most of them's dead now, but their young'uns might still work here."

"Not all of them's dead." Idalene leaned forward and tapped the photo in front of Maxann. "Not that one right there, anyhow."

They leaned in to get a closer look. It was a girl about twelve, standing in the back at the end of a row of young men, her sharp features beautiful in an intelligent, foxlike way.

"Is that you?" Lottie May looked at Idalene like she'd made some kind of wonderful discovery.

Idalene grinned. "Not bad, if I do say so myself."

"How old were you?" Laurel picked up the picture and stared at the girl. It seemed impossible they were one and the same.

"I come back here when I was twelve year old. Lied about my age and they let me in 'cause I was tall and didn't need to stand on a box like the little ones."

Oh, my God, Laurel thought. Sixty-three years, and look how proud she was. "What are you going to do when you retire?"

"I'm going to sit home and eat candy and watch soap operas all day long." She made a joke of it, but when she laughed there was a raggedness in her voice, a sense of desperation that broke Laurel's heart. But what could she do? What could any of them do?

"You can't do that," Maxann said. "That's Percilla's dream."

"Hardy har har." Percilla took out her lipstick and a small mirror and reapplied that terrible pink shade. "You'll be laughing out the other side of your mouth when me and Rex is off on a cruise and you're ninety years old and still working in the winding room."

JUST AS he finished his barbecue sandwich, Dan heard Steve holler, from behind the counter, "Hey, beautiful!" Dan looked up to see Maxann coming through the door. Oh, shit, he thought. The one night he took Jill up on her offer to keep him company at supper and one of Pansy's friends had to walk in. Maxann went up to the counter to give Steve her order, and Dan kept one eye on her and one eye on Jill, who'd been talking nonstop since they sat down.

Sure enough, after Maxann ordered, she looked around the restaurant and saw him. Dan wanted to slide under the table when he saw her eyebrows shoot up right before she headed in his direction.

"Well, Dan Champion," she said, stopping at the end of the table. "What are you doing here?"

"Hey, Maxann," he said. "Just having a bite of supper."

Maxann gave him a look that said *I'll get back to you in a minute*, then turned to the other side of the booth. "Who's your little friend here?"

"Hey, I'm Jill," Jill said, and held out her hand, that big mouthful of teeth so white against her pink lips.

Maxann ignored the hand and said, "Hey there, Jill. I'm Maxann Cannon. I'm a good friend of Dan's wife, Pansy. Do you know her?"

Jill started to answer but Dan jumped in first. "Jill's our secretary, mine and Ralph's," he said.

"Uh-huh," Maxann said, nodding once with her mouth open, eyebrows raised. "Well. How is Pansy? I need to get out there and see her."

"About the same," Dan said, feeling the guilt fade as he started to get mad. What business was it of hers to check up on him? Her of all people, the one who went through men like Popsicles.

Steve hollered across the restaurant, "Maxann, your barbecue's ready."

Without turning, she hollered back, "Okay." She gave Jill one more hard look, then glanced at their nearly empty plates. "Dan, if you're getting ready to go, I'll walk out with you." She kept standing there, waiting for him, drilling holes in him with her eyes.

Dan shot a look at Jill, who sat there with a stupid grin on her face, perky as always. He wiped his mouth on a napkin and reached for his wallet. "I guess it is time to be getting home." He threw a twenty on the table and stood up. "Jill, thanks for keeping me company," he said. She kept sitting there smiling as he put on his jacket and followed Maxann out of the restaurant.

Maxann stopped at his truck and turned on him. The neon JOJO'S BBQ sign glowed red behind her head and lit up her face. Her eyes flashed in the dim light of the parking lot and he felt just a little bit scared. She hopped on the tailgate of his truck and he knew there was no getting away from her till she'd had her say. He threw up his hands and said, "Don't start. We was just eating."

"Uh-huh," Maxann said, shaking her head. "Dan, Dan, Dan."

He put his hands on the truck, feeling the rust patches where the paint had peeled off. She needed a paint job, and that tailgate needed fixing too. Ever time he went over a bump it banged down. But after twenty years, this truck was like his best friend. "What do you want, Maxann?" he said.

"I'm just curious," she said.

"It's none of your business."

"Well, you're the husband of a good friend of mine, and that makes it my business."

"Maxann, why are you making me feel guilty about having supper with somebody? That's all it was."

"I ain't making you feel nothing." She set her sack of food on the tailgate next to her and buttoned her sweater. Dan shivered and realized it had got cold since the sun went down.

Maxann pulled a pack of cigarettes out of her pocket and held it out to Dan. When he shook his head no, she took one, lit it, and inhaled hard. "I bet this ain't the first time, is it?" she said. "I could tell just by looking at her face, she thinks she's got you on the hook."

"That's crazy. We work together, and besides that, she's young enough to be my damn daughter."

"Well, she meets all the criteria, then."

He turned his back on her and leaned against the truck.

Maxann paused, then spoke softly, her cigarette smoke curling over his shoulder and into his face. "What're you doing, Dan, working on a replacement?"

"You don't know nothing about nothing," he said.

"I know what I seen just now. You may not have romance on your mind, but that little gal does. She's already planning the wedding and spending your money, big boy."

"Horseshit," he said. It bothered him to talk ugly like that to a woman, and he took a deep breath and tried to calm down a little bit. "Listen, sometimes I work late and then stop here for a bite of supper. Is that a crime? And if I like to have a little company while I eat, that ain't a crime either, is it?"

"Yeah, and next thing you know you end up in that motel down the road, and then she's pregnant, and then life as you know it will be over. It's the oldest story in the world, you fool. Shit, Dan, go home."

"I do go home. Ever night. Ever goddamn night." He was getting mad again, but it rolled out of him and he couldn't stop it. "I bring Pansy home from Kitty's and she stays on that couch all night with the TV on and the lights out. Then I take her back to Kitty's in the morning. If I try to talk to her, she just looks at me or else closes her eyes and pretends she's asleep. I keep trying to help her, but she don't do nothing but lay there, and I'll tell you what." He hesitated, not wanting to say what he was about to say. "I'm tired of it, that's the truth. I don't think I can stand it much longer. It's got me at the end of my damn rope." He slammed his fists on the side of the truck. His whole body was shaking and he had the terrible feeling he might be about to cry. He rubbed his hands up and down his thighs, trying to get calm.

Maxann didn't say anything, just kept sending them smoke signals over his shoulder.

"I miss her, dammit." He said it so low he didn't think she could hear him.

"Oh, honey," she said with a sigh. "I know." He heard a scuffling noise and realized she was scooting across the tailgate toward him. When her hand touched his back he jumped. She rubbed circles between his shoulder blades, and it felt so good to have a woman's hand on him again, like when he was a boy and his mama rubbed his back to help him go to sleep.

"Dan, you big old baby," she said, and he tensed. "Now, don't get mad again. I'm trying to tell you something. You're just like I was with Floyd. You know that man done everything for me, and it never occurred to me to take care of him back. And then he got sick and I had to. And, oh, that made me so mad. It wasn't supposed to be that a-way. But he couldn't help it, no more than Pansy can. She's sick. But Dan, you're lucky. Pansy's going to get better, so don't do nothing foolish like I done, take up with the first thing you see. That's how I ended up married to that asshole Johnny after Floyd died, and you know how long that lasted. You got to think straight now. Think about all the times Pansy's took care of you when you needed it. It's a two-way street, old man."

She was right. He knew it, hadn't even needed her to keep talking, because he knew all of it the minute she walked up to the table in there. What was he doing here? All he wanted to do was go home and sit on his deck and drink a beer and look at the stars. No, he wanted something else too. He wanted Pansy to sit out there with him. He wanted to play Hank Williams and laugh when she hollered at him to turn down that shit-kicking music. He wanted to get in the bed with her at night and have her scoot up against his back and put her little cold feet on his leg. And she would again. He knew that, he believed it. If he didn't, he'd go crazy and have to go to the doctor himself and get a prescription.

And then all of a sudden he knew what to do, couldn't believe he hadn't thought of it before. He grabbed Maxann's shoulders and give her a big kiss on the mouth. "Thank you, honey," he said, then jumped in the truck, barely giving her enough time to clear the tailgate before he peeled out of the parking lot and headed home.

10

As soon as she was sure Pansy was asleep, Kitty went to her bedroom and got the bottles of pills Dan had brought the night before. She'd hidden them in her dresser drawer just to be safe. She tiptoed through the living room, even though Pansy always slept the whole morning and nothing, not even the door slamming or the phone ringing, woke her up. Kitty left the TV on to hide any noises she might make in the kitchen. It took her a few minutes to open the dang childproof caps, but then she finally got them and took two capsules from each bottle, just like Dan told her. She wasn't even going to try pronouncing the names of them pills. The names didn't matter as long as they worked. She studied the pills, trying to decide what to put them in. The best thing would be something hot, something with a strong taste, but it also had to be something Pansy wouldn't turn away from, which was the hard part. She couldn't hardly even stand to eat no more, just toast and crackers and chicken broth. It'd have to be the broth. Kitty got a pot out and turned on the burner. It embarrassed her to death to get it out of a can, but she didn't have a chicken to cook, and she didn't want to wait. Pansy needed her medicine now.

It took a while, but the capsules did melt all the way once the broth got boiling. Kitty dipped out a little spoonful. It looked all right. She blew on it and tasted, closed her eyes and smacked her tongue against the roof of her mouth. Not bad. It might have a little whang to it, but she could say Pansy's taster was messed up because of being sick. Kitty tasted again, hoping that little lick of hormones and depression medicine wouldn't work on her system. At her age, she'd got way past the need for anything like that. She couldn't get over the things they had nowadays to make life easier. It was a push-button, pill-popping world, all right.

She left the pot on low heat and went to check on Pansy. Still asleep. Kitty turned the TV off and went to sit by the window with her embroidery. She liked the house quiet, did not like to run the radio or the TV during the day. The daytime was what she called her working hours, and she didn't need no distractions. Even though she'd been retired from the plant for twenty years, she still kept the same hours: up at five o'clock, breakfast, dressed and ready by six. From six to seven she had another cup of coffee and read the paper. Then she went to work. Now that she was retired, she spent her days sewing, gardening, canning in season, and reading. She'd do her sewing in the morning, little alterations jobs she took in to make spending money. She also made christening gowns for babies, gowns with embroidery and smocking and sometimes beads and lace. They run a picture of one of them in the paper one time and people made a fuss over her for a while, called it a work of art, which embarrassed Kitty to pieces. It was just a little old baby dress, after all.

Right at noon she'd have her dinner, just like if the plant whistle still blew to let them know when it was time to eat. After lunch she sat down with a book or a magazine and read. Well, she'd read for about five minutes, till she couldn't keep her eyes open no more, then she read the inside of her eyelids for about thirty minutes. After reading time, Kitty went back to her sewing. In the spring and summer she worked in the garden early mornings before it got too hot and in the evenings when it had cooled off some, and did her sewing in the heat of the day, sometimes sitting by a window, sometimes on the front porch where she could catch a breeze. She and Garland had never put air-conditioning in the house, because them window units made too much noise and run the power bill up too high, and they couldn't afford to install central air. They made do with natural.

Depending on what she was fixing for supper that night, Kitty would start cooking sometime between four and five o'clock and have supper on the table at six on the dot. Once she'd eaten and washed the dishes, she took a bath, put on her gown, fixed herself a dish of ice cream—fudge swirl—and sat down to watch *Wheel of Fortune* at seven-thirty. She loved *Wheel*, loved Pat Sajak, loved Vanna White in spite of her sometimes trashy clothes. "You can just tell," she used to tell Edith, "that them is two nice, regular folks. They're steady workers—been in the same job for years. They're friendly, got a good sense of humor, well-groomed and tidy in their appearance." The real reason Kitty loved *Wheel*, though, was because she could win at it. *Wheel* was her game, and *Jeopardy!* had been Edith's.

When Edith was living, they always watched *Jeopardy!* at seven and *Wheel* at seven-thirty. Edith was the *Jeopardy!* champion. Kitty just couldn't think fast enough. With *Wheel*, she usually had a few minutes to study the puzzle and figure it out. It took patience and attention to detail, not Edith's strong suit. Edith would sit on the couch with her feet on the coffee table—it was one of the compromises they'd come to after Edith come to live with Kitty that Edith could put her feet up if she took her shoes off first. Kitty would sit in her rocker by the window, looking out at the road like she didn't particularly care who won or lost, but really she was wound up tight as Dick's hatband, impatient for her show so she could wipe that smug look off Edith's face.

Right at the opening music of *Jeopardy!*, Edith would look at Kitty with that sly grin of hers and say, "Are you ready for me to slay you tonight, Kitty?" And then she'd laugh an evil laugh that bubbled up from her belly like gas. Every night. It drove Kitty crazy. It was just like when Andy Griffith used to do the commercial for Ritz crackers. Kitty hated the way Andy said, "Go-o-o-o-o-d cracker, good cracker!" so she'd turn the sound down on the TV, but then Edith would do a perfect imitation of Andy and keep doing it until Kitty had to leave the room with her hands over her ears.

During *Jeopardy!*, Edith would holler out the answers and then look at Kitty and wait for Alex Trebek to say she was right, which she always was. Edith was smart. She bragged how if she ever got on *Jeopardy!* they'd have to kick her off after a while because she'd never lose and folks would get tired of watching her win. One time Kitty tried to argue with her and said, "Edith, you would not win either. Why, you'd lose the first day because you never remember to put the answer in the form of a question. If Alex says, 'This capital of France is known as the City of Light,' you're supposed to say, 'What is Paris?' But you'd just holler, 'Paris,' and then Alex would say, 'Ohhhhhh, sorry, Edith. You forgot to phrase it in the form of a question.' "

"You're crazy," Edith said. "I'd just look at him and say, 'Paris. Isn't it?' That's in the form of a question. Isn't it?"

Somehow or other they'd managed to put up with each other in this house for twenty-five years, and sometimes Kitty had felt closer to Edith than she had to her own husband, which come from them growing up and growing old together. It wasn't a bad arrangement. When Edith's husband, Lamar, died and Edith had to sell their house and find a smaller place, it never entered Kitty's mind at first to invite her to move in, even though Garland was dead and she had plenty of room. Then one night Edith come for a visit and they was sitting on the front porch and she was telling how hard it was finding a place she could afford and out popped the words just like that without no warning. Kitty told her, "Well, Edith, I don't see why you can't come here and live with me."

The truth was, she'd been so lonesome since Garland died that the thought of having some company seemed real good, even if that company sometimes got on her last nerve. There was an adjustment period, and there was times Kitty would've gladly cut off Edith's head just to shut her up, but mostly they got along fine. Edith didn't want nothing to do with Kitty's garden and sewing and cooking, and Kitty didn't want nothing to do with Edith's record playing and dancing.

The best part was, Edith did make Kitty laugh, and she could put up with a lot for that. She missed Edith, missed her something terrible, and every night she took her time eating and washing dishes and all, drug it out so by the time she sat down to watch TV, *Jeopardy!* was over. She always turned on the TV right when the audience was yelling, "*Wheel. Of. Fortune!*"

———

PANSY SAW Laurel coming, the damn box in her hands again. She couldn't figure out how the girl had got so nosy. The last thing Pansy felt like doing was looking at little pieces of paper her mama had saved for no good reason. But here come Laurel every evening, making her sit up on the couch so she could sit down too and get into that box. Pansy liked the nights Laurel went off to the library. It was easier with just Dan there. He watched TV and let her lay there and didn't expect her to sit up and talk.

Laurel had pulled out a stack of papers and was spreading them across her lap and Pansy's too. "Mama, why do you think Maw Bert would keep these old feed bills?"

Pansy pretended to be watching the news. "Lord, there ain't no telling." Her own voice sounded like it came from far off, from somebody else's mouth. "She probably kept ever piece of paper that come in that house."

"Cotton seed," Laurel said, and looked up from the paper. "Did Grandpa Dill grow cotton?"

Pansy nodded. "All these fields around here was cotton and corn and tobacco." She could see him now, her daddy, behind a mule and a plow, or dragging a sack down the rows, the boys spread out around him with their hoes or sacks. He wouldn't let Pansy get out of school and come help like he done with the boys. No, he said, no girl of his was going to slave in a cotton field, and he meant Bert as well as Pansy, his two girls in that house full of boys. He couldn't save her from the mill, though, wasn't there to save her. She often wondered where she'd be now if her daddy had lived, if the boys hadn't married and gone off and left her and Mama there by themselves.

"Look at this, Mama, there's something on the back." Laurel handed one of the bills to Pansy and she stared at the pencil drawing, the fine lines and shading combining to create a portrait of a young woman. "It's Mama," Pansy said, taking the other pages from Laurel and looking through them. She'd seen other drawings her daddy had done, just doodles on napkins and envelopes, but she knew these were his too. "They're all her."

Only they showed a mama Pansy didn't remember ever seeing. Jealousy like a sharp, unexpected pain pinched her heart. Her daddy must've seen this woman, must've known that sweet smile, that gentle look. What happened to the woman her daddy had drawn? Pansy wanted her, that other mama, one who could inspire Daddy to draw this, one who could show such love and tenderness with her whole face. She needed it—had needed it as a child and needed it even now. Pansy handed the papers back to Laurel. No use wishing for what could never be. "I'm tired," she said.

Laurel put the papers back in the box, closed the lid, and set it on the coffee table. "You rest, Mama," she said, then stood over her.

Pansy had closed her eyes but could feel Laurel's stare, her fear, her concern. Without opening her eyes she said, "Are you going to start supper?"

"I'm going," Laurel said, and Pansy felt her move away, then heard the radio come on low in the kitchen, then the sound of Laurel getting out pots and pans. She let out the breath she'd been holding and opened her eyes, comforted by the dimness of the living room with just a rectangle of light from the kitchen door at one end. It comforted her the same way she felt comforted as a child, laying in bed listening to her mama in the kitchen on a cold winter morning, starting the fire in the woodstove, starting the coffee, breaking eggs.

Daddy and the boys would've already gone out to feed the stock and do the milking. Her mama would come to the door and say, "Get up, lazybones," when Pansy would lay there an extra minute, dreading throwing back the warm weight of the blankets to let the cold air in. She'd count to three, throw off the covers, run to the kitchen, and stand shivering next to the stove by the ladder-back chair where her mama had hung her school clothes so they'd get warm too. Pansy would dress by the stove, then set the table.

When Daddy and the boys would come tromping in, their breath still steaming, their cheeks red with cold, Mama would make them wash, then serve up a big breakfast of eggs and grits and sausage and biscuits and gravy, and they'd all sit around the table together and eat, not saying much. It was too early in the day for that. Then it would be time for school, which Pansy had loved, except for eleventh grade when she had so much trouble with science and math.

Only once had she complained about having to go, and when she did her mama turned on her, her anger quick and surprising as a summer thunderstorm. "Girl," she said, "don't you never let me hear you complain about getting to go to school. Not never. It's a privilege and you better remember. It'll be over soon enough as it is."

At the time Pansy had hated her mama. She'd only gone to tenth grade herself and had no idea how hard it was, how everything but art made her head hurt. And what use was algebra and chemistry and English literature to a girl heading into Revel Mill when she graduated, same as the rest of her family? None of it was practical, especially not the art, although she had sure thought it was back then, had thought maybe she could go to art school and find some way to make a living with it. She could see now where all that come from. Her daddy.

How come her mama never showed her those drawings of her daddy's? Why did she save them just to keep them hid in a box? The easy answer was that her mama was a pack rat, saved everything, as if all the buildup of papers and clothes and ruined pots and pans and mismatched dishes and knickknacks and doodads was proof of her still being alive, still mattering. She used to fuss if Pansy wanted to throw away so much as an old *TV Guide*. "I might need it," she'd say of old bread bags, pieces of string, rubber bands, tinfoil washed and refolded after being used. Living through the Depression had something to do with it, that need to get the good out of every little piece of tinfoil and string, to not waste one iota of anything useful, but it was also more than that. Her mama needed things, needed to accumulate things, have them piled around her. Needed, not wanted, but needed.

Pansy had never understood it. That stuff just made for a lot of clutter, took up space, kept her mama from seeing the walls, the floor, the furniture. Kept her from seeing what it would be like empty. When they moved her to the nursing home and sold the house, Pansy had walked through it empty one last time. It was just a little house, only four rooms, a tar-paper shack, but it was home, and seeing it empty had hurt more than she could have imagined. But it had been only a little taste of the feeling she had now that Mama was dead and she was an orphan.

ALBERTA

I'd sit there at night after I got the young'uns to bed and feel him
watching me. I didn't know he was setting there drawing me on
the backs of them old feed bills, which was about the only kind
of paper we kept in the house, really. We saved anything having
to do with our finances. I thought he was figuring, trying to make
ends meet. I wasn't so much interested in his doings, anyway. I
was too caught up in my own misery to care about him or
anybody else. Too many children and too much work and not
enough sleep and no dreams, that was the recipe for my
unhappiness. I kept having child after child, and got to where I
didn't even make much effort at naming them when they come. I
let him do it.

Having growed up on a farm, I knowed what was causing
them babies, and I reckon I could've stopped him, but I was
selfish. That was the one thing in my life I took pleasure from
and I did not want to give it up. I never felt so good as when he
was inside me and the whole rest of the world just went away for
a while. Of course, it always came back too soon, and he'd fall
asleep and leave me all alone in it again. Then I hated him. And
coming right after loving him, that hate would frighten me so. As
I laid there by him, unable to sleep, my heart would beat
practically out of my breast. I loved my husband. I did, in my
own way. Lots of folks felt sorry for him, felt he could've done
better, said I was cold to him, but nobody knows how it is
between a man and a woman when they're alone together. It's
nobody's business but theirs.

I admit I could've been a better wife, but at the time it was all
I could do to get through the day. I can see now that he was
struggling as well. It wasn't just me. He seemed to handle it
better, though. Most times I was blind to his suffering, but there
was moments when the veil of misery I lived behind lifted and I
seen him on the other side. One time, I remember watching him

come down the road from town looking so tired and downhearted, I didn't think he'd make it across the yard and into the house. He'd been to the bank to try and borrow money against the farm just to get us through that winter. We'd been married about fifteen years by that time and had eight children to feed. I watched him come toward the house, watched him through the kitchen window, and knowed he'd been turned down.

"Wipe your feet," I said when he come through the door, and he did, then took off his hat and coat and hung them on the back of the door. He sat down at the table and started sweeping circles on it with his hands, little ones at first, then bigger and bigger till he was stretching clear across the table to reach. There wasn't a crumb on that table. He just done it out of habit.

I watched him a minute, then turned back to the stove to finish supper. He'd killed a rabbit that morning and I'd made a big pot of stew with the meat and had a pan of corn bread in the oven. I stirred the pot and said, "Wasn't any good, was it?"

"Nope," he said, and kept on rubbing the table.

"I told you," I said. We was already mortgaged, so why would the bank give us any more money? I reckon he hoped maybe they'd take pity on a family with eight children. It was so quiet in that kitchen, except for the bubbling pot and the sound of his dry palms on the table. "Lord, will you quit that," I said. "You're driving me crazy."

He quit, then said, "I sold ten acres to Willard Jenkins."

I got real still then. Ten acres? He sold ten acres of his daddy's precious land? I would've thought he'd sell one of the young'uns first. "How much?" I said.

"Five hundred dollars."

Five hundred. That might get us through, pay for food and fuel and seed in the spring. We'd have to be careful, though. Couldn't nobody get sick, at least not sick enough to need a doctor.

That'll have to do," I said. That's all I said, with all I knowed
of his family and how much the land meant and his promise to
his daddy to keep it in the family. As the only child, the land was
all his, his legacy and his burden. I had always thought it unfair of
his daddy to expect so much. Dill was only one man, and he had
to work a job in the mill just to pay taxes on the place. But no
matter how hard he had to work, he always swore he'd never sell.
Losing that ten acres broke his heart. He still had a hundred and
twenty left, but that was the beginning of the end of it. He
seemed to know already that times would stay hard, and every
year he'd have to sell more and more, until finally all that was left
was the eight acres Pansy and Dan lives on now.

Dill's mother died when he was five years old, struck by
lightning as she walked home from a neighbor's during a
thunderstorm, leaving him and his daddy to fend for themselves.
He didn't have no memory of her alive. His living memories was
of his daddy. Every time he walked that land, he seen his daddy,
clearing trees, plowing fields, chopping cotton, shoeing mules,
baling hay. His daddy's very blood was in that ground, and I
knowed what that meant to Dill. But I didn't say nothing that
night, nothing but "That'll have to do." Why didn't I go to him?
Why didn't I put my hands on his shoulders and say something
that might help, something simple? "You're a good provider,
Dill." That would've been enough.

But I just stood there. In a few minutes, he started rubbing
the table again, that old oak table his daddy made for his mama,
the same table they laid her out on when she died, the same
table his daddy was laid out on when he died in his sleep the year
me and Dill got married. I believe Dill was trying to say sorry
with his hands, sorry to his daddy for selling the land, for letting
him down. I could feel his daddy in that house then, in the walls,
the floors, in every stick of furniture, and for the first time in a
long time I felt somebody's sadness besides my own. Dill's and
his daddy's sorrow run through that house like a cold, wet draft,

and I shivered and moved closer to the stove. I couldn't do a thing but just stand there, stirring that pot.

There's a drawing Dill done of me that night. He had a real talent for drawing, for making things look like what they really was. Only there's one thing different, one thing that is not right. Instead of staring down into a bubbling pot, my hair stringy around my hot face, he's got me looking over my shoulder at him, my face bright and framed with golden brown curls, looking at him as tenderly as some mother might look at her sleeping child. All his drawings of me is like that. He'd draw me while I cooked, or washed dishes, or bathed a baby, or swept the floor, and always he pictured me with that bright face, them soft curls, that tender smile. He seen something that was never there. I never looked like that. My hair was always straight and brown and limp, my face was always ruddy from work or standing over a hot stove, and if I smiled at all, I didn't know it. It was all made up, all just some dream he had.

11

THE ORGANIST HAD BEGUN GOING THROUGH HER SONG list again and the groom shifted from foot to foot, big drops of sweat running down the sides of his balding head and onto his pink cheeks. The entire church sat quietly, the only noise the rustle of people shifting in their seats and the occasional cough. Laurel looked at Hap, who shrugged, then looked behind her. That young redheaded preacher had excused himself and gone looking for the bride when she failed to appear on cue, but it looked like he wasn't having any luck. Maybe Melanie was having second thoughts, just as Laurel had on her wedding day. Listen to your little voice, Laurel thought, returning Hap's smile and hoping Melanie could pick up on the message. If you're not absolutely sure, then for God's sake, don't do it. It's better to be alone than to wish you were.

Finally the preacher, scrawny and freckled and too young to drive much less perform a wedding ceremony, came back looking stunned and, after a conference with the groom and his parents, announced in his surprisingly deep radio-DJ voice that the wedding had been canceled. He then asked that the bride's family and friends please remain. During the announcement the groom's parents had hustled him out of the church double-quick, followed by row after row of his family and friends until now the entire groom's side sat empty, the white satin bows on the ends of the pews hanging lopsided. Laurel wanted to laugh, thinking if the church was a boat, it'd surely tip over right now. Everybody on the bride's side sat waiting for further instructions from the preacher, but he only looked at the floor and shook his head.

The poor groom, Laurel thought. He'd looked so shocked, so embarrassed. He probably never in a million years thought Melanie would ditch a great catch like him, not gorgeous but cute in a round-faced, boyish way, and a doctor to boot. Percilla must be throwing a fit. It was a wonder she hadn't tried to drag Melanie down the aisle by the hair of her head.

Hap lifted his arm from the back of the pew behind Laurel and leaned forward, hands between his knees. "What do you think happened?" he whispered.

Laurel shrugged. "No telling. But I bet they're having to give Percilla tranquilizers about now." Watching Hap sit there and fidget, it was so easy to imagine them ending up together. If she was a stranger and walked in and saw them sitting there, she'd think they were married, had been married so long they didn't have much to say to each other anymore. It was the female curse—obsessed with planning the future instead of living in the moment. She could predict the engagement, the wedding, the rest of their lives. All she had to do was go along. But somehow, good as that picture looked with Hap in it, she couldn't get excited about being in it with him. Not that there was anything wrong with him. She couldn't complain about someone so handsome, successful, and charming, could she? Except now that they'd been dating a few weeks, they'd run out of things to talk about. What would she do with a man she couldn't talk to? He caught her staring and smiled and winked in that cocky way of his that reminded her so much of Scott, that look that said, *I know you want me, baby*. God, it was irritating.

Dan, who'd been fidgeting on the other side of Laurel ever since he sat down, stood halfway and said, "I'll be back in a minute," then straightened and headed toward the back of the church. He was probably going to see about Rex. Laurel had smelled whiskey on Rex's breath when he was talking to Dan in the vestibule earlier. Good Lord, drunk at his own child's wedding. Although maybe he'd had good reason, maybe he'd seen this coming.

Three rows up, Maxann turned around and waved, her eyebrows raised as if to say, *Can you believe this?* Lottie May said something to her, and Maxann looked back at Laurel and stuck her tongue out before turning to face the front. They could've passed for mother and daughter, Laurel thought, Lottie May tiny and white-headed, Maxann tall and blond and younger-looking from the back.

"Ladies and gentlemen, may I have your attention please." The preacher had finally raised his head and seemed to be focusing on a point up in the balcony.

A door in the choir loft opened then and Rex stepped through, his upper body thrust forward as if he'd been pushed. Dan followed, then got beside him and held his arm until he got steady. He guided Rex down the steps and over to where the preacher waited. What in the world? Laurel looked at Hap, who was sitting up straight now. *This is getting interesting*, he mouthed, and nodded toward the front.

When he saw that Rex was steady on his feet, at least for the moment, the preacher faced the congregation again. "Ladies and gentlemen, it appears there will be a wedding after all." He nodded at the organist, who shrugged in confusion and started the wedding march, then lifted his hands, palms up. Everybody rose and faced the back of the church.

At a nod from the preacher, Craig Johnson, the single remaining usher, opened the door and stood back as Carmen stepped through, her entire face as red as the church carpet. She marched to the altar, her strapless pink tulle dress swishing violently as she passed, and took her place on the side opposite her father, then stood glaring toward the back of the church, her bouquet of pink roses and baby's breath dangling from one hand.

Okay, Laurel thought, we've got one bridesmaid. Now, who the hell is the bride? In the shadows of the vestibule, she saw something white move, then step forward, and there, framed by the double oak doors, stood Percilla, a lacy veil covering her face and hanging almost to the hem of her white satin mother-of-the-bride dress. Laurel's hand flew up to her mouth, and she wished her mama had felt good enough to come today. She was going to hate having missed this.

Percilla lifted a bouquet of white and pink roses to her chest and started down the aisle. It was Percilla's moment and she was milking it, taking tiny steps, smiling at everybody on the way down. She was the queen and they were all her subjects. Laurel couldn't help smiling back. Every woman deserved to be queen for at least a day, and Percilla's joy was contagious.

As she came closer, Laurel could see that the dress fit perfectly. Percilla must've been wearing a decent bra and a girdle for a change. Instead of looking fat and dumpy, she was full-figured, voluptuous, positively radiant. Suddenly Laurel could imagine how she must've looked years ago before all the extra padding. Under the veil, her face was framed with a white rose above each ear, and by some miracle she had chosen to wear mauve lipstick instead of hot pink. Laurel hoped somebody had asked the photographer to stay. Percilla would want to remember this.

Rex seemed steady on his feet until he caught sight of the bride, did a double take, and took a step back. Dan caught him and led him forward to stand in front of the preacher. Percilla reached the altar at last and reached for Rex's hand. Carmen crossed her arms over her chest, looking furious. Laurel had been afraid she'd be miserable at this wedding, but it was turning out all right.

Once the congregation was seated, the preacher announced that in lieu of their daughter's wedding, which had been canceled due to circumstances beyond their control, Rex and Percilla were taking the opportunity to renew their vows. They also were asking that everyone join them at a reception at the country club immediately following the ceremony. Then the preacher opened his Bible and began to read. Laurel wondered if the ceremony was really written there, word for word. She'd never bothered to check, not even for her own wedding. She wondered if Percilla felt the same crazy excitement and terror standing up there, renewing her vows, as Laurel had felt the day she stood there with Scott.

Percilla said her "I do" loud and proud, with a grin thrown over her shoulder toward the bride's side, and then the preacher turned to Rex. "Do you, Rex Dover, take this woman to love and to cherish, in sickness and in health, till death do you part?" When Rex didn't answer right away, the preacher looked up from the Bible. "Rex?"

There was a long silence until Rex swayed and a gasp went up in the church. Dan caught him again and whispered something in his ear. Oh, God, Laurel thought. He's so drunk he can't even remember to say *I do*.

Finally his mouth opened in slow motion and it felt like everyone in the church became one mind, willing him to get the words out this time. His throat worked. And then he belched, the longest, loudest belch Laurel had ever heard in her life. It went on for what seemed like a full minute, after which Rex put his hand over his mouth and said, "Excuse me." Giggles broke out in the pews. Percilla hissed, "Rex!" and yanked on his hand.

The preacher, the look on his face indicating that Rex's breath was less than fresh, whipped out a quick, "I now pronounce you man and wife," then looked at Percilla. "You may kiss the groom," he said, then muttered under his breath loud enough for everyone to hear, "if you can stand it."

Percilla lifted the veil over her head, looking behind her for help from her bridesmaid, but Carmen had disappeared. All that remained was her bouquet on the floor. Percilla didn't let it slow her down, though. She grabbed Rex's lapels and turned his mouth mauve with a long, lingering kiss. When she pulled away, Rex stood there surprised for a minute, then hollered, "Well, hey, baby!" and wrapped his arms around her, his face in her neck. The bride's side cracked up then. They all began to applaud, couldn't help it, and Rex and Percilla took a bow before weaving their way down the aisle, grinning like newlyweds.

At the reception, when Laurel heard that Melanie had eloped with her boss, the Al Davis of Al Davis Plumbing, she had the inexplicable urge to jump up and down and cheer. It made no sense, getting that excited for a girl she barely knew, but it felt like Melanie had run off not only for herself but for Laurel, for all women who walked down that aisle because they thought they couldn't make it without a man.

As she swayed in the middle of the dance floor with Hap, both of them drunk on champagne, his chin in her neck, Laurel felt a freedom she hadn't felt in a long time, probably not since puberty. She wasn't worried about looking stupid, or about whether she was too fat or too short or too boring. She just was. With her hands resting lightly on

Hap's waist, she floated through the evening, thinking only, This is nice. I'm enjoying myself. But it's not everything. It's not my life. There is so much more, so much.

Percilla

Daddy always made a fuss over me. Too much, Mama said. She said he never once got foolish over the boys being born but bawled like a baby when I come along. Maybe men are always all their lives scared to show too much emotion toward another man, even their own sons, and have to direct it all at the girls to keep from being thought unmanly. Or maybe boys just ain't that interesting to their daddies till they get old enough to play ball. I don't know. Rex was the same way with our girls, foolish over them. He seemed to think he was the big protector and now he had something worth protecting, something that was all his. Boy, he found out different when they started growing up, just like my daddy did. Little girls leave a trail of broken hearts, and the first and the worst is always their own daddy.

Of course, I thought my daddy was the be-all end-all when I was little. I still thought the world of him after I got grown, but not in the same old way. He was tall to me, though I'm taller now than he was, and he was dark and handsome and strong and brave, everything little girls need in a daddy.

I was the only girl, so it was me and Mama, though Mama was always so run-down and wore-out looking I think it'd been a long time since anybody thought of her as a girl. It used to make me so mad that she wouldn't try and fix herself up a little bit, but she always said she didn't have time to be pretty, she had too much to do. Now I'm older I understand better what she meant. I don't just wake up in the morning already pretty like I done when I was eighteen and twenty years old. It takes work, but it's worth doing. Even though I've put on a pound or two here and there, I still make the effort to wear nice clothes and fix my hair and put on makeup every day. Some women think when they get a man they can give all that up, but it's just the opposite. After the wedding is when you need it even more, not just to keep the man interested, but to keep yourself interested too. If you quit being interested, everybody else will too. And a little attention never hurt nobody.

My wedding was such a disappointment to me. I always wanted to wear a long white dress and march down the aisle with everybody looking at me, but then I got in the family way and everything happened so fast, and besides that we didn't have no money for a fancy wedding. Just wore my Sunday dress, a plain old blue thing, and stood up in Mama's living room with her and my brothers as witnesses. Didn't have nothing for a reception but coffee and a little old pound cake with lemon icing, and it already had a piece cut out of it. I never had nothing for myself, but when I married Rex, I made up my mind I would.

Marriage was exciting for about two weeks, then I seen what it was going to be, the same old thing ever day. A girl needs excitement in life. The day you can't get a man's attention just by walking in a room is the day you ought to just curl up and die. Even when you get old, you have to keep yourself up, keep in practice, because you might be a old woman, but at least you'll look pretty good to all the old men. If Rex goes before me, I don't intend to sit home in black and wait for my turn. No, sir. I'm going out there and play the field, which is what I should've done and would've done if I hadn't got myself pregnant. I was lucky to get Rex, though, considering the baby wasn't his. He's been real good about it, and Carmen don't never need to know her real daddy got killed in a knife fight when she was six months old. I took that as a sign that I had done the right thing marrying Rex. Then I went and had Melanie so Rex would have one of his own, but I quit after that, and thanked the Lord every day for birth control.

That's where my mama went wrong, having all them young'uns. Of course, maybe she didn't have a choice back then. I don't know. I can't help thinking she could've found a way. I learned real quick the best birth control is a headache. It's a wonder Rex didn't check me into the hospital. Mama just didn't know how to manage men and that's why Daddy was all the time stepping out on her. I don't blame him near as much as I do her. If a man ain't getting it at home, he's getting it somewhere, don't ever doubt that. The only one I do hold against

him is that Dot Ramsey. He made a fool of himself over that woman
and it wasn't even love, couldn't have been, because she wasn't
nothing to love, just a spindly towheaded little thing thought she was
better than him. No, he just wanted what he couldn't have, and that's
something a man can't help. He's born with that. She knowed what
she was doing, teasing him, making him wait. Of course, he was the
bossman with a family to support, and she had a husband to take
care of her. The whole thing embarrassed Mama to death, especially
when Dot come to the house. She brung Maxann with her for some
reason, and I remember having to set there in that living room with
her while Mama and Dot talked in the kitchen, Dot telling Mama she
never had nothing to do with Daddy, and Mama crying and saying
she believed her.

   Me and Maxann knowed each other from school, but we never
went in the same groups. They was just something about the real poor
kids like Maxann, how scrawny they was, their stringy hair and
hand-me-down clothes, that made you want to look the other way
when you seen them in the hall. She set there that day and give me the
meanest look, if looks could kill I would've been dead. I didn't see
what call she had to look at me that way when it was her mama the
one causing all the trouble. I said, "What you looking at, you hateful
thing?" and she said, "I don't know, I ain't figured it out yet, you ugly
bitch." Well, it don't take much to light my fuse and she lit it. I went
over there and drawed back my arm and smacked her right across the
jaw. I almost hated that I'd even touched her, because a lot of them
poor kids had lice and scabies and all kind of diseases. It was worth it,
though, when I seen my fingerprints on her cheek. "You ain't fit to
come in this house," I said. "You take yourself out on the porch." She
was on me then, and it was like trying to get a mad cat off of you. She
climbed all over me, clawing and biting, ripping my new dress and
pulling my hair. It scared the lights out of me, having somebody that
little and puny fight so hard. We must've made some noise, because
Mama and Dot come running in and separated us. Maxann didn't
look much different from when the fight started, but I was a mess,
crying and carrying on over my ruint dress. Dot told Mama she was
sorry and grabbed Maxann's hand and jerked her out the door. That

satisfied me some because it looked like Maxann was in for a
whipping. It wasn't too long after that Dot got beat near to death by
her own husband. Another woman that just didn't know how to
handle her man.

In that respect, I reckon Mama and Dot had a lot in common.
They was both smart women, so I never understood why they had so
much trouble in that one area. It ain't hard to figure out, really. Men
boil down to two things: their belly and their pecker. Nothing
complicated there. Now, you want to talk about complicated, it's
women that's hard to figure. Most women think too much, for one
thing, and it ain't healthy. I'd much rather be doing something than
thinking about something. I just go on and do whatever it is. I'm more
like a man that way. Daddy loved that about me, and so does Rex. I
speak my mind like a man, and men like a little sass. They like it
when you show them who's boss, as long as you don't make them look
bad in front of their buddies.

The first time Daddy took me to the Moose Lodge, I wasn't but
about four years old. He liked to go there Friday nights and set around
with his buddies, have a drink or two, play some cards. He'd worked
hard all week and he deserved to cut loose a little bit. A lot of times he
went by himself because Mama was too tired. That night he tried and
tried to talk her into going and she just kept saying no. So Daddy said
if she wouldn't go, he'd take me. Mama throwed a fit, said he wasn't
taking her baby in no beer joint, but he just picked me up and went
out the house with her hollering from the door. She was real big with
Mickey then, couldn't hardly get up off the couch by herself, and we
only had the one car, so they wasn't much she could do about it.

It was dark in there, and smoky. Men and women sat at tables
with brown bags of liquor and bottles of Coke and ashtrays. The
jukebox played country songs and people talked loud, their mouths
open real wide. Everybody smelled good and looked pretty and
laughed a lot, and I loved it. Daddy went over to some of his friends
and set me up on the table in front of him. Somebody said, "Who's
your date, Mike?" and Daddy said, "This here's my little princess,
Percilla Sue." Another man said, "She sure is sweet." And right out of
the blue, I turned to him and said, "I ain't sweet neither. I'm full of piss

and vinegar." I don't know where that come from, but, Lord, did they laugh. It got to where Daddy took me with him whenever he could get me past Mama, and somebody always made sure to say something about me being sweet, just to get me to answer back about being full of piss and vinegar. I made the mistake of saying that to Mama one time, and she took a hickory to my legs and said she better not never hear them words come out my mouth again. I never could figure out why it bothered her so much when Daddy didn't seem to mind.

That's been the story of my life, though, other women being so jealous of all the attention I get from men. I don't let it bother me none. I just keep on being me. I've always been like that, not caring what other people think. Like that time I joined the union. I was married and had two girls in school and a steady job, but what did I have to look forward to ever day? What did I have to get excited about? It was awful. I was so bored with my own life it scared me to death. Then I met George, and I guess you could say we had a little affair. He worked in the dye house and told me if I'd join the union and help him, then he'd make me shop steward when the union got voted in at the plant. Of course, I didn't really care nothing about being no shop steward. We used to meet at his headquarters at the Dogwood Motel out on 74 and, Lord, you talk about being fired up. Trouble was, we ended up in that bed so much we never got a lick of work done.

Of course it didn't work out. No, sir. Them people was too ignorant to know what was good for them. Why, you'd a thought I was asking them to join the Communist Party or something. Then the word come down that John Dollar had talked to George's bossman. He told him, "Get rid of that son of a bitch," and sure enough, two weeks later George was gone, let go, they said. Grady give me a little talking to, let me know real quick he wouldn't stand for no more bullshit. I'd been there a lot longer than George, which I reckon is the only thing that saved my job, that and Grady being sweet like he is. It was years before they quit calling me Norma Rae behind my back, and I only seen that dang movie one time and I don't look a thing like Sally Field.

Seems like ever good thing in my life don't last. Daddy dying in that wreck when I was eighteen, right after me and Rex got married, and then Mama gone of cancer right when I needed her most, when them girls of mine was babies, then George getting run off, and now Rex, who has got to where he's just about impossible to live with. I don't understand that depression of his hanging on so long. It ought to be over by now. It's been two years since Pilgrim closed. Ain't no reason he can't go out and find work and get back to his old self, I don't care what that doctor says. I felt bad for him at first. I know a man's job is more important to him than just about anything. But it's wearing on my nerves now. My daddy wouldn't a never let himself come to such a pass. No, sir. He would've done something. Sometimes I think the only thing keeping Rex alive is me telling him to get up and do this and do that. He can't even think for himself no more. I still love him, but he ain't turned out to be no kind of a man. My daddy always said, when the going gets tough, the tough get going. He'd be ashamed to see me married to Rex the way he is now. I'm ashamed myself. There's times I wish so bad my daddy was here. I never have missed Mama as much, but, Lord, I miss Daddy. Sometimes you just need your daddy, you need somebody to call you their princess and set you up on a table for people to admire. You just do.

SPRING

You are not alone.

12

The weather was warm for April but not too hot yet, and the shade on the screen porch was just the right temperature. Laurel rocked and stared out into the yard, gradually relaxing until she felt almost peaceful. Lottie May's yard was a busy place, so many different wild things to look at. She'd seen all kinds of birds, although the only ones she recognized were robins and cardinals. A little lizard she thought was called a skink soaked up sun on a stump in the yard. Two gray squirrels skittered around and around the trunks of the oak trees at the edge of the yard, chasing each other in a weird squirrel game, or maybe a mating ritual. It was spring, after all.

The late-afternoon sun slanted in at a low angle, casting light high and creating shadow below so that the purple irises and pink geraniums around the well house looked as if they were underwater. The whole afternoon seemed liquid gold and green, and Laurel realized she felt almost happy. Wait a minute. Not almost. Was there such a thing as almost happy? She was happy. It was a revelation, a feeling she'd been without for so long she'd forgotten to miss it, that sense that life was good, the world was beautiful, people weren't all bad. If only she'd realized sooner that all she needed to regain a sense of contentment was a haircut and a home-cooked meal made by somebody besides herself. She'd been doing all the cooking for herself and her parents, and enjoyed it, but it sure was nice to be waited on for a change. Lottie May had been asking her for weeks to come over to supper, and Laurel kept resisting, saying she had to get home and see about Mama. But tonight for some reason she hadn't felt like going home, wanted to do something different, something to go with her new hair. Big adventure, she thought, having supper at a friend's house. It seemed fitting, though, that she be here tonight. A drastic hair change was a major event for a woman, and Lottie May was the one who'd inspired her. It was no big deal, really, but somehow seeing Lottie May, at her age, embracing change like that, she wondered about herself, how attached she was to her own comfort zone and how much that scared her.

She ran a hand across the back of her neck, shook her head so the soft curls swished against her cheeks. She couldn't recall the last time she had hair this short. Scott had liked it long. Most men did, though Laurel couldn't understand why. She felt free and so much cooler, so much sexier with these bouncy curls instead of the heavy, dead weight of the same hair she'd been carrying around since high school. She'd been afraid she might cry when she heard the scissors start cutting but instead watched a big smile come across her face in the mirror. It was impossible to take herself seriously sitting there covered with an apron, hair falling all around her, country music blasting on the radio, and Nicky the hairdresser telling in great detail all about how her mama had gone blind in one eye because of a detached rectum. It had taken all her willpower just to keep from busting out laughing, not so much at Nicky's use of the wrong word but at how much fun it was to be immersed in this real world of real people in all their crazy, flawed, fascinating humanity.

Thunder rumbled in the distance and the wind picked up, rustling through the trees in Lottie May's front yard. The sky in front of the house was still that vivid blue made even bluer by the sharp contrast of huge white clouds, which meant the storm must be coming from behind her. Laurel loved storms, loved everything about them—trees thrashing, rain pouring, thunder cracking and booming overhead, the shock of lightning. Then the subsiding, the gradual fading away, the water dripping from leaves, air cooler, distant thunder again, this time calmer-sounding, like a grumpy old man rather than an angry god.

Storms made her feel safe for some weird reason. She always jumped when the thunder got close, but she felt enclosed and protected too. Maybe it was because she was always inside. If she ever got caught outside in a storm she probably wouldn't enjoy it quite as much.

She'd always hated being at Maw Bert's during a storm. She unplugged everything in the house and wouldn't talk on the telephone or go near a window, made them sit on the couch holding a feather pillow to protect them from lightning. She'd never been able to explain why a feather pillow would keep away lightning, just told them to hush and sit still.

Storms with her mama were fun, though, especially if the power went out. She'd light the big fat pillar candle with angels carved on the sides that she kept on the coffee table, then they'd sit on the floor at her feet while Mama told scary stories like the man with the golden arm or I want my toe bone. She loved her mama so much during those times, loved how exciting she made the story, how safe they felt sitting there with her and Daddy. Something scary inside to take their minds off what was scary outside. She felt like her mama could do anything then, even magic.

Thunder boomed again, closer this time, and dark clouds pushed across the sky in front of the house, giving the whole world a darkgreen cast.

The screen door squeaked open and Lottie May leaned out. "You better come in the house," she said. "It's fixing to woo-woo."

Laurel laughed. "What?"

"That's what Nisco says. He couldn't say *thunder* when he was little, called it *woo-woo*."

"I think I'll sit out here just a few more minutes, unless I can help you?"

"No, supper'll be ready directly. Lord, I wish it would rain."

Thunder cracked and a jagged length of lightning reached down to the ground next door on the other side of Idalene's house. Laurel jumped out of the rocker. "Okay," she said. "That's enough for me."

She followed Lottie May to the kitchen, taking in the shabby but neat living room as they passed through. Pictures of Nellie Belle and Nisco and her other kids and grandkids covered one wall, the TV took up another, and over the couch hung a picture of a white-haired man in a black suit sitting at a table praying. Laurel was almost positive Maw Bert had had that same picture in her house. The walls were knotty-pine paneling and the floors looked like oak. Considering the house had probably been built when the mill opened, it looked pretty good, a basic four-room mill house: living room and bedroom on the front, kitchen and bedroom on the back, with a third bedroom that had been added on just off the kitchen. It was lower than the rest of the house and had a step down into it.

"Nisco!" Lottie May hollered. "Get washed up. Supper's ready." She turned from the stove and waved her fork at the kitchen sink. "You can wash up over there, honey."

It was like an oven in the kitchen, which was appropriate since the heat came from the woodstove. How did they stand it? She took her time at the sink because it was cooler there with the breeze blowing through the open window. There was no hand soap, so Laurel squirted Joy into her palm and lathered up, the lemony smell filling the air around her. Through the window over the sink she could see into Lottie May's and Idalene's backyards. Both had big gardens with neat, well-tended rows of lettuce and onions, and it looked as if somebody had just set out tomato plants. Beyond the gardens each yard had a shed, and then up a little hill behind some bushes and small trees ran the railroad track, and beyond that, beyond those trees, was the plant, the old smokestacks just visible above the tree line. Their whole world was defined by that place, it seemed, even when they weren't in it.

As Laurel and Nisco waited at the table, Lottie May started spooning something out of a pot.

"What is that?" Laurel said.

Lottie May turned her upper body away from the stove, spoon in hand, denim apron around her waist. "Chicken and dumplings," she said with a smile, reminding Laurel so much at that moment of Maw Bert that tears came to her eyes. God, nobody had made chicken and dumplings for her since Maw Bert went into the nursing home. She hadn't even made them for herself, because she could never get them to come out like Maw Bert's.

"I think I'm going to cry," Laurel said, making a joke of it so she wouldn't feel so foolish. "Maw Bert used to make chicken and dumplings for me all the time."

"Oh, honey," Lottie May said. "That's all right. I cry ever time I smell strawberries, because Ed loved them so much."

When they'd finished eating, Lottie May put some chicken and dumplings in a Tupperware bowl and sent Nisco to carry it next door to Idalene's. "And don't you stay over there all night neither," she told him.

After he left, they went out on the porch to cool off, leaving the dishes in the sink. It was so peaceful, no noise in the neighborhood except dogs barking every now and then and somebody mowing grass down the street. The storm had passed without raining on them.

Laurel leaned forward in her rocker to get a better look at Idalene's house, which was almost identical to Lottie May's. "I didn't know y'all were such close neighbors."

"Yeah," Lottie May said. She had a habit of rubbing her hands over and over the arms of the chair while she rocked. It was a wonder the wood hadn't worn completely away. "Ever since we found out we was sisters, I been living here next to her. She helped me get this house."

Laurel stopped rocking. "Y'all are sisters?"

"Oh, yeah, honey, did you not know that? Well, half sisters, had the same mama. But we was raised up by different people."

"Why?"

"You tell me and we'll both know. Idalene don't like to talk about it and I was just a baby when it happened."

Laurel was trying to picture them side by side, trying to see resemblances, but it was impossible. "But surely, close as you are, she would've told you something."

"Well, honey, we might be close, but Idalene, she likes to keep her distance."

A screen door slammed next door and Nisco came running across the yard, screaming, "Meemaw! Meemaw!" Lottie May jumped up and met him at the end of the porch.

"Lord, young'un, what?"

"Idalene throwed her supper up all over the floor. Then she slid down in it. I think she's sick."

"Oh, Lord," Lottie May said, rushing down the steps after Nisco. Laurel ran behind them, not sure what she could do except get in the way.

They stopped, breathless, in the kitchen doorway, and Idalene turned from the sink, giving them a hateful look. The seat and legs of her pants were soaking wet, and she was wringing out a wad of paper towels. "What?" she said, then squatted and started mopping up the floor with the paper towels.

"Here, honey," Lottie May said, bending over her. "Let me do that. Why don't you go change your clothes?"

Idalene smacked at her hand and missed. "I don't want to change my clothes. I'm fine. Y'all just go on back home now, you hear?" Idalene glanced back at Laurel. "I thought I seen you go in over there. Your hair looks good like that. Young girls ought not wear their hair up in a bun. Makes you look old."

"Thank you," Laurel said. "I think." She'd only worn her hair on top of her head a few times, when it was really hot out.

Lottie May had backed away from Idalene and stood watching her intently. "Are you sure you're all right?"

Idalene sighed. "Yes. It's just one of them twenty-four-hour bugs, so you'uns better get on out of here before you catch it."

"It stinks in here," Nisco said.

"Nisco!" Lottie May said.

Idalene laughed, and the transformation from sourpuss to a woman almost girlish and carefree was amazing. "It sure does, young'un, but a little Lysol will take care of that. Now, scoot."

They made their way slowly out of the house, and Laurel noted how different Idalene's living room looked than Lottie May's—no family photos, no doodads, no knitting in a basket beside the couch. It looked like a furnished room for rent.

Back on Lottie May's porch, settling into the rocking chairs, Lottie May hollered, "Nisco?"

"Yes, ma'am?" he hollered back, his voice coming from the direction of the backyard.

"Nothing!" Lottie May hollered back. She turned to Laurel. "I just like to make sure where he's at." She'd brought her knitting out with her and Laurel watched the needles sliding through the loops of yarn.

She remembered evenings like this from childhood, only she was on the other end, one of the kids in the yard answering her mama's call. She used to feel so sorry for the grown-ups, stuck up there on the porch with nothing to do but talk. But it was nice on the porch, peaceful, and she leaned back and rocked, letting the peace of twilight sink into her.

"I'm real worried about Idalene," Lottie May said after a few minutes. "That's the third time this month I've seen her sick to her stomach. Seems like she's been feeling bad ever since she retired."

"Has she been to the doctor?"

Lottie May snorted. "Idalene? Go to a doctor? She'd as soon lay down and die as give money to a doctor. That woman pinches a penny till it squeals."

There was a rumbling in the distance and Laurel wondered at first if it was another storm. Then she realized it was a train. She'd forgotten about the tracks so nearby.

The train used to run by Maw Bert's house, and Laurel would lay there at night, listening, then reach over and touch Maw Bert's back to make sure she was still there. Then she'd fall right back to sleep. For some reason Laurel felt near to tears again. She must be hormonal. Crying over a damn train, she thought. Stupid, stupid.

The train got louder and the floor vibrated under their feet. It shook the whole house, rattling the windows in their frames. After it had passed into the distance, Lottie May said, "My first husband, Ed, died right here in this house."

Wait a minute, Laurel thought. How did we get from Idalene to Ed? Was this what happened when you got old, your mind just jumped around from topic to topic, no rhyme or reason?

"Died at five minutes to six, right yonder in that green chair. Just set down and died, and him not but twenty-six year old. Doctor said a blood clot hit his brain."

Night was coming down and Laurel was glad to have it to hide her face in. Lottie May sounded so sad, as if it had happened yesterday instead of years and years ago. "I'm sorry," Laurel said.

"I tell you what." Lottie May stopped knitting, stopped rocking. "I had me the best husband ever walked this earth."

Laurel waited, figuring there was more, but that was it. Lottie May sat back, rocking and knitting again, nodding slightly as if she'd managed to make an important point. Wasn't she supposed to follow up with an example, something to illustrate what made him the best husband on earth? For some reason, Laurel really wanted to hear that story, wanted to know what it took to make a woman love a man that hard and that long even after he was dead. Or maybe it was because he was dead. Maybe if he'd lived they'd have ended up divorced too.

Laurel thought maybe what she really wanted to know was how could you tell if love would last? How did you ever trust your own judgment again after being betrayed by a man who promised to love you and be faithful? Until there was some kind of test, some guarantee of a positive outcome, she would play it safe, spend her days at work and her evenings with people she could count on, people like Lottie May. She would embrace the rocking chair, the front porch, the library— hell, she might even take up knitting—all the accoutrements of a well-adjusted spinster lady in a small town.

Lottie May

I have to say, I love Nellie and Nisco the best of all of them. I can't help it. Course I love my other young'uns. Course I do. But Nellie's my baby I had with Ed, and even though she ain't all there, she's all I got left of him, her and Nisco, who's starting to look a whole lot like his grandpa now he's outgrowed his baby fat. Ed, he was my true love, and if he hadn't of died, I never would've looked at another man, especially not one like Butch Holt. But for some reason, after Ed died, I felt desperate to get married again. It was like I couldn't catch my breath when I was all by myself, just me and the baby and nobody else in the world to care if we lived or died.

Maybe if I'd had me a mama, maybe I wouldn't of panicked the way I did and married the first man to come along and ask. A mama might've moved in with me, kept me company, watched the baby while I worked, told me life is hard but what don't kill you makes you stronger, told me everything was going to be all right. A mama might've done a lot of things.

Not that Mr. and Mrs. Dooley wasn't good to me. They was. But they never let me forget I wasn't theirs. I don't think they done it to make me feel bad. They was just such honest people, I think they didn't want to tell me a lie or try to be something to me that wasn't true. They was more like a aunt and a uncle than a mama and daddy, though they raised me from the time I was a baby. There was always that separation between us that I couldn't never get past. I think now maybe they always thought one day my daddy might come back for me and so they was afraid to love me too much. But he never did come back, and now I reckon he's dead too.

My life has turned out just fine, though. I can't complain. The Lord has blessed me. I got a good job, I got healthy young'uns and grandyoung'uns, I go home to my family every night and not a empty house like poor Idalene. No, I can't complain. And ever since that sorry Butch went off for the last time with no intentions of coming back, well, ever since then I feel sort of like a weight's been lifted off of

me, like I'm free to do what I please now. I don't have to take nothing
from nobody.

Now, I ain't got nothing against men. I like men. They're good
company, and most of them are good providers. Even Butch, sorry as
he was in a lot of ways, he always sent his paycheck home, every
week, regular as the mail. That's how I knowed to name his young'uns
like I done, for all the places he sent money from: Nebraska, Missouri,
Aloha, Maryland, Natchez, Tennessee. I reckon he's still up there in
Tennessee, settled down with that woman he took up with all them
years ago. That's what the young'uns tell me, anyhow. I don't ask. He
ain't my business no more.

I believe at this time of my life, I am done with men as far as a
personal relationship goes. I'm done with all of that. I reckon once I got
through the change, that's when it just left me, that need for a man,
and I don't miss it, not one bit. I feel like I have such a full life, and
plenty to do, plenty of people to take care of and love.

To be honest, I believe part of the reason I don't care if I ever meet
up with a man again is because these last few years I feel like I got Ed
back with me, and I wouldn't trade nothing for that. It's like I couldn't
have him while I was with Butch. I'm ashamed to admit I never did
love Butch, but I was faithful, which is more than I could say for him.
And I was so busy raising all them young'uns and making ends meet,
Ed and all that part of my life just got shut away somewhere inside of
me. And I reckon that's how it had to be or the pain of it might've
killed me, might've made me lose my mind.

But now, even with Nellie Belle and Nisco to look after, even with
my job at the plant, now I got time for Ed again, and the surprising
thing is, it don't hurt at all. It's the sweetest feeling, just looking at his
picture, remembering him, remembering myself the way I was back
then. I feel like a fool, dwelling on romance at my age, but that's truly
what we had. I know I've had a hard life and it shows, but there was
a time I could turn some heads. My hair was long and brown and
curly all down my back, and I wasn't big as nothing, but I had a good
figure on me, a woman's figure from the time I was thirteen. I got a lot
of looks, and sometimes more, from boys and men, but I never had eyes
for nobody but Ed.

He didn't know it then, but I picked him out for mine that very first day of first grade. My eyes went right to him, like I knowed him already, knowed him better than my own self. We was good friends for the longest time, and it wasn't till high school we started courting. He was a hard one to catch, but then, the good ones always are.

That's something I don't see how Idalene has done without, having somebody to love. Anybody else would've latched on to me and my young'uns, but not her, no, sir. I ain't never seen nobody so independent. If it wasn't for Nisco, I'd probably never even set foot in her house. But even Idalene can't keep that young'un out. He never met a stranger, that boy, and he loves Idalene about as good as he loves me. She'll tell him stories and sometimes there'll be something about my mama and daddy, things she remembers but I can't. I feel ashamed of myself, using Nisco that way, but it ain't hurting him, and Idalene is so durn stubborn.

Nisco's the only reason I know my mama, Dorcas, growed up in a lumber camp in the mountains somewhere, ended up there when her daddy got a job cutting timber while her mama done wash and cooking for the loggers. When she was little, Dorcas'd sing and dance around the campfire for them loggers. She'd sing them old ballads like "Lord Lovell" and "Barbara Allen," and, Lord, they eat it up. I can just picture her, a little girl with long brown hair like mine holding her skirts out and swinging back and forth, the fire casting a shadow up against the trees, all them big old men sitting around on stumps, not talking or making a sound, caught up in the sound of her sweet voice carrying through the dark night.

That's something I have got good at in my life, with the Dooleys, with Ed, with Mama—taking whatever little bits gets throwed my way and making the most I can out of them. It's like stretching a piece of meat to make more than one meal. If you ain't got much to start with, you're grateful for every little scrap and it all tastes good, even when you're down to the bone and starving for more.

13

Pansy woke to an empty house. She didn't know how she knew it, because Kitty's house was always quiet, but somehow she knew. How long since she'd been alone except to go to the bathroom or take a shower? Months, she reckoned. What had happened to her? She used to relish her time alone. Sometimes she'd send Dan to the store or to run an errand just so she could have the house to herself for an hour or two, and she'd always encouraged his Saturday morning loafing when he went to the dump, then stopped at Hardee's for breakfast with his buddies.

She pushed the covers off her legs and sat up on the couch. Kitty had opened the windows to let fresh air in, but it gave the room a chill. Pansy shivered, then stood up and wandered into the kitchen. It wasn't really cold. She'd just been still for too long. She went through the empty kitchen to the back door and looked out. At first she didn't see anything but grass and the garden, corn about a foot tall. Then she saw something move and realized it was Kitty, stooped over putting something in the ground. Dan must've come and tilled the garden for her. The soil was a rich brown color from all the years Kitty had cut the red clay with cow manure. The garden patch ran twice the length of Kitty's little house and half the width.

Pansy stepped outside into the sunlight, and it felt so good. Her toes stretched against the warm concrete of the porch and she closed her eyes, waiting for the tiredness, dreading that feeling that made standing seem like a terrible effort. But it didn't come. She took another step to the edge of the porch, then went down the steps and into the grass. It had grown deep and thick, green as summer corn. Dan would need to get over here and mow soon. Pansy looked up at the sky, electric blue, and the clouds, puffy and white. Everything was so beautiful, so alive.

Kitty looked up and saw Pansy and grinned. "Morning, glory," she said.

Pansy walked across the yard, straight into the dirt of the garden, and stood ankle deep in it, wiggling her toes so they squirmed up like worms.

Kitty was barefoot too. "Feels good, don't it?"

"Yes, ma'am, it sure does," Pansy said. Her voice seemed to have come back inside her head, like it was really her talking again. "What you planting?"

"Putting in some more collards and turnip greens. Got some more onion sets too."

"Give them to me. I'll do it."

Kitty grinned at her. "You don't never get over raising your own food, do you?"

After a few minutes of squatting to plant the onions, Pansy sat down and scooted along the row on her butt. "My legs is weak," she said.

"It ain't no wonder," Kitty said. "You been laying on that couch all this time. If you don't use something, it'll quit on you."

"That's the truth," Pansy said. She finished the row of onions, then leaned back on her hands and watched Kitty doing her row of salad greens. She did it so perfect, like a little machine—bend, poke the hole with her finger, drop the seeds, cover them up, take a step back, bend, repeat. Pansy reckoned Kitty must've been doing this from the time she was old enough to walk. It was good to wake up and see that things hadn't changed, the world was still like she left it, only spring had come.

When Kitty finished, she straightened up and bent backward to stretch out her back. "Oh, Lord," she said. "That'll put kinks in you. I'm getting too old for this." She squinted at the sun overhead, then looked at Pansy. "I believe it's getting on toward dinnertime. I'm going in the house and fix us a bite."

"All right," Pansy said. "I just want to set here in this warm sun for a minute."

"All right, honey," Kitty said.

Pansy looked up with her eyes shut, daring the white heat of the sun to blind her. God, she had missed being outside.

"Pansy?"

She didn't know how long she'd been sitting there, and Dan's voice sounded far away above her head. He looked so big and old and worried. The tiredness came back a little bit, but not as bad. "You're just in time for dinner," she said.

He held out a hand and pulled her up. "Good. I'm starving."

"Me too," Pansy said. "I feel like I ain't eat in a month."

They started across the yard, Dan looking at her sideways. She could feel him next to her, wondering, and for the first time in a long time, she didn't feel like smacking him. He said, "You act like you feel better today."

"I do feel better," Pansy said. It felt so good to say that and mean it. When they got in the kitchen, she saw a look pass between Kitty and Dan and got the feeling they were keeping a secret from her, but she didn't care enough to find out what it was. Not yet anyway. "You know what?" she said. "I think I want me a sandwich to go with that soup today."

LAUREL SAT in the car a long time, working up the nerve to go in. After Maw Bert died she thought she'd never have to come here again, never have to sit by another dying woman. Oh, God, she didn't want to go in there and see Idalene hooked up to machines, tubes running out of her arms, so doped up she might as well be dead already. But she had to go, because that's what friends did.

A few months ago she probably would've laughed to think of her and Idalene being friends. But ever since Idalene retired, she'd been going by to see her, and she and Lottie May had been trying to talk her into taking some short trips, to Grandfather Mountain or Tweetsie, maybe even up to Cherokee to gamble. They still considered Laurel the gambling expert just because she'd lived in Vegas for a while.

She'd tried to get Maxann to come with her tonight, but she had something at Charlie's school. And they'd decided not to tell her mama yet, afraid it might set her back when she'd just started acting like she felt better. Without her mama there as a buffer, she didn't know if she could've stood the stranger Maw Bert became at the end, cussing them one minute and crying for them the next.

She didn't know what she was so worried about. That couldn't have happened to Idalene, not this quickly. Laurel had just eaten supper with her and Lottie May last week and she was fine, complaining about Lottie May's cooking as usual and eating like a horse. How could the woman have stomach trouble one day and a death sentence the next?

She'd stopped at the drugstore and bought Idalene a box of chocolate-covered cherries, because she couldn't think of anything else and Idalene loved them so much. What was she thinking? Was she going to walk in there and say, *Hey, Idalene, sorry to hear you're dying. Have some candy.*

Okay, Laurel, she thought. Get a hold of yourself. Just get out of the car and walk in there and be a grown-up and deal with it.

If Idalene had to be in a nursing home, this was probably the cream of the crop, at least on the outside. The two-story brick building sat next to a patch of piney woods and was surrounded by dogwoods that in the spring looked like a layer of snow suspended in midair. This time of year, however, everything was green, but it all looked black in the yellow light of the parking lot.

The front door swung wide before she reached it, and a tall, skinny old man, his thick silver hair standing straight up, held it open for her.

"Good evening," he said in a hushed voice. After she got through the door, he said, "If you'll tell me the name of your beloved I'll be glad to escort you," and held out his arm.

Laurel stared at the long arm, the sleeve of his black pinstripe suit hanging from it like a curtain. Her beloved? The man kept his elbow in the air, so she took it and said, "I'm here to see Idalene Stevens."

"Oh," he said, looking a little uneasy. "Miss Stevens is in the corner room. Right this way."

The old man's long legs could've carried him down the hall a lot faster, but he kept his steps small and slow. Laurel was short but not that short. She tried to speed things up a little, then felt guilty for dragging him and slowed down. He had to be at least eighty, and she couldn't remember ever seeing anybody so skinny—not skinny enough to look sick, just one of those gangly types with more arms and legs than he knew what to do with, like a giant insect. She studied the enormous hand at the end of the arm she held, surprised to see that the nails were manicured. Not what she'd expect from a man who looked like he'd be more comfortable in a pair of overalls.

As they moved down the hall Laurel glanced into the rooms with open doors, looking quickly away if the occupant caught her staring. The sight of those people propped up in hospital beds, TVs blaring and dinner trays across their laps, brought back too many bad memories of Maw Bert's last years. She'd died upstairs in the critical-care unit but spent the previous two years down here. Laurel hated for anybody to end up in a place like this.

The old man stopped in front of a closed door. "Here we are, ma'am," he said, but was nearly drowned out by a loud, cackling laugh from the other side of the door. Laurel glanced at the old man's face and saw a look of absolute panic.

"Excuse me, miss," he said. "This is as far as I go."

"Thank you," Laurel said, and watched him take off down the hall, eating up the distance with his long legs. The laughter had stopped and she knocked on the door.

"Come in if you have to," Idalene hollered.

Laurel opened the door and her mouth almost dropped open. Joe Clark sat at the foot of Idalene's bed with her feet in his lap. In the dim light they looked like a scene from some exotic fairy tale, a courtesan in pink nylon and curlers and her eunuch in gray unform with a gun on his hip. She was even more surprised to find herself feeling a little jealous.

"Hey, stranger," Idalene said, lifting her head off the pillow to wave in the direction of a chair by the bed. "Sit down and take a load off."

She didn't look as bad as Laurel had thought somebody dying of stomach cancer would look. Thank God. She took a seat and glanced over at Joe.

"Hey," he said, not a bit embarrassed to be holding an old lady's feet in his lap, his big hands wrapped around them like he was operating a crane.

"Y'all know each other, don't you?" Idalene said.

"Oh, yeah," Laurel said. "Joe's my bodyguard." It made her smile to watch him turn red. Somehow or other, every time she went to the library to get out of the house for a while, Joe was there too, and he always seemed to be leaving at the same time she was and always insisted on walking her to her car.

"Uh-huh," Idalene said, leaning back in her bed with a satisfied look on her face. "Did Pepper bring you down?"

"Pepper?" Laurel said. Idalene must've meant the old man who'd led her down the hall. "Yeah. When he heard you laugh, he looked like he'd seen a ghost and took off."

For some reason that tickled Idalene and Joe something fierce, and Laurel just looked from one to the other, waiting for them to quit laughing.

"Oh, Lord," Idalene said. "You know Washington's Funeral Home? Well, he used to work there, and one of his jobs was opening the door and escorting people to whichever room their visitation was in."

"Oh," Laurel said. "That's why he called you my beloved."

"He thinks we're supposed to be dead. First time Lottie May come out here, I was asleep and he brung her up to the bed and stood there with her for a minute. He says, 'Don't she look good? So peaceful.' About that time I woke up. I said, 'Dammit, Pepper, I ain't dead yet and I wish you'd quit rushing me.' Poor old soul. He ain't right. Ain't been back inside this room since. Which is probably a blessing, because they say he's bad to walk off with things that don't belong to him. I reckon he thinks we don't need them no more since we're dead."

Laurel had no clue what to say to that, so she shook her head and smiled. Joe picked up one of Idalene's feet and went to work with toenail clippers, the nails so yellow and thick he had to practically saw through them with the clippers. When they finally did snap free, they flew off in all directions and Laurel prayed none would land on her.

"It's a pretty sad state when you get to where you can't even cut your own toenails," Idalene said.

"You wouldn't deny me the pleasure, would you?" Joe said.

Idalene cackled again. Good answer, Laurel thought.

"You look good," Laurel said. "How are you feeling?"

"Oh, I feel all right, I reckon. They got me on this painkiller where I just push a little button whenever I need some and it shoots right in my veins." She held her arm out so Laurel could see where the needle was taped down. "I go as long as I can stand without it, though. Don't want to get addicted."

Laurel and Joe exchanged looks, thinking the same thing, and Laurel wanted to cry. Why hadn't Idalene gone to the damn doctor when she first started feeling bad?

"All done," Joe said. He put the clippers in his shirt pocket. "If you're wanting these polished, you better get Laurel to do that."

Idalene held up her feet and studied her toes, wiggling them back and forth. "No," she said. "Men don't like painted toenails, do they, Joe?"

Joe stood up and brushed some clinging toenails off his pants. "I don't notice paint much," he said. "What bothers me is when the toenails get too long and claw your legs. Anyway, you'll have to ask your visitor when I bring him tomorrow."

Good grief, Laurel thought. I can't believe we're having a conversation about women's toenails. And she wondered exactly whose toenails he'd been referring to. Not that it was any of her business. She'd just thought a man who spent his free time in a library wouldn't be having any problems with women's toenails.

"Tomorrow," Idalene said, nodding, and a look passed between her and Joe that Laurel didn't understand.

He pulled the sheet and blanket over Idalene's feet and let his hand rest there. "I'm going to take off now. You holler if you need anything, okay?"

"I will."

"Laurel," Joe said, nodding to her. He paused at the door and looked back. "Whatever you do, don't let her talk you into rubbing lotion on her feet. You'll be here all night."

After he left, Idalene sighed. "That boy," she said.

"How do you know Joe?"

"Oh, me and a friend of mine used to go hear his band play all the time."

Joe was in a band? She couldn't picture that. "What kind of band?"

"Bluegrass, honey, the only kind they is. That boy can pick a banjo like the devil. You ought to go see him sometime. They play out at the Ponderosa near about every Tuesday and Saturday night. Course, I only went on Tuesdays 'cause that's bluegrass night. Saturdays they play country so folks can dance."

The Ponderosa. That was the club Maxann mentioned whenever she tried to talk Laurel into going dancing with her. When she'd still been dating Hap, she'd never even considered going with Maxann, but now that she'd cooled that relationship, maybe she should reconsider. Just because she wasn't interested in dating didn't mean she couldn't dance. And the closer Charlie's graduation got, the more depressed Maxann acted, not talking and cutting up like her usual self, not even picking on Percilla as much. Laurel figured it would do them both good to get out and let their hair down.

"Well, I hope Joe didn't leave on my account," Laurel said.

"No, no. He don't never stay too long. We'll set here and watch *Andy Griffith* and laugh while I eat my supper. Have you ever seen the one where Opie knocks his baseball in the haunted house and Barney and Andy have to go after it? That's the one we seen today. I declare, I love that Barney Fife. He don't have to say a word to make me laugh, just makes them rubber faces." Idalene pushed a button to raise the head of her bed higher. "What you got in that poke?" she said, pointing to the bag in Laurel's lap.

"Oh, I forgot. I got you a little something. Lottie May said you didn't want flowers."

"No, ma'am. I don't want to sit in here watching nothing else die." Idalene pulled the bag open and peered in, then stuck her hand in and pulled out the box of chocolate-covered cherries. "Well, thank you, honey. I love these things." She set the box on the bedside table.

"You're welcome," Laurel said, feeling bad that she hadn't been able to come up with something better than candy. Idalene had turned her attention back to the TV, where another *Andy Griffith* was coming on, and Laurel couldn't think of anything to break the silence. How could she make small talk when Idalene was dying?

A commercial came on and Idalene picked up the remote and clicked the TV off, the silence becoming even louder. "I don't like the color episodes," she said. "Things went downhill after the black-and-white." She leaned her head back on the pillow, staring off into a corner of the room as if a black-and-white Andy Griffith had appeared over there. She shifted in the bed, tensed and groaned, then waved Laurel back in her chair. "It's all right. Just time for me to push my little button is all."

As the painkiller pumped into her arm, Idalene's body relaxed visibly, even though Laurel imagined that she couldn't possibly be feeling the effects of the morphine that quickly, could she? Maybe just knowing relief was on the way was enough to make the pain bearable, knowing the suffering would end.

Idalene turned on her side, her face relaxed. "When I'm dead," she said, "I don't want to be buried. I know I'll be dead and won't know nothing, but I can't stand to think of being under the ground in a box. If they buried you natural so everything would fall apart quick, I wouldn't mind so much, but nowadays they pump you full of chemicals and seal you up so you'll be there forever. Don't that just make your skin crawl?"

Laurel shook her head, her mouth drawing down into a grimace. "I haven't ever thought about it," she said. Just talking about it now makes my skin crawl, she wanted to say.

"Well, you're young yet. But I'm telling everybody so there's no question. I want to be cremated. I've done paid for it and all."

Why are you telling me this? Laurel thought, hoping she didn't look as uncomfortable as she felt.

Idalene yawned, showing black holes in the back where teeth used to be. "Oh, I'm getting sleepy. I sure could've used some of this stuff back when I was working and couldn't sleep because my legs hurt so bad." Her arm flopped toward Laurel and she wiggled her fingers. "You stick to your desk job, honey. Don't never go out on that old cement floor and kill your poor legs."

Laurel wondered if Idalene had meant to hold her hand. She hesitated, then hooked her fingers over Idalene's and squeezed. "I won't," she said, knowing that was one promise she could keep.

Idalene squeezed back, closed her eyes, and Laurel thought she'd fallen asleep until she said, "It sure did feel good having a man's hands on me again. Even if it was only my feet." Her eyes opened and stared into Laurel's, but she seemed to be looking long and deep into something beyond Laurel. "I surely have missed that ever since Mr. Arthur got too old and sick. It was my only comfort."

Her eyes closed again, and Laurel sat quietly until Idalene's breathing became regular and even. She wondered who this Mr. Arthur could be. As far as she knew, Idalene had never married and she'd never mentioned a boyfriend. *Boyfriend* seemed like the wrong word to use for somebody that age. But if he'd had his hands on her he must've been more than a friend.

Awake, Idalene's face was always moving, talking, scowling, laughing, and she hardly looked sick at all. But asleep it went slack and Laurel saw the hollow cheeks, the sagging skin, the dark bags under her eyes. Though she'd always looked a good bit younger than her years, now it appeared that age had caught up with and then passed her. Even her body seemed to have shrunk, and she lay curled into herself the way a fern curled up its leaves at night.

Laurel had trouble reconciling this person with the picture in her mind of the strong, healthy woman standing in the middle of the winding-room floor, laughing at a good joke or cussing a machine. It was so hard to watch somebody go down like this. It made it hard to remember them the way you wanted to after they were gone. She hated seeing Idalene weak and helpless, just as she'd hated seeing her Maw Bert that way. It shook the whole foundation of her world, seeing somebody she counted on to always be strong reduced to a shriveled shadow of themselves. How was she supposed to go on in the face of that? Where did all that strength go? Where was she supposed to get hers from now?

Idalene started breathing heavily through her mouth and Laurel figured it was safe to leave. She eased the door shut behind her and leaned against it, closing her eyes against the fluorescent lighting. Why did they have to use that kind of light, anyway? It made everybody look bad, and the light was cold and indifferent and that was the last thing you needed more of in a place like this. Laurel wanted to find some rocks and chunk them at the ceiling until all those long white bulbs were smashed and the only light came from the exit signs over the doors at either end of the hall.

She saw Pepper making his slow way down the hall toward her. He must give return service as well. Laurel pushed away from the door, thinking she'd meet him halfway, then let herself fall back against the door again. His job seemed so important to him, better that she let him do it. Besides, it'd do him good to face his fear and come on down here to death's door.

Idalene

I hate for Mr. Arthur to see me in this nursing home, but I can't stand not to see him again, and Joe don't mind bringing him. Mr. Arthur, he won't ask that daughter of his, because he'd have to tell where he was going and why, and he won't do that. He's too proud to be explaining himself to anybody. Which I reckon is one of the things I like about him. He keeps himself to himself. It's a wonder we even got together, the way we are, so independent, and fierce about it too. And the fact we have kept it to ourselves for so long is a miracle, really, especially seeing as how we've knowed each other just about our whole lives, growed up together. But he married young and it wasn't till after his wife died that we got together.

When we started working at the plant, we was just young'uns and our families couldn't afford for us to go to school and not bring in that paycheck ever week. My cousin, the one I lived with after Mama died and I run off from the orphanage, he said school wasn't nothing but a waste of time nohow. Said it didn't matter what I put in my brain because it was my hands I'd be using to make my way in the world. He was right too. Him and his wife wasn't much on hugging and kissing young'uns, but they did give me something I could use for the rest of my life, which was common sense. Look at things the way they are and not the way you wish they was and you'll get along all right.

That has stood me in good stead over the years. I've many a time tried to drill it into Lottie May's thick head, but she was born a dreamer just like Mama and always will be one, I expect. I can't even wrap my mind around us two coming from the same mama. Maybe if Lottie May had growed up the way I did, she wouldn't have turned out so dreamy and impractical. Marrying that no-account Ed Gamble, then that even more no-account Butch Holt, she just set herself up for disappointment. I learned early on from the bad example of Mama's life. Do not get married and do not have children. Once you do that, your life ain't your own no more and you're just at the mercy of all these other people.

Of course, the romance of it is awful hard to resist when you're young, the beguilement of love and marriage and babies and all that. But I was strong, that's one thing I did get from Mama, and as I got older I come to see I was right. It ain't romance a body needs in this life. It's companionship. And that's what I have had with Mr. Arthur all these years. We been good companions and have took care of each other in all the ways a man and a woman do, and I mean all the ways. He wanted to get married at first and give me a terrible time about it for several years, even though he couldn't stay mad and always come back to me. I think he'd marry me this minute if I said yes, but he takes me the way I am. I ain't never even used his Christian name outside of my bedroom. Somehow that was the only place it seemed right, the place where we was as close to married as we ever got.

We kept each other from being lonely and didn't need to be married or live in the same house to do it. I almost feel bad having kept it a secret, because if more women knowed how nice it can be like this, they might give it a try themselves and be a lot happier. I know folks see me alone, no young'uns to look after me in my old age, and feel sorry for me. Well, the hell with that. I'm not lonely and I don't need nobody to take care of me. I have provided for myself just fine, with Mr. Arthur filling in the gaps.

He's going to have a hard time when I'm gone, and I don't know how in the world to get him ready for it. His daughter takes care of him, food and clothes and medicine and all, but she don't talk to him or touch him. He's so alone there in that house with his own family, it breaks my heart. The only thing makes me feel less bad is knowing he won't suffer long. His time's a-coming too and then, with any luck, if there is a heaven like Lottie May says, there'll be a mill hill there too and we'll move in our little houses and take up right where we left off. I can't think of no heaven better than that.

14

"WELCOME TO THE SMOKE PIT," MAXANN SAID AS SHE led Laurel through a huge doorway and out onto a loading dock. She went down a short flight of brick steps and sat near the bottom, then looked up at Laurel. "Well, come on, take a load off."

Laurel moved carefully down the steep steps toward Maxann. A breeze lifted her hair and the cool air and the quiet washed over her like a balm. She sat down with a sigh and watched Maxann light up a Marlboro.

"We're early," Maxann said, then drew so hard on the cigarette that her cheeks sucked in. She blew smoke out away from Laurel. "In a few minutes there'll be fifteen people out here and this whole thing'll be full of smoke. It'll look like one of them hollers up in the mountains where my mama come from, all full up with mist on a cool morning."

Laurel leaned her elbows on the step behind her and sat back to look at the rectangle of blue sky above them. Who knew it was such a beautiful day? In the office the closest she got to natural light was passing the window on the way to the bathroom.

"Well," Maxann said, and leaned back against the steps next to Laurel. "Charlie's going to be graduating from high school in about six more hours."

"That's right," Laurel said. "Are you excited?"

"I reckon. You know what pisses me off, though? His sorry daddy says he can't come. Says he's got to drive a truck to New Jersey tonight and can't come to his own son's graduation. That son of a bitch has known about it for a year. You'd think he could take one day off work. But that's typical of Bruce."

"What did Charlie say?"

"Oh, he acted like he didn't care, but I know his feelings is hurt. Sometimes I wonder how he turned out as good as he did."

"You might've had a little something to do with it," Laurel said, hoping to get a smile out of Maxann. But it didn't work.

Maxann threw her butt on the ground and mashed it. "We better get back to work."

Three women Laurel recognized from quality control came out on the platform above them and lit up, blowing smoke in the other direction as Laurel and Maxann passed.

"Listen," Laurel said before they went in. "Charlie's leaving for the beach in the morning, right?"

"Yeah."

"Why don't we go out tomorrow night, then? You don't have a date, do you?"

"No, and thanks for the reminder."

"Well, you keep threatening to take me to the Ponderosa and I figure it's time to bite the bullet. Besides, Linda wants me to find the band for the Labor Day picnic, and I've been thinking about hiring Flint Hill." She didn't bother to mention that she'd also been thinking about Joe Clark ever since that night at the nursing home.

"All this time I been begging you to go and you decide now is the time?"

"What can I say? I've been busy."

Maxann stared at her hard. "I don't need no pity date," she said, then nodded. "All right, then. You be at my house at seven o'clock tomorrow night, and bring your dancing boots."

WHEN SHE got out of the car, Laurel stood there thinking this was the last place two women should go alone on a dark night. Maxann had just driven them halfway across the county, down a long and winding country road, past farms and woods and more farms to get to this? A barn with a porch? A set of wide, shallow wooden steps led up to two huge doors with black iron handles. Laurel wouldn't even have known it was the Ponderosa if Maxann hadn't told her. There were no signs, neon or otherwise. The only advertisement was word of mouth and, of course, the music. Though the sound was somewhat muted, absorbed by the walls, the building seemed to pulse with a beat and the bass throbbed through the air. There were no windows, but Laurel didn't need to see inside to know that a lot of people were in there making a racket almost but not quite loud enough to drown out the sound of crickets.

"Hot damn, listen to that!" Maxann did a little clog dance right there in the parking lot, her red cowboy boots kicking up gravel. "Come on, I'm feeling lucky tonight." She stopped and looked back at Laurel. "Well? I can see the grass growing under your feet. Let's go."

Laurel realized there was no way she'd get Maxann to leave now. She'd have to call a taxi to get home. They probably didn't even run taxis out this far. Good God, what was she thinking, letting herself be dragged out to a place like this? A bunch of drunken rednecks line dancing to country music. Then she remembered it was her idea. She must've been nuts.

Maxann, decked out in skintight Levi's and a red halter top, marched over like a country drum major and took hold of Laurel's arm. Laurel could smell the cigarette smoke and the Jontue. "Laurel, honey," Maxann said softly, as if she were talking to a panicked horse. "How long was you and that boy married?"

"Almost fifteen years."

"Lord God. No wonder you don't know what to do. Well, you just follow me and it'll come back to you. Before you know it, you'll be beating them off with a stick." Maxann grabbed her hand and dragged her across the parking lot and onto the porch. Two men in jeans and boots and cowboy shirts, both middle-aged and balding and obviously plastered, blew out on a wave of music just then, almost knocking them over. They looked Laurel and Maxann up and down, apologized, held the door open so they could enter, and followed them back in.

Maxann flipped her hair over one shoulder and smiled at the men, then elbowed Laurel and started laughing and snapping her fingers in time to the music.

Oh, great, Laurel thought, and wondered who she'd be lucky enough to end up with, Abbott or Costello.

They went to the bar and ordered drinks, a beer for Laurel and a whiskey sour for Maxann, who tossed it down and then quickly got rid of Abbott and Costello by dragging Laurel down the bar to sit near two guys she recognized from the plant. Laurel remembered seeing them but couldn't remember their names.

"Laurel, this is Bobby and Woofer."

"Yeah, you work in the dye house, right?" she said. Shaking hands didn't seem to be appropriate in this setting, so she held on to her beer.

They nodded and then all of them turned to look at the dance floor. It was too loud to make conversation, anyway. Laurel didn't know country music, but the band seemed pretty good. They sounded real country, the old honky-tonk stuff her daddy loved. The room made her think of the words to one of his favorite songs: *Dim lights, thick smoke, and loud, loud music.* The dance floor was crowded with couples dancing, laughing, hollering back and forth to each other. The layer of smoke hanging just below the low ceiling seeped down into Laurel's hair and clothes, and she knew she'd have to shower before she went to bed.

When the band started a new song, Maxann hollered and jumped off her stool, grabbed Bobby's hand, and pulled him onto the dance floor with her. Woofer looked Laurel up and down, then turned his shoulder to her and scanned the room. That's all right, Woofer, Laurel thought. I don't want to dance with you either, buddy. And what the hell kind of name is Woofer, anyway?

The song was a fast one, and Maxann and Bobby two-stepped around the dance floor like they'd been dancing together for years. Laurel had to admit it looked like fun. Maybe she'd take some classes, then come back and give it a shot. The older couples looked so cute together, a lot of them wearing matching shirts and hats. This was it for them, the big night out. A couple of beers, some dancing, then home in time to get a good night's sleep before church in the morning. There were people about her own age out there too, some couples all over each other and in serious need of a motel room, some looking bored and eyeballing other partners across the floor. Laurel drained her beer and ordered another. If she had to get drunk to make it through this night, then so be it.

By Laurel's third beer, Woofer had abandoned her altogether and she got tired of trying to look happy sitting there alone. She noticed people standing near the stage, watching the band, and circled the dance floor to join them, thinking she might not feel so conspicuous that way. As she got closer, she recognized the bass player, Bushy Cook. He caught her eye and winked, then nodded to his right. There was Rusty something-or-other, also from the plant, on pedal steel. And Joe Clark, playing lead guitar. The whole band except Joe must work at the plant, so it seemed only right that she should hire them for the picnic.

Joe looked up and saw her but didn't nod or smile. Did he always have that serious look on his face, that wounded squint? Maybe he was too focused on his playing. Or maybe he thought he had to make himself look tough to override the cupid's bow mouth and the dimple in his chin.

They finished the instrumental and immediately cranked up another song, a slow ballad. Judging by the noise level, Laurel got the impression this crowd would get rowdy if the music ever stopped. Music to soothe the working man and woman. Joe leaned into the mike and sang, his voice a rich baritone. "*Crazy arms that long to hold somebody new.*" He sang with his eyes closed, and Laurel felt free to stare, couldn't seem to stop, as a matter of fact, and jumped when she felt a hand on her shoulder.

Maxann yelled in her ear, "Why ain't you dancing?"

Laurel shrugged and smiled and yelled back, "Nobody asked."

"Hell, if you wait to be asked you'll never dance." Maxann grabbed Bobby's hand and pulled him forward. "Here, dance with Bobby. I'll go find me somebody else." She flipped her hair and smiled at Bobby, then disappeared into the crowd.

"Listen," Laurel said. "I don't really know how to do this. Don't feel obligated."

"Oh, hell, don't worry about it," Bobby said. "I can show you."

She looked around for a place to set her beer.

"Bring it," Bobby said, grabbing her free hand. He was already clogging a little bit, itching to get back on the floor. It felt weird to have a strange man's hand on her neck, but everybody else danced that way, a modified version of a waltz being the closest comparison she could come up with. She didn't know people had gone back to touching while they danced. Last time she'd gone dancing was in college, and back then you didn't touch the guy until after the dancing.

With the slow song and a good partner, she picked up the shuffling step, keeping her eyes on her feet to make sure she did it right and didn't step on Bobby's toes. Between songs she finished her beer and got rid of the bottle. The next song was faster, but the step was the same and Laurel was able to quit watching her feet. When her eyes met Bobby's, he grinned and spun her around. It felt like being on a ride at the fair, swinging out into space and back again, his hand at the back of her neck keeping her from flying off, and the freedom of it made her laugh. She quit worrying about looking stupid and just danced.

Later, when they turned on the canned music so the band could take a break, she and Maxann found a small table against the wall and Maxann immediately propped her feet on a chair. "Lord, my dogs is barking," she said, and started to say something else but her mouth just hung open as she stared toward the tables on the other side of the dance floor. Laurel looked too, but she didn't see anybody familiar, nobody except Grady with a woman she didn't recognize. The woman, probably in her late forties, had on a long, slim jeans skirt and white blouse, and her silver pageboy swung against her cheeks when she threw her head back to laugh at something Grady said. Grady turned then and saw Laurel and waved and Laurel waved back; then she saw his eyes go to Maxann. His smile disappeared and he nodded once, then turned back to his lady friend. Maxann's boots hit the floor and she turned to the table and emptied her glass in one deep swallow. "I'm going to get me another drink." She swayed a little when she stood up. "You want one?"

Laurel shook her head and held up her half-full beer. Maxann turned and pushed her way through the crowd on the floor. Laurel couldn't believe all this time she'd never noticed Maxann and Grady had the hots for each other. Her mama had said something to that effect a long time ago, but Laurel hadn't thought about it since. Just keep on going, she thought as she watched Maxann sashay by Grady's table on the way to the bar. Don't stop and let him see you're jealous. Make him wonder.

After Maxann passed him without speaking, Grady said something to the woman and stood up. He took a quick look at Maxann at the bar, then headed toward Laurel. Oh, Lord, she thought, this ought to be interesting, wondering if he'd be able to make his getaway before Maxann got back.

"Hey there, young lady," he said. Laurel had never seen him out of his usual uniform of navy cotton-blend pants and golf shirt. He looked good in his jeans and white button-down. Suddenly she could imagine him as a younger man, a slim, baby-faced farm boy shirtless on a tractor in the middle of a cornfield. Maxann must be crazy, not pouncing on him when she had the chance.

"Hey, Grady," she said, a little embarrassed by the picture she'd just conjured in her mind.

"I just wanted to ask how your mama's doing."

"She's doing better, thanks. Today's the first day she stayed home by herself for a little while." Another reason Laurel had been glad to get out of the house, to give her mama and daddy some time alone together.

"Well, that's good. I'm glad to hear it. We sure do miss her." He looked behind him, then at the chair Maxann's feet had been on. "Can I sit a minute?"

"Sure."

He sat on the edge of the chair, looking determined, though his cheeks flushed red when he saw Maxann coming back toward the table. Laurel figured he must've decided to bring Muhammad to the mountain.

Maxann stopped and gave him a quick look before turning to Laurel. "If I'd known you was giving seats away to any fool that walked by, I would've made you go get the drinks." She slid past Grady and into her chair.

"Maxann," Grady said. Their eyes met and they stared for a long time. Maxann turned away first, her face pale, and took a sip of her drink. Grady seemed to relax then, as if getting the initial contact over with had been the hardest part.

Even with the loud music and people talking and hollering all around, it seemed very quiet at their table. Finally Laurel couldn't stand it anymore. She leaned across the table so Grady could hear her. "I love your house," she said. "Maxann pointed it out to me on the way over here."

Maxann had not only pointed out the two-story white farmhouse but had even pulled into the circular driveway to show Laurel what she called his yard art. "He ain't home," Maxann said. "And even if he was, he wouldn't care." They'd wandered around the yard and Maxann had showed her an old claw-footed bathtub full of purple and white petunias, two bedpans with hens and chicks, a full-size, rusted-iron bed frame surrounding several tomato plants. The main attraction, though, was a row of old work boots—laces missing, tops flapped open, round toes pointing out—that lined the sidewalk leading up to the front porch. Bright orange and yellow marigolds grew out of each one. "Ain't that the tackiest thing you ever seen," Maxann said, laughing in a way that let Laurel know she thought it was actually wonderful.

They even went up and sat in the two wooden rockers on the front porch, enjoying the last of the evening light, and Laurel couldn't understand why Maxann looked so at home there. "I get the feeling you've done this before," she said.

Maxann sighed, her eyes closed as she rocked. "Grady's been real good to my boys, used to take them hunting, do man kind of stuff with them, you know. Sometimes I'd sit out here, waiting on them."

Laurel had been dying to ask why she didn't let Grady do man kind of stuff with her, since they were both available and obviously had a lot in common and lived right down the road from each other and worked together. But then she thought that might be the reason right there, familiarity breeding contempt, or at least indifference.

But now she could see it was anything but indifference. These two were crazy about each other and for some reason neither one would give in to it, and she didn't know either one well enough to figure out why.

"Well." Grady stood up and leaned toward Laurel. "I reckon I better get on back. Tell your mama we been thinking about her."

She nodded. Maxann didn't look up from her drink until he'd gone, then she watched until he reached the other woman. "Son of a bitch," she said, quietly the first time, louder the second.

"Maxann!" Laurel looked around to see if anyone had heard, but the music was so loud, it was a wonder she'd heard it herself.

Maxann finished her drink, staring at the dancers as they stomped and spun past the table. "Goddamn son of a bitch!" She got up and headed for the bar again, not bothering to ask if Laurel wanted a refill this time. She came back with two drinks and polished them both off in about five minutes.

"Maxann, you might want to give it a rest," Laurel said. "I don't think I'm strong enough to carry you out of here."

"No problem." Maxann turned her purse upside down on the table and everything spilled out, including the car keys, which she slid across the table toward Laurel. "Just come back and get me in the morning. And bring coffee."

Laurel didn't know how to drive a straight drive, and didn't need to try after the beers she'd had, but she put the keys in her pocket anyway. She didn't want Maxann getting behind the wheel either. "Maxann," she said, watching as she gathered the other stuff that had fallen out of the purse and put it back, "I am not leaving you."

Two hours later she was about ready to change her mind. She'd had a couple more beers to keep Maxann company, then cut herself off when she realized Maxann had no intention of winding things up. The band was still playing, but it was almost one in the morning and a lot of people, including Grady and his lady friend, had gone home, or somewhere besides here. The few couples left on the dance floor seemed to be holding each other up as they swayed to the music, and a couple of loud guys, including Bobby and Woofer, still hung out at the bar. Laurel realized she should've figured out how they'd get home before she had those last beers. She felt too fuzzy and relaxed to figure it out now.

"I'll tell you a secret," Maxann said. Her eyes had that dead look, like she'd gone on automatic pilot while the rest of her slept somewhere deep inside her head, just waiting for her body to follow.

"Listen!" She slurped her drink, sloshing some over the side of the glass, then wiped her hands on her jeans. "Listen," she said.

"What?" Laurel wanted to take a tissue and reach over and wipe the mascara from under Maxann's eyes, the way her mama used to lick a tissue and wipe dirt off her face when she was a kid. She didn't think Maxann would appreciate it, though, or even allow it.

"Did you hear what I said?"

"Yes, you've got a secret. What is it?"

Maxann leaned closer and cupped Laurel's face in her hands and squeezed her cheeks. "Look at you." She shook Laurel's face back and forth. "You're cute as a button, ain't you? I used to be cute like you. I used to could get any man I wanted."

Laurel pulled her face loose and leaned back from Maxann's whiskey-sour breath. "Maxann. You still can. There's men here that'd give money just to drink your bathwater."

"Oh, yeah, I know. But that ain't enough for some men. Oh, no, not for Mr. High and Mighty Grady Valentine."

Laurel decided listening to Maxann rant and rave all night had earned her the right to a little nosiness. "Did you and Grady used to go out?"

"Go out? Honey, the only going out that man does is with his trac-tor. He comes home from the plant and works till it gets dark and then eats his corn bread and milk and goes to bed. And he wants me to do the same, spend the rest of my life sitting on that damn porch talking about work and dirt and what we're having for supper."

So it had gone beyond going out. He'd asked her to live with him, maybe even marry him. "Well, you sure did seem to enjoy rocking on that porch when we stopped by there tonight."

Maxann gave a little burp, then muttered, "Shut up, smart-ass."

Laurel sighed. "Okay, then, what's this big secret you were going to tell me? And I hope it's not that you're crazy about Grady, because that was obvious the minute y'all looked at each other." She giggled. "Across a crowded room. All right, all right, I'll shut up."

"I don't think I should tell you my secret now." Maxann put her head down on her arms, and Laurel wondered if she was crying or maybe passed out.

"Maxann?"

Her head jerked up. "All right, fine, I'll tell you. But you got to promise to keep it to yourself."

"I promise."

"Well, what you and Grady and the rest of this bunch don't know is that I am"—she hiccuped, then leaned closer and whispered—"a witch." She laughed and slapped the table so hard her drink sloshed over again. "That's right. That's my secret. What do you think of that? Guess I ain't just some old rip you feel sorry for now, am I? Guess you ought to have a little more respect for old Maxann now, don't you?"

Maxann's head fell forward onto her arms again, and this time Laurel was pretty sure she'd passed out. Just to be sure, she put a hand on Maxann's head and rolled it to the side. Yep, eyes closed, mouth open, snoring slightly. Great. She pushed Maxann's drink to the other side of the table so it wouldn't get knocked over if she woke up thrashing, then leaned back in her chair. Jesus H. Christ on a cracker. How in hell did she end up here in Redneck-a-lina with Maxann the middle-aged witch drunk as a skunk, and herself not far behind?

The band stopped playing then and they announced last call at the bar since the club would be closing at one o'clock. Oh, great, Laurel thought, wondering if she could sober up and teach herself to drive a stick shift in fifteen minutes. She glanced around the room, looking for a familiar face, and saw Joe Clark, hatless at last, packing up his guitar onstage. What the hell? He was a cop. It was his duty to serve the public, and if she wasn't the public, she didn't know who was. She looked back at Maxann to make sure she was still asleep, then got up and went over to the stage.

"Hey, you," she said, hoping it sounded flirtatious and not just drunk.

Joe straightened and stared down at her. He looked like a giant up on that stage. "Hey," he said.

"Listen." She took a deep breath. "Listen, we need a ride." She turned and pointed at Maxann. "I can't drive a stick, and plus I'm just a little bitty bit drunk. Could you give us a ride?" She smiled up at him. "Please?" How could any man resist that?

His mouth twitched as he glanced from her to Maxann. When he squatted down and stared at her, she had to take a step back. The giant's pretty face had got close and made her a little dizzy.

He smiled and said, "Just let me finish packing up, okay?"

It took both of them, one on either side, to half drag, half carry Maxann to the car. She didn't wake up even when they banged her head against the door loading her in the backseat. Once they got her in, Joe opened the passenger-side door for Laurel and she slid in, embarrassed about the way she'd tried to entice him into driving them home, embarrassed that he knew she was in no condition to drive, embarrassed that she had got herself into this position. As he slid behind the steering wheel and started the car, she put a hand on his arm. "Thank you for doing this. I know it's a pain in the butt."

He looked at her briefly, that worried squint still on his face. Was it all black and white with him, either serious or goofy? She wished he'd smile or do something to help her feel less like a pathetic drunk. "I'm glad to do it," he said. Then he did smile, just a quick flash before he turned his attention back to driving.

Laurel leaned back in the seat and closed her eyes. She felt tired but good. Satisfied, that was it, she felt satisfied after a night of dancing, drinking, laughing, and people-watching, and now here she was being escorted home by a big strong policeman. A nearly perfect evening. The only thing missing was the anticipation of what might happen at the end of the drive home. But that would be wrong, so wrong. They were library buddies. He was her bodyguard, walking her to the car, chatting for a few minutes. She didn't want to ruin it.

Then again, maybe he thought she was off-limits. He'd seen her out with Hap a couple of times when they stopped in at the café and he was there at the counter, eating a burger and reading a book. But first she had to figure out why she was even thinking about this. Was she interested in Joe? When she'd just ended one ill-conceived relationship? Trouble was, Hap had gotten on her nerves, expecting her to drop whatever she had planned, which admittedly wasn't much, maybe a movie with Maxann or supper at Cecil and Lisa's. She'd been content with one date a week, and sometimes even that felt like too much. He'd become so needy, calling nearly every night. Scott had been the same way when they dated in college, always wanting to know where she was and what she was doing, showing up unexpectedly on nights she just wanted to sit home in her nightgown looking awful and watching TV. It had bugged the shit out of her, but then he asked her to marry him and she forgot to be irritated. It had taken Hap to make her realize that she'd been irritated a lot during the last fifteen years, and she'd be damned if she'd let another man do that to her now.

But Joe didn't irritate her. He didn't talk all the time. Like now, they were riding in complete silence, no talking, no radio, and it was comfortable. She didn't feel like she had to fill up the silence. She could just enjoy it. Something else was going on tonight, though, something she hadn't counted on. She wanted to touch him, wanted to scoot over next to his warm body and lay her head against his arm and put her hand on his thigh, feeling the muscles flex as he pressed the accelerator.

Her eyes flew open and she checked to make sure her hands were still in her lap and hadn't strayed across the seat. Oh, God, she thought. This is terrible. I'm sitting here thinking of repaying his kindness with a roll in the hay, or a roll in the backseat once they got Maxann out. Oh, God.

Laurel said, thank you, thank you, in her head when they pulled into Maxann's driveway a few minutes later. She was almost safe from making a fool of herself. But then he cut the engine, cut the lights, and rolled the window down. They sat there, not talking for a minute, and Laurel started to relax again. He hadn't leapt from the car to escape her, so maybe she hadn't disgusted him completely.

"Listen to that," Joe said, and Laurel rolled her window down too. Every now and then the deep booming of a bullfrog cut across the wall of sound created by thousands, millions of crickets singing in the darkness. Maxann had left the porch light on, and when Joe shifted so that he faced her at an angle, Laurel could see his smile, the dimple in his chin.

"I love a night like this," he said softly. "My grandpa used to take me out frog-gigging at night, and sometimes we wouldn't even look for frogs. We'd just let the boat drift and sit there and listen."

That was all it took, him sitting there so sweet and serious. Against her will, it seemed, every single molecule in her body was pulled toward him, like straight pins to a magnet, their collective force so

strong she lost control of her own body. She could only watch helplessly as her hand lifted, the fingers touching his cheek, his chin, his
lips. Then the hand cupped his warm neck and pulled, until she didn't
have to pull anymore. His mouth was on hers and he copied her move-
ments, cupping her neck and pulling her closer and closer, her body
sliding along the seat toward him until she was practically in his lap.
A part of her sat back, surprised, but most of her had gone beyond
thinking.

When he pulled his mouth away, she tried to follow, but he put
his hands on her shoulders. Breathing heavily, he leaned his forehead
against hers. "Oh, man," he said. "I didn't see that coming."

God, he smelled so good, like cedar. She studied his cheeks, his
nose, his mouth, and then she couldn't help herself, she leaned in and
touched her tongue to the dimple in his chin, tasting the salty man
taste of him, and then he was kissing her again, pressing her back
against the seat, and Laurel lost her mind, couldn't have stopped if
she'd wanted to, and she didn't want to, didn't want to so badly that
she almost cried when he pulled away from her again and got out of
the car. Hands limp at her sides, she watched him stand there, arms
braced against the hood. What had just happened here?

When she'd got her shaky legs under control, she got out and faced
him across the hood. But before she could say anything he raised his
head and said, "I'm sorry."

"What are you sorry for?" There was a tug-of-war going on inside
Laurel, part of her wanting to make him feel better and part of her
wanting to smack him for being sorry.

Joe came around to her, his face back to serious again. His hands
reached, but he pulled them back. "I don't want to take advantage," he
said. "It wouldn't be right."

Oh, God, Laurel thought, chivalry now? Go ahead, take advantage,
please, she wanted to scream. I'll forgive you in advance.

"It's not just that you're a little tipsy." He put his hands in his pockets and Laurel knew it wouldn't take much for her to change his mind.
He had his own tug-of-war going on. But he looked so sweet, so concerned. "I know it's probably not my place to say this, but maybe it's
too soon. It hasn't been that long since your divorce."

What? Not only was he being the strong one, the chivalrous one, but now he was also being sensible and mature? Suddenly she felt like a balloon with all the air let out and was surprised when she didn't go limp and fall to the ground.

He reached out to her then, touched her cheek. "But when you're ready, you just give me a sign, okay?"

All she could manage was a nod, then together they unloaded Maxann and got her into the house. After they laid her on top of her bed, Laurel walked Joe to the door.

"I'll bring the car back in the morning," he said.

Laurel nodded and stood there after the door clicked shut, listening as he drove away. Then there was no sound except the crickets and those crazy bullfrogs. She made sure the door was locked, then went down the hall to check on Maxann. She looked like a giant Barbie, minus the big boobs, lying there snoring on top of her pink bedspread.

Laurel went back to the living room and lay on the couch, staring at the dark shapes of unfamiliar furniture surrounding her. She hadn't been this drunk in a long time, so drunk she felt boneless and floppy and terribly, terribly fragile. Sleep was pulling her under and she couldn't think about what had just happened. There'd be time enough for that tomorrow.

In the Garden." Wasn't that the name of Kitty's song? Pansy rolled over on her back and stared up at the stars. The dirt felt soft as powder between her fingers, and the rustling of the corn all around seemed to be saying something she couldn't quite make out, but it was something good.

"I come to the garden alone," she sang softly, thinking how Kitty always said that song was like a waltz with Jesus. For the first time in a long time Pansy didn't feel alone or lonely. She felt surrounded. Not smothered like she'd felt the last few months, but surrounded, enveloped in something warm and safe and big, much bigger than her or her fears or this garden or this town or this world. She sang louder, not worrying what anybody else might think. Who cared? There was absolutely nothing wrong with what she was doing. She wasn't hurting anybody, not even herself. The only difference between her and everybody else was that she wasn't scared anymore. Driving around all day, she'd figured that much out, at least.

Lord, she had missed driving, hadn't realized how much until she got behind the wheel that morning. Now all those months she hadn't gone anywhere seemed like a prison sentence. It must be that hostage mentality she'd read about. While you're in the prison it don't seem that bad, but once you're out, Lord have mercy, how did you ever stand it? All that time just laying there on Kitty's couch, sleeping, staring into space. Was that really her? She'd got in that car today without knowing where she wanted to go or what she wanted to do. She just went, enjoying the freedom of driving around all day, just driving, going wherever she pleased, stopping at Hardee's for lunch, then driving some more, seeing the world again through new eyes.

When she got back home and seen Dan in the light of the living-room window, sitting there watching TV like always, she just couldn't stand to go in. Not because of him, but because she didn't want walls around her again, not just yet. That freedom had been so nice, and she wasn't ready to give it up.

So she'd kicked off her shoes and thrown them on the front porch, then wandered across the yard, the grass tickling her ankles. There was no moon, and once she got away from the house, it felt like the dark swallowed her up, made her invisible. It felt so good, moving through the night like a ghost, almost forgetting her own body. She walked through the hedge and into Kitty's yard to the edge of the garden, then stepped over pepper plants and between tomato plants until she was inside the rows of corn, stalks rustling as she brushed by them, all the way into the heart of the garden. The dirt felt so good to the skin of her feet that she got on her knees, then on her belly. Propped on her elbows, she leaned down and smelled the dirt, the dark mineral smell of it, and felt the heat of the sun still in it, rising up into her.

Lord, I am blessed, she thought, rolling over on her back, fingers sifting dirt. Truly blessed to be out here in this peaceful night, to see the stars, to smell the corn, to hear the crickets. It was a gift so beautiful she wanted to paint it.

Her whole body went still, as if her mind required every ounce of energy she had at that moment. She hadn't thought about painting anything but a wall or her toenails in so long. Where did that come from? It scared her so bad to even think about it, but walking right next to that fear was something else. She felt younger than she had in a long time, like she could do anything. She might be a grandma, but she wasn't old and she wasn't dying. And maybe it was natural that it should come back to her now, when she seemed to have got on the other side of her midlife crisis or whatever it was.

When she heard a voice whisper, "Pansy?" she froze, thinking at first the corn was talking back to her, which meant she really was crazy and would have to be sent to Broughton. Then the voice called again and Pansy realized it was Dan. For one second she laid there, stiff and quiet, resenting him being there, ruining her solitude. But just as quick as it come, the resentment passed, because she could picture him there, lost and bewildered on the other side of the corn.

"*Oh, Danny Boy,*" she sang. "*The pipes, the pipes are calling, from glen to glen, and down the mountainside.*" It'd been so long since she sung that to him. She used to go looking for him in the shed or in the yard or the pasture, singing that song to get his attention.

He found her then, come and stood over her, and she felt him more than saw him, knew he was mad and hurt and confused and most of all terrified.

"Pansy?" he said again, and it was all there in his voice, the wondering where she'd been all day, the anxiety that she might never be his old Pansy again, the fear he wouldn't be enough for her anymore.

"I'm here," she said.

"Pansy, where the hell have you been? We been worried to death."

We, Pansy thought. Why couldn't he just say *I* was worried to death? He always had to have a buddy. "Who's we?" she said.

"Me, and your children, and Kitty. Don't you even care we was all worried about you? Your note didn't say nothing about where you went or when you'd be back. How do you think that made us feel?"

"I'm sorry, Dan," she said. "I didn't mean to worry nobody. There was just something I had to do today."

"What?"

Pansy sat up, pulling her knees to her chest and wrapping her arms around them. "I just needed to get out for a while, that's all. I just went driving around."

Dan hunkered down next to her. "Well, why didn't you just say so?" he said, using that patient voice he'd been using on her the last couple of months, even though she knew behind it he was irritated at her. She didn't see why she should have to explain herself to him. Wasn't she a grown woman with her own car and her own money?

Dan's knees must've started to give out on him, because he grunted and sat down in the dirt next to her, stretched his long legs straight out in front of him, the joints in his knees and ankles popping. We are getting old, Pansy thought, surprised that it didn't bother her more. It made her happy to think of the two of them falling apart together.

"I was really worried," Dan said, the patience and the irritation gone. He just sounded tired.

Finally, she thought, an *I* instead of a *we*. Seemed like the minute they got married they both quit being an I and became a we, forever and ever, amen.

"Hey," she said, finding his hand in the dark and patting it. "Remember how we used to go riding in your truck when we was dating? I loved when we'd park in a field somewhere and lay in the bed of the truck and look up at the stars. Remember that?" She laid back down, then reached up and pulled at Dan's arm. "Come on," she said, and he laid on his side next to her.

She thought about the dream she'd had all them months she was sick—or whatever she'd been, crazy maybe—the dream where she was in an airplane and scared to death it was fixing to crash. Dan was there too, flying the plane, and he looked so calm, but it seemed like she knew something he didn't. She knew that plane was going down. So she hit the eject button and shot up out of there into the sky, and all she could see for a long time was white. Then after a while she was able to look down and see her house and the plant and everything, and it all looked so little. She floated awhile, thinking, *Is that my life? That little thing way down there?* But the closer she floated back down, the bigger things got, and then she began to see it all clear again. The dream always started out so scary, but by the end she felt peaceful, until she woke up and remembered that she hadn't bothered to worry about leaving Dan in the plane, and in the dream she never knew if it had crashed or not. She'd left him without meaning to.

Dan sighed. "I reckon I just don't understand you anymore."

"Dan, you know I didn't mean to get like that, don't you? I couldn't help it." Pansy got on her knees and pushed him onto his back. He was as invisible as she'd felt earlier; they were both invisible in the dark. Her fingers did her seeing for her, reading the stubble on his jaw and neck, tracing his soft lips, tangling in his thick hair.

She put her lips to his ear and felt him shiver. She whispered, "You understand me, you crazy thing. You understand me perfect. You're the only one that does." Her fingers moved down his neck, his chest, wriggled between the buttons on his shirt, pulled at his chest hairs. "Hey," she said. "Remember what else we used to do in the back of your truck?"

"We got a perfectly good bed in the house," he said, but made no move to get up.

"We certainly do," Pansy said, swinging a leg over his hips. "Now, be still and let me have my way with you." She unbuttoned his shirt from the belly up and pushed it off his shoulders, her mouth going where her fingers had been. Dan groaned and grabbed her hips, wanting to roll her onto her back.

"No," she said, pushing his chest, holding him down until his hands let go. He got still, waiting for her, and she sat back. She thought about the corn and how, during the heat of the day, the sides of the leaves curled in, protecting themselves from the sun. Then when it got cool they rolled out flat and broad and open under the evening sky, ready to catch the dew. That was how she'd always felt with Dan, like that corn, like she didn't have to curl in on herself and hide with him. Those nights in the back of his truck, she laid down and held out her arms and let him cover her, listening to the wind in the trees, watching the stars over his shoulder, feeling like nothing could touch her but him, and he would never hurt her. She wanted him to know that feeling too. That's why they were here tonight, in the garden. She'd called and he had come. Smiling to herself in the dark, she bent to him slowly, covered his body with her own.

Alberta

I didn't never marry no job till I got married. No, sir, I had plans of my own. But then Dill come along and seemed like I just lost my mind some way and didn't even care about getting it back. Oh, God, I loved that man, loved him so much I could eat the dirt right out of his heel prints. And the whole time there was this other part of me sitting up inside my head watching everything that was going on and shaking her head at me, disgusted. But I slammed the door on that girl so I wouldn't have to see her. Sometimes she'd get in a panic and nearly beat that door down, wanting me to let her out, but I wouldn't open it for nothing. Dill'd come close and I'd breathe him in and that door would slam shut and nothing else mattered.

We'd meet by the river after our shift, in that same place I first seen him. Nobody ever come down there that time of day. They was all home getting their suppers. I'd tell Mama I wanted to go to Kitty and Edith's room at the boardinghouse. She didn't like me a-doing that, but I reckon she felt like I ought to have a little bit of fun in between working at the mill and working at home. That's all most people done then was work, from the time we got up till the time we went to bed. I reckon she figured I was too tired to get up to anything I shouldn't. But with Dill I forgot about being tired. I forgot everything but how sweet he talked, and the way his big old black eyes looked at me like they was trying to soak me up, and how he made me laugh, telling stories about different ones in the mill, doing voices and acting out things, and sometimes he'd even jump up and do a little dance and I'd lay there in the grass with the river making music on the rocks behind him and just laugh till I couldn't breathe. Then he'd fall down beside me and put his mouth on mine and his breath tasted like sweet corn and tobacco and I tried to eat him up with my mouth, my hands, my whole body, wrapped myself around him like I was starved to death.

Before Dill, all I ever thought about was leaving the mill, saving my money, and going to that teacher college. Every week I give Mama and Daddy my paycheck and was glad to do it, but I took the dollar they give me for spending money and put it in a box under my bed and the rest of them knowed not to touch it. That was my college money. Dill didn't make me forget all that, not at all. Being with him made me feel like it was closer than ever. I could just see us getting married and moving to Greensboro and him getting a job at one of them mills there while I went to school, and we'd rent us two rooms in the top of some boardinghouse and I'd come home at night and cook his supper and study my lessons while he read the newspaper. Then we'd listen to the radio and go to bed. We'd have our own furniture, nothing fancy, just a table and two chairs and a bed, pretty curtains at the windows, two big feather pillows and one of Mama's quilts on the bed. Oh, I had it all pictured, how it'd be. We talked about getting married once in a while, but he never talked about my plans or any he might've had.

Then I found out I was going to have a baby and, Lord, it scared me so bad. I wasn't even worried about Mama and Daddy and what they was going to do. I was just so mad at myself for not thinking of that. But then I calmed down and thought about it and started getting all excited, thinking there wasn't no reason we couldn't go on and get married right then and go on to Greensboro. All I could think was my life was finally fixing to start, my real life. We could put a baby bed in our two rooms, and I pictured Dill sitting and rocking the baby, singing to it, while I sat at the table with a lamp shining a soft light down on my schoolwork.

One day by the river—it had got cold by then, too cold to lay on the ground—we sat next to each other on a big old oak tree stump and I told him. I says, "Dill, we're going to have to get married now." He took my meaning right off and got this worried look on his face. He wouldn't look at me, just stared at the ground, and I wanted to know what was down there more important than me.

"Give me a minute to think," he said, so I got quiet. Finally he says, "All right," like he just figured everything out. "Here's what we'll do." He put his arm around me and hugged me close, told me not to worry, said everything was going to be all right, said we'd go to town and get married Saturday, said his daddy would move out of the big bedroom and let us have it.

I stood up then so I could think straight. "No," I said. "No, Dill." He looked up at me, them eyes smiling and confused. "Dill," I said, "I don't want to live with your daddy. I don't want the big bedroom. Don't you remember me talking about Greensboro and the teacher college?" I got down on my knees in front of him and held on to his hands. They felt so warm next to mine. I told him we could get married and go together, and he could work and I could go to school till the baby come.

He leaned back from me, looking at me like I was a young'un caught telling a lie. "Honey," he said. "That was just talk. You know you can't do that, not now. And I got Daddy to take care of, and the farm. I can't leave my land."

I got mad then, for I could see he meant it. I scraped up a handful of dirt, black and damp around the foot of that stump, and held it out to him. "This is more important to you than I am?" I put a hand to my belly. "It ain't nothing but dirt, Dill."

He shook his head at me, said, "Honey, come on, now."

I took and flung that dirt in his face as hard as I could. We sat there staring for a long time, and I could tell he wanted to smack me for that but he didn't. The dirt stuck to his eyelashes and in his beard but he never reached up to wipe it off. Finally he said, "Alberta, you got to grow up now." He said it so gentle, but hard too, like a man on a skittish horse might talk. "You got to quit talking foolishness. We're going to get married and live on the place and start a family. That's how people do, honey."

If I hadn't loved him so much I would've got up then and run and got my box of money and went to Greensboro by myself. No telling where I would've ended up, dead in a ditch or teaching in a school somewhere. But I couldn't leave him. I could not make myself get up and turn my back. That starved place was still there and he was still the only way I knowed to keep it fed. I put my face in his lap and held on to his legs and cried the hardest I ever cried in my life. While I cried, he petted my hair and hummed a little song, I think it was "Blessed Assurance."

Behind my closed eyes, in that little corner of my mind, I seen that door open up and that girl, that other me, stood there holding a picture in her hands, the picture of my two rooms with the pretty curtains and Mama's quilt, and she took and ripped it in half and throwed the pieces on the floor. Then she stepped back and shut that door her own self with no help from me.

I never seen her but one more time after that. It was years later, after me and Dill had got married and had two more babies. It didn't last long. Seemed like something in me was just bound to keep her shut up there, couldn't bear to see that look on her face, that look that said I got just what I deserved, which was nothing.

16

LAUREL'S HEAD WAS SPINNING BUT NOT HURTING nearly as bad as she'd expected, so she opened her eyes, held on to the back of the couch, and slowly pulled herself into the upright position. She sat very still, waiting to see what her stomach was going to do, but it seemed okay. Her lips had stuck together during the night and she scraped her teeth over them to remove the scum. Good Lord, she thought, it looks like Martha Stewart's been here. The living room was a perfectly coordinated feminine dream, with peach and pink cabbage-rose fabric on the couch and chairs, peach drapes and lace sheers at the windows, pale green plush carpet. A Martha Stewart trailer—wouldn't that be an oxymoron?

She leaned back and put her feet on the coffee table. Somewhere a cuckoo clock counted to ten. What time had they gotten in last night, or was it this morning? She couldn't remember. Either way, it was too early for cuckoo clocks. Maxann must still be dead to the world, because no sound came from behind the closed door down the hall. Laurel finally decided she couldn't go back to sleep and couldn't wait for coffee. Groaning, she got to her feet and shuffled into the kitchen.

The sun coming through the window behind the breakfast nook blinded her and sent a pain shooting behind her eyes. She closed the blinds, then turned back to the kitchen and opened cabinets until she found coffee and filters. Just the smell of Maxwell House when she opened the can made her feel more human. As she leaned against the sink and waited for the first cup to drip, she noticed that the kitchen was just as pretty and feminine as the living room. The blue-and-white checked and ruffled curtains echoed the blue-and-white tile floor and made the whole room seem cozy, like Aunt Bea's kitchen on *The Andy Griffith Show*, a place for visiting as well as cooking and eating. Charlie had probably done his homework at that little table while Maxann made him peanut butter cookies. No, that was too much of a stretch, and, anyway, Charlie was too old for cookies and milk. They probably opened a bag of Doritos and some salsa.

Laurel envied Charlie his postgraduation beach trip, a true rite of passage, the first trip away from home without adult supervision. She hoped he wouldn't get too drunk or, worse, thrown in jail. Laurel had gotten drunk for the first time on her graduation trip, though she'd felt guilty about it the whole time, as if her mama and daddy had a crystal ball and could see exactly how she was polluting herself and would rush down to Myrtle Beach, kick in the door, and drag her home. She had to admit there'd been a part of her that wished they would. Not really—the humiliation of that happening in front of her friends would've been too high a price. And she'd had fun, she and her girl-friends lying in the sun all day, drinking and flirting with boys all night. But Laurel was cursed with the inability to forget what it all meant, that graduation trip, and the feeling of loss that went with it. Sure, she still had the rest of the summer at home with her family and friends and she'd probably be sick to death of them by next week, but after the summer she'd head to Chapel Hill and college and life would never be the same. Maybe being the first to leave the nest made it harder somehow.

It'd been a long time since Laurel had gotten drunk, though she'd been pretty good at it in college. She hadn't even gotten drunk when Scott left, although if ever there was a good reason to get shit-faced, that was it. She'd been shit-faced last night, though, no doubt about it.

As she sat blowing on her coffee to cool it, she heard a groan and a few minutes later the sound of the toilet flushing. Maxann made it to the kitchen door and stared at Laurel. Her hair looked like a cyclone struck it, and the circles under her eyes were so dark they looked like smeared eyeliner. Maybe it was smeared eyeliner. Neither of them had been sober enough to remember to take off their makeup last night.

"You look like hell," Maxann said. The blue *My Baby Is American-Made* T-shirt hung down to her knees and the shoulder seams reached almost to her elbows. "Did you sleep all right?"

"Like a log," Laurel said. "Of course, I probably could've slept on a cement block last night and never noticed."

"You tied one on last night, didn't you?" Maxann said, and laughed.

"You're one to talk. We had to load your dead ass in the backseat." Laurel wondered at the new comfort level she felt with Maxann. Did getting drunk together bring the boundaries down? There was nothing to hide behind when they both looked and felt like hell and knew it.

Maxann raised an eyebrow. "We?"

"Joe Clark. He drove us home."

"We we we, all the way home," Maxann said, looking over her shoulder at Laurel as she poured herself a cup of coffee. "And did anything happen with you and Old Joe Clark?"

Laurel's face got hot. "No, nothing happened."

"Bull and shit. You're telling me there was no exchange of fluids whatsoever?"

"God, Maxann, what a romantic you are."

"Ha! Romance is for sissies." Maxann leaned back and pulled her hair up off her neck and held it on top of her head. "This hair's getting on my nerves so bad. I think I'm going to chop it all off like you did. Now, are you going to sit there and tell me nothing happened last night?"

"I kissed him. That's all."

"You kissed him? Well, maybe there's hope for you yet. How was it?"

"Nothing. It was a mistake."

"Uh-huh. Your face wouldn't be turning all shades of red if it was nothing."

"I don't want to talk about it," Laurel said, watching as Maxann drained her cup. How did she stand to pour it down her throat like that, hot as it was? When Maxann set the cup down, Laurel stood and said, "You want some more?"

"Sure. Listen, don't be embarrassed because you was the one that had to start the kissing. I'm sure he didn't mind. As a matter of fact, I imagine he joined right in, didn't he?"

Laurel didn't answer, just poured the coffee, handed Maxann her cup, and sat down again.

Maxann grinned and blew on her coffee. "Don't make me beat it out of you, now."

"He turned me down, all right? Are you happy now?"

"You're shitting me."

"Pretty embarrassing, huh?"

"Honey, being horny is nothing to be embarrassed about. You're a grown woman and it comes with the package. And there was Joe, a big old healthy man, so you jumped him. It's perfectly natural."

"I did not jump him. Not exactly."

"Well," Maxann said. "Look at it this way. It's like eating doughnuts. Don't laugh. You go along not thinking about doughnuts, and you might not even be that hungry, but one day there you are at the grocery store and you see that Krispy Kreme box and all of a sudden there ain't nothing in the world you want more than a doughnut, so you buy yourself a box, eat three in the car on the way home, get sick to your stomach, and leave the rest for somebody else. But if you don't eat one, you'll wake up at two o'clock in the morning thinking about them damn doughnuts, but the grocery store's closed and you ain't got nothing but crackers. God, now I want a doughnut."

"Maxann, have you ever noticed how you always compare men to food? Like last night you said you had a taste for Bushy Cook."

"Well, Laurel, have you ever noticed how women that don't have a man tend to get fat? Percilla, for example."

Laurel started to say, *But Percilla's married*, then remembered being married was no guarantee of an active sex life. Her last six months with Scott had proved that. No wonder she was horny.

"Poor old Percilla Sue." Maxann seemed genuinely sorry, which surprised Laurel.

"What do you mean?"

"Old Rex ain't much use to her since he got laid off. He's on a bunch of medication for his nerves and depression and all. And on top of that, he's bad to drink."

"Yeah," Laurel said. "I smelled it on him at the wedding."

"She makes do at work, though." Maxann raised her arms over her head, stretched and yawned. "She's the hand-relief queen."

Okay, Laurel thought, too much information. Time to change the subject. She hesitated, then decided to be direct. "So, what's going on with you and Grady?"

Maxann's head whipped around and she glared at Laurel. "Grady? Not a damn thing. Why?" Her face had turned as pink as her bed-spread.

"I don't know. Don't you think he looks a little bit like Jimmy Stewart?"

"Jimmy Stewart was butt-ugly."

"He was not. How can you say that? A woman could do a lot worse than Grady." And Maxann, Laurel thought, you have, several times.

"What are you talking about Grady for? Ain't it bad enough I got to spend forty hours a week with the man?"

"Fine," Laurel said, deciding it'd be better to save the Grady questions for a time when they weren't both hung over and irritable. "By the way, you said something very interesting last night."

"Do I want to know what it was?"

"You said you're a witch."

"Oh, hell, is that all?" Maxann got up and went to the window, her bedroom shoes scuffing on the tile floor. "My aunt Maggie used to say we come down from witches in Scotland or some shit like that. Said we had powers over men." Maxann opened the blinds to let the light in, then looked over her shoulder at Laurel. "Where's my car?" she said.

"Joe's got it. We couldn't fit in his truck, so he left it at the Ponderosa. Don't worry, he's a cop. He'll bring it back this morning and then I'll take him to his truck."

"Aha," Maxann said. "Smart girl. You better hit that shower before he gets here. You don't want him to see you looking like that, do you?"

"Shut up," Laurel said, but she got up and hurried toward the bathroom. Behind her, Maxann laughed and turned on the radio. Before she shut the bathroom door, Laurel heard, *"Fly, robin, fly, up up to the sky."* Seventies music, not what she would've chosen for a hungover Sunday morning. Was there any music that did fit this occasion? Maybe the theme from *The Poseidon Adventure: "There's got to be a morning after, if we can make it through the storm."* She turned the shower on and stepped in, and her body sagged in relief. The warm water felt so good on her head, her shoulders, everywhere. She used Maxann's shampoo and soap to wash away the smell of smoke and whiskey and sweat, then stood under the water and let it beat down on her.

When she closed her eyes, the memory of kissing Joe played on the insides of her eyelids like a movie. Oh, God. She groaned and covered her face with her hands. How could she have done that? It wasn't like her at all. But she couldn't control it. It was as if she was going through withdrawal from some drug and then suddenly somebody offered her a free sample and, since nobody was around to catch her, she took it, a little taste of what she'd been craving without even being aware that she craved it.

She'd read an article not long ago that said chemistry between two people was a real thing, and being in love was actually just being addicted to hormones or pheromones, at least at first. And a woman she'd worked with in Vegas used to talk about how she'd been depressed ever since she left her all-male office to come work in their all-female office. She said even though there was nothing sexual between her and her coworkers, the hormonal soup created by men and women working together kept her energy up, made her look forward to coming to work every day.

Maybe that's what I'm missing, Laurel thought. But did she really want to lose herself in that fog again? Look where it had gotten her with Scott, so blinded by her need for him that she couldn't see how miserable they made each other. By the end of the marriage, she was more addicted to him than in love with him. He'd become a habit, and a period of withdrawal—uncomfortable, even painful—was necessary before she could get on with her life. Much as she hated to admit it, Joe was right about that.

And yet, even though it had gone bad, it must've provided some vital nutrient she needed and was starved for now, starved enough to throw herself at poor Joe. Last night at the Ponderosa, being around those men, even men she had no interest in, Laurel had felt something in her sit up and take notice. Even now, with a hangover and an embarrassing memory, she felt more alive than she had in a long time.

Maxann

I ain't no witch, 'cause if I was there'd be a whole lot of things turned out different in my life, starting with my mama. If I had any kind of power she'd still be here and that damn Claude would be the one in the ground. Ain't no such a thing as witches or magic or special powers. It's all just what you got in your own body, your brains and your two hands and feet and what they can do.

The first thing I remember about Mama was her taking me to work at the Alamance Diner with her 'cause she couldn't afford no babysitter. She'd set me in that high chair close to the jukebox so I could hear the music good, then she'd go on and do her work, which was waitressing. If I'd ever get to crying, she'd put some grits or some applesauce on my high-chair tray, and boy, I'd go to town eating and making the awfulest mess you ever seen.

And laughing. She said I laughed all the time, and she felt like I should've got a paycheck same as her 'cause folks come there to eat just so they could play with me. I reckon I liked all the attention, and I was happy. Funny how you don't remember the happy times, though, at least not as clear as the bad. The time I remember clearest is the day Mama quit.

She had to leave me at work while she run to the store for her boss, Tom Stines. They'd run out of something, I don't recall what, and it was right before dinnertime, their busiest time. Mama give me some grits and run out the door and Tom was supposed to watch me. Well, I know I was young, but I still remember Mama going out that door and leaving me, waving bye-bye through the window before she turned and headed on down the street. When she didn't turn right around and come back, well, I reckon I realized she wasn't playing no game and I got scared and set in to hollering and carrying on, wanting my mama, you know. Old Tom, he come over and at first he was nice and tried to feed me grits, but then I reckon he got irritated, and the more I cried, the madder he got. Finally he started hollering at me to shut my mouth and quit being such a baby, which is what I was, for Pete's sake. I hollered and he hollered.

To this day, I still remember how them grits felt in my little hand, cold and wet and mushy. I drawed back my arm and throwed them at him just as hard as I could. They hit old Tom square in the face and he looked so surprised, well, I couldn't do nothing but laugh. I laughed and laughed. That is, till he jerked me up by the arm and started calling me a little bastard, which I was but didn't know it at the time or even what that word meant. I screamed at the top of my lungs, and about that time the door opened and Mama come running in. The look on her face when she seen him holding me up by the arm like that, Lord have mercy, it's a wonder he didn't drop dead right then. Mama wrapped her fingers around his wrist and he let go of me right quick. She grabbed me up out of the high chair so fast my feet got hooked up under the tray and pulled my shoes off. She didn't stop to get them, though, just marched out the door. I heard old Tom a-begging, "Come on now, Dot. Don't go off mad. I didn't hurt her." When Mama still didn't turn around, he hollered, "Goddammit, Dot, that whistle's going to blow any minute now and that dinner crowd will be in here wanting to eat. Come on now!" Mama stopped then and turned on him. "Well, you should've just thought of that before you ever laid a finger on this young'un of mine." He hollered, "Fine, don't bother coming back." Mama said, "You go to hell, you son of a bitch!"

That's when Mama went and got her a job over at Revel. She didn't want to because she never wanted to leave me, but it couldn't be helped. It was the only job in town. So instead of feeding them millhands, she become one of them. Old Tom come sniffing around again a couple days later, saying he was sorry and wouldn't Mama please come back. He brung my shoes back and had a little doll for me that I wanted so bad, but Mama wouldn't let me have it. She told him she wouldn't take that kind of treatment off nobody.

Which makes it hard for me to understand what all happened later, how she ended up with a man like my stepdaddy. I guess it had to do with my being a bastard and her wanting me to have a real family, a family name. She even went and had three more young'uns with that son of a bitch to seal the bargain. I guess I was about three when she married him. It wasn't long after she left the Alamance and started working at the plant. That's where she met him. He thought he was better than her because he finished high school and come from a nice neighborhood instead of the mill hill. He wasn't too good to go to bed with her, though. They never are. I don't have a whole lot of memories from that time. I remember my teachers in school and when my brothers was born, but most everything else is blurry, like ten years all run together in a couple of days.

The next strong memory I have is the night Mama left him. I don't even like to say his name because all it brings to my mind is a picture of pure meanness. You can't even say Mama left him. Claude Ramsey beat her out with his fists. He beat her pretty regular, anyway, but never bad enough to make her bleed. But that night she made the mistake of trying to stand up to him when he wouldn't give her money for our school clothes, and he beat her down. She was laying there bleeding on the floor and Claude and the boys just standing there looking at her like she was taking a nap or something. When I seen that Claude wasn't going to do nothing, I run across the road and called the police. Well, they wasn't nothing but a gang of Claude's old poker buddies, drinking buddies, you know, so he just told them Mama fell and hit her head on the coffee table, and they stood there looking at her for a minute and then turned around and left. The sorry bastards. Ain't no coffee table I ever seen could do that kind of damage to a human body. For all I knew, all of them beat their wives too. Maybe they had some kind of lodge for it and had regular meetings to decide how to back each other up if it ever come out what they done.

Well, then I run across the street and called a ambulance, though I didn't know how in the world we'd pay for it. They come and carried Mama to the hospital and said if I hadn't called when I did, Mama would've laid there and bled to death. It was all they could do to keep her alive, anyhow. It took her so long to get well, and she never did get *back right again. I think she wished she had died. They wouldn't let me go stay with her at the hospital, but wasn't no way I was going back to Claude's house, so I went to my aunt Maggie's. I didn't really like her much, but at least I wasn't afraid of her. That's where Mama come too, after she got out of the hospital weeks and weeks later.*

Claude wouldn't let her have the boys. She begged for them, but they was the only things he could hold over her head, so he kept them. And them just little bitty shits too, three, five, and seven years old, too young to be kept from their mama, but that's exactly what he done. Mama went ahead and divorced him, and then it wasn't long before he remarried, some poor little fool that didn't know no better, just as stupid as my mama was.

I keep hoping to hear one of these days that he's dead, that somebody beat the hell out of him in a fight and killed him dead as a hammer. That's what I hope.

I felt bad for them brothers of mine, but I had to concentrate on looking after Mama and me. She wasn't never able to go back to work, but she got disability and I worked after school and weekends at the mill, sweeping and stuff, and Aunt Maggie didn't charge us no rent, so we done all right.

In my life I remember two main feelings. One is mad-as-hell-and-scared-shitless, which seemed to start the day Mama left her job at the Alamance and ain't hardly let up since. The other is what I call the high-chair feeling, which I wouldn't never tell nobody else because it sounds so stupid. It don't feel stupid, though. It's the best feeling in the world, and some nights that's what helps me get to sleep, closing my eyes and remembering what it felt like to be that baby with a trayful of grits, a jukebox full of pretty music, a roomful of interesting people, and a mama always where I could see her, a mama who come by every once in a while to wipe my chin and blow a raspberry on my belly.

The biggest mystery to me, one I can't seem to give up trying to figure out, is where my mama went. Not the one that set like a zombie staring off into space until the day she died when I was sixteen. Not that mama. I'm talking about the one I knowed first, the one that told off her bossman and quit her job and stomped right out of the Alamance without a thought for where my next pair of shoes might come from. If Aunt Maggie is right and we are witches in our family, then why can't I figure these things out? Seems like it'd just come to me somehow. She always said it skipped a generation and had skipped my mama, meaning I would get it, but I think it must've skipped me too, because I don't see nothing but what's right in front of me.

17

THE EARLY-AFTERNOON SUN SLANTED ACROSS THE TOP of Idalene's bed and she laid there squinting as if even in her sleep she felt it, blinding. Pansy had gotten so used to the routine, she didn't even have to look, just reached behind her and turned the wand to close the blinds. Every day as the bars of light disappeared and the puckered skin between Idalene's eyebrows relaxed, Pansy was grateful she could at least do that much for her. Closing the blinds and sitting with her a couple hours every afternoon, that was it. Not enough, not nearly enough.

When her mama was in here that last year, Pansy hadn't been able to take off work during the day like this, but she come every evening, made sure she ate something, sat with her even though she couldn't talk and hardly ever opened her eyes. It was about the only time she'd ever seen her mama without that worried look on her face, the one like Idalene's when the sun hit her eyes, and it had took a stroke to do it. It made Pansy feel so tender toward her, seeing her laying there sweet and helpless as a baby. She brushed her hair, held her hand, read to her, talked to her, waited with her for what they both knew was coming. Hard as it'd been, she wouldn't trade nothing for it, that time with her mama.

As usual, Kitty had fallen asleep sitting up in the padded vinyl chair, hands in her lap still holding a little silver crochet hook and a white doily. Pansy wished she could do that, just sit there with her chin on her chest and doze off. It must be so nice to feel that relaxed all the time. There had to be some perks that come with age, and she hoped that was one of them.

The last thing she felt like doing these days was sleeping. She'd slept enough for two lifetimes. Now she woke up restless and ready to get up and do something, but not any of the things she'd done before, not going to work and cooking and cleaning, even though all them things still needed doing. But right now Laurel was handling all that, and Pansy was selfish. She wanted just a little more time, and she'd decided she was going to take it. Time to be in her own house by herself for the first time in her life, time to visit Idalene, time to help Kitty in the garden. For now that was all she wanted, all she could handle, and if Dan didn't understand, well, there was nothing she could do about that. She knew he was confused, wondering why she hadn't picked up right where she left off now she was feeling better. She couldn't explain it herself. She just knew it wasn't time yet, just like she knew it would be soon enough. That was one thing Dan had never been good at, being patient. It was high time he learned.

Idalene groaned and shifted in the bed, the pain finding her even through all the drugs. Pansy got up and stood over her, studying her face, wondering if she should call the nurse. She'd seemed all right when they first got there, had eat all her lunch and talked to them like her old self. This was the first time Pansy had seen her feel the pain in her sleep like that. Idalene got quiet again, still deep asleep.

"Is she all right?"

Pansy turned away from the bed and nodded. Kitty's hands had took up right where they left off on the doily, doing their work without her even having to look. They sat quiet for a few minutes, listening to Idalene's breathing, and Pansy watched Kitty's quick fingers making loop after loop, around and around. She never had got the hang of fine needlework like that.

"I knowed her mama, you know," Kitty said in a low voice, like she was telling a secret.

"You did?" They'd been coming here all these weeks and this was the first time Kitty thought to tell her that? "Idalene told me before she come to Russell she lived in the orphanage up at Wolfpen."

Kitty nodded. "That's right. That's where they sent her and the boys after Dorcas died."

"The boys?"

"Her brothers. She had three little brothers. Well, there was four, but one died. They was the cutest little rascals, and, Lord, she bossed them just like she was the mama. They minded her too."

Idalene had brothers? She'd never said one way or the other, but Pansy had always thought of her as an only child. Idalene had always kept herself a little bit apart from everybody else, even in the picture Laurel had showed her, the one of Idalene the year she started at Revel. That made it hard to picture her in the middle of three brothers, but Pansy wanted to see her that way, wanted her to not be so alone in the world. She shivered as the air-conditioning came on with a whoosh and wished she'd remembered to bring a sweater.

"What about their daddy?" Pansy said.

"Hunh," Kitty said. "That no-account D. L. Spofford? That was the sorriest man ever drawed a breath. They was better off at the orphanage. I've always wondered what ever happened to those boys."

"The only family I ever knew her to have is Lottie May."

Kitty shook her head. "Ain't that something? We all thought that baby died when Dorcas did."

"How'd she die?"

"She got shot. They shot a bunch of people that day, killed three or four."

"Shot? By who?"

"They never did find out. One of them mill police Old Man Revel hired to keep down the union organizers. They was over at the Gum Branch schoolhouse having a rally, and them thugs waited for them to come out and just started shooting. It's a miracle your mama didn't get killed too."

"Mama? What was she doing there?"

The crochet hook stopped for a second, then continued on. "Oh, honey," Kitty said, then was quiet for so long, Pansy wondered if that was all she was going to say.

"Poor old Bert," Kitty said at last. "If it wasn't for that Bruno she might've learnt to be happy. She had so much to be thankful for, a husband and healthy young'uns, a good job and a roof over her head and enough to eat, and that was back in a time not everybody could say that." She let the doily rest in her lap but kept her eyes on it, as if lifting them might break the thread of the story she'd just picked up.

"When she seen him it was like something sparked up inside of her, something that'd been damped down since her and Dill got married. That Bruno, Lord, well, he was handsome and had a way of talking—he could sell Popsicles to the Eskimos, as Edith used to say—but he was a devil too, setting Bert and Dorcas at each other the way he done, letting them fight to see who'd work the hardest for him and that durn union. Got Dorcas in the family way and would've got Bert that-a-way too if she hadn't already been carrying, and turned out he had a wife and six children up there in Philadelphia. And that's right where he went back to, didn't give a fig for poor old Dorcas or that baby or none of her young'uns, didn't give a durn about Bert neither, and her half out of her mind with grief when he left here and then again when her baby come stillborn. It was a terrible time."

She stopped then and looked up at Idalene's long body stretched out under the blanket. "I reckon them young'uns got the worst of it, though, especially this one." She shook her head and started the crochet hook again.

Pansy sat back in her chair, not knowing what to say. As bad as she felt for Idalene, all she could think about right now was her mama loving another man besides her daddy. If she was honest, there'd been a few times she looked at other men herself and wondered what it might be like, but never once had she been tempted to trade Dan in, not even for a minute. But apparently her mama had been tempted, more than tempted, ready to go if this Bruno called. And Pansy and her brothers owed their family to their mama's little stillborn baby, or maybe to the selfishness of that union man? No, she wanted to believe it was more than that. Something had kept her mama here, kept her from following that man, something she couldn't get anywhere else, and Pansy knew that something was her daddy.

And what about her daddy? What had he done? But of course she knew. He waited it out, just like every year when her mama had her bad spell. He sat and held her hand and said, "This, too, shall pass; this, too, shall pass." He said it like a prayer he believed with all his heart, and he made Mama believe it too, because the bad spell always did pass, and her mama always did come back to them.

"I probably shouldn't have told none of that." Kitty put her cool fingers on top of Pansy's hand. "Edith used to get so mad at me for telling things."

Pansy put her other hand over Kitty's. "Well, Edith worried too much."

"She did, didn't she," Kitty said. "That old rip."

"Who you calling a old rip?" Idalene's voice come out a croak as she lifted her head to see better.

Pansy jumped up and put a pillow behind her head. "Look who's awake," she said. "You want a drink of water?"

"Yes, Lord, my mouth's dry as a chip."

Pansy poured a cup of water and held the straw while Idalene drank, thinking of all the people she'd done this for over the years: her children, her mama, Dan's parents, and now Idalene. Some got well, and some didn't, and Idalene wouldn't. It was just something she had to accept. The worst part of it was feeling so damn helpless. She hadn't been able to do nothing for her mama, and there was not a thing she could do for Idalene either, nothing except be here. She shouldn't be the only one here, though. If Idalene had family besides Lottie May, why weren't they here?

"Idalene," Pansy said, trying to decide if she felt up to being barked at by an old woman who didn't like people messing in her business. But it was her business, the business of a friend. "Idalene, do you ever hear from any of your brothers?"

Idalene, straw still in her mouth, rolled her eyes up to look at Pansy. A long second passed and Pansy watched her go from surprised to mad to sad. Oh, Lord, she thought. The barking would've been easier to take.

Idalene laid her head back on the pillow and turned her face away. "I don't even know where they are," she said. "And that's for the best. Now, why don't y'all go on home. I know you got things to do, and I'm tired."

Pansy looked over at Kitty, who wrapped the doily around the crochet hook and stuck it in her bag. They said their good-byes, even though Pansy hated so bad to leave Idalene alone like that. But she'd already turned on her side, facing away from them. At the door, Pansy stopped to look back and her heart twisted at the sight of the back of Idalene's head, her hair all matted from laying on it for so long. Tomorrow she'd bring a curling iron and some hair spray and fix that head. It was the least she could do.

ANDY GRIFFITH again? Was that the ideal way to spend the last days of your life? Idalene must think so. Tonight's episode was the one where Opie accidentally killed a mama bird with a slingshot and then had to take care of the babies. Laurel sat on one side of the bed, Lottie May on the other, waiting for the show to be over so they could talk to Idalene. When Andy finally said, "Yeah, but don't the trees seem nice and full?" Idalene hit the mute button.

"That's my favorite one," she said, taking off her glasses so she could wipe her eyes. "I love when Barney talks that bird talk."

Idalene put her glasses back on and scooted up higher in the bed. "I'm glad y'all is here." She looked like some kind of exotic bird plucked of its feathers, her head cocked to one side, her hair white at the roots and red the rest of the way down. Laurel was amazed how alert Idalene was tonight. She'd slept through most of the last few visits.

"I got something for you to read, both of you." She reached under the covers and pulled out two folded sheets of hospital stationery, handed one to Laurel and one to Lottie May. "Now, read them and don't say a word."

Laurel looked at Lottie May, wondering if she knew what Idalene was up to, but Lottie May shook her head, looking equally clueless. Laurel opened her letter and read:

> Dear Laurel,
> I am not a writing woman, but I figure I best set this down on paper. I'm leaving you my house and everything in it.

Laurel looked up at Idalene, opened her mouth, but Idalene's hand flew up and she pointed in Laurel's face and said, "Anh!" It was the same nasal warning Laurel's mama used when Laurel was little and about to do something she wasn't supposed to. She went back to the letter.

It's only for you, now, not nobody else, not even Lottie May, so don't try and give it to her. I've took care of her and Nellie Belle and Nisco.

I talked to your lawyer friend Hap Luckadoo, and he's got all the legal papers about everything. Don't give him no money, 'cause I done paid him.

You're a single woman like me, so when I got to thinking who my house could do the most good for, you come to mind. You might not want to live there, so go ahead and sell it if you'd rather have the money. It won't matter none to me. But I got a feeling you might like a place of your own about now. I got a feeling it would do you good.

Sincerely,

Idalene S. Stevens

"Idalene, this is wonderful of you, but I cannot take your house."

"Anh!" The finger came up again. "If I'd wanted to talk about it I wouldn't a wrote a letter."

Laurel looked helplessly across the bed at Lottie May, who sat looking at her own letter, tears running down her face.

"Now, don't start that boohooing or you'll have to leave." Idalene played with the hem of her sheet, a pleased little smirk on her face. She's enjoying this, Laurel thought, enjoying being the benefactress, and who were they to deny a dying woman?

Laurel folded the letter and put it in her purse. There was no point trying to talk to Idalene now. She'd have to talk to Hap and figure out what to do. God, she hoped he wouldn't ask her out again. She didn't feel like dealing with that.

Lottie May had gone to stand by the edge of the bed, the letter fluttering in her hand. "Idalene, this is so much money."

"Yes, it is. I hope you appreciate it."

"I do," Lottie May said. "It's real nice of you." She raised her head then and looked Idalene in the eye, something Laurel had hardly ever seen her do. "But there's one thing I'd rather have than all the money in the world."

Idalene picked up the remote, held it in the air as if she meant to turn the TV on again, then laid it down again. "What?" she said, as if she already knew and didn't want to deal with it.

The sound of their breathing filled the silence, expanding it like a bubble until Laurel couldn't stand it anymore and said, "What? What do you want, Lottie May? Ask her."

"I want to know about Mama," Lottie May said, her voice trembling.

"That's what I figured."

Lottie May flinched as if the harshness of Idalene's voice was a physical blow, but stood patiently waiting.

"Well," Idalene said at last, still not making eye contact with Lottie May. "What do you want to know?"

Lottie May hesitated. "Well, what did she look like?"

"Look like?" Idalene looked straight at Lottie May then. "You want to know what she looked like, go look in that mirror over yonder. Lord God, the first day I laid eyes on you when you come to work at the plant, I like to had heart failure. I thought Mama done come back from the grave."

Lottie May's hand rose slowly to her own face, as if she could see through her fingers.

"Your eyes is different, black like that Eye-talian daddy of yours, but the rest of you is all her." Idalene leaned back against the pillows, staring at the blank TV. "You talk like her too. I swear, I was so glad when you got old. I used to couldn't even look at you without getting a cold chill. But once you got older than she was when she died, it wasn't so bad."

"What was she like?" Lottie May said, leaning closer to the bed.

Idalene sighed and closed her eyes. "She was tired, that's what she was. Y'all need to go on now. I done pushed my button and I'm getting sleepy."

Lottie May looked so disappointed, Laurel wanted to slap Idalene, except that she looked pretty bad herself. She thought of that day not long ago when she and Idalene sat in separate bathroom stalls, each oblivious to the other crying in the next stall. She seemed so alone now, gone past the point of wiggling her fingers under the wall to ask for toilet paper or anything else.

Lottie May picked up her purse and went back to the bed. "You need anything?"

Idalene's eyes opened and she stared at Lottie May for a long time. "Come back tomorrow," she said finally. "I'll tell you then."

Idalene

I'm glad I ain't dying in the wintertime. It's bad enough to lay here and die period without having to see everything around me dead too. Watching out that window, I seen everything turning green again, summertime coming on, and I feel peaceful. Ever since I was a little gal I have hated wintertime. I don't like to be cold. It keeps me from being able to think about anything except how cold I am. I don't like to be too hot neither, but if I had to choose, I'd pick hot over cold any day of the week. That's one of the reasons I never have cared for the beach. It's either too hot or too cold.

One time in the middle of this real hot summer, Lottie May says to me, "Idalene, I want my young'uns to see the ocean, and I'm tired of waiting on that Butch to come home and take us, so let's me and you take them." Well, I tried to talk her out of it. I had been to the ocean myself with Victor Stevens right before he got shipped overseas and killed in France. I didn't figure it'd changed that much since then. I was so foolish about Victor, but I was in love for the first and thankfully last time in my life. Being in love ain't all it's cracked up to be. Mainly it's a pain in the ass because it makes you do things you'd otherwise be too smart to do.

What I done was, I talked Victor into running off to Myrtle Beach to get married. He didn't want to, wanted to wait till he come home from the war, didn't want to take a chance on saddling me with a cripple or leaving me widowed with a fatherless child to tend to. All of which I didn't appreciate at the time but did later when he didn't come home, especially when I seen what all Lottie May went through with that Butch circling through only just long enough to breed. It was like something in him knowed ever time she got pregnant, because that's when he'd take off, knowing his work was done.

I loved being with Victor, but I sure didn't love that ocean. You talk about cold, that wind whipping across that water cut to the quick. It was miserable on that beach. And I didn't love it no better when me and Lottie May took her young'uns down there. We went for three days, and it was the longest three days of my life. I wore myself out standing on that beach in the hot sun, watching them young'uns go in that big old water, not knowing if they'd come out again. Lottie May kept saying, Lay down here with me and rest, but I couldn't, not so long as they was in the water. What she didn't seem to understand was how it wouldn't take nothing for one of them waves to fling itself over the head of one of her babies and carry it off. She wasn't paying a bit more attention than nothing. "They're fine," she said. "Ever one of them knows how to swim, Idalene. They're just like fish. And they know how to holler for help too."

Poor Lottie May. She can't help being so ignorant. She's always had somebody to look after her, so she don't know what a awful responsibility it is taking care of people. It don't hit you till something bad happens and, even if it wasn't your fault, that burden is on you for life, like a tiger on your back, and you can't never never never shake it off. But Lottie May has led a sheltered life. She ain't never had nothing bad happen to her except for Ed dying. That was bad, but it was only the one thing. She don't know how lucky she is, always having had a nice home and enough to eat and shoes on her feet.

I can't even remember calling a house a home, we moved around so much. We'd just get settled good when Daddy'd hear of another mill that paid more and off we'd go. It wasn't till after Daddy left for good we finally settled down in one place. Mama couldn't find work at first, and Daddy, he never sent us a nickel. We didn't even know where he was. At least that Butch let Lottie May know where he was most of the time and sent money. Mama didn't have nobody but us young'uns, and we wasn't much more than five little mouths to feed. Finally at last she heard they was hiring on at Revel and we moved to Russell and she got a job right off.

Since I was the oldest, she'd leave me in charge when she went to work ever afternoon. She worked second so she could tend to us most of the day and I could go to school for a little while. She'd leave a pot of beans and a cake of corn bread on the stove for our supper, tell me to get the little'uns to bed by eight o'clock, and then lock us in the house. They didn't have day care back then.

I got to where I liked being in charge. I kept everybody busy doing little chores and playing games. The evening would always pass pretty quick, though it was ten long hours before Mama got home. She'd run down that hill from the mill, through the black part of town and on to where our little house set on the edge of a big woods. I reckon it was two miles. The house ain't there no more. They tore it down. Should've tore it down long before we ever moved in it. Anyhow, the little'uns would be asleep by the time Mama come, but I always waited up. When I'd hear her key in the door, I froze at whatever I was doing and waited to see who come through. It was always her, but I reckon I couldn't help being nervous in case one day it wouldn't be.

Mama always said to me, "Hey, little mouse, you been keeping house?" and I'd set with her while she eat a bite of supper and then we'd go to bed. Then Mama got up before daylight to cook our breakfast and do the wash and other chores she had. If she got five hours of sleep a night, I'd be surprised. The main thing I remember about her is how tired she looked. People nowadays don't know what tired is.

Mama had lost two babies in between Peanut and the last one, Richard. One died before it was born, and the other'n died of croup. I reckon that's why we all made such a fuss over Richard. Just the fact he lived seemed like a miracle. We all called him Sonny Boy, after that song, "Climb up on my knee, Sonny Boy, though you're only three, Sonny Boy." We loved that song and we loved that Sonny Boy. He was the sweetest thing and hardly ever cried, and he'd smile when he seen me leaning over his bed. I reckon he thought I was his mama too.

When he was a baby I'd milk the goat and feed him, because Mama couldn't come home from work to nurse him. Then when he got

to where he could eat regular food, he'd eat beans and taters right
along with us, I'd just mash his up good. He follered me everwhere,
and the first word out his mouth wasn't Mama, it was I-dee, that's
what he called me, I-dee, 'cause he couldn't say Idalene yet.

We went along real good for a while, didn't even miss our daddy.
The only bad time was in the wintertime when it got so cold in that
house. They was cracks between the floorboards big enough to see
through to the ground, and that wind whistled up through there some
nights and froze us half to death. We'd set as close to the stove as we
could stand, with blankets wrapped around us. That was the only heat
we had. I always made sure Sonny Boy's bed was closest to the stove. I
didn't never want him to know what it felt like to be cold. But then one
day he got sick with a little croup and I tried to make him stay in the
bed, but he would not do it. Ever time I turned my back he'd climb out
and run and hide somewhere, and then I'd hear him just a-giggling
and have to go hunt him. He had the prettiest blond curly hair, and
when I'd put my hand on his head, it felt so soft and slick. Anyhow,
that little cold wouldn't leave him, and I reckon it turned into
pneumonia, though we couldn't be sure because we couldn't afford to
pay no doctor. It was awful in this world, the sound of that terrible
barking cough coming out of that little young'un.

One night Mama come in the door and she took one look at me
a-setting next to Sonny Boy's bed and she come a-running. I said,
"Mama, he won't wake up. He's been asleep like that since five
o'clock." I hadn't never been so scared in my life. She picked him up
and his little head dangled back and this sound come out Mama's
mouth like something in there was getting killed. She squeezed him
against her and turned her back to me and started rocking back and
forth. She done that a long time. Finally at last she laid him back in
his bed and covered him up and petted his head. She said, "Sonny
Boy's dead, Idalene." So then I knowed. I had not kept that baby
warm enough and so he died. I had killed my little brother. Mama
didn't hold it against me, and I still watched over the other three when
she was working, and it got to where they hated for Mama to leave
because I never give them a minute's peace. I watched ever move they
made, and if they so much as sneezed I put them in the bed and made

them stay there. I wasn't but eight year old myself, but I was big enough to make them mind.

After Mama died, it ain't no wonder the boys didn't want to have nothing to do with me at the orphanage. I reckon they decided they didn't have to listen to me no more. So when I got to be twelve year old I left there and come back to Russell to live with Daddy's cousin and went to work in the plant and stayed. Mama never wanted us to have to work in a cotton mill like she done, but I liked it. I liked making my own money and I liked being independent. I didn't need nobody and, most important of all, didn't nobody need me.

SUMMER

Bloom where you're planted.

18

Pansy felt guilty, thinking about Dan and Laurel at work while she was out driving all over the countryside, but she might as well enjoy it while she could. Once she went back to the plant, she wouldn't have this kind of freedom anymore. Already Dan was treating her like nothing had changed. But he'd find out soon enough. Some kind of switch had been flipped and wasn't no going back to the old Pansy who spent every waking minute seeing to somebody else's comfort.

But she didn't want to think about Dan now, didn't want to think period. It was a beautiful morning, the sky so blue, the trees so green. The August heat made the whole world shimmer. Pansy had always loved summer best, loved the aliveness of it.

She was glad she hadn't taken the interstate, or superhighway as Idalene used to call it. She liked going slow, enjoying the view as she drove past fields of corn green and higher than a man, pastures full of black-and-white milk cows. Then came little white mill houses, then brick ranch houses, everything getting bigger and closer together as she came into Granite Springs. It wasn't a big city, but compared to Russell it was huge. Pansy pulled the directions out of her purse and checked to make sure she was on the right road. And just a few minutes later, there it was, Spofford Amoco. That easy, she'd found Idalene's brother.

Laurel had gone to the library and looked up phone numbers for Spoffords in Wolfpen, where the orphanage used to be, and Granite Springs, the nearest city, and it'd taken Pansy only an hour or so of calling to find this brother, William, who owned the Amoco station, and surely he'd know about the rest. Why hadn't Idalene tried all those years? And now it was too late.

The station was small, one of the old Amoco's that hadn't been remodeled into a six-pump convenience store and where they still actually worked on cars. The doors to the double garage were open and Pansy could see a blue car up on the lift inside one, stacks of tires piled high against the walls behind it.

A man in blue coveralls walked out of the station to meet her, something that hardly ever happened anymore. Everything was self-service these days. Peanut—his name sewed in red thread on the left breast pocket—stood about the same height as Pansy, five three, and was built like a bull—great big shoulders and a tiny little bottom half. Even though he must be in his sixties at least, he walked quick, like a much younger man. As he came toward her, he wiped his hands on a dirty rag, which only seemed to spread the grease further.

"Help you, ma'am?" he said.

"I'm looking for a man named William Spofford."

He smiled as if he'd remember where he knew her from in a minute. "That's me. I'm him."

"You're William?"

"Yes, ma'am."

Oh, Lord, Pansy thought, I've found him. She could even see a resemblance between him and Lottie May, the nose, the shape of the face.

"And you've got brothers named James and Carl?"

He squinted at her. "Ma'am? Did you just call here a couple days ago?"

How did she go about telling him now that she'd come face to face with the man? It was too hard. She should've told him on the phone, that would've been easier. But when she tried, when she heard his voice, heard him answer the same questions she'd just asked him, she couldn't even speak and had hung up on him. It was not something to be done over the phone. A decent person would tell something like this in person. It was common courtesy.

"I'm so sorry I hung up on you," she said. With the sun beating down on the top of her head and heat radiating up from the pavement, she felt like she might melt right here next to her car. Was it really that bad, or was she having a hot flash? She pulled a Kleenex from her pocket and blotted the sweat on her forehead. "Could we go inside and talk for just a minute, please?" She hoped he had air-conditioning in that dirty little office.

He led her inside and moved a stack of newspapers off a chair so she could sit, then turned the fan on the desk so it would blow on her. He leaned against the desk, arms crossed over his chest, waiting.

Pansy didn't know how else to start, so she just blurted out, "Do you remember having a sister named Idalene?"

He cocked his head to one side, a confused look on his face. "Well, yes, ma'am. But I ain't seen her since we was young'uns. Do you know her?"

"I did." Pansy hesitated. "I hate to be the one to tell you this, but she passed away last week."

His eyes closed, light blue eyes so much like Idalene's it was scary, and his chin swung in slow motion toward his chest. He stood there, his head hung down, for a long minute.

"What happened?" He looked more stunned than sad, and if Pansy had known him better, she would've hugged him.

"It was stomach cancer." Pansy wanted to say Idalene didn't suffer, but that would've been a lie and the family deserved the truth. "She went pretty quick, and there was a lot of people that loved her and took good care of her. We didn't know about y'all or we would've called."

He put a hand to his nose and squeezed it, then sniffed hard and shook his head. "I wanted to look for her after I got grown, but Carl and James said no, she wouldn't want nothing to do with us. Since they was older, I figured they knew what they was talking about. I wish now I had of tried." He pushed away from the desk, ready to walk her outside. "I sure do appreciate you coming to tell me in person like this. Makes it easier, knowing she had friends."

"Wait," Pansy said before he could start for the door. Might as well get it all blurted out while she was on a roll. "There's something else. You've got another sister. Well, a half-sister. Lottie May."

"A half-sister."

"Yes. The one you thought died with your mama. She didn't. Didn't die, I mean." Poor Peanut, he really looked confused now, like a little boy trying to do math in his head. Pansy spoke as gentle as she could, using the same voice she'd used to calm her young'uns down from a bad dream. "She lives in Russell and works at Revel Mill with me. And she did work with Idalene."

"Yeah, but I don't understand something. How did Idalene find her?"

Oh, Lord, Pansy thought, she could hear what was really behind that question and it broke her heart. Why didn't Idalene look for them too? "She didn't. It was just a coincidence. When Lottie May come to work at Revel, Idalene said she looked so much like your mama she knew it had to be her. She'd heard that the baby lived but didn't know what happened to it till then."

"My Lord," Peanut said, resting his butt against the desk and looking around the office. "I can't quite get my mind wrapped around it."

"It's a lot to take in," Pansy said, nodding, glad then that she'd come, that she was there to see the look on his face, the surprise and the beginning of a kind of hope. "Idalene wanted y'all to get together," Pansy said. "It was her last request, really." She'd never said it in so many words, but when Idalene didn't snap Pansy's head off for asking about the brothers, it was like permission in a way for Pansy to do what she liked with the information.

"Lord, yes," Peanut said. "I want to meet her, and I know Carl will too. He lives right down the road here, but James is in California. He ain't been in very good health the last year or so, and I don't know if he can get out here. But I wouldn't feel right going without him."

"Well," Pansy said. She stood up, knowing he'd need some time alone to digest all this, to call his brothers. "Why don't y'all talk about it and give me a call." She wrote her name and number on the back of a grocery receipt and handed it to him. "I would give you Lottie May's number, but . . . well, the truth is, she don't know about y'all, and I was afraid to tell her in case I couldn't find you." She hadn't wanted to tell him that, hadn't wanted him to know Idalene never told her own sister about them, but she had to protect Lottie May. If she found out she had brothers only to lose them, it would break her heart.

"Pansy Champion," he said, and looked up from the paper. "Well, Pansy, I surely do thank you for what you done."

As she got ready to pull out onto the road, Pansy glanced in her rearview mirror and saw him there behind her next to the pump, tiny and sad, like those little gnomes Lottie May kept in her yard. She waved, but he was already turning away. He'd been shocked, and rightly so. It was a lot to take in, especially at his age. She hadn't had the heart to tell him the rest, that Idalene had been cremated and that very afternoon Laurel and the girls would be scattering her ashes in the river, just as she'd requested. Pansy had been hoping to make it back in time herself, but in a way was glad she wouldn't. They'd had a viewing and a funeral, and she'd said her good-byes even before that. Just like with her mama, she'd had to let Idalene go a long time before she actually left this world.

LAUREL EYED the stretch of tall grass and weeds between the pavement and the edge of the river. No telling what all kind of snakes or bugs were in there. If it hadn't been so hot she would've worn her knee-high snow boots. She just hoped jeans and tennis shoes would be enough of a barrier between her and any critters that might want a taste of her. She'd started sweating and her T-shirt stuck to her back, but there was no shade behind the loading dock. If they didn't hurry she'd be nothing but a puddle when they got there.

Bushy Cook came out on the loading dock and saw her standing below him. "Hey," he said, and made no move to go back in the warehouse.

"Hey," she said back, feeling nervous. She'd been hoping nobody would see her. She didn't think they'd get any flak about it but figured it was best to keep it to themselves just in case. "I'm waiting for somebody," she said, even though he hadn't asked.

"Oh, right," he said, in a way that made her think he knew what they were getting ready to do. Maybe Joe had told him.

Bushy went back in and Laurel looked toward the gate. Finally. Lottie May led the way, a small white plastic bag in one hand. Oh, God, Laurel thought. Those are Idalene's ashes in that bag. She wished they'd put her in an urn or something besides a trash bag. It didn't seem dignified enough.

Percilla and Joe followed Lottie May, Percilla talking a mile a minute and batting her eyelashes up at Joe. Laurel's heart thumped up in her throat at the sight of him. While she'd accepted that her mind and emotions weren't ready for a relationship just yet, her body was a different story. But she could handle it. Once she'd gotten past her initial embarrassment, Laurel had been grateful for Joe's clear head that night at the Ponderosa. They'd pretended those kisses never happened and had fallen into their same old routine at the library and on their visits with Idalene. They were friends, and that was something Laurel needed more than anything else right now.

"Where's Maxann?" Laurel asked when they got closer.

"She went to get her gloves out of the car," Lottie May said.

"Gloves?" It hadn't occurred to Laurel until just then that they'd be using their hands. She wished she'd thought to bring her own gloves, tried to think if she had a pair of Isotoners in the car.

Joe said, "I can carry the bag if you want me to, Lottie May. The ground's kind of rough."

She handed it to him, and it seemed even smaller in his hands. That used to be a person, Laurel thought. How could it all boil down to one little bag of ashes?

Maxann came running up, red-faced and out of breath, pulling on a pair of black winter mittens. "Sorry," she said.

Laurel felt glad then that she hadn't thought of gloves, wondering how it made Lottie May feel to see Maxann putting them on. She turned and started stomping through the grass, hoping to scare off any snakes, not sure why she was mad all of a sudden. Joe caught up with her, bent toward her. "Listen," he said. "This is probably a bad time, but I need to tell you."

Oh, God, she thought. What now?

He put a hand on her arm and said softly, "Mr. Arthur died last night in his sleep, real peaceful. His daughter called me this morning."

Laurel stopped and looked down at the weeds. That sweet old man who'd cried so hard at Idalene's funeral she'd been afraid he would pass out, he was dead. A dragonfly flitted past her knees and she lifted her head and watched it zip off toward the river. The light had changed in the last week or so and, in spite of the heat and the long days still ahead, she was reminded of fall. The world was changing all the time, all around them, and most of the time they were too busy to notice. There were so many things that went unnoticed, people too, and Laurel felt glad and relieved that Idalene and Mr. Arthur had found each other. She reached out and touched Joe's arm, then continued on toward the river.

Even in the middle in full sun, the river looked dark and slow. The dry summer had brought the water level low, exposing roots and rocks on both sides. Joe braced his foot against a root and helped them down the steep bank and onto a narrow strip of muddy beach. They stood there a minute, and Laurel was beginning to wonder if she should make the first move, when Lottie May reached out and took the bag from Joe. Her hands clenched around the plastic, holding it tight against her belly. When she spoke, her voice came out higher than normal, as if any minute she might break down. "Idalene said when she was little, her and the other young'uns used to sneak out when their work was caught up, come down here, and go fishing. Said it used to make the bossmen so mad, but what could they do? They wasn't nothing but children." Lottie May's fingers worked at the twist tie holding the bag closed, but she couldn't seem to twist it the right way.

Laurel stepped over to her. "Here, let me." When the bag was open, she looked at Lottie May, waiting for a signal of some sort, but Lottie May just stood there crying, tears running under her glasses and down her cheeks. Laurel looked at Joe, then Percilla, then Maxann. They all just stared back, as helpless as she was.

Finally Maxann said, "Oh, hell," and came over to Laurel. She stuck a hand in the bag and brought out a mound of gray, lumpy-looking ash. She looked at it a minute, then dropped it back in the bag, ripped off both gloves, and threw them on the ground. As she lifted out another handful of ashes, her mouth opened as if she intended to say something, but she got choked up and instead held her hand over the water and let the ashes sift through her fingers. A slight breeze blew them onto the mud at her feet. "Dammit," she said. "I wanted her to go on the water."

She scooped out another handful and Percilla whined, "Don't take them all."

Maxann gave her an irritated look. This time she waded into the river, shoes and all, until the water reached her knees. The ashes landed on the water, floating a little ways before sinking underneath. Maxann looked back at them. "Well," she said. "Come on. It's only water."

They hesitated, looking at one another, then down at their feet. Laurel took a step, her foot sinking even deeper as water soaked in. These shoes will never be white again, she thought. The river was full of red-clay mud, and already the shoe looked slightly orange. She took another step and when she looked back, Joe had taken Lottie May's arm before stepping into the water with her, and Percilla followed. She didn't look happy, but at least she came.

"Be careful," Maxann said. "There's some slippery rocks on the bottom."

When she reached Maxann, Laurel handed the bag to her and stuck her hand in before she lost her nerve. Once it touched the ashes, she didn't feel grossed out anymore. They felt soft and lumpy and kind of gritty, like fireplace ashes. Hell, she thought, those ashes were probably cleaner than her hands. She held them cupped in both hands and waited for the others to take some.

As Lottie May took hers, she said softly, "I know we had music at the church funeral, but would somebody say a word, or at least sing something?"

Laurel looked at Joe. He was the musician in the group, after all. She wondered if he'd pick one of the bluegrass songs he'd done at Idalene's funeral. That had been an experience, a bluegrass band playing a funeral. But Idalene had known what she wanted, and she'd made sure she got it. As the ashes drifted from Joe's fingers, he sang, *"In the sweet by and by, we shall meet on that beautiful shore."*

A breeze blew through the trees, the leaves waved, and downstream, diamonds of light flickered across the water. The air felt cooler in the middle of the river, as if they'd left the heat and humidity of

August on the bank. Laurel saw it there, that heat, waiting. The brick walls of the plant shimmered in it.

It wasn't that long ago the sight of that place made her feel sick and trapped—the walls, the fence, the bricked-up windows. But somehow over the last few months it had changed. Or she had. Now it was simply work, which had come to be so much more than a job. The outside didn't matter. When she pulled into the parking lot every day, she wasn't thinking prison, she was thinking about what she had to do that day, and thinking about things she wanted to tell Maxann or Lottie May, or her mama, thinking about the latest crazy thing Percilla might've done. The plant was only a prison if you let it be. For some people it was home. It had been Idalene's home for sixty-three years, her home and her family. She hadn't been alone at all. And if heaven was the place a person had been happiest in life, like Idalene believed, Laurel figured right now she and Mr. Arthur must be sitting in their yard chairs on a shady hillside somewhere, listening to bluegrass music, drinking beer, eating cold fried chicken, watching the world go by. It made Laurel feel good to think about all the different ways people had of loving each other, and it gave her hope that love, if it was tended properly, really could last.

When the song was done, they turned back toward the bank and Laurel took Lottie May's hand. They were halfway there when there was a grunt and then a loud splash. She turned and saw Percilla on her butt, water up to her waist.

"Oh, Lord," Lottie May said, her hand covering a smile. Maxann didn't even try to hide. She stood there and laughed out loud. Joe looked helplessly from Percilla to Laurel.

"Don't just stand there." Percilla held her hands in the air like a child who wants to be picked up, her face red as a beet. "Somebody get over here and help me up!"

Joe waded over, took her hands, and pulled, but her feet kept slipping on the rocks. He squatted to get better leverage and put all his weight into the pull, then ended up on his butt across from Percilla.

He shook water off like a dog, grinning like he couldn't think of anything more fun than sitting fully clothed in the middle of a river. "I believe Idalene's having some fun with us," he said.

"Well," Percilla said, touching her hair to make sure it hadn't got wet. "That'd be just like her." She must've decided she'd have an easier time getting up by herself, because she turned over and got on her hands and knees.

Maxann stepped cautiously over to Percilla and held out her hand. Percilla took hold, got one foot under her, then the other, then slowly straightened. "Thank you," she said, holding on tight. "Now, don't let go."

They proceeded slowly, holding hands, slipping and catching each other several times before they made it back.

Lottie May said, "Lord, Percilla, honey, them pants'll never be white again."

Joe still sat out in the river, staring up at the sky, at the trees, a contented look on his face.

"What in the world are you doing?" Laurel said when they'd reached the bank and turned to wait for him.

"I heard something a minute ago and I'm trying to figure out what it is. Listen."

They got quiet and listened and a minute later heard a high-pitched, chattering squeal, like a squeaky wheel on a speeding shopping cart.

Laurel looked at Maxann. "What is that?"

"Lord," Maxann said. "I don't know."

"I'll tell you what it is," Percilla said. "It's a whistlepig."

"A what?" Joe said.

"A groundhog," Laurel said, remembering her conversation with Rex at the Christmas party.

Suddenly there was a splash, and the women saw an animal the size of a small dog—a small, fat, ratlike dog—scuttle up the opposite bank. Joe must've seen it too, because he leaped up, then slipped and fell again before finally getting to his feet.

"What you running for?" Percilla hollered. "It's just a groundhog. It won't hurt you."

He practically walked on water getting out of the river, then stood next to Laurel and looked out toward the place he'd been sitting. "It's not the groundhog I'm worried about. It's the copperhead." The word *copperhead* was enough to make them all, Laurel included, turn tail and run, squealing, up the bank. When they got to the top, they stood together, laughing and breathing hard. Joe came up next to them and pointed toward a big rock in the middle of the river. "It jumped off that rock and started swimming right toward me," he said. "I can't believe we didn't see it before."

"I'm glad we didn't. Let's get out of here before we see another one." Maxann turned and started high-stepping through the grass, Percilla on her heels.

Lottie May still faced the river and Laurel stood with her, waving Joe on when he gave her a look that asked if he should stay. She put her arm around Lottie May's shoulders and they stood there together, not speaking but saying good-bye.

19

THE CANVAS WAS SO WHITE, THE LIGHT FROM THE BED-
room window bounced off it and hurt her eyes. She turned the easel to
face the room and stood looking at it. It was still blank, still waiting.
She'd got so excited about the idea of painting a picture, going to the
store and getting the paints and the palette and the easel and the can-
vases, and now here she was with nothing to paint, no idea how to pro-
ceed. It'd been too long, that was all. She was crazy to have thought she
could do it again. She ought to just go on back to work like a normal
person. But still she kept standing there, waiting.

The bedroom window overlooked Kitty's garden, and Pansy could
see her out there picking beans. Early that morning after Dan and
Laurel left for work, she and Kitty had eaten breakfast at Kitty's
kitchen table and then went their separate ways. Kitty wanted to get
through the rows before the sun got too hot, and Pansy was dying to try
her paints. She'd put on a pair of shorts and one of Dan's old shirts, a
bright blue one the color of the sky over the garden, and now stood
barefoot in front of the easel, waiting.

What did she used to paint in high school? Things she loved—trees,
people, houses, fields. If she just had some of those pictures now, if her
mama hadn't thrown them in the trash the summer after Pansy graduated. It still made her mad to think how calm her mama was, saying she

didn't need to be fooling with that nonsense no more now she was a working woman. Pansy knew they weren't great paintings, but they were treasures to her. Well, no sense dwelling on that. She didn't have all day, and she wanted to get done and cleaned up before Laurel and Dan got home from work. She wasn't ready to tell them what she was doing yet, didn't want to hear them being all supportive about her taking up a hobby. Was that all it was? Somehow the word *hobby* didn't have enough feeling in it, but Pansy couldn't think of anything better.

The one painting she did remember was one of her daddy in the field at his plow, hat pushed back on his head the way it was when he wanted to see how far he'd come, eyes squinting far down the row just plowed. That was how she remembered him still, even without the painting, because that was where he was happiest, out on his land. She thanked God every day he never lived long enough to see all but these eight acres of hers and Dan's sold off.

She could probably paint that one again but couldn't get excited about it. It was done, in the past. She wanted to paint something in her life now. She watched Kitty bend and pick, bend and pick, and thought about painting her, good old Kitty who was so sweet and took such good care of her. She could paint Kitty in the beans with the corn tall and green behind her. Pansy loved corn, especially loved to drive past big fields of it under a big blue sky. It made her think of being at the beach, where nothing cut into her view of the ocean and the sky. She was always pointing cornfields out to the kids when they was little, not wanting them to overlook something so beautiful. One time when Laurel was about twelve, she was sitting in the front seat acting bored and she said, "What is it with you and corn, Mama?" It took Pansy back so, she didn't know how to answer. She thought everybody felt the way she did about it, or they would if they really looked. She couldn't explain it in words. The night Dan had found her in the corn, she'd made him understand without words, hadn't she? Wasn't that the best way for a man and woman to communicate, the closest they could come to speaking the same language?

Yesterday she hadn't understood what made her pick up acrylic paints, but now she knew. She was going to paint that corn, and the sky, and her and Dan under it, and that called for sharp, clear colors.

She didn't start right away, just sat still and let the picture develop in her mind first, getting more and more excited as it come clear how to do it. Lord, she couldn't remember the last time she felt this good, this happy, this alive. No, wait, yes she could: when her babies was born. All that life had come out of her and she couldn't think of no better feeling. Her hands shook as she reached for a tube of green paint and twisted off the lid.

HER ARM felt like it was fixing to fall out of the socket, so she put the brush down and looked at the clock. She'd been standing there two and a half hours and it felt like five minutes, except for her sore muscles. A big smile come across her face and she couldn't help it, she liked what she saw. It would take a while to paint the whole picture, but she had the outlines of things down and could imagine the finished picture as if it already existed: corn, dark green and mysterious; a purple-black sky filled with white stars; on the right side of the corn patch, two heads, a man and a woman; on the left side, two sets of feet, all the toenails painted green. She might have to change one set of feet. Dan wouldn't like to see himself with painted toenails. That was easy to fix, though. Their eyes needed to be bigger to show them trying to see every last star as they laid there side by side. The corn was like the covers on their bed, or like their body, something they shared and there was no way to tell where their separate parts connected. But they still had their own heads and feet, and she decided she wanted to see their shoulders and hands too. She could paint that in later.

Her stomach growled and she remembered Kitty was making fried chicken for dinner, and Pansy felt like she could eat a whole chicken all by herself. She could eat and sit and talk to Kitty a little bit, all the time feeling happy knowing the picture was up here waiting on her to come and finish it.

WHAT SHE needed now was a frame, something to set it off just right. It'd have to dry a couple days first, but she wanted to be ready to show it to Dan and Laurel. She was so nervous, thinking of them seeing it when they got home from work, but also excited. She had her keys in her hand, measurements on a piece of paper in her pocket, when she remembered the pictures in the storage room of the shed, pictures that had belonged to her mama and had nice frames. Before she spent any more money, she ought to check and see if one of them would fit. They were old and probably too big, but it wouldn't take a minute to look.

She cranked the car and got the air-conditioning going so the car would be cool when she got in, then went to the shed. It was like an oven inside, but she didn't bother turning on the fan since she wouldn't be there long. The storage room was even hotter, and sweat ran down the middle of her back and the sides of her neck. Laurel never had got out here and gone through all this stuff like she said she would, but then again, she worked so hard, especially these last few weeks getting ready for the picnic. It didn't seem fair she had to come home every night and cook. There was no reason Pansy couldn't do that. She'd been missing her kitchen anyway. She'd start tonight and have supper on the table when they got home.

She picked her way through the boxes and found the pictures leaning against the wall on the other side. The wooden frames felt grimy under her hands as she flipped through them, remembering. Most of them had been in the house since her daddy was a boy, and she'd never stopped to wonder if her mama had loved or hated them. There was a great big long one of the Last Supper that had hung over the bed in Mama and Daddy's room. And a smaller one of a white-haired man in black praying at a table—that one had hung in the kitchen. There were two pictures she remembered from the living-room walls: a print of a red gristmill by a stream, and one of two big horses hitched to a plow, the rows humped up red and dusty behind them, and beyond that a row of trees showing the first green of spring. It had been her daddy's favorite, and on winter nights after a long day's work in the mill he'd sit in his chair after supper and just stare at it.

All the frames were too big, though, and she let them fall back against the wall, then looked down at one that'd fallen over. Pansy saw Jesus staring up at her from a frame made of what looked like gray barn wood. It was smaller than the rest and just might fit. It would need cleaning and maybe a mat, but it should work, and it was the perfect material for her picture. She turned the frame over, bent the nails up, and picked at the corner of the picture with her fingernail to lift it up. Expecting to see dirty glass, she saw instead more white, then looked at the front of the picture she'd just turned over. That's not Jesus, she thought. That's Daddy.

And then it sank in and she recognized the picture, her own brush strokes, her own name in the corner, *Pansy D.* Oh, Lord. How had it got here? Had her daddy saved this one, hid it from her mama somehow? But no, that was impossible. She remembered taking this picture out of the box under her bed and looking at it after her daddy's funeral. Oh, Mama, she thought, why did you have to hide everything from us? And why save this one? Maybe she couldn't stand to burn a picture of her own husband, but there had been others of Dill and she'd burned those. Hadn't she?

Pansy's hands shook as she laid the picture on top of Jesus and set it carefully aside. She grabbed the gristmill picture and undid the back. Nothing, just the mill inside. The same with the praying man and the plow horses. Oh, please, oh, please, she thought as she lifted the Last Supper and turned it over. The nails on the back were fastened down so tight she had to get a flathead screwdriver to pry them up.

But there, under the cardboard backing, there was her treasure, all the paintings she'd kept in that old coat box under her bed, the ones her mama had claimed she burnt in the oil drum in the backyard. She lifted each one and laid it on top of a box until they were spread around her, thirty of them at least. She sat on a box in the middle of them and just looked, forgetting the heat and sweat and dirt and everything else. She saw her daddy in the barn, in his chair, coming down the road from work; her mama at the clothesline, making a bed, milking a cow; her brothers on the porch and on the tractor; her house; her school; her art teacher, Mrs. Young; and Dan, in overalls, in his Sunday suit at church, in his truck. It was her life, her young life anyhow, spread out for her to see.

They weren't great pictures. Good, but not great. The loss of something precious only made it grow more beautiful in the imagination over time, the same way her most precious memories of her young 'uns were of the times when they was small, the times that had been gone the longest and when they had been freshest and newest and most innocent.

She couldn't paint like that girl now if she tried, and she didn't want to try. It was better to be on the other side of that kind of innocence, to the point you knew what you did and did not have control over. That's what struck her about these paintings: their innocence. She'd been so young, so blind to the fact that just because she was a good girl and worked hard didn't mean all her dreams would come true.

It wasn't fair that people, especially girls, was brought up to believe that. There was so much more involved than just simple living right. There was the hand of God, not to mention the hands of the other people in your life, people who loved you but showed it in ways you couldn't begin to understand. And if you didn't have no encouragement, the chances of pushing off them other hands and finding your own way was pretty small. She'd done better by Laurel, though, kept her hands off as much as she could stand, let Laurel decide what she wanted to do, where she wanted to go, who she wanted to be. The jury was still out on that, though, and all Pansy could do was wait.

WHEN SHE got home and found the car running but no Pansy in sight, Laurel panicked. She ran through the house calling for her but got no answer. Oh, God, she thought. She's snapped. She's run off somewhere and it's all my fault. I should never have let her stay home alone.

She went back to the carport to turn off the car, then went around the house, thinking maybe she was working in the yard, even hot as it was. At the open shed door she hesitated, afraid of what she might find, but then she heard a noise and stepped inside, the heat falling on her like a wet blanket. She heard the noise again, a rustling from the storage room. "Mama?"

Pansy looked up, her nose red and her clothes dark with sweat.

"Mama, how long have you been in here? You could get heat stroke." Laurel stepped closer and noticed the paintings spread out around Pansy. "What are these?" She picked up the one closest to her, a watercolor of Maw Bert's house, the two maple trees in the side yard on fire with orange and yellow leaves, the sky bright blue overhead, the details sharp, almost like a photograph. Then she saw the name in the corner, *Pansy D*.

When she raised her head, Pansy said, "Well, what do you think?"

"Where did these come from?"

Pansy leaned to the side and pointed to the Last Supper picture leaning against the wall behind her.

The disciples? Oh, God, Laurel thought, please don't let my mama be having a nervous breakdown.

"I come out here looking for a frame and found this." Pansy held up the Jesus picture so Laurel could see.

The disciples AND Jesus? It was worse than she thought. Why couldn't her daddy hurry up and get home?

"I found one in here and the rest in the Last Supper."

Laurel shook her head. "I'm still confused, Mama. Why didn't you ever show these paintings to us? Why did you hide them?"

"I didn't hide them. Mama did."

"Why would she do that?"

"Lord, honey, you tell me and we'll both know. She told me she burned them all."

Had she entered the Twilight Zone? Her Maw Bert burned her own daughter's pictures? That didn't sound like her. "Maw Bert told you she burned these pictures and then she hid them from you?"

Pansy nodded, pulling her T-shirt away from her chest. She went to the window and opened it, stood there fanning herself with her hand. "Am I having a hot flash or is it hot as hell in here?"

Laurel went to stand next to her at the window. "It's a wonder you didn't pass out. It must be a hundred degrees in here. Why didn't you take this stuff in the house and look at it?"

"I don't know. I reckon I just got carried away."

"Did Maw Bert ever tell you why she hid them?"

Pansy looked at Laurel a long time, long enough that Laurel started to feel uncomfortable. Finally she said, "That was all such a long time ago. The important thing is I found them." She hesitated. "I found that letter too. The one about the scholarship."

Was she mad? Laurel couldn't tell. "I'm sorry I read it without checking with you first, Mama." She took a deep breath. "Why didn't you ever tell me?"

"Tell you what? That I won a scholarship? Honey, if I'd ever known about it myself I sure would've told y'all."

"What?" Could the grandmother she knew, the one who took her to the library and read to her and played tea party with her, could that woman be the same person who hid her own daughter's scholarship letter and treasured paintings? It didn't seem possible. A feeling of rage rose in her chest, something she'd never thought she'd feel in connection with Maw Bert. Why didn't her mama look upset too? Even though she'd had more time to absorb it, deal with the betrayal, she should still be furious. "Mama, aren't you mad about this? Don't you want to know why?"

Pansy shook her head. "What's the point in getting mad?"

"I don't know. I just don't understand how she could do that to her own daughter."

"Listen," Pansy said. "I've had my times of being mad at Mama, Lord knows I have. But all that was a long time ago, and I know in my heart Mama done the best she could for me. I can't be mad at her for that, can I? I wouldn't trade one minute of the life I've had for no scholarship in the world, and that's the truth. And now I got these back, I feel like Mama's trying to tell me something. She couldn't burn them. She wanted to but she couldn't, because she knew how much they meant to me. She saved them for me, and I think she knew I'd find them, someday."

In the light of the window, Pansy looked younger somehow, like a weight or a worry had been lifted, something specific that she wouldn't tell Laurel, something that had been there a long, long time. Seeing her mama like this was worth more than the answers to any questions Laurel might have about Maw Bert. She pushed them to the back of her mind, thinking maybe there'd be time for them later, but maybe not, and that was all right too. The hardest part was knowing her mama had been denied her dream, and seeing her accept it so easily. But maybe that was how it worked. Maybe one generation opened the door and it was up to the next generation to walk through it. That's what Laurel had done, with her mama's help, she had walked through that door, gone to college. And now what? She must be such a disappointment.

"Oh, Lord," Pansy said, looking at her watch. "Your daddy'll be home and I ain't even started supper."

Laurel nodded. She understood her mama was back and stronger than ever, it seemed, and Laurel was grateful, so grateful. The only problem was, where did that leave her?

With the stack of paintings and the Jesus frame in her arms, Pansy headed out the door and Laurel followed, relieved to get out of the heat of the shed. Laurel stopped to pull the door shut behind her but Pansy kept going, and the further away she got, the smaller Laurel felt, the sensation of shrinking making her want to holler, "Mama, wait!" But she wasn't a little girl anymore. She could make her own way now, and she knew it was time, no matter how lonely it might feel getting started.

Pansy stopped behind the house, at the edge of the big rectangle of dirt that Dan had kept tilled and free of weeds for two summers now. Laurel knew he'd been hoping Pansy would go back to her garden this year, but it was too late for planting now. Pansy squatted, the pictures balanced on her thighs, and took up a handful of dirt, let it sift through her fingers. She turned her head toward Laurel. "I reckon this ground's set idle long enough," she said. "Next year I'm going to make it even bigger." She stood, dusting her hand against her shorts. "And you can help me."

Laurel stopped halfway to the garden. She thinks I'm still going to be here this time next year. Am I? She honestly couldn't say, but at least thinking of the future didn't fill her with dread the way it had back in the winter. Maybe she would be here next summer and help her mama with the garden. What was wrong with that? Maybe she'd still be working at the plant too. Maybe she'd move into that house Idalene left her. Maybe she'd get married and have kids. Maybe she'd go back to school. Maybe she'd take up painting herself. It seemed to run in the family. Or she could write a book. That editor had liked the news releases she did on the plant anniversary, said she was a good writer. The point was, she had options, right here in Russell, all kinds of options.

She went the rest of the way to her mama, smiling, and Pansy said, "What you grinning at?"

Laurel threw her arms around Pansy, paintings and all. She inhaled the blend of her mama's sweet pear shampoo, turpentine, and sweat, making a memory to remind her how it felt to be still, to live in the moment, to just breathe and let go, and wait, and see.

ALBERTA

All the things I done, Pansy never understood I was trying to save her from heartache. She ain't never had to suffer nothing like me, she's led a blessed life, always had plenty to eat and nice clothes to wear and didn't never have to work in the fields. She don't know how lucky she was. By the time I got up as tall as the plow handles I was out there working same as Daddy and the boys, when I wasn't in school. Only reason Mama wasn't out there too was because she always had a baby to tend. We plowed and planted and hoed, and Mama stayed back and kept house and cooked the meals. If people nowadays had to work like that, they'd die.

Pansy's daddy, he spoiled her, and I let him. Might be she'd appreciate what all I done for her if she'd had to work like a man all her life. That mill job would've looked mighty good to her then. I couldn't do nothing with him, though. He said no girl of his was going to work in the field like a man, said mine and Pansy's job was in the house and keeping a garden. I wonder if he would've felt thataway if I hadn't give him all them boys first. Probably not. Probably would've had me and Pansy both out there a-helping him, and then see if she would've thought her daddy was so perfect.

He acted like I ought to be happy to finally get me that girl child after all them boys, and I was happy at first. But seemed like when she started growing up she changed some way and I couldn't see her as a little girl no more. I seen when she started filling out and looking at boys at church, and I felt like I wanted to lock her up in the house and never let her out. I hadn't never knowed before how clear it is to other people, that change from girl to woman, and so I knowed my mama and daddy must've seen it in me and they didn't do a thing to stop it. They ain't much you can do to stop a child growing up, making the same terrible mistakes, but I done the one thing I could do, which was keep her home with me. It won't hard when Dill was still a-living, because she was her daddy's girl, followed him everywhere. When he passed, she was at the age where other girls in her class was going on car dates and wouldn't nothing do but for her to start that too, no matter how I argued it with her.

Finally I got tired of having Dan's feet under my table every night of the week, so I let her go. Wasn't long before she graduated high school and I knowed if I could just get her graduated and get her a good job in the mill, then I could relax. She'd be safe. I knowed she'd go on and marry Dan, all I had to do was look at them together to see that, him watching every move she made and her lighting up like a Christmas tree every time he come on the place. I knowed she'd be safe because she'd be satisfied with him.

The thing that worried me more than her a-getting married was her all the time talking about that durn art teacher of hers, that Mrs. Young. She put ideas in Pansy's head that had no place there, telling her she ought to go to college and study art and then come back and teach it in the school. I purely hated that woman for doing that to my girl. She ought to have knowed we couldn't pay for no college, couldn't hardly afford to let Pansy finish high school. If it hadn't been for all the boys sending money after their daddy died, we might've starved to death.

But Dill, he made me swear Pansy'd finish school, said she wouldn't amount to nothing in this world without her education. This from a man that didn't finish sixth grade and didn't want me to go to college myself. I shouldn't never have let her go that last year with that Mrs. Young loading her up with how talented she was and what a wonderful teacher she'd make. Then Pansy'd come home talking about how this one and that one was a-going to college, never asked to go herself, but I could see it there in her face, that wanting to go. Wanting something she knowed she couldn't have. I believe Mrs. Young didn't have no young'uns of her own and used other folks' to lay down her dreams on, and that won't right. I never done that to Pansy. I never had no expectations for her, or made her feel like she had to do nothing but be a good person. I didn't want her to bear that burden.

And she was happy, a real happy girl all the time. She understood we was poor and couldn't do like some, and she made the best of what we had. I remember one year at Christmas we didn't have no money for presents for the young'uns, so the church brung us out this box of used toys, most of them way past fixing. It made me so mad. I told Dill to take it out back and burn it before the children come in from school. I'd rather my young'uns had nothing than a box of trash. But he didn't. He carried it out to the barn and hid it and worked on some of the things he thought he could fix.

Not long after that I seen Pansy come walking toward the house with something under one arm. I said, "What you got there, baby?" And she held out this little doll and, oh, it was pitiful, that doll, one arm gone and no clothes on its little cloth body, the head cracked and the hair and eyes all chipped. I reached out for it, said, "Baby, you don't want that old thing," but she wouldn't let me take it.

"It's mine," she said. "I found it and Daddy said I could keep it."

Well, that made me mad right there, him giving her something from that box after I told him not to. I held out my hand. "You give me that doll right now," I said, "before I stripe your little legs."

Pansy had always minded so good and never argued like the boys done, but that time she didn't. She took off to the barn hollering for her daddy, and of course he let her keep it, wasn't nothing I could do. He took some brown paint and give it new hair and eyes. He couldn't do nothing about that missing arm, though, so Pansy made up a little story about how the doll had been laying in the windowsill and the window fell and cut off her arm. I got so tired of seeing that dirty thing I made it a dress and some little shoes out of a flour sack to match a dress I'd made for Pansy.

She named it Daisy and carried it everywhere she went till it was hanging together by just a thread or two, its little head hanging off the back of its neck and the stuffing showing. She wouldn't give it up, even when I told her I couldn't sew it back together no more, because there wasn't nothing left to sew. So I had to take it one night when she was asleep. At first I couldn't make myself throw it on the fire, for I knowed how much it meant to her, but I also knowed it was fixing to fall all to pieces and then how would she feel, seeing that?

I dropped it in the stove and closed the lid so I wouldn't have to see it burn. Of course Pansy cried for a week over that, but she soon got over it and I knowed I'd done the right thing, just like I done with that letter that come when she was at the beach with Eloise. What would've been the point of her knowing she got that scholarship when she knowed she couldn't go? I knowed Mrs. Young had done it, applied for that thing, because Pansy wouldn't have wasted her time on such foolishness. So really it was that Mrs. Young I was hiding that letter from, not Pansy.

I put it away, thinking one day down the road when Pansy was married and had babies of her own I'd pull it out and say looky here and she'd say, "Oh, Mama, I'm so glad you never showed me that. It would've broke my heart." And then I'd tell her, "Honey, I know," and finally at last I'd have a reason to tell her how I happened to know the right thing to do, how I knowed about having your heart broke by wanting what you can't never have, and she'd see all I ever wanted was to be a good mother and do for her what mine never done for me.

20

With a million and one things to do and that damn Linda nowhere in sight, Laurel wondered if she'd make it through the day. Every time she turned around, somebody wanted something, an answer to a question or a signature or directions. She'd been out in the sun too long and her head was starting to hurt, but the pig people were still setting up the food and the stage still hadn't been set for the band tonight. If one more person came up to her and tapped her on the shoulder, she'd scream. She deserved five minutes to herself, five minutes to sit and think and make sure everything was under control.

She found a folding chair on the covered stage, the only shade in the middle of the field, and sat down, fanning herself with her clipboard. The Labor Day picnic always fell on the hottest day of the year, and this year was no exception. The trees surrounding the field looked so cool and inviting, or the shade under them did, and she thought of the little lake behind those trees where she used to swim as a kid, but there was no time for swimming today.

The pig cookers had been set up in the shade on the side of the triangular field closest to the picnic tables. The caterers, the same ones who'd done the Christmas parties and picnics for the last ten years, had also set up long tables covered with white cloths to hold the food.

Laurel had ordered enough pig and potato salad and baked beans and slaw and hush puppies and rolls and sweet tea to feed everybody at least twice. And as usual the ladies had come through with desserts, all heat-resistant things—brownies, Rice Krispies Treats, cookies, pound cakes. And later, when there were enough kids here to volunteer to sit on the buckets while the men cranked, they'd have homemade ice cream. The back of Grady's truck was loaded with watermelons and parked by the horseshoe pit behind the picnic tables. Laurel could just see the gleam of those green melons and wished she had one right now. She needed to be drinking water but hadn't had time to stop and refill her bottle.

For the last hour she'd been on the opposite side of the field, over by the row of display tables, checking in entries for the employee arts-and-crafts show. She'd put a notice in the last newsletter requesting that all employees who wanted to enter something arrive early today, and there'd been a steady stream, so many that the tables had filled up and she'd had to send some of the guys back to the plant for more.

It was amazing, the number and variety of entries. Most of the crafts were some sort of needlework—macramé, crochet, quilts, needlepoint, cross-stitch, and knitting, including one of Lottie May's sweaters, but there were also ceramics, the most interesting of which was a ceramic owl piggy bank with a working clock in its belly. Laurel wondered if that was a subtle way of saying time is money. There were wood carvings of animals and birds; cloth dolls the size of a six-year-old; beer-can wind chimes and birdhouses, including one in the shape of a church; Christmas ornaments made of beads; and paintings, quite a few more than she'd imagined.

In addition to traditional landscapes and still lifes and portraits, there were also paintings on sweatshirts, hats, and shoes (mostly ribbons and flowers); on wooden furniture (again, mostly ribbons and flowers); on a Harley-Davidson (the gas tank a dark purple with a gold eagle, wings outstretched); and on sand dollars (tiny beach scenes with lighthouses or ships). How did these people find the time and energy to do this stuff?

The only entry missing was her mama's. When Laurel left the house that morning, her daddy had been helping get the pictures into rough frames he'd hammered together the day before. She'd never seen her mama so excited, and it thrilled Laurel to see her that way, so happy and alive, especially after the last few months. She'd come back to them and then some.

Bushy Cook came tromping up the steps, carrying amplifiers. "Hey," he said, breathing hard. "I just seen your mama in the parking lot. She's looking for you."

They must need help getting the pictures carried in. Laurel got to her feet and moved the chair to the side of the stage. Good timing, Mama, she thought. If Bushy was here to set up for the band, that meant Joe couldn't be far behind, and she didn't need that distraction. Whenever he was around she couldn't seem to think straight, even though she'd sworn she wanted him only as a friend. Yeah, right, the little voice in her head said. Who are you trying to convince?

When she got to the parking lot, she couldn't see her mama and daddy at first because they were surrounded by a group of about twenty-five people Laurel had never seen before. They crowded around the back of her daddy's truck, and then each one stepped back, holding one of her mama's paintings. What was she doing, selling them? Laurel hurried over to the truck. "Mama? What are you doing?"

Pansy looked over and told her to wait just a minute, then picked up the last painting, one covered with a white pillowcase. Dan slammed the tailgate and Pansy handed him the picture, then took Laurel's arm and said, "Come here. I want you to meet somebody."

Something was up, she could tell. Her mama radiated so much nervous energy, Laurel was amazed her hair didn't light up like one of those fiber-optic Christmas trees, and it wasn't just about the paintings.

They stopped in front of a short, stocky old man who had stepped to the front of the group with the paintings. He must be their leader, Laurel thought, wondering again who all these people were. Then she noticed the man's blue-and-white striped work shirt, and specifically the name on the pocket. *Peanut.* Her mouth fell open.

Oh, my God, she thought, her hand flying to her mouth. Something inside her started jumping up and down. She took her hand away and hugged her mama. "Oh, my God," she said. "They came, they came." She turned back to Peanut, meaning to shake hands, but threw her arms around him instead. "Oh, my God," she said again, unable to think of any other words for how she felt. She pulled back, embarrassed, but Peanut didn't seem to mind being hugged by a complete stranger and held on to her hands. But then again, they weren't really strangers. They had Idalene and Lottie May in common.

She couldn't help staring at him, looking for resemblances. She saw Idalene's sharp blue eyes, though his had more of a twinkle, and Lottie May's little button nose. "I'm Laurel," she said.

"I knew it," Peanut said. "You look just like your mama. Now, that's a pretty woman." He winked at Pansy. "I'm William, but everybody calls me Peanut."

He turned then to another short gray-haired man, almost his twin, who stood next to a thin, white-haired man in a wheelchair. "This is Carl and James, my brothers. And the rest is all our wives and young'uns and grandyoung'uns."

Laurel shook hands with the brothers, waved to the others, still stunned. "I'm so glad y'all could come," she said, thinking it was a very good thing she'd ordered the extra food. This bunch looked like they could do some damage to a pig. She turned to Pansy. "Mama, how did you do it?"

Pansy laughed and shook her head. "I didn't. Peanut called this morning and said James had got in yesterday and they was ready. I knew by the time they got to Russell, Lottie May'd already be here, so they just come on to the house and followed us."

Oh, my God. Laurel looked at them all again, the Spoffords, Lottie May's family, standing there holding her mama's pictures, looking hot. It was a miracle. Was that too grand a word? She didn't think so. "Come on, y'all, let's get you out of this sun."

After they dropped the paintings off at the arts-and-crafts display, she and Pansy led the family across the field to the picnic tables under the trees and then went looking for Lottie May, Dan trailing behind them.

They found her sitting in the shade at the horseshoe pit, watching Nisco, and sat beside her for a minute, trying to act nonchalant. Laurel looked at Pansy over Lottie May's head, wondering what to say. She couldn't just blurt out, *Oh, by the way, Lottie May, your long-lost broth-*

ers are here. She was about to ask her to come help her do something, anything, when Pansy spoke up.

"Lottie May, I want you to come and look at my pictures and tell me what you think."

Lottie May squinted up at her. "Well, I got to keep a eye on Nisco here."

"I'll stay with him," Dan said.

"That's right," Pansy said. "Dan can watch him."

Lottie May pushed herself up off the bench, though she didn't seem real thrilled with the idea. "All right, honey. Nisco, you mind Dan, now."

Nisco's "yes, ma'am" echoed behind them as they headed back up the tree line to the picnic tables. Laurel kept glancing over at Lottie May, trying not to get caught staring, wondering if she could sense what was about to happen. This felt big, huge, and Laurel hadn't even realized it until she saw Peanut standing in the parking lot a few minutes ago.

"Why are we going this way?" Lottie May said. "Ain't the pictures over yonder?" She pointed across the field.

"Yes," Pansy said. "But let's stay in the shade and go around. It's too hot out there."

"Lord, Pansy," Lottie May said. "Are you still having trouble with them hot flashes?"

Pansy grinned at Laurel over Lottie May's head. "Yes," she said. "They're just awful."

Peanut, James, and Carl must've seen them coming, because they'd walked a little ways away from the rest of the Spoffords and stood waiting next to the brick barbecue grill. Laurel wished she had a camera to get a shot of those three old guys. What a picture. And what must Lottie May think, coming face to face with three grinning old men she didn't know?

They stood there for a long few seconds, staring at one another, like some showdown in an old Western, Lottie May looking from Laurel to Pansy in confusion. Her mama's mouth was pinched together and she was trying hard not to cry, so Laurel realized it was up to her. "Lottie May," she said. "This is William and James and Carl Spofford."

"Howdy," Lottie May said, nodding at them before she looked up at Laurel like a child waiting to be told what to do next.

"You don't recognize us, do you?" Peanut said.

"Well, how in hell could she?" James said, wheeling himself closer. "We ain't even met her yet."

Lottie May smiled, her face intent as if she was trying to identify the men in front of her. Bless her heart, Laurel thought, she thinks she ought to remember.

"Lottie May." Laurel's throat seized up then. She was no more use than her mama, both of them standing there trying not to cry. She gave Peanut a helpless look and he took over. He stepped closer, his hands reaching out and then pulling back. He crossed his arms over his chest and put one hand over his mouth, overcome for a minute. When he could speak, he said, "You don't know us, but Idalene was our sister. And you are too. Our half sister."

The smile fell off Lottie May's face, and Laurel worried that maybe it would be too much for her. Maybe they should've told her earlier, given her time to prepare herself. But it was too late now. Laurel nodded. "They are, they're your brothers," she said. "Mama found them."

"Yeah," Peanut said, laughing. "She pulls in my gas station one day, says, 'I'm looking for William Spofford,' and I says, 'That's me, right here I am.' And this here is my brothers, James and Carl." He waved an arm behind him. "And yonder is a whole bunch of wives and young'uns and grandyoung'uns."

Lottie May looked where he pointed, then back at him. "I got brothers?" she said, then whirled around and hid her face in her hands, crying as if her heart would break.

Peanut stepped up and gently touched Lottie May's shoulder. "Come on, little sister," he said. Laurel and Pansy stepped back to give them some privacy, and a few minutes later the brothers led Lottie May over to where the rest of her family waited.

Laurel put an arm around her mama's waist. "I don't know why we're crying," she said. "This is a good thing."

"Well," Pansy said. "Sometimes that breaks your heart more than the bad stuff." She pulled out two tissues and gave one to Laurel. "Now, come with me. I got something else to show you."

Pansy made Laurel close her eyes when they got to the arts-and-crafts area, and it took Laurel a minute to realize what she was looking at when her mama said, "Open." The display panels in front of her were full of her mama's paintings, all those familiar faces and places, Grandpa Dill and Maw Bert and their house and her uncles. The one in the middle was different, though, practically jumped off the panel. It was done in brighter paints—acrylic, maybe, instead of watercolors. Laurel moved closer and studied it, then looked at her mama, her face questioning.

Pansy nodded, and Laurel looked at the picture again. It was clearly her mama and daddy, at least their faces. She didn't think she'd ever seen her daddy with painted toenails. She put her finger on them and looked at her mama again. "Has Daddy seen this?"

"Not yet."

Laurel looked at the painting again, taking in the vivid colors of corn and sky, the young faces of her parents, their bare shoulders making her wonder if the picture was inspired by actual events. She couldn't imagine them getting naked in the garden like that, but then, they'd been around a long time before she came along. There was probably a lot she didn't know about them.

"So this is why you went looking for a frame that day." She'd never stopped to question what made her mama look behind those old pictures of Maw Bert's. "Mama, I love it."

"Well, that's good, because it's yours."

"Mine? But don't you want to keep it?"

"No, I painted it for you. To remind you."

Remind me of what? Laurel thought, but when she opened her mouth to ask, Pansy interrupted. "Honey," she said, "I better go find your daddy before he hears about them green toenails from somebody else." Something in her voice made Laurel look back and there was Joe, coming straight toward her. Pansy had already started across the field away from her. What in the world had she meant when she said the picture was to remind her? Remind her of what?

Joe stopped in front of her, that serious look softened by the beginnings of a smile. "Hey," he said. "I been looking for you."

It pleased her so much to hear him say that, she had to turn away in case he could see it there in her face. "My mama painted this," she said, then felt embarrassed, realizing he'd look at the painting and see what she saw, two potentially naked people in a cornfield at night, which meant they either had done or were about to do something naughty.

He didn't say anything for a minute, and she raised her head to see him studying the picture.

"I like it," he said. "Especially the corn."

"You're as bad as Mama," Laurel said. "All my life, she's tried to get me to look at the corn, look at the corn."

"Well," Joe said, his head tilted as he continued to study the picture. "Corn is pretty, especially the way she's painted it. It looks like it could jump up and walk off by itself. But it's like a cover too, and they look like they enjoy being under there together."

That's it, Laurel thought. Joe had figured it out before she did. It was a marriage, her mama's and daddy's. Like a garden, it took hard work, but look how beautiful it could be when both people got down in the dirt together and put their whole selves into it. Her mama had wanted to give her something she couldn't put into words, and she had. She'd given her hope. Laurel smiled up at Joe, not caring anymore if he could read what was in her face, counting on him to recognize a sign when he saw one.

WHEN THE band started playing, the chairs facing the stage began to fill up, but Pansy stayed put. The air had cooled off considerably since the sun went down, but she still didn't feel like moving. The hard wooden bench of the picnic table was just as comfortable as those folding metal chairs, and they could hear the music just fine. Dan sat next to her, rubbing her back, and she didn't want to risk spoiling her good mood by moving an inch. Maxann and Grady sat across from them, watching the band and pretending not to notice each other, and Percilla was at the other end of the table polishing off a piece of pie. Lottie May was still with her family, and Laurel had gone off to check on the food and the displays again.

Dan's hand dropped away from Pansy's back and she looked up at him, then turned and saw what he saw, poor Rex staggering up behind

Percilla. He'd been drunk when he got there, and apparently he had a bottle in the car, because he'd been getting steadily drunker all day. He stopped and stared down at the top of Percilla's head, his mouth working as he tried to get the words he wanted. He put a hand on her shoulder to steady himself and said, "Come on, baby, give me the keys." He'd been asking for them on an hourly basis.

Percilla didn't even look up from the pie, just said, "No, Rex, you're too drunk to drive." She chewed and rolled her eyes so Pansy, Dan, Maxann, and Grady could see. "The car's unlocked. Why don't you go sleep it off?"

Pansy couldn't imagine what might be going through Rex's mind, but it couldn't be good. She'd probably get mad too if Percilla used that smug tone with her. Rex's mouth opened and stayed open for half a minute, then he closed it and wandered off again in the direction of the parking lot.

"He sure does drive me crazy." Percilla laughed. "I told him fifty times not to come if he didn't want to stay the whole time. I want to see the fireworks."

"Dan'll take him home," Pansy said. She glanced at Dan and he nodded. She figured he wouldn't mind getting out of here himself. He didn't care too much for these picnics anyway.

"Oh, he's too drunk to know what he wants." Percilla pushed her plate away and leaned her elbows on the table. "He'll lay down in the backseat and go to sleep."

"Being out of work is hard on a man," Dan said. Pansy could tell he didn't like to see Percilla treat Rex the way she did. It was hard on both of them, though, Rex being out of work and Percilla having to live with a drunk.

"Well, it ain't no easier on a woman," Maxann said.

"I have to say, I'm glad to be back at work," Pansy said. "That sitting home all day ain't all it's cracked up to be."

"I wouldn't mind a little taste of it," Percilla said.

"The only difference between work and home for you is there ain't no TV at work," Maxann said.

"You think they're going to lay off again this year?" Dan said, looking across at Grady.

Grady shook his head. "I haven't heard anything."

"Ha," Maxann said. "I think some people knows more than they're telling."

Grady just smiled and looked down at his hands.

It's not Grady that knows more than he's telling, Pansy thought. "A little bird told me we better enjoy this picnic, because it's probably going to be the last one." There, the seed had been planted, and maybe now Laurel wouldn't feel so guilty. She'd come home from work one day last week, all tore up because she heard John Dollar and Linda Gibson talking about how the plant might be sold and then shut down and they'd all lose their jobs. Then when she asked him about it he said she better not say nothing to nobody. Laurel couldn't understand why Pansy didn't get more upset herself, and it was all Pansy could do not to laugh. Laurel had no way of knowing they'd been hearing that kind of rumor for years, and they all knew one day sooner or later it would come true. But what was they supposed to do in the meantime? The only thing they could do about it was show up for work every day and hope the job would still be there tomorrow.

Maxann raised her eyebrows and lifted her chin. "Right. And has your little bird told you anything else?"

"Nothing definite."

"Who are y'all talking about?" Percilla looked from Pansy to Maxann to Grady and back to Pansy.

"Nobody you know," Pansy said.

Percilla looked like she wanted to keep on pushing to find out, but Pansy gave her a look that shut her up. "Well," Percilla said. "Whoever it is, they're just borrowing trouble. Ain't no sense worrying about it till it happens."

Maxann pulled out a cigarette and lit up. "Well, excuse the hell out of me," she said, blowing smoke up into the air. "But I happen to think a little further ahead than my next meal. If I get laid off, I'm screwed."

"What about them training programs at Russell Tech?" Percilla said. "If I get laid off, I'll just go over there and get myself retrained."

"For what?" Maxann said. "Do you see any new companies coming in here? And let's say I do get retrained. Who's going to hire a fifty-three-year-old woman when they can get a twenty-year-old to do more work for less pay and less benefits? I got a bad feeling I'm going to end up working at Burger King in a paper hat."

"Well," Pansy said. "At least we'll all be over there together, there or Wal-Mart."

"I can just see you in that cute little Burger King outfit," Grady said to Maxann. "I'll drive through your window."

"Old man, you ain't driving through nowhere. You're going to be behind me shoveling up my fries."

"I can't work in all that grease." Percilla rubbed a hand over her cheek. "My face'll break out."

Maxann laughed. "Well, then, I reckon you better start practicing saying, 'Welcome to Wal-Mart.' You know the bad thing about working in one of them places? You end up getting bossed around by these little old boys young enough to be your grandchildren."

"Uh-oh," Dan said.

Pansy looked up and saw a gray figure swaying in the shadows behind Percilla, then realized it was Rex.

"Are you back again?" Percilla said.

Rex didn't speak, just stood there with his hands in his pockets like some kind of bum. Somebody that shit-faced ought to keep his hands free in case he fell, Pansy thought.

"Percilla, baby," he said. "I'm going to ask you one more time to give me them keys."

Dan stood up. "Come on, Rex, buddy. I'll run you home."

"No!" Rex said, still staring down at Percilla's head. "I can take my own car and go to my own house my own self."

Percilla looked up at him then. "Rex, let Dan take you home."

"Percilla!" Rex swayed so far to the right that Dan put out his hands to catch him. He swayed back in the other direction, then got himself steady. "Percilla, honey, do you know what *Rex* means? It means *king*. That's me, baby, your king. Don't you know that? Now, give me them keys."

People at nearby tables were starting to stare and Percilla must've noticed, because she swung her legs over the picnic-table bench and stood up to face him. "Rex, get a hold of yourself. Do you hear me?" She grabbed his arm, but he shook loose and stepped back from her. "I am your king," he said.

Lord, how embarrassing. Pansy didn't want to stare but she couldn't help it. It was like watching a train wreck.

Percilla turned back toward the table, getting ready to sit down again, and in that split second Rex took his other hand out of his pocket and called her name. When she turned back to him there was an explosion of sound and a flash.

Pansy jumped. What was that? She wished there was a rewind button on that moment, feeling that she'd missed something. They'd all missed it, even Percilla.

Rex, his arms hanging by his sides, said, "Percilla, honey, can I have the keys now?"

Percilla looked down at her belly, then back up at Rex. "Honey, you've killed me," she said. She slumped onto the bench and Rex looked around at them all, his face terrified, his eyes wild.

Dan said, "Rex, wait," and took a step toward him, but Rex pushed past him and ran.

Things speeded up then. Dan ran after Rex, Grady hollered he was going to call an ambulance, and Pansy and Maxann jumped up and went to stand by Percilla, staring at the blood blooming on her shirt. A crowd started to gather around them, people just standing there watching Percilla bleed.

"I'm scared to touch her," Maxann said.

"He's killed me," Percilla said.

"No, honey, you're going to be all right." Pansy put her arm around Percilla's back. "Do you want to lay down?"

Percilla shook her head. "If I lay down I might die." She sat with her back against the picnic table, and Pansy and Maxann sat on either side of her, propping her up till help arrived. It was all they could think to do.

Suddenly the music stopped and Pansy heard Laurel's voice, asking if there was a doctor or nurse in the park. Dan must've found her and told her what happened. Before she could finish her announcement, there was a loud noise, then static, then Rex's voice echoed across the park.

"Percilla, honey," he said. "Are you all right?"

Pansy gently pushed Percilla's shoulder so she tilted toward Maxann, then got up and ran to the edge of the field and looked toward the stage. Rex was up there with Laurel, and he had a gun. Her heart pounded so hard she could feel it in her ears. Her baby was up there with an armed crazy man. She started through the crowd, which had abandoned Percilla and gone to watch the stage. Rex swayed in front of the fallen microphone stand while Laurel stood a few feet away. She looked so calm, like she stood next to a crazy man with a gun every day of her life. Behind Rex, the band stood frozen, their instruments still in place. And heading up the steps on the other side was Dan. Oh, Lord, Pansy thought, what are you doing? She kept moving past the rows of chairs and up to the edge of the stage where she could see Laurel's face, surprised but not terrified. She knew Rex, knew he wouldn't hurt a fly. But she also knew he'd just shot his own wife, saw the gun in his hand.

Rex bent and picked up the microphone stand, set it back in place, and put his mouth up to it. "Percilla?" he said, his voice breaking.

Dan stood on the edge of the stage, his whole body poised and aimed forward, ready to move in and either talk or tackle, Pansy couldn't tell which. Then she noticed Joe slowly easing the banjo strap off his shoulder and over his head. That's right, he was a policeman. He'd know what to do. He wouldn't let anything happen to her baby.

Rex breathed heavily into the mike, then started talking again. "Honey, I'm sorry," he said. "I didn't mean it. Did somebody call a ambulance?"

Joe had the banjo off now, but Dan held up a hand. Pansy figured at this point the only person Rex posed any threat to was himself, but there was always the chance he could trip and the gun would go off. And here they were in the middle of nowhere. It'd take the cops and the ambulance forever to get there. Dan and Joe were both out of uniform and had no weapons.

"All I wanted was my car keys," Rex said. "I just wanted to go home because I'm tired. You know I still love you." He looked over at Dan. "I do. I still love her."

Dan nodded and said, "I know, buddy."

"I know what you're thinking," Rex said. "I know she's let herself go these last few years. But you know what, buddy? Fat women need love too."

People started laughing. Pansy looked around, amazed. Did they think this was part of the show? Where was the damn ambulance?

"Dan, remember riding the cotton wagon to the gin when we was little? Well, that's what it feels like, son, riding on top of that cotton. A fat woman ain't got no sharp edges."

The crowd laughed again, and Pansy felt like if she'd had that gun she might've shot somebody herself.

Rex looked down at the gun in his hand, shook his head, looked back at Dan. "That's something can't nobody take from me, is my woman, because I still love her even if I did have to shoot her. They've took my job and my health and everything else, but they can't take my woman."

Rex was crying now, his head tilted back, his mouth open. "I don't understand it, Dan." He shook his head and rubbed his eyes. "Why don't our government care about us no more? The big shots always saying we got to help our neighbors. Well, I'm all for helping my neighbor, but I don't think I ought to have to give my neighbor my job so he can feed his family when I can't feed mine. The government cares more about the damn Mexicans and Chinese than they do us. They got us by the balls, boys."

The speakers flared up suddenly, squawking and squealing with feedback. Rex spun around, looking for the source of the noise, then dropped the gun and put his hands over his ears. In a flash Joe moved in and grabbed the gun, while Dan went and put his arm around Rex and started talking in his ear. Joe put the gun in the waistband of his jeans, then went over to Laurel. He said something to her and when she nodded, he put his arms around her.

Thank you, Lord, Pansy thought, watching Dan lead Rex down the steps and over to a chair, where he sat down heavily and Dan stood by him. Pansy went to the foot of the stage in front of Laurel. "Honey, are you all right?"

Laurel pulled away from Joe, her eyes wet, and nodded. "How's Percilla?"

Pansy looked over her shoulder, unable to see back to the picnic table, then heard the sirens. She looked back up at Laurel. "I don't know, but I'm going to go see."

By the time she got back to the picnic table, the rescue people had Percilla on a stretcher and were loading her into the ambulance. When they got her inside, she tried to sit up and they had to push her back down.

"Be still, honey," Pansy said.

"Where's Rex?" Percilla hollered, panic in her voice. "I want Rex."

Maxann got up in the ambulance and sat beside her. "Hush, now, lay back. Rex is fine. Dan's got him." She looked down at Pansy. "I bet they don't allow smoking in this thing, do they? I know I'm going to need me a cigarette before this ride's over."

"We'll get the car and follow you as soon as we can," Pansy said just before the paramedics slammed the doors shut and took off, siren wailing. As she left the shelter of the trees, two police cars came bumping across the field toward the stage. Idiots, she thought, ruining their shocks. Why didn't they slow down? Didn't they know this used to be farmland, and under all that pretty green grass the land had hardened in the shape of long, plowed rows, ready to offer up corn again if it ever got the chance?

ALBERTA

He used to sing me this song: "Alberta, what's on your mind? Alberta, what's on your mind?" That's all the words he ever sung. He hummed the rest, a pretty tune, sort of sad and tender. It wasn't till years after he died that I ever heard the whole thing. My baby boy Calvin gave me a record album by Doc Watson, that blind man from Deep Gap. Calvin didn't know I didn't even have a record player in the house. He went right out and bought me one and played that song for me. He thought I'd like it because of that song with my name. He didn't remember his daddy singing it to me. Calvin was so pleased with himself I didn't have the heart to tell him I would never listen to that song again. I won't never forget the words, though, the ones Dill didn't sing. That blind man sung, "My heart is so sad 'cause you treat me so bad. Alberta, what's on your mind?"

Dill always sung that with a smile on his face, sung it to try and pull me out of a bad mood. Sometimes it worked and sometimes it didn't. I wonder if he even knowed all the words. Maybe he just heard the Alberta part somewhere and latched on to that, never bothering to learn the rest. I think if he'd known, he would've picked another song. He never was one to hold a grudge or make nobody be any different than what they was.

It got to be his theme song for me when I disappeared inside myself and he had to haul me back. That song was like the worm on the end of a hook, him the hook with his fingers under my chin tickling or his nose in my hair. It was such a little thing, but it always brung me back. I got behind my eyes again and he'd be there with a smile and another question and before I knew it we'd be at the table with the children and for a little while everything would be all right.

Being by myself was what brought it on mostly. Too much quiet, nothing to distract me but work, and that only occupied my hands. There was many times I come to myself in the middle of the afternoon, Dill at work and the young'uns in school, and I'd find the dishes washed, the beds made, chickens fed, cow turned out, wash on the line, and supper cooking, and I had no idea who done it all.

Losing your life inside your own mind don't feel like loss at the time. I didn't dwell on where I'd been, only on the wonder of being back, the newness of everything each time. I'd think to myself, How can I still be here? It's the same as with sleep, only most folks don't think much about it. I lay down, I close my eyes, I drift off, but where do I go? I know where my body is, but where is the part of me that thinks and feels and knows things? Where does she go? And why does she always come back?

I lived with that waking sleep for a long time, up until after Dill died. Then I woke up and stayed awake the rest of my life to the hurt that never went away. I had done terrible things, and I reckon my punishment was a long life. But I had suffered too, as much as anybody, maybe more. Yet they was the ones at peace, while I stared down a long, dark tunnel of years with no light at the end, no salvation. I thought of taking my own life, but the atonement for the life I had took so many years before was already too heavy a burden. I couldn't bear no more.

All the times Dill sung that song to me, he never once got a answer or even acted like he expected one. What would he have done if I'd told him? Maybe I knew and that's why I didn't say. The words never once formed in my head to tell. I wouldn't allow it because I knowed if I ever did, they'd somehow find their way to my chest, then my throat, then my mouth, and then they'd fly free and I'd have no secrets left, nothing to keep Dill's lips at my ear, his breath thawing the froze place in my brain like warm water will thaw froze fingers till they burn back to life and remember how to work again.

I thought I loved him, Bruno, but I didn't. All I loved was what I thought he could do for me, which was get me away. I have lost my mind so many times, but that was the worst. And keeping it to myself all that time made it grow bigger and bigger in my memory, so big I couldn't help but see it ever day of my life, the white schoolhouse, the big windows, Bruno and me and her, Dorcas, and her big with his baby, and me with nothing, no hope of ever getting out of the life I had got stuck in, Dill and the young'uns like deep mud sucking me down, trying to drown me. The only solid thing that day was the gun.

Dill begged me not to go, said he knowed the mill police would be there and somebody might get hurt. I made up my mind then and took that pistol from the drawer where Dill kept it, stuck it in my pocketbook. That weight hung on my arm all through the meeting, all through Dorcas singing her damn songs and Bruno giving his speech. I stayed in the back and followed Dorcas out, and then there was the sound of shots and screaming, and I couldn't see nothing for the smoke.

There was nothing solid for a long time after that, everything was like a dream, and then there was Dill again, and children. And after a long while, there was no more Dill.

I took to reading again, after all them long years away from it. It was the only thing rested my mind, give me back that waking sleep, enough to get me through my life and out of this world, and I have never looked back, for what good does it do. I lived, I died, and now there is nothing, not one blessed thing, Dill, on my mind.

21

No wonder Idalene was able to save all that money, Laurel thought. She hadn't bought anything new since the sixties. Her TV even had knobs. There was so much she needed—new furniture, for one thing. As grateful as she was for Idalene's old stuff, she looked forward to replacing the couch and the TV and getting some bookshelves in here. She didn't understand how people lived without bookshelves, without books.

She couldn't seem to settle down tonight. She should be tired after helping her mama empty the storage room last night and run the yard sale this morning. They'd gotten rid of most of Maw Bert's junk and a lot of their own. Her mama planned to turn that room into a workroom for herself, and her daddy was probably still out there trying to get that wall knocked out so he could install bigger windows. It tickled her to death to think of them out there, him with his saws and her with her paints, but in a weird way it made her feel lonely too.

She went to the kitchen and flipped on the radio Idalene had left on top of the refrigerator. Randy Travis twanged out, singing about his love being deeper than the holler and stronger than the river. Laurel flipped the dial past hard rock, easy listening, NPR, rap. Nothing appealed to her, so she put it back on Randy. At least he was familiar.

That's what she was missing, the familiar, something comforting.

She wandered into the bedroom, Idalene's old room, all brown and white: white walls and brown curtains, maple spool bedstead, dresser, and chest of drawers. The hardwood floors were scarred in places and could stand a good buffing, but they were so much better than carpet. Really, all this room needed was color—maybe a nice, soothing blue paint for the walls, different curtains, a new bedspread. The rest of the house needed perking up too, but one thing at a time. Between work and fixing this place up, time would pass, and before she knew it she'd be used to everything and wouldn't feel so lonely.

The window in this room faced Lottie May's house, and Laurel could see that all the lights were off, except that little lamp she kept on in the living room, the one next to that green chair where her husband had died. It was good to know they were over there, even if they were asleep. Lottie May was going to teach her how to knit, and Laurel was going to find a place to take Nisco riding. The boy was crazy for horses, just like she was at that age. And next spring Laurel was going to have her first garden, had already got seed catalogs and started planning. Joe had promised to come over and till it for her, and she'd promised to cook him supper. Anything beyond that, they'd have to see. She was in no rush, and the wonderful thing about Joe was that he wasn't either.

The smaller bedroom was furnished with twin beds, a small table between them and a chest of drawers on one wall. Idalene probably never used this room except for storage, which was probably what Laurel would do too. She had to weave her way through the stacks of cardboard boxes full of books to get to the bed. When she sat, the mattress squeaked, startling her. It was a little unnerving being in a house alone. It embarrassed her to realize this was probably the first time she'd ever slept in a house by herself. Thirty-six years old and finally getting a room of her own in a home of her own. It was about time.

Her hand reached out to the top of the carton nearest her, lifted the flap. Inside were old textbooks from college English, not something she was interested in revisiting right now. She wasn't even sure why she'd saved them. She stacked them on the floor and opened another box. Cookbooks. Laurel slid down on the floor, pulling boxes to her and opening them, stacking books around her in two- and three-foot towers. Before long every box was empty and the floor looked like it had sprouted book stalagmites, all different heights and configurations. She sat cross-legged in the middle of them and let her eyes slide down the stacks, reading titles and authors, greeting old friends.

That's what her books felt like, old friends, and she felt less alone among them, surrounded by them. They comforted her in some way she couldn't define. Of course, she could never tell anyone that, because it sounded crazy. How could inanimate objects be your friends? And yet it was true. Everywhere she and Scott had moved in the years of her marriage, she never felt at home, and had actually suffered a kind of physical ache, until she unpacked her books and put them out where she could see them.

It was funny, she hadn't thought about it until now, but she hadn't felt that ache since she came back to Russell. She supposed she'd been too busy to think about anything much. Between work and family and friends, life had gotten so full. God, would wonders never cease.

Nothing would ever take the place of her books, but having a few real people in the mix made for a nice change, people who could listen and talk back, people you could touch and who could touch you. She looked down in her lap at the worn copy of *Jane Eyre*, one of her favorites. She'd always identified with Jane, her independence hiding her longing for home and family. And if she was Jane, who would the other girls be? Scanning the titles around her, she knew she wouldn't find any to match the stories she'd found in her friends. They hadn't been written, might never be written, a thought that made her ache. Didn't women like her mama and Idalene and Lottie May and Maxann and even Percilla deserve to have their stories told, the same as Scarlett O'Hara or Jane Eyre? Was that what had inspired Charlotte Brontë to write her book, the unthinkable possibility that this woman's story might go untold?

Laurel spent the first night in her new home curled up on the floor under a blue, red, and yellow striped afghan Lottie May had given her, her head resting on a fat leather-bound copy of *Little Women* she'd read a hundred times since she got it for her tenth birthday. She dreamed of blue walls and a bed with a white candlewick spread, white lace curtains at an open window, the smell of cedar, the sound of a far-off train.

Epilogue

GOOD LORD, LAUREL THOUGHT, I'M MORE EXCITED than they are. She could barely sit still. It had something to do with watching their excitement, being with them on their first plane trip, their first trip out of state, their first girls-only trip. It must be one of the delights of having children, experiencing the wonder of everything all over again through their eyes.

"Oh, Lordy," Lottie May said, still clutching the pocketbook she'd held in her lap ever since the *fasten seat belts* light went out hours ago. "Ever time I look down and see clouds, I can't help thinking, *It ain't right, it ain't right*. If the Lord had wanted us to fly, He would've give us wings."

"What do you call that thing out there?" Maxann said, pointing out the window. She sat between Lottie May and Percilla on one side of the aisle while Laurel and Pansy sat on the other.

"I can't stand to look at that wing neither," Lottie May said. "It's too stiff. If it moved a little bit, I might feel better."

"If it moved a little bit it might fall off," Maxann said, going back to the *People* magazine she'd bought in the airport.

Laurel leaned forward and looked over at Lottie May. "Why don't you pull your shade down and take a little nap before we get there." It wouldn't be much of a nap, though, because they were due to land soon. But the girls wanted to go straight to the casino, and she was afraid Lottie May would be too exhausted to enjoy it.

"No, I don't want to miss nothing," Lottie May said, tightening her grip on the pocketbook, which contained, among other things, a little Ziploc bag of Idalene's ashes. Since it was Idalene's money paying for the trip, Lottie May said the least they could do was take her along. Laurel hadn't wanted to let Lottie May pay for it, none of them had, but she'd bought the tickets with some of the money Idalene left her, said they should consider it an early Christmas present from her and Idalene.

"They Lord, would you look at this?" Maxann held up the magazine, pointing to a picture of a movie star in a dress that seemed to be made of nothing but Saran Wrap and a few strategically placed sequins. "Can you believe people goes out in public in such as that?"

"Trashy," Lottie May said.

"I think it's pretty," Percilla said. "Did y'all remember your sparkle outfits?" She pulled the front of her T-shirt away from her stomach to draw attention to the shiny silver threads mixed in with the blue spandex.

Laurel had told them they'd need one good sparkle outfit to wear to the Tom Jones show, but it looked like Percilla had gone and got herself a whole wardrobe of them.

"Oh, yes, honey," Lottie May said. "Mine's got gold sequins all over it." She bent over her purse and looked at Pansy. "Did you ever find you one, honey?"

When Pansy didn't answer, Laurel poked her with an elbow. "Mama, did you hear Lottie May?"

"What?" Pansy pulled away from Laurel and gave her an irritated look.

Laurel knew Pansy wasn't trying to keep the plane in the air through sheer force of will like Lottie May, but she couldn't understand why she'd been sitting there staring out the window for the last half hour. "Mama, are you all right?"

Pansy sighed. "I'm fine. Just been sitting here worrying."

"About what?" Laurel said.

"What if we get fired? What if Grady finds out we ain't really sick?"

"Oh, honey, don't you worry about that," Maxann said. She closed the magazine and put it in the pocket on the back of the seat in front of her, then stretched her legs out. "I had me a little talk with Grady last night and told him all about it. He said not to worry, if anybody asked he'd tell them we all caught something Percilla brought home from the hospital."

"Don't blame it on me." Percilla put a hand to the side where she'd been shot.

"You talked to Grady last night?" Laurel turned in her seat so she could see Maxann's face. It had turned red.

"We had supper at Western Sizzlin', that's all." Maxann stared down at her fingernails like they were the most fascinating things in the world.

"Did he pay?" Laurel said, ready to pounce.

"Yes. So?"

Laurel hooted. "Then it was a date. I can't believe it."

"Halleleujah!" Pansy said. "It's about time."

"Did you give him some sugar?" Lottie May said, taking her eyes off the wing long enough to wink at Maxann. Percilla didn't say a word, just reached for the *People* magazine.

Maxann slumped down in her seat. "Y'all shut the hell up, okay?" She snuck a look at Laurel, then went back to studying her fingernails, grinning like a monkey.

Laurel let her head fall back against the seat, grinning like a monkey herself. She didn't understand it. Here she was, going back to Vegas, going to court to finalize her property settlement, going to say good-bye forever to her marriage, to Scott and their life together, and she was having a wonderful time.

When the pilot announced their descent into Las Vegas a few minutes later, Laurel reached for her seat belt, so glad they were flying in at night, wanting them to see the lights and the glamour, not the ugly concrete and dust of daytime Vegas. "Y'all look down there," she said. "There it is."

"They Lord!" Lottie May said. "Would you look at all them lights? I'd hate to pay that power bill. Is that all gambling places?"

"Yes, ma'am," Laurel said. "See that big green glowing building? That's the MGM Grand. That's our hotel."

Percilla practically laid in Maxann's lap, trying to see out the window as they circled Vegas. "I'm going straight to the casino and put a quarter in a slot machine," she said. "Rex told me to do the first one for him."

It still amazed Laurel that they'd got back together, that Rex was already out of jail, doing community service, dried out and clean of any drugs except aspirin, looking ten years younger. What amazed Laurel even more was Rex's take on the whole episode. He'd told her daddy, "Well, buddy, it's a hell of a way to get your health back."

"Me too," Maxann said, pushing Percilla off. "I hope one of us wins big."

"Yeah," Percilla said, waving her *Beating the Odds in Vegas* book. "And I hope it's me."

Laurel leaned her head back and closed her eyes, content to just sit and listen to them talk, loving the sound of their voices around her.

"All I want to do is get my feet back on the ground," Lottie May said. "I feel like a seed cast on the wind."

"Me too," Pansy said. "I've had enough."

"We'll be getting right back on again Sunday," Percilla said. "You'll be right back in the wind."

"That's all right," Lottie May said. "Long as I'm blowing toward home."

Acknowledgments

I owe this book to three inspirations who shared their stories:

Jamie Pryor, who was so good to me even though we never met and whose story made me laugh and cry and gave me a key to this book.

Marie Moore Neese, my dear and delightful friend and neighbor who doesn't think of herself as a teacher but has taught me a lot, particularly about the art of living.

And especially, Pat Eaton, whose voice I hear in my head talking about women and work, who keeps me writing about mothers and daughters. Mama, if this story could be told in a picture, it would be the look on your face the day we went to J&C and I asked how it felt to be back. I hope I got it right.

Plant Life grew out of two words, and for them I am indebted to the Title Master, Kelly Jerome Duncan, the best brother in the world, who will always get first crack at naming my books and is available for hire.

Many thanks to Jackie Cantor, a heroic editor whose patience and support allowed time and space for this story to grow, and whose kindness, vision, and careful pruning helped the novel find its true shape. Thanks also to Kathy Lord, for that amazing green pencil and those yellow sticky notes asking all the right questions.

I am forever grateful to Joelle Delbourgo, a remarkable agent and writer's champion, who changed my life and whose continued faith and support mean so much to me.

Thanks to my best friend, Joy Patterson, for inviting me on the big birthday trip, and thanks to Joy, Tamara Barringer, Crystal Patterson, Lori Fuller Niver, and Windy Batten for a whopping good time in Vegas. I only hope the girls in *Plant Life* have as much fun as we did and are lucky enough to get kissed on the jaw by Wayne Newton.

Brother-Man Silas House, thank you for sending me Jane's poem, for writing such great honky-tonk scenes I had to try one myself, and for being a true friend, inspiration, and companion on this writing path.

Ben Bulla helped in so many ways, particularly by sharing his wonderful book *Textiles and Politics: The Life of B. Everett Jordan: From Saxapahaw to the United States Senate*. Thanks, Ben, for taking me to Glen Raven, for good stories and good fellowship, and most of all for friendship. Thanks also to June Bulla, good neighbor, friend, and hard-core Carolina fan even in the losing years, who makes the best cheese straws, zucchini bread, and Italian cream cake in Alamance County.

I am grateful to three outstanding poets whose words inspired and sustained me during the writing of this novel: Jane Hicks ("First Day Photo"), Ron Rash (*Eureka Mill*), and Mike Chitwood (*The Weave Room*). Thank you for finding the poetry in the lives of working men and women and writing it so beautifully.

There is much great material about mill folk, but two books were especially informative and inspirational: Jacqueline Dowd Hall's *Like a Family: The Making of a Southern Cotton Mill World*, and Victoria Byerly's *Hard Times Cotton Mill Girls: Personal Histories of Womanhood and Poverty in the South*.

I owe so much to the kindness of these folks who helped along the way:

Karen and Don Ward and Roger Gant were so gracious and generous with their time, knowledge, and attention when I visited their plants.

Raymond Stewart gave me lots of firsthand information on modern-day plant life.

Alex Horstman kept me company at lunch one day and shared great insights and information about painting and art.

John R. Fuller and Amy Hembree befriended me at Sewanee and patiently answered my many questions about what it's like to be a police officer.

Tamara and Brent Barringer very kindly explained legal procedures in a way I could understand and didn't charge me a dime.

Alice Cotten and the folks at the North Carolina Collection at UNC Libraries provided all kinds of resources and helped me find the mill-worker stories I was looking for.

The following libraries were wonderful places to read and write in the company of other book lovers: Davis Library and Wilson Library at UNC, Chapel Hill Public Library, Graham Public Library, and Bogue Banks Public Library.

Thanks to Linda Hobson and the North Carolina Writers Network for the opportunity to read from this book at the spring conference and for your ongoing support of Tarheel writers. I'm also grateful to the Sewanee Writers Conference for a Tennessee Williams Scholarship and the opportunity to work on part of this book with some amazing writers and teachers.

Thanks to these friends and family for support and encouragement, for great lines and stories, for being there: Darnell Arnoult, Debbie and Tim Atkinson, Mary Atkinson, Darrell and Marie Barrett, Felicity Callis, Patsy Cole, Michael Croley, Elizabeth Duncan, Bill Eaton, Becky Hart, Bill McAllister, Matt Mielke, Sandra and John Patterson, Bonnie Perkins, Billy Joe Price, Dolores Price, Gary Price, Lisa and Jimmy Rogers, Lee Smith, Anita and Glenn Stedham, Nancy Stratton, Diane Sutera, Amy Trester, Nicky and Gilbert Turner, and countless other kind folks who generously shared information and stories about cooking, cussing, smoking, loving, dancing, dying, mill life, and just life in general.

And finally, thanks to my writers group, Virginia Boyd and Lynn York (as well as our much-missed long-distance member Darnell Arnoult and honorary member Silas House). Without your love and faith and support and occasional butt-kicking, this book would never have been written and I'd probably be locked up somewhere with an incurable case of Second Novel Panic Syndrome. Even if I could do it without y'all, I don't know if I'd want to.

About the Author

PAMELA DUNCAN was born in Asheville in 1961 and raised in Black Mountain, Swannanoa, and Shelby, North Carolina. She holds a B.A. in journalism from the University of North Carolina at Chapel Hill and an M.A. in English and creative writing from North Carolina State University in Raleigh. She lives in Graham, North Carolina. Her acclaimed debut novel, *Moon Women*, is available in paperback from Dell.

Please read on for a preview of
Pamela Duncan's next novel...

THE
BIG
BEAUTIFUL

by

Pamela Duncan

A Dial Press Trade Paperback

On sale April 2007

The Big Beautiful

"IN THE TRADITION OF FANNIE FLAGG
AND REBECCA WELLS...
DUNCAN IS A FROM-THE-HEART,
QUIRKY STORYTELLER."
—Publishers Weekly

PAMELA DUNCAN

Author of *Moon Women* and *Plant Life*

The Big Beautiful

On sale April 2007

Prologue

THAT BABY GIRL RAN TO THE OCEAN THE SAME way she ran to somebody she loved, arms flung wide, mouth open and laughing, ready to grab the whole world and squeeze it all to her little self. Cassandra didn't run after her, just stood watching, wishing she wasn't too old and fat to do like Catherine. She breathed deep through her nose, taking in the smell of salt air. Was there anything better than that smell, and the feel of salt air and salt water on your skin?

Catherine had only waded in up to her knees, but she was shivering, probably more from excitement than cold. It was still well over eighty degrees. Well, they wouldn't be able to stay out much longer or it'd get dark on them. Cassandra looked up and down the beach. Wasn't anybody much out this time of day, everybody gone to eat, or inside getting ready to go eat.

That's where Ashley and Ruth Ann and Betty were, getting ready. Up there laughing and talking and unpacking. Cassandra always felt so young and foolish around them, like another young'un in their eyes. She'd made up her mind not to care anymore, though. She and Catherine just had different priorities. There were more important things than unpacking and talking and getting cleaned up for supper. It was their first day at the beach for heaven's sake. They didn't need to be spending it in the house.

Catherine squealed like a pig and pointed up at the sky. Cassandra looked up too and saw a rainbow so pale it was nearly invisible. It started behind them in the direction of Morehead City and stretched way out over the ocean, ending in a big pile of white clouds on the horizon. Rainbows always made her think of her mama, the only person she'd ever known that didn't get excited about seeing one.

Cassandra waded over next to Catherine and they watched a bunch of pelicans fly low over the water. Fishing, Cassandra reckoned. Then some seagulls screamed behind them and Catherine jumped and grabbed Cassandra's leg. Cassandra picked her up in one arm and turned to point at the gulls. "Them's just seagulls, honey. Don't be scared." A man was throwing bread from his deck and had about twenty gulls treading air over his head.

"Birds," Catherine said.

"That's right. Birds."

Catherine laid her head on Cassandra's shoulder and they turned to face the ocean again. The soft sound of waves whooshed around them, and Cassandra figured it wouldn't be long before Catherine conked out, all worn out from excitement. They ought to go in, but Cassandra couldn't bear to, not yet. It was her favorite time of day and she wanted to watch the last light on the water, then all the shades of blue and gray blending as night slowly slowly settled over the ocean.

A fish jumped out of a wave right in front of them and Catherine's head popped up. "Fish!" she said, pointing.

"Yes. A big old fish."

Every time a wave welled up, they could see bunches of fish swimming through it. The last rays of light from the setting sun turned the water blue-green, and the fish looked like little silver shadows inside the wave. It was amazing how they kept going straight ahead even while the waves broke. Cassandra wondered what made them so determined to get wherever it was they were going. Some instinct probably, something unexplainable.

No matter how many times she came down here, the one thing she never got over was the amount of life at the beach. She didn't remember noticing it when she was younger. But now it jumped out at her everywhere, life all over the place, wildlife and not so wild. So much to see. All kinds of birds and fish, and the little white-almost-clear crabs that watched you back, walking sideways across the sand and disappearing down a little bitty hole if you even breathed.

She made a mental note to look up that crab in the nature book she got at the gift shop in Salter Path last time she was here, back in April. Already she'd learned the names of coquinas and mole crabs and terns and skates and barnacles. It was like they had a whole different vocabulary down here. All that life going on, things most people didn't pay a bit of attention to. Too busy getting a tan or talking or swimming. Even the wind felt like a live thing here, always moving and changing and causing everything it touched to move and change too. Cassandra felt like anything could happen at the beach, like all she had to do was be patient and the wind would bring something her way, something unexpected but good, something that would change her life forever.

JUNE

She had been forced into prudence in her youth.
She learned romance as she grew older—
the natural sequence of an unnatural beginning.

Jane Austen

Iʔ

IT WAS LOOKING AT HER FEET THAT DID IT. SHE blamed that magazine article on dreams she'd read in the doctor's office the other week, the one where this woman said if she didn't like what she was dreaming, she just looked down at her feet, and when she looked back up, poof! New dream.

So every night for a week she went to sleep saying over and over *look at your feet, look at your feet*, but once the dream started all she could do was stand and watch, and every night it was the same. She watched herself marry a man whose face she couldn't see, and the preacher said, "Do you Charlotte take this man?" but she couldn't open her mouth to tell him her name was Cassandra. Then she lifted her veil and saw the groom was Mr. Collins from that movie *Pride and Prejudice*, which meant she wasn't Lizzie, or even Jane. She was Charlotte Lucas, the one that settled. The one that married a man she didn't love just to have a husband. Cassandra had wanted to change that dream so bad, turn the bride back into herself and Mr. Collins into Mr. Darcy.

No, wait, not Mr. Darcy. Dennis. Her groom was Dennis, and this was no dream. This was her wedding and it was time to wake up. From the corner of her eye she could see A.J.'s legs in his white tux as he waited to escort her down the aisle. They looked like the legs of a soldier in dress uniform, like that picture of Marshall from when he was in the Marines, the one Mama had kept on the dresser, right next to the picture of Daddy in his army uniform, both so handsome. Cassandra had always dreamed of her daddy walking her down the aisle, but he hadn't lived long enough, or maybe she'd taken too long. A.J.'s left leg twitched back and forth like it was hearing music none of the rest of them could hear, fast music saying, "Let's get this show on the road."

Staring at the white satin pumps that matched her dress, she wondered why they even made shoes with pointy toes. People's feet were not pointy. As a matter of fact, they were more rectangular than anything, or at least hers were. Fred Flintstone feet.

All right, Cassandra, she thought. That's enough feet and dreams. She took a deep breath and forced her head up. The first thing she laid eyes on was Ruth Ann, making a face that didn't need any translation, an irritated look saying, "What are you doing?"

All Ruth Ann's young'uns were there too—Ashley with her belly pooched out, Keith holding Catherine, who looked so cute in her little white lace dress that would probably be filthy before the day was out, Angela and David and their two boys, and Alex. Then there were all her brothers and their families, and all of Dennis's family, every one staring like she just landed from Mars.

The last person she let herself look at was Dennis. Standing up there cute as a button in his white tux, hair stiff as a board from all that gel he used, that long skinny finger pushing his glasses up his nose every ten seconds. She'd begged him a million times to get some new glasses that didn't cover up so much of his face, but he wouldn't do it. At least two or three times a year he lost his glasses leaning over a grave—when he started sweating, they slid right off—and he said it would be crazy to spend a bunch of money replacing fashion frames all the time.

Dennis winked and smiled and oh, he was the sweetest thing. She did want to marry him. Didn't she? Of course she did. She smiled back, thinking okay, now, now I can do it. One of her feet even moved forward.

But then the organist caught her eye, or rather her hat did. None of the other women wore hats, ever, but Joyce Perkins never went without one. Her mama had thin hair and everybody figured Joyce must be losing hers too. The hat was ice blue with big navy flowers in front, colors that matched her dress. She looked like the hydrangea by Cassandra's front porch. Joyce sat with her fingers poised over the keys, raised her eyebrows at Cassandra, then nodded. Cassandra wanted to holler, "No! Wait!" but Joyce's fingers hit the keys and the music blared out and she froze again.

A.J. took hold of her elbow and whispered, "Ready?" She shook her head no, but then that prissy Aubrey started pushing from behind, saying, "Go! Go! Go!" in a real low voice. That little hussy, Cassandra thought, all she cares about is following her durn schedule and having everything turn out just so. At rehearsal the night before, Dennis had to take her outside and calm her down so she wouldn't pinch Aubrey's head off for telling her how to walk. "She's just doing her job, honey," Dennis said. "We want to get it right, don't we?"

Oh yes, we must get it right. Why, if something was to go wrong, oh horrors! Cassandra hadn't wanted a wedding planner in the first place, especially not that uppity Aubrey. She didn't see what was so complicated about walking down the aisle.

Aubrey pushed again and Cassandra fought off a smile, tickled at the thought of that munchkin back there trying to shove her up the aisle, Aubrey the tugboat and Cassandra the oil tanker. One advantage to being a full-figured gal was if she didn't want to move, then they by God couldn't make her.

She heard whispers then, people probably wondering what in the world she was doing, holding up the wedding like that, her own wedding. What was she doing? Wasn't this what she'd wanted her whole life and been afraid would never happen? Cassandra, she said to herself, this is your wedding. Buck up now and get on with it. You're not a little girl anymore playing paper dolls. This is real.

Maybe that was the problem. She was still in shock. After all those years of waiting and hoping and nothing ever happening, just when she was getting used to being an old maid, along comes Dennis, who told her after they'd been dating a while that he made up his mind about her the minute she walked through the door of the funeral home. What woman wouldn't want to hear that? But so much happened so fast—Mama dying, getting engaged, selling the house and the daycare, planning a wedding. A lot of the time Cassandra had felt like one of those little toy divers at the bottom of a fish tank, frozen underwater, just watching while everything rushed past her.

"Give me a minute," she whispered to A.J. and he raised a finger to Joyce. She quit playing and the church got quiet, except for the rustling as people fanned themselves with the wedding programs. Some time during the night the air conditioning had broken and nobody could get it to work in time for the wedding. Cassandra had suggested having her brother bring in the giant fan from his garage, but Aubrey had pitched a fit and Ruth Ann said it would blow them all away and drown out the vows. If only she'd listened to Dennis and got this over with on Valentine's Day, back when it was still cold weather. But no, she wanted time to lose more weight. No amount of weight was worth this, though, melting inside a sauna of a dress.

Cassandra took a deep breath and lifted the skirt to let some air circulate under there. Sweat trickled down her back, probably making a big sweat stain on that white satin, a stain everybody would see and bust out laughing over, one that would never come out, just like the one on her high school graduation gown. Only two people in the whole gym came out with giant sweat stains on their backs, her and Butch Randall, a linebacker on the football team. Not her most ladylike moment.

The dress was bad enough, that heavy satin that did not breathe, but then add on the layers of underwear and petticoat and pantyhose and they might as well have wrapped her in plastic and covered her with a fur coat. The hose were the worst, right up against her skin, and they were white to match the dress. White stockings only made her legs look fatter, what A.J. called baloney legs, the same size around from thigh to ankle. She hadn't even intended to wear any since the dress was floor length, but Ruth Ann said people would still be able to see the tops of her feet and it was plum tacky to go bare-legged at a wedding.

Why did getting married have to be so uncomfortable, anyhow? They ought to have worn matching denim outfits like that couple in the paper last week. Or black leather like that couple on the news, the ones that got married on the back of a Harley in Myrtle Beach.

A.J. pulled on her arm again, and she could feel all eyes on her, burning. Still she couldn't move, not with her feet swelling up like that, like little loaves of bread dough rising, just like Aunt May's. At family reunions when she was a little girl, she'd sit on the floor at Aunt May's feet, fascinated by how the fat on top plumped up between the sides of her shoes. She'd always wanted to poke her finger in that fat to see what would happen, thinking it would be soft and squooshy like the Pillsbury Dough Boy, but she never had the nerve. She just sat there, looking at feet and hems and creases in pants legs, listening to the grown-ups talking and laughing over her head, loving Aunt May's cackling laugh, wondering if you had to have a big belly to laugh like that. It made Cassandra feel happy and safe, made her want to grow up to be just like Aunt May. And damned if she hadn't, fat feet and all. Except Aunt May wasn't an old maid who still lived less than five miles from where she was born.

Well, Cassandra thought, she wouldn't be an old maid if she married Dennis. And the word *if* hissed through her brain like a hot skillet dropped in a sinkful of dishwater. If she married Dennis.

There came a ringing in her ears then and she wondered if she might be fixing to pass out, which was something nobody in her family ever did except from drinking, and even that was rare. Her people didn't get the vapors like Southern belles in romance books. They were sturdy and strong, especially the women. But oh, how she wished she could be a fluttery belle right now, Scarlett or Melanie or whoever, just have everything go black and then wake up laying on a big bed in a nice cool dark room all by herself.

She really was feeling dizzy all of a sudden, so she closed her eyes and leaned back just a tad so if she did fall, she'd land on Aubrey. Think of something calm, she thought, something cool and soothing. And then she saw it, blue, deep sparkling blue, and it took her a minute to realize it was the ocean, the big beautiful ocean on a cloudless summer day, whitecaps icing the tops of the waves, sea oats bending in the breeze.

She'd wanted to go to the beach on their honeymoon, but Dennis said it was too far, so they were going to Asheville for the weekend instead, to stay at the Grove Park and visit Biltmore House, which Cassandra had seen a million times already but Dennis never had because when he was a little boy his daddy was always working, and now he was always working. Since his daddy was cutting down on his hours, Dennis didn't have any back-up and couldn't afford to take a whole week off. She'd told herself it didn't matter where they went as long as they were together, but she could see now that was a load of crap. She hadn't been to the beach in over a year, not since that last time with Ruth Ann and the girls, and she wanted to go.

A.J. poked her and whispered, "Honey, come on. It's time to shit or get off the pot."

How romantic. But he was right. It was time. She looked up at him and nodded and he winked. What was the deal with men winking, anyhow? It made her feel like a little kid. He must've nodded at Joyce because she started up the organ again. Cassandra wished now she'd got piano music. Organ music always made her think of funerals, or altar calls. Somebody save me, she thought.

She looked at Dennis and smiled her biggest smile. Poor feller, he looked right red in the face. She felt her feet move, slowly, but they weren't doing that step-pause, step-pause Aubrey drilled into her last night. Instead they shuffled side by side until they'd done a complete 180 and she couldn't see Dennis or the organ or anybody else. And suddenly she could breathe again. A little breeze came through the open doors, blew through the veil onto her face. Ah, so cool. She could use just a little more of that before she got married, a little more of that breeze. Moving now toward the church doors, toward that wind, she could see more and more blue sky, then green grass, the white sidewalk, the black limo that mercifully did not have the name of the funeral home painted on it. Dennis, bless him, used those removable magnetic signs, said kids wouldn't want to go to a prom in a funeral-mobile.

The organ was still going, and she fell automatically into a step-pause, step-pause perfect enough even for Aubrey. Her dress rustled against the doorframe and then she was floating, down the steps onto the sidewalk, the heels of her shoes clicking on the concrete. She'd loved that sound when she was a little girl. It made her feel so grown up.

A low buzzing hum followed her like a swarm of bees, then she realized it was the sound of voices. They got louder and louder, so loud she lifted her dress to walk faster and was practically running by the time she grabbed the bumper to slingshot around the front of the car. Somehow she got herself and the dress stuffed into the driver's seat. She slammed the door and felt for the key in the ignition, then remembered Dennis kept it under the mat. Like that wasn't the first place a thief would look. Which made her a thief, she thought as she leaned down and felt under the mat, then sat up with the key in her hand.

Don't look back, she told herself, don't look. But her head turned of its own accord and there they were. The church had emptied out and they stood bunched up on the steps and the sidewalk, staring like cows. They didn't look real, somehow, looked more like a picture of people in an album, photos of somebody else's wedding. Cassandra half expected to find her own face looking back at her from that crowd, a guest at yet another wedding not her own.

Ruth Ann stood out front, arms crossed over her chest, the blue chiffon skirt of her matron of honor dress blowing around her skinny legs. Cassandra couldn't make out what she was saying to A.J. out the side of her mouth, but the look on her face said, "I am not believing this." A.J. pulled at his tie, grinning like a monkey, like Cassandra had done something that tickled him so good. The rest of the family just looked confused and concerned, and Dennis's family too. Except his mama. If looks could kill, Cassandra would be wounded, the way Maria was glaring at her. His daddy had taken off his glasses and was polishing them with a handkerchief, shaking his head. When she saw Dennis pushing through to the front of the crowd, she panicked and started the car, thinking he'd run after her, but he stopped, just stopped and stood there. He looked like somebody in a movie that'd been shot between the eyes but his body didn't know to fall down yet.

His black eyebrows pulled together and his mouth moved, made the shape of her name. A wave of guilt rolled over her and nearly pulled her under, but when Dennis took a step toward the car, panic got back in the driver's seat. She hit the electric door locks, put the car in drive and took off. Drive, just drive, she told herself. Don't think. Just drive. She checked the rearview mirror to see if anybody was following but couldn't see a thing because somebody had written all across the back windshield in shaving cream. It took a minute to figure out that it said, "Happy Ever After."

They must all be going crazy, must think she was crazy. She had to go back there and fix it, make it all right. But her foot stayed on the gas.

Dennis, he'd handle it. He was good in a crisis. Hell, it was his job to make things easier in a bad situation. She'd seen him do it a million times, help people say goodbye. He'd been so sweet to her and Ruth Ann when they went to make their mama's funeral arrangements last year, handing them Kleenex while they cried, bringing them water while they looked at the casket catalog, giving them advice about which outfit to bring in. That was the first thing she liked about him, how sweet he was, how he always knew exactly the right thing to say. By now he'd probably shooed everybody back to the church, saying, "Folks, it's too hot to be standing out here. Why don't we go to the fellowship hall where it's cool and have some refreshments."

She should be grateful for a man like that. He was probably saying exactly the right thing now, something to make himself feel better as well as everybody else. "Don't worry," he'd say, laughing a little bit like he knew her better than she knew herself. "It's just nerves. She'll drive around the block, get herself calmed down and then we'll start over." And he'd believe it too.

Ruth Ann must be about to split out of her skin, wondering what was going on. She always thought she knew everything too. She was probably sitting there with her lips mashed together, thinking, "I told her. And now she's gone and wasted all that money on a wedding that ain't going to happen." A.J., he loved it when something unexpected happened and was probably still laughing. Her brothers and their wives would wait a while, drink punch and eat chicken nuggets and peanuts and mints, and then they'd look at their watches, tell somebody to call them if Cassandra came back, and go on home. Ashley and Keith, they were probably thinking about their own wedding last summer and how different it was from today, how everything had gone just perfect and everybody cried like a baby because Ashley and Keith belonged together.

But didn't she and Dennis belong together too? Up until a few weeks ago, she'd been sure of it. And besides that, she was tired of watching from a service road while everybody else zoomed by on a highway, getting married, having kids, getting on with their lives, making it look so easy she figured there must be something wrong with her.

Well, here was the proof, as if she needed any. Driving a stolen car in her wedding dress on the way to nowhere. Proof she was crazy, proof there was something bad wrong with her, proof she was meant to be an old maid. No, worse than that. A spinster, like that joke she'd heard her daddy tell: What's the difference between an old maid and a spinster? An old maid is a woman that ain't never been married. A spinster is a woman that ain't never been married, nor nothing.

I guess it's "nor nothing" for me, she thought, surprised she wasn't crying over it. She ought to be ashamed, was ashamed, but there was something else too, relief and some kind of energy that made her feel like she needed to mop floors or hoe the garden to work it off. But she couldn't go home and do any of those things, so she kept on driving.